DARK WEB

T. J. BREARTON

Published 2015 by Joffe Books, London.

www.joffebooks.com

This book is a work of fiction. Names, characters, businesses, organizations, places and events are either the product of the author's imagination or are used fictitiously. Any resemblance to actual persons, living or dead, events or locales is entirely coincidental. The spelling is American English.

ISBN-13: 978-1511614467

For my family.

PROLOGUE

Sitting in the cab of his plow truck, Lenny Duso lit the half-smoked cigar. The mug of coffee Mary had made fifteen minutes before sat steaming in the cup holder on the dashboard. The truck rumbled and the heaters blasted, but it was still cold. Lenny wore the full Carhartt jumpsuit and a large floppy hat Mary told him made him look Russian. The stogie lit, he clamped it between his teeth and rubbed his bare hands together for warmth. It was a cold night. Three a.m., and only a couple of degrees out. The snow was falling straight down — that granular, sugary kind of snow which piled up quick.

Lenny had twelve residential clients in the small town of New Brighton deep in the Adirondack Mountains. He plowed them out for twenty-five bucks a pop. Most of them were older people; all the young ones either had their own plows or shoveled out by hand.

He dropped the gear shift into drive and the big Ford started rumbling down his driveway. He watched his nice little modular home recede in the mirrors. In the warmer seasons you could hear the river burbling through the trees. Now the water was mostly sheathed in ice.

He reached the end of the driveway and made the turn onto Bluff Lane, a short street that fed into River Street. From there he took River over to the main route, 9N, hung a left and was on the way toward his customers.

Lenny puffed on his cigar as the old Ford got up to speed. His first customer was just a mile and a half down the road. The state plows had been out, but the conditions were already worsening; that sugar-snow kept stacking up, and those big boys would be working until morning.

He reached over and grabbed the mug of coffee. It was a travel mug, stainless steel, a present from his daughter this past Christmas, when she was home from college. He took a sip, relishing the flavor, silently thanking his wife for getting up so early to make it. Mary knew how to make coffee. They'd been married for almost forty years.

Their eldest was a son, Francis. Francis went by the name Frank. Frank was older than Shalene, the college student, by three years. Aside from these basic facts, Lenny didn't like to think about his son all that much. At least he knew where the boy was. County jail was only a few miles away.

Lenny was trying to avoid thinking about Frank any further — holding the coffee in one hand, the smoldering cigar in his teeth, windshield wipers drifting back and forth to sluice away that grainy snow — when he saw the shape in the middle of the road.

He set the coffee in the holder and immediately began to slow down. Up ahead, smack in the center of 9N, near one of the few street lamps, a dark lump lay in his path.

Lenny's gaze shifted to the rear view mirror. No one was behind him. He looked out the driver's-side window and saw only darkness. Few people lived on this stretch of 9N. Street lights were staggered here and there as you neared the intersection of Pike and Main in the small town proper, but that was it.

He came to a complete stop. He set the cigar in the ashtray, thought better of it, and then stubbed it out. He kept his eyes on the lump. A fresh eddy of snow and wind churned up 9N toward the truck, dusting the shape on the road. *Someone hit a deer*, he figured. *They hit it and just moved on*. It happened all the time.

The storm was supposed to continue into the next day. *The Farmer's Almanac* had predicted a cold winter, and it had been, with the temperature hovering around zero or below for weeks at a time. The woodstove in Lenny's home had been crackling non-stop since December, and it was now mid-February. Lenny was proud to have heeded the *Almanac* and bought two extra cords of firewood. Other folks were running out already, but he had enough to last until spring. Whatever it was lying there in the road would soon be frozen rock-solid, if it wasn't already. Someone could slam right into it, sending them swerving off the road and into the trees.

"Dammit," he swore. The truck was just starting to get warm and now he had to go out into the cold. He reached around in the seat beside him and found his gloves. He pulled them on and tried to ignore his escalating pulse. Not much riled Lenny, but something about the way that shape looked, now that he was closer to it, moiled the coffee in his stomach.

He didn't think it was a deer. Not really.

He opened the door and lowered himself out of the Ford, grunting as he went. He slammed the door shut. The sound was swallowed up by the blanket of snow. To his right, an impenetrable tree line of pines and spruce. To his left, an empty field with trees set far back. Wild forests covered a lot of this region.

The land was passed down generation to generation. His mother had given birth to him sixty years ago in his parents' home up on Rabideau Way, a sprawling fifty acre farm that his father had inherited from his own father. Granddad had come down from Canada as a young man and worked the woods by torchlight, alongside the Scots and Irish and Dutch who first logged the region in the late 1800s. This was how New Brighton was first settled; many properties were over a hundred acres apiece. That unholy cop John Swift had a sizeable plot too, not far away, handed down by his own grandfather.

Lenny looked further down 9N. He could see the first house there in the distance, a little white double-wide with smoke spewing from the chimney. Maybe two hundred yards away. The Hamiltons were an elderly couple in their seventies. He had some sort of dementia; she was a cat fanatic and into those little figurines you put everywhere in your home until it looked like you'd been invaded.

Lenny stepped in front of the Ford. The headlights beamed over the plow and into the falling snow. The shape was motionless, sprawled right across the center line. Dead. You just knew when something was dead. The stillness of it was unlike anything else, even a rock. It was more than stillness, it was an absence. It was something heavy, pressing on your chest.

He left the sanctuary of the plow truck and started walking towards the shape. He didn't have a cell phone. His wife and daughter had been nagging him to get one for years now. He didn't see the need. He knew just about everyone in town, how every street turned and curved, who grew up in which home. The only people he didn't know were some of the newcomers. Each year, New Brighton had a few arrivals, young people working for the county, the social services, hospital, or jail, or up at the college in Plattsburgh. Some of them even worked from home on their computers, doing things he didn't know much of anything about.

He had a CB in the truck. Channel 9 was reserved for emergency communications and traveler assistance and he could contact County Dispatch if need be. First he wanted a closer look. Lenny took a couple steps towards the shape in the road, the snow falling so thickly now that it was collecting in his bushy eyebrows and wetting his beard. He flexed his gloved hands and stopped again, just a few feet from the unmoving presence.

It was definitely not a deer or a moose. Something stuck out at an angle, and even covered in snow, there was no mistaking it. It was an arm. With a bare hand. There was a dead body in the middle of the road.

He looked at the hand. The snow on it was translucent, crystalline, as if the body still had some warmth and was melting it.

"Jesus," Lenny said. He regretted taking the Lord's name in vain, but he figured the Lord would forgive him this transgression, given the situation.

The body had to have been there only a short time. Judging by the accumulation, the last state plow had thundered through maybe fifteen minutes ago.

He took another step forward, and an alarm went off in the back of his mind — he shouldn't contaminate the scene of a death, accidental or not.

So he squatted down, his knees popping like a couple of firecrackers, and got a better view of things, but from a safe distance.

Whoever it was, the head was turned away from him, as if looking back down the road. This was a small mercy. The body was on its side, the arm up and out at that weird angle. Had someone just walked out here and fall down dead? It was cold — the person didn't have the right clothes on. It was hard to tell, but it looked like he or she was wearing pajamas. Could have succumbed to the weather. Really, though, there was no use in speculating. He stood back up, and was about to return to the truck and get on the radio, when he saw headlights appear along the road, coming from the direction of town.

Probably they would have a cell phone; he didn't think the things worked out here anyway, another reason not to bother with getting his own, but he didn't know for sure. He would wait and see, and then use the radio if need be.

He walked towards the oncoming vehicle, giving the shape on the ground a wide berth. He held up his hands and started waving. He didn't want to chance the car hitting the body.

He glanced over at it. From this angle he could see part of the face. That same crystalline snow covered it, twinkling in the light of the single nearby street lamp. His heart thumped against his chest as he stared. The dead person's eyes were open, staring out through the mask of white powder.

Lenny turned his gaze away. He didn't like the anxiety he was feeling now. He wasn't used to surprises. He had his routine, he had his home, his wife. He'd raised his children. Sometimes they didn't turn out the way you wanted — Frank was a troubled young man — but Lenny had done his best to provide.

The oncoming car was starting to slow down, and Lenny gave his arms a fresh wave in the air. He walked, toward the vehicle, away from the body.

Still fifty yards away, the car came to a halt. Lenny squinted through the snow. It was a sporty, compact car. Sleek, dark blue, or maybe black — hard to tell under the light of the street lamp and the headlights blinding him. He considered who it might be. The county buildings were all in the other direction. The mental health facility, the hospital, the jail, were all back in the direction from which the car had come. The other way, 9N wound off into the night, with a full ten miles before the next town. Maybe they were coming home, then. Perhaps a nurse who'd finished her shift.

But the car just sat there in the distance, engine idling. Lenny raised a hand and shielded his eyes from the brilliance of the headlights.

The vehicle suddenly jerked forward. It made a turn in the road, drove to the shoulder, stopped, and started backing up. Whoever it was, was leaving the scene.

"Hey!" Lenny shouted. He waved his arms again. The headlights had swept across his body and then plunged into the thick forest. The car continued backing up, stopped, and then turned and accelerated away in the other direction.

"Hey, hey!"

It was useless. He watched the red taillights shrink away in the swirling snowstorm.

Lenny lowered his arms and headed back to the plow truck. Time to get on the CB and call County Dispatch, get the cops and an ambulance out there.

As he moved back towards his vehicle, he kept his eyes on the Ford, careful not to look at the face again, those lifeless eyes watching the taillights recede into the night. Then the overhead street lamp clicked off, enveloping that face in darkness.

PART ONE

THE BODY

CHAPTER ONE / TWO MONTHS EARLIER

The plane carrying Mike Simpkins rose off the hot tarmac. He was on his way across the Sunshine State to his home on the east coast, in Stuart. Mike and his wife and three kids had lived in Stuart — Turtle Bay condominiums — for six years. Their two youngest had been born down there and were native Floridians.

Florida was a great place to live. Even under the unrelenting hammer of the sun, Mike had found himself working the Gulfstream Horse Racing with a smile on his face. The sweat had poured down from his hair and soaked his shirt, but he hadn't cared. The tropical heat was good. Salty breezes, boiling sunshine, even alligators — these were the reasons he'd moved south in the first place.

But nothing lasted forever.

The pilot, an older man named Craig, brought the prop plane up into the unbroken blue sky, talking to Mike over the headsets they were both wearing. Mike was the only passenger in the tiny Cessna.

"You said you're moving back north? New York?"

"Yeah, that's right. The wife got a teaching job at a college there. Been a while since she's worked; she's been taking care of the kids."

The pilot shot him a quick sideways glance. "Maybe it's none of my business, but I'm flying you across the state here, away from one of the biggest horse races in the south . . ."

Mike laughed. "Yeah, I know. I'm a pretty big deal, huh? Nah. The company I work for was struggling; got bought out." Mike watched the ground far below for a moment; the golf estate communities had given way to miles of swamp as they flew a path over the everglades. No man's land, he thought.

The pilot continued. "The buyout didn't include you, is that right?"

"Correct. It didn't include me. This fancy little airplane ride is their way of hoping I don't raise a stink."

He'd tried to remain upbeat. He'd started as a Utility years ago, a guy who wrangled cable for cameramen, and it had been a struggle to work his way up. If the film business was tough, the broadcast TV business was tougher. He'd freelanced for a long time as a Utility, sometimes as a Grip, supplementing his income as a bartender, carpenter, and landscaper. He'd even sold vacuum cleaners for a short time. Always pining to be a cameraman, but it had gone the other way — he'd gotten more into the managerial side of things; he discovered an aptitude for wiring and technology. Rand-Burr, a production company based in Miami, had picked him up as a fiber tech manager after he'd worked his first gig at the *Gulfstream Park and Casino* seven years before. He'd been on salary since, and with benefits. The job had been contingent on his relocation to Florida, where the company was based. So he'd packed up his family — just the three of them then, with one bun in the oven — and they'd moved to the warmer climate, never looking back.

But the north hadn't finished with them.

"So . . . what?" the pilot asked. "You got work in the city then?"

"No, not New York City. Upstate."

"Oh. You mean like White Plains; in there?"

White Plains, thought Mike. To the uninitiated, "upstate" meant a few miles north of Manhattan. There was a whole state up above the city, one that stretched up to Canada, that abutted the entire westerly border of Vermont.

"Further north: New Brighton," Mike explained. "Up in the Adirondack Mountains."

"Oh you mean the boondocks," the pilot said, chuckling. He shot Mike another quick look, in case he'd taken offense.

"That's right. Chopping wood, shoveling snow, hunting for the abominable snowman."

The pilot was banking the plane and peering out the small windshield, no longer quite paying attention to the conversation.

Mike didn't begrudge the pilot his remark about the boondocks. People often laughed at the remote places, just harmless teasing. But the more he thought about it, the more he felt the sting of failure, a gnawing in the back of his mind that told him the move was somehow a sign of weakness. That he had failed as a man and as a provider.

He wasn't too confident he'd be able to pick up work back in the north — Lake Placid wasn't far from New Brighton. Placid had twice hosted the Olympics and still held world-class events each year at the facilities — which were still standing — but jobs were scarce and it was a competitive business, a you-had-to-know-the-right-people type affair. They even said the structures were in bad shape, no longer up to competition standards. People were leaving the region in search of better jobs. The idea of sliding backwards in his career and having to wrangle cable again as a Utility was not a prospect he relished. The alternative, having to rely solely on Callie's income, was even worse.

They had no buyer yet for their Turtle Bay condo. They'd already bought the house in New Brighton and made the first mortgage payment last month. They'd intended on selling the Turtle Bay condo furnished, and buying new furniture for the New Brighton house once they'd gotten there, figuring that shipping everything would be just as expensive and more of a headache in the long run.

"You said you got three kids?" The pilot was leveling out the plane. Mike could see the east coast of Florida on the horizon. It was amazing how fast flying was, even in a prop plane. He looked at the control panel, they were doing 150 knots. He guessed that was about 175 miles an hour on the ground.

"Yeah, three kids. Two girls, one stepson. Teenager."

"That's great, man. I never had kids."

"No?"

"I read some study recently that said people without kids are happier. Does that ring true?"

"I saw that study. I think it was more that *couples* felt more fulfilled in their relationships — they had more time for one another if they didn't have kids."

"Yeah, right," the pilot said, nodding. "I never got into that, either." He broke into a wide grin.

Mike smiled back. He understood not wanting to get attached, even not wanting to have kids. He was an only child himself. But after meeting Callie, that had all changed.

She'd had her son Braxton with another man when she was twenty-four, a rock-and-roller with an anger management problem. They weren't married, and Braxton had been a surprise. Mike had been a shock to his own parents; both middle class, a mother with health issues, a father who liked his freedom. Mike had always felt an unspoken connection to Braxton because of this. But life with a child when you weren't the biological parent was often dicey, to say the least. Mike and Braxton had experienced some turbulence.

Just as he had that thought, the prop plane dropped in the sky for a moment, and Mike's stomach floated.

"Sorry 'bout that," said the pilot. "So, when do you make the move?"

"Tomorrow."

The pilot arched his eyebrows. "That soon, huh?"

"That soon."

Mike gazed out the window at the coast drifting slowly towards them. It was December, warm even for Florida this time of year, and sweat was drying on Mike's shirt in the cool cockpit of the plane.

"Well, good luck, pal," the pilot said.

"Thanks."

The pilot started the descent. Mike felt something flutter in his chest.

Here we go, he thought.

A whole new life about to begin.

* * *

For the trip north, the family took both vehicles, each towing the largest size U-Haul pod rentable. The girls rode with Callie, while Mike and Braxton drove together. Mike wanted to visit his father along the way. Jack Simpkins had retired to St. Augustine ten years earlier. St. Augustine sat on the east coast of Florida about thirty miles south of downtown Jacksonville. It was the oldest continuously occupied European-settled port in the continental United States. Ironic, Mike often thought, that his father had wound up there, an Irish boy from the Bronx. Retirement did strange things to people.

Mike and Braxton made the trip mostly in silence, Mike listening to the radio, Braxton on his Sony laptop, ear buds in, intent on an online game called *The Don.*

"Dad," he said suddenly, "I need you to pull over."

Mike glanced at him. They were trucking along at seventy miles an hour on a major interstate.

"Braxton, bud, we're on the freeway. You gotta go to the bathroom, or what?"

"Yeah. Sort of. Pull over." He sounded urgent.

"Brax, I can't just pull over. On the shoulder you mean?"

"Wherever, Mike. Quick."

Mike glanced in the rear view mirror. It was early, just before nine o'clock, but the traffic was already thick. He took another look at his son and saw that the boy's face was drawn, his expression haunted. Braxton pulled his ear buds out and they fell onto his laptop keyboard. He hastily brushed them aside, closed the computer, and set it down at his feet. "Quick, or it's gonna get messy in here."

Mike flipped on his blinker. He was in the middle lane, where he liked to travel. There was an SUV hovering fairly close to his back right, so he stepped on the gas, made the lane-switch, and then started slowing down, his blinker still flashing. The SUV blared its horn as it overtook them on the left-hand side.

Mike edged over to the shoulder. There was nothing but trees alongside the road. He guessed that they were near the Turnbull Hammock Conservation Area. They'd passed a sign for Mosquito Lagoon about half a mile back. Before he'd even brought the truck to a complete stop, Braxton opened the door and jumped out.

"Braxton! Jesus!"

Mike slammed on the brakes. He checked his mirror for traffic and jumped out. He ran around the front of the pick-up just in time to see Braxton leaning over the grass, hands on his knees, hunched forward.

Mike blinked and stood still for a moment, watching as Braxton heaved up whatever he had in his system — Braxton had picked at his eggs and toast that morning in his usual fashion. Now, what little he'd allowed to enter his system was splattered on the ground.

A gossamer strand of drool hung from the boy's lower lip and Mike put a hand on his shoulder. He expected

Braxton to shrug it off, but he didn't. The two of them remained motionless for a moment, traffic rushing by, buffeting the truck and U-Haul.

"Fuck," Braxton said softly.

Mike opened his mouth to reprimand the boy, but then decided to keep quiet; just for once he could let an F-bomb pass.

This thought brought his wife to mind. They'd set off after Mike and Braxton, both because Callie and the girls were a little slower to get things together, but also to allow Mike and Braxton a little bit of time alone with Jack, Mike's dad, before the girls descended with their usual whirlwind chaos. They were maybe fifteen, twenty minutes behind.

"You okay? Your stomach upset?" Stupid question.

Braxton didn't respond. He just stayed bent-over, staring down at what had come out of his body.

"You feel hot? Like you've got the flu?"

"No," Braxton said, and now he stood upright, and Mike's hand slipped from his son's shoulder.

"Easy. Just take it easy."

"It's hot out here," Braxton said.

Mike looked around. There were hazy clouds slowly boiling on the horizon. It was muggy, seventy-five degrees and climbing. The air was fragrant with the oil and raveling asphalt of the road, which was cracked and broken in places. He could also smell the trees of the Conservation, sweet in the humidity, with traces of midnight jasmine, their nighttime scent burning off under the bright, bustling day. He was going to miss Florida. Then the wind shifted and he detected the acrid, bilious smell of Braxton's vomit.

"Come on, let's get back in the car where it's cooler."

Braxton turned and walked back to the truck. Mike took a couple of quick steps and got there ahead of him. The passenger door was still flung open. He touched Braxton gently on the small of his back as the boy climbed into the vehicle.

CHAPTER TWO / TWO MONTHS EARLIER

After the bright day outside, the condo was gloomy. There were deep shadows in the corners, monochromatic furniture, everything just the way it had been the last time Mike had visited his father. How long had it been? About six months. He always planned to visit more often, but it was still a four hour drive. It was always Mike that made the visits happen, lately at Callie's prompting. She wanted the girls to get to know their grandfather, and for Mike and Jack to patch over the dark hole which had come to characterize their relationship.

Good luck, honey. Mike thought. He loved her for trying. But women couldn't understand about sons and their fathers. That all their lives, sons were condemned to seek their father's approval. And when a father betrayed a son's trust, it never fully returned.

Jack Simpkins had always worked for the NY Transit Authority. He and Mike's mother had lived in the same rent-controlled walk-up in Manhattan for over thirty years, right up until she had succumbed to cancer. He'd put in long days his whole life, working hard and drinking harder. He'd gone out to a bar a few blocks from his home nearly every night. But he'd left behind everything and everyone when he moved to Florida to retire.

Jack looked at Mike. "You all packed?"

Mike nodded. "Yup. What we couldn't pack, we shipped. What we couldn't ship, we sold. Callie's pretty good on eBay."

As if on cue, Mike's phone buzzed in his pocket. He knew it was his wife. "Hold on, guys," he said.

Putting the phone to his ear, he walked away, leaving his father and his son together. He moved deeper into the dark of the condo.

"Hello?"

"Hey. How you guys doing?" his wife said.

"We're good. Just got to Jack's. How are you and the girls?"

"Reno just told me a joke. Where do hamsters come from?"

"I don't know, where do—"

He heard Reno shout from the backseat, "Hamsterdam!"

Mike smiled. He could picture his daughter in her pigtails, an open book on her lap. Her sister Hannah, beside her, strapped into a massive car seat.

He spoke in a low voice. "Braxton been sick? Did he say he was sick?"

"He's not feeling good?"

"He just threw up alongside the interstate. Seems fine now. He's never gotten car sick, right?"

"He puked? I mean, really threw up? What did he throw up?"

"Hang on," Mike said. "Let me sort through the sample I took with me."

"I mean . . ."

"Just food. Just breakfast. Nothing alarming."

"What was he doing?"

"What was he doing? Sitting and playing his game on the laptop."

"Could be motion sickness."

"Yeah," he said.

"I'm sure he's fine, babe. Thanks for letting me know."

His wife insisted they share all information, especially about the kids, and it was usually Mike who did the worrying. His wife was tougher. Part African-American, part French, part English, copper-toned and honey-haired, Mike joked that this made Callie part superhero. At least, the mixed descent seemed to make her resistant to illness.

"Okay," he said, glancing towards the kitchen, and his father and son. Then he added in a louder voice, knowing they would hear him over the car speakers, "Hi, girls!"

"Hi, Dad," Reno called back.

"Ah-dadda," Hannah said.

"Okay," Callie told him. "Love you."

"Love you, too."

He hung up. Right away, he felt the worry start to worm its way in. Despite all Callie's common sense, a sick kid was a sick kid and that always made you feel a little scared.

Mike went back into the kitchen where he found Braxton sitting on a stool at the kitchen counter, eating a sandwich. That was good, Mike thought. The kid had an appetite. Maybe whatever it was had passed.

Braxton had bangs that usually hung in front of his eyes. His hair was brown, but his mother had allowed him to highlight it with blond streaks. He dressed in skater clothes — Vans sneakers, RUCA t-shirts, Volcom Stone hooded sweatshirts, Bulldog pants. Tight pants tapering down at the ankles, a t-shirt hugging his thin frame, a baggy hoodie over top.

Jack was bent over, rummaging around for something in the cupboards. He stood up and looked at Mike. "You got all the numbers? Water, electric, fuel oil?"

"Yeah, Pop. I do."

"You change the address so you can keep tabs on the 529 account? I don't want them calling me."

"Yes, I forwarded all correspondence. You won't be hearing from them."

For a moment Mike wondered if his father would ask Braxton how he felt about returning to the North Country after so many years; if he remembered being there as a small child. Or maybe ask Mike if he planned to stop and visit any of the old gang on the way up, like Bull Camoine on Staten Island. But he didn't.

"Hope you find work up there. You'll need the money. House like that, it takes a beating in the winters."

"How are things around here?"

Jack sniffed. "It's the same everywhere you go. People are all the same."

Jack closed another cabinet, apparently not finding what he was looking for. He went over and opened the broom-closet door.

"So, Pop . . ." Mike said. "We're hoping you come and visit us this summer."

"Too cold up there for me. Been there, done that."

"But, Pop, that's why I'm saying *in the summer*. You can stay in Braxton's room. The girls are bunking together, but there's a full basement. I'm hoping to finish it off; I'm sure I'll get to it by the summer, and Braxton is going to love crashing down there. So . . ."

Mike's dad didn't appear to be listening. He withdrew from the closet with something he'd gotten off a high shelf.

"Hey, kid," he said to Braxton.

Braxton looked up from his food.

"C'mere."

Braxton got off his stool and went over to his grandfather. The older man faced the younger. They were not blood, but Mike suddenly saw a striking resemblance between the two of them, some essential similarity, and he felt his chest swell with emotion.

Jack handed Braxton a small package that said PETZL on the side. Mike realized that it was a headlamp.

“I used to work down in the subway tunnels. Swear by these. It’s a lot darker up where you’re going. So this will help you see your way around.”

Braxton took the package from Jack and examined it. It was the kind of headlamp which had an elastic band and an LED light. Mike saw Braxton smile.

“Thanks.”

Mike felt a shiver of pleasure run down his spine, as Jack ran his hand through the kid’s hair, something Braxton usually shrugged away from. Jack’s calloused fingers brushed it out of his face. “It’ll help keep this gob out of your eyes, too.”

And Braxton laughed.

CHAPTER THREE / PRESENT DAY

"Swifty, what do you make of this?"

John Swift heard his name and looked up from where he was squatting next to the snow-covered body. Alan Cohen, the Sheriff's Deputy, the first on-scene after the emergency call, was pointing to something in the powdery drift alongside Route 9N.

John Swift sighed to himself and stood up, feeling old all of a sudden. The snow pattered down on his coat, sounding like a crackling fire. He longed to be home by the wood stove, with Kady resting her head on her front paws beside him. Anywhere but out here in the cold at three a.m., with evidence vanishing under the snowfall, and more bunny and deer tracks than tire or foot tread.

Swift went over to where Alan Cohen was standing, hands on his hips, facing the direction of Marshall Hamilton's open field. Cohen looked down at something near his feet. A piece of cardboard was sticking out of the snow. Swift squinted down. "Looks like trash, Alan. I'll have my CSI bag it, though. Thanks."

"Sure," said Cohen. Alan Cohen was a relatively young, eager deputy. He was well-meaning, but spent most of his time doing pick-up orders for the county mental-health clinic. He looked completely out of place at a crime scene.

Swift clapped a hand on Cohen's shoulder. "Thanks," he said. Cohen smiled, staring down at the cardboard as if he'd cracked the Lindberg case.

As Swift walked away he saw ambulance lights spreading color in flashes, so that the forest on the other side of the road seemed to pulse red. He stared into the woods for a moment, stopping in his tracks, hypnotized. Then the moment was over, and he looked back-and-forth along route 9N.

More troopers had arrived and set up blockades at either end of the crime scene, giving them a core scene of about two hundred yards to work with. But no one was coming. This time of night, in the middle of February, snow like this beading down, you'd have one car coming along every ten minutes. But as dawn approached, traffic would increase. They would have to set up a detour two miles back, onto an inconvenient circuitous route around New Brighton.

Swift forced himself to look back at the body. The EMTs who arrived first had detected no pulse, and initial assessments were that the body had been in the snow for at least fifteen minutes. Short enough that the corpse still radiated some heat, but long enough that the brain was surely dead, the life irrecoverable. They needed to wait for the official declaration from the coroner, who was on his way, probably wrested from deep sleep like Swift had been.

And here were his headlights, stabbing through the snow, turning it to black particles in the beams.

* * *

"Deceased," said Hal Woodruff, crouching next to the body. Woodruff was in his early seventies, silver-haired, dressed in a thick winter coat.

Swift looked at the arm sticking up in the air. "Recognize him?"

Woodruff shook his head. "Never seen him. Don't know him, doubt I know the family."

"First impressions?"

Woodruff sighed. His eyes gleamed in the headlights that illuminated the scene. "Not good. I don't see any blood. Arm is sticking out at a weird angle, but . . . I don't know . . . he could have landed like that or something; fell over."

Swift knew where Woodruff was going. There were three possibilities. Firstly, natural causes — a heart attack, stroke, aneurism, pulmonary embolism, something like that. The kid could be a diabetic. Didn't have his meds, got in a fight with the parents, ran away from home, went into insulin shock, froze to death. The second possibility was an unnatural cause, such as drugs or alcohol in the system. The third was foul play.

A state trooper was taking a statement from the plow-truck driver, Lenny Duso, who'd discovered the body. Duso had reported that a car had arrived at the scene shortly after he'd come across the body and then turned and sped away.

That alone made foul play grimly probable. And worst of all, the decedent in the road was just a kid. Barely a teenager. Maybe thirteen years old.

The parents would have to be contacted. Swift knew it wouldn't be Woodruff who talked to the family, it would be him.

Which was shitty.

"When do you put time of death?"

"Offhand? I'd say it was recent. Just stiffening with rigor now, no lividity yet, still some warmth emanating from the skin. It's faint, but it's there." Woodruff looked at Swift again with those old-man eyes that hurt Swift somewhere deep inside of him. "This just happened," Woodruff said.

"Alright," Swift replied. He felt something buzzing against his chest — his cell phone, stuck in an inner pocket of his winter parka. Swift went over to the trooper who was interviewing Duso. He pulled out his phone and glanced at it. It was a new email notification.

"Oh for God's sake," he muttered. He'd only gotten the phone recently, a top-of-the-line smartphone, when they became mandatory within the department. A week or so ago the phone had offered him "push notifications," and he'd asked a co-worker who said that he did. He realized now that it meant his phone buzzed every time he received an email. But it was his personal account, so he didn't bother to check it, merely glancing at the time.

It was 3:23 a.m., Duso's emergency call had come in twenty minutes ago, and about a half inch of snow had fallen in just the last few minutes, probably two inches since the call. Highway Department plows would want to come through any time now. They would have to be diverted.

The trooper looked up as Swift came over, and his eyes widened expectantly.

Swift asked, "You got the description of the vehicle?"

"I did, yes."

Duso started talking. "I told him what I saw. I told him it was some little Jap—"

Swift held up his hand. "And we have coverage at exits 30 through 33?"

"That's correct."

"Let's get units out to Route 73, in case they knew they were spotted and decided to stay off the Interstate."

"Yes, sir."

Swift started to turn away, then looked at Duso. "Thank you for your . . . quick reaction calling this in."

Duso's expression was hard to read, concealed by his gnarly beard. "I did what any good American ought to do. You know, I look to serve justice, not the bureaucracy." His eyes narrowed, no doubt hoping Swift would feel the sting of his little barb. When Swift said nothing, Duso went on, "I would have chased those sons of bitches down myself, but you know, again, you gotta play by the rules, or if the rule-makers don't like it, there you go off to the stony lonesome."

Swift nodded sympathetically. In his mind he could see the sands slipping through the hourglass. There was no way he was going to get into a political argument with the likes of Lenny Duso. Hal Woodruff had made the death pronouncement, and everything needed to move quickly now. No time for Duso's moralizing. "You did just fine," Swift said. "Thank you."

He hurried away before Duso could bend his ear further. He returned to the body, twenty yards away. He heard the grumble of an engine and saw a set of headlights approaching. He hoped it was his Crime Scene Investigator. He was going to need more people on this, and fast.

Woodruff was still on his knees next to the dead kid. Swift pulled his phone out. The cold bit into the skin of his hand as he dialed and held the phone up to his ear.

Woodruff was not a forensic pathologist. The nearest medical examiner was in Plattsburgh, about forty miles away, a consultant who did some work with the college, but ninety percent of her gigs came from law enforcement. Swift listened to the recorded message in the medical examiner's office and left a voicemail. The approaching headlights drifted over to the side of the road. He put his phone back into his pocket and watched the CSI get out of the vehicle. He could only imagine what she was thinking. A crime scene in the middle of the road, in the middle of the night, under a snowfall that just kept coming.

CHAPTER FOUR

Brittney Silas had on a big puffer coat with a fur-lined hood, yet she still looked numbed by the cold as she approached the crime scene. The bitter wind hunted the gaps in Swift's own jacket as he watched the CSI squint through the flashing reds and blues of the state-trooper vehicles, taking in the scene before her.

She located him in the commotion and came over. Despite the ditch hour, she looked alert and present. The rumor about Brittney Silas was that she was a tough woman, a take-charge type. As far as Swift knew, she was single, never married, no kids. She'd been a Crime Scene Investigator for thirteen years. It didn't exactly make her a veteran, but she was experienced enough. She worked all over the county, but lived nearby, the one positive in a night filled with negatives.

"John, how are you?"

"Like I took a tumble on an honest bet. Busier than a one-legged man in a butt-kicking contest. I've got more."

Her gaze was roving, taking in the whole scene, finally landing on the lump of snow in the center of it all.

Swift's eyes followed. "I'm guessing you're going to be able to get your photographic log, your narrative log, barely an in situ diagram, and you're not going to have much of a latent print-lift log."

She seemed unfazed. "Did you have Mr. Woodruff bag the hands?"

Swift blinked. He could feel the snow on his eyelashes. "No. Left everything for you just the way it was."

"Let's get him to bag the body's hands immediately." She moved off fast, and Swift hurried to get in step with her.

"How do you want to handle this?" he said.

"Well, let's start to process. We'll work up to the body, just the way we're supposed to." She seemed to be talking to the night, to the relentless weather, as much as to Swift. Within another couple steps they were next to Hal Woodruff, Deputy Cohen, and the body.

Brittney turned on a high-wattage smile for Hal Woodruff. "Hi, Hal."

"Hi Brit."

"Decedent identified?"

"No ma'am."

She put her hands on her hips. Swift saw she was wearing snug ski gloves. CSIs had been referred to as Evidence Techs not long ago, a term they surely resented. The scene was Swift's to control, but he could already feel Silas insinuate herself. Her breath plumed out in front of her. She looked around. She peered into the trees, then she rotated around and looked at the field. Now she was looking down the length of route 9N, at the house in the distance. "When's the last time you worked a DB case?"

Swift thought back. "Two years," he said. There had been a suicide in the woods. A man around his own age, late fifties.

"Okay," she said. "Hal, let's check for an ID."

"Probably too young for a driver license," said Swift.

"Yeah?"

"Yeah. Before this layer of snow here, we could see the face better. Young male, Caucasian, about 120, 130 pounds, somewhere between twelve and fifteen years of age."

"No wallet, no ID, nothing in his pockets," said Hal. "Think he's wearing pajamas."

"Thanks, Hal." She walked away from the body. Swift followed. As she walked she pointed to Lenny Duso, who was watching them from beside the trooper's car.

"That's our discoverer?"

"That's him."

She pointed beyond, into the road.

"And probably we've driven all over the tire tracks. The vehicle he said turned around and hightailed it out of here."

"Yes, ma'am."

She shot him a quick look, and Swift realized he was on the defensive. "We had to approach somehow," he said.

"Wish we could have protected a little more of the core scene."

"Deputy Cohen was the first to arrive. Then two of my troopers, and then I got here."

She said nothing and he could sense the tension rising between them. "I'm sorry, Ms. Silas, but this is the best we got. This is a pretty major route here."

"Have to turn the vehicles around."

"We're rerouting traffic, yes. In two hours, there's going to be twenty cars trying to come through every minute."

"Too bad for them. Processing the scene can't be rushed."

"I know it can't, and, Ms. Silas, I'm not trying to fight you here. But we're in the middle of a blizzard at three o'clock in the morning. I don't think you're going to be tagging a whole lot to take back to the lab. That body is the most important piece of evidence, so the sooner we can get to it, the better."

She stopped walking and faced him directly, frowning up at him. They were near one of the vehicles, which washed one side of her in thin white light. "Do you think this is a homicide?"

"My kneejerk reaction? Yes. But I can't say for sure. I've got to put my worksheet together. I need you to document the scene as best you can, given these conditions. It's going to be your chain of evidence. But we do need to get an ID on that kid and find out who his parents are. Start questioning his friends, family, associates. Someone was here, according to a witness, who did a one-eighty right over there and took off."

"They weren't just scared by what they saw? Maybe someone just didn't want to get involved?"

"I don't know. Anything's possible."

"Well you made the call, detective. You think there's foul play, that this is a crime scene. But this kid could have walked here, could've been driven here, could've been lowered from a helicopter for all we know. The scene can tell us that. I need to find what I can, before it vanishes under all this white stuff. As you keep pointing out."

"Understood," he said quietly.

"You don't sound happy, Detective Swift."

"Happy? I'm happy. There's a handful of homes within a half mile of here. My guess is that, no, he wasn't flown in by chopper, but he came from one of those homes. But I have no ID. If I had an ID, I might be better prepared to give someone the worst news of their life. So in the next few minutes, see if there's any ante-mortem data in all this shit that can tell me whose dead kid is lying there before I go knock on their door."

She stood looking at him, the snow falling between them; the lights sweeping through.

Her voice was softer. "Gotcha," she said. Then a pause. "I liked the line about the one-legged man."

CHAPTER FIVE

Deputy Alan Cohen pointed down Route 9N at a small white house in the distance. "Looks like Mrs. Hamilton is already up," he said.

Swift turned and saw a woman standing on her porch, a tiny figure from this distance. One of his troopers had already headed over and was nearing her driveway, trudging through the powdery snow.

"I'll be back." Swift started walking towards the house. It looked like there was no more postponing the inevitable.

He'd planned on questioning the Hamiltons as soon as possible — they were really the only neighbors close enough to have seen anything — but waking people up in the middle of the night to ask them what they knew about a dead kid lying in the middle of the road? He didn't think the kid had come from their house — he knew the Hamilton family and their kids and grandkids, and the dead body in the road didn't fit the profile of anyone there. And there was little chance they could help identify the vehicle that had fled the scene, or its driver. An older couple, in their eighties, they had surely been sound asleep. Only now had all the lights and commotion disturbed one of them, half an hour after Lenny Duso had called Dispatch.

The woman and the trooper both watched him approach. He tried on a smile and climbed up the two steps onto the porch. He kept his voice low, almost to a whisper.

"Hello, Mrs. Hamilton."

"Is there someone out there?"

Swift glanced at the trooper, a man with the uncommon name of Koby Bronze. Bronze was young, twenty-five years old. His open expression communicated to Swift that he hadn't said much to the woman yet.

"Yes," Swift said, turning his gaze back to Mrs. Hamilton. "There's a young man. Unfortunately, he's passed away."

She put a hand to her mouth, and her eyes widened. "Oh no. Oh dear," she said through her fingers. Swift got a look at her. She wore a long winter bathrobe, pale pink, and slippers on her feet.

"It's very cold out here, Mrs. Hamilton."

"Lorraine."

"Lorraine. We can come back later in the morning and talk to you. No need to alarm yourself with this. Everything is safe; we're here now and we're going to make sure we get to the bottom of what's going on."

"I see . . ."

He gave her another smile. "Did you hear anything that woke you up? Any voices out there, or maybe a car, something like that?"

She still had her hand to her face. "I don't sleep very well. My husband snores. I woke up and saw the lights coming through my window." She took her hand away from her mouth and pointed with a knobby finger at the police lights. "Those."

"That's fine. Thank you, Lorraine." Swift glanced at Trooper Bronze, conveying with a look and a slight jerk of his head that the trooper should help the woman back inside and calm her down. He started to turn and leave the porch.

"It's a young man?"

He paused, and faced her again. "Yes, ma'am. About thirteen years old."

Her hand returned to her mouth. Swift saw that it was shaking a little, the fingers quivering, patting against her lips. "Oh no," she said again.

"You think you know who it might be?"

She nodded, almost imperceptibly.

Now he was all attention, his nerves taut. "Who?"

"Only thirteen-year-old lives around here is from the new family."

"The new family?"

"They moved into the Getty place." She'd been looking past Swift at the scene further up the road, but Lorraine Hamilton now turned in the other direction. She pointed shakily. "Next house down."

The Getty place. He knew the name. An older couple, same generation as the Hamiltons, had owned the house, and both had passed within a year of each other. If he remembered correctly, their place had sat unlived in for a time. It wasn't far away. He'd mentioned to Brittney Silas that there were a handful of homes nearby, but he'd thought the Getty place was still vacant.

He peered into the darkness for a moment. He could see a single light in the distance, vague, obscured by the falling snow. A porch or walkway light, perhaps. He looked back at Lorraine Hamilton. "Are they home, do you know?"

"I'm not sure. I think so. They're a nice family. Came over and introduced themselves — the woman brought cookies."

"When was that?"

Swift took out his notepad and clicked a pen.

"Oh, a month ago, I guess. Maybe two. I'm sorry."

"No, it's okay. This is very helpful. I'm sorry this is the middle of the night."

"I don't sleep very well. It was after Christmas, though."

"So they've been living there for maybe two months. Got it." Swift looked over his shoulder back at the scene in the road. The figures there were small in the distance, but he thought he could see Hal Woodruff at the center of the activity, and Brittney moving around, carefully examining every detail. The on-call mortuary service had been notified. It would arrive in the next half hour and would transport the body to the forensic pathologist in Plattsburgh. As soon as the high and mighty Ms. Silas felt ready, anyway.

Swift didn't know whether he should immediately go on to the decedent's possible family home, or back to properly take control of the investigation. The body had been found on a New York State Highway, which made it a State concern, though the first-responder had been Alan Cohen, from the Sheriff's Department. The nature of the call, however — *body in the middle of the road, possibly teenager . . . witness says he saw a car speed away, not a hit-and-run though, body was already there* — had been sufficient for the State Police to alert BCI Investigator Swift about a possible homicide. Swift had arrived minutes later. Now he was lead investigator and had to coordinate all those involved. He and Silas had done the walk-through, and had reassessed scene boundaries — she was willing to redirect traffic for miles; he had to do something to mitigate that. Hal Woodruff, the coroner, had checked for pulse, respiration, reflexes, and pronounced the teenager deceased, but beyond that, Woodruff was out of his depth. A homicide investigation needed to move quickly and be light on its feet. He would have to cut Hal loose and extend medico-legal jurisdiction to Brittney for now, entrust her with the chain of evidence custody.

She would need support — documenting, photographing, collecting evidence and being responsible for it — to ensure it wasn't tampered with, lost, stolen, or anything else. In this case, that it wasn't swallowed up by all the damned snow. It was a lot to ask of one person. Swift knew what it was like to carry such a burden.

Crime Scene Investigators like Brittney, who worked for the State troopers, were a relatively new addition to the proliferating law enforcement departments. When Swift had started as a State Police Detective twenty years earlier, detectives did all the leg work. He could still feel that stress, that sense of being torn apart, needing to be in all places at once. It had never really gone away.

He felt sick. Soon he would have to confront a family with the death of their child.

Swift returned his attention to the elderly woman. "Mrs. Hamilton, thank you. Please let Trooper Bronze escort you back inside. Stay warm. We'll be in touch."

He turned and stepped off the porch and back out into the snow. He turned in the direction of the Getty place.

CHAPTER SIX

Something woke her up.

Callie sat up in bed, rubbing at the skin beneath her eyes. It had taken her forever to fall asleep, fitfully, beset by strange dreams. She turned and checked the time on her phone on the bedside table. It was quarter of four in the morning. She listened for Hannah, who now shared a room with Reno and was still prone to waking up in the night. Hannah had slept in the same bed with Callie and Mike until she was almost two. Reno had spent less time co-sleeping; she was in her own bed by the time she was barely a year old. Callie and Mike had agreed, over months of often emotional dialogue, that this would be their last child. Since then, there had been an unspoken reluctance to transition her to another room. They were savoring every moment. But while co-sleeping might have its developmental advantages, it could be a strain on the marriage. While Callie and Mike had gotten somewhat inventive with ways to share crucial marital one-on-one time together, more often than not simply sleeping peacefully beside one another was all they needed. Hannah would rotate around in the bed throughout the night like the hour hand on a clock, her little pudgy feet winding up in Mike's face, or sticking through Callie's ribs. It was disruptive for both of them.

Callie swung her legs out of the bed. Mike was still asleep. He was the deeper sleeper, and while he didn't have her ability to nap and drift in and out of sleep, he had the enviable ability to sleep through all the Florida storms and hurricanes.

Her feet touched the cold floor. The small woodstove that had been alive with roiling, dark orange flames was now a dim red glow.

She listened intently. She heard nothing, but left the room nonetheless, her bare feet whispering across the hardwood floor.

It was chilly — and quiet.

Callie had forgotten about the dark and cold, and the profound silence of the North Country. Outside at night, the wind moaned, and there was a sense of empty space, but also of things living out there in the snow and trees, keeping to their own. A deep thrum of life in the crisp, unvarnished landscape of the night forest. She remembered it from her childhood. When the other girls were penned up inside talking to one another on the telephone, she would put on her coat, slip outside and take in the air. She somehow understood that the Adirondacks were a special place, removed from the rest of the bustling, packed-together world.

She passed through the kitchen and turned down the hallway towards the kids' rooms. There was no sound, but she felt uneasy. Something was leading her, drawing her forward with invisible pulleys that cinched around her, like her skin, dry in the cold mountain air.

She suddenly had an overwhelming urge to stop walking, turn around and go back to bed, slip under the covers, pull them up over her head, and sleep. To escape. But she went on.

She stopped at the girls' room, which was first on the left. The door was ajar, as per usual, and she pushed it open further. She leaned in and listened to the girls breathing. Reno was a deep sleeper like her father; her breath whistled softly through her small nose. Hannah was more difficult to hear, and Callie tip-toed further into the room, where the baby was sleeping soundly, her breathing coming through her mouth in little *haa* exhalations. She'd been stuffy-nosed lately.

But Callie was still tense. Back in the hallway she turned and, heart beating, walked the few paces to Braxton's bedroom. His door was closed.

She turned the knob and swung the door in. There she saw the cool, blue glow of the computer screen on his desk. He had probably snuck out of bed and been doing something on his laptop, and that was what had awakened her. Her heartbeat slowing, she was already preparing a short, whispery lecture in her mind when she saw that he wasn't in his bed.

He wasn't even in the room.

She glanced at his desk again. His MacBook had some sort of character on the screen, a cartoonish figure that looked like someone from a mob movie. There was a caption next to the character which read, *What're You, Sleeping with the Fishes? Get Back In There!*

Braxton's chair was pushed away from the desk, and there were a few papers lying beside the computer.

She wheeled around and left the room. She walked back down the hallway. The bathroom was off from the kitchen. She had passed it on her way to the girls' room but couldn't remember whether it had been open or closed. She usually kept it closed so Hannah, if awakened, wouldn't wander in and start splashing around in the toilet bowl.

The door was shut. She raised a hand and rapped softly. She whispered, "Brax? You in there?"

There was no light coming from under the door, so she opened it and looked in. The bathroom was dark except for a night light plugged into the wall.

She went into the living room and looked on the couch, but he wasn't there, either.

She didn't know what to do. She was stumped. She was a little angry, and she was scared. She turned and walked quickly back to his room, not so lightly this time; her footfalls pounded the wood as she advanced down the hallway. Maybe he had just been burrowed under the covers and she hadn't seen.

Or, she thought, *he's out smoking.*

Just the one time she'd detected the scent of cigarettes on his clothes, but she'd also smelled something else; the unexpected, rather bright scent of fabric softener. She didn't think many kids came home from school smelling like their clothes had just been exhumed from the washing machine, and when she went through the pantry and discovered among the fusty bundles of dirty clothes a missing spray bottle of the stuff, she'd realized he'd been covering up. This had been over two months ago, though, before they'd moved, and since then she hadn't noticed anything, despite sniffing his jackets and shirts on a regular basis. Still, she could have missed it.

Back in his room, she saw for certain that he wasn't there. She stood in the center, and debated whether or not to put on clothes, go outside and catch him in the act, or stay here in his room, like some mob boss from the game he played online, and wait for his return. Mike would go ballistic if he knew Braxton was smoking, but Callie had smoked on and off for years, and knew how hard it was to stop. Mike didn't smoke because Mike never *had* smoked. It was simple — if you didn't start, you didn't get hooked. And if Braxton was sneaking one here or there, maybe she could ward off the demon nicotine before it really sank its teeth in.

Even as she thought this, a nameless fear crept over her. It took a moment for her to become aware of the faint red pulse that seemed to live in the room. She looked closely at the wall beside her and saw that it was flashing red; very faint, but unmistakable. Now the fear welled up into her throat, and she spun around, went to the window above his desk and pushed back the short curtain.

She stopped breathing. Outside, quite a distance away but close enough to be visible, what looked like half a dozen police cars were all out, parked in the middle of the road, their lights flashing.

Callie drew a sudden, trembling breath. She rushed from the room, displacing the papers on Braxton's desk.

Oh God, oh no, oh God, keep him safe, tell me he's safe, that he went outside to look at the lights, that's all, he went outside to look.

She jogged down the hallway and back into the living room, turning towards the bedroom to wake Mike. She was almost at the kitchen door when there was a soft knock behind her.

She stopped in her tracks, frozen. Her thoughts vanished like things shot out of the sky. Far away a voice told her a deep truth. It was connected to the knowledge that our birth, our life, our death are what they are, all inevitable and impermanent. What would follow was only a drama arising out of attachment. The storm and tantrum of the ego.

Callie turned around slowly, and faced the door on the other side of the living room. The one that led to the cold, dark outside.

The soft rapping came again, perhaps a little more urgently.

She stood still. The moment drew out like a blade, until the knocking resumed.

She found herself drifting towards the door, as if propelled by some unseen force. But she knew. Death was on the other side.

CHAPTER SEVEN

Callie was not in bed beside him, but Mike considered that perfectly normal: Hannah still woke up in the night and sometimes Callie would crawl into bed with her to get her calmed back down, and then fall asleep herself.

His dreams hung in his mind like the after-image of a movie. There was a homeless man who lived near the Hirschl and Adler Galleries in Manhattan, just east of Central Park. He had a tent that rippled in the bitter cold. Nearby was a townhouse that had sold for millions of dollars.

Mike remembered the man and his long, Slavic face and nappy beard. Mike had brought the homeless man a battery-powered heater one particularly brutal winter.

The dream, the image of this man still hanging over him, Mike swung his legs out of the bed and stood up, rubbing his eyes. Then he became aware of voices from the living room.

Callie was up talking to someone. Braxton?

Mike walked out of the room, and, as he moved through the dark kitchen the voices grew clearer. He heard Callie take a deep breath, and then let out a moaning wail.

The sound sent a tremor down the column of his spine, and he quickened his pace.

In the living room there was his wife, as he had never seen her before. She was a tangle of arms and legs, and she was being held by a man standing just inside the doorway.

Mike registered two things as he approached them: His wife was somewhere between fainting and trying to get out the door. The man holding her back was a cop. He just had that look. If Callie sensed Mike behind her, she didn't show it. Instead, the low sound coming from her throat mounted to a mad shriek, and she redoubled her efforts to get past the man blocking her way.

"Callie!" Mike called. His voice sounded strangled. He took her by the shoulders. Only then did she seem to become aware of his presence, and turned and fell into him in a heap. Over and over again, she said, "Let me get out there. I have to get out there!" Her breath was hot against his neck. She grew rigid and pushed away from him, repeating more loudly: "I have to *get out there*!"

Mike looked beyond her at the man in front of him. "What's going on?"

"Sir, my name is . . ."

But his words were lost amid Callie's shrieks, as she broke loose from Mike and pummeled at the cop, knocking him backwards.

The entrance had two doors, a main door and a storm one. The main door was still open behind the man, and the storm door, which swung outward, did nothing to break his fall as Callie charged into him. The two of them went sprawling onto the porch outside. At the same moment, Reno came into the room behind Mike. "Mom?"

Mike spun around and moved instinctively towards his daughter. He had no idea what was going on, but he knew he needed to protect his family. He scooped Reno up and moved quickly into the hallway with her in his arms, as Callie and the man disentangled themselves on the porch.

"Mom!" Reno was yelling now, too. "What's wrong?"

Mike shushed her. "You'll wake your sister."

He stopped just short of her bedroom and held her away from him so he could look into her eyes. She was only six, but she was smart, intuitive; you could get nothing past her. "I don't know what's happened yet," he said. "But I need you to stay right here for just a minute. Let me go help Mommy."

"Mom!" She looked past him, trying to catch sight of her mother.

"Reno," he said firmly. "Please, honey. I'll come right back for you. *Stay here.*"

He set her down on the threshold to her bedroom. Miraculously, Hannah was still asleep in the darkened room. Mike left Reno and turned away. Passing Braxton's door, he stuck his head into the room.

Gone.

The computer was lit up. A criminal-looking character stared out from the screen. The room held a faint, red pulse. Lights from outside. Cop lights. Ambulance lights – *God no.*

He turned and retraced his steps down the hallway, passing Reno, who stood where he had placed her, her little face contorted with confusion and fear. It pained his heart to leave her. But he had to see to Callie.

"Right back," he said as he passed her and ran a hand over the top of her head, across the soft, tangled hair.

He pounded back to the living room. The man at the doorway was holding Callie, who had quieted down. She was saying, "Why? Why won't you let me?" in a breathy whisper.

Any moment, he thought, and she'll start shrieking again. Callie was emotional; she had a short fuse, and was a bear of a mother. Now, her instincts were firing on all cylinders. Mike got his arms around her and drew her back into the house, expecting renewed protests.

But she seemed to soften as she felt his arms around her. The cop, covered in snow from his fall, came in behind them, the storm door swinging shut. He met Mike's eyes as they all retreated from the entranceway. And then Mike saw behind him the red lights dousing the trees, turning the snow pink in rapid-fire flashes.

The cop shut the main door. Mike held fast to Callie, who was now quietly weeping.

"I'm Detective John Swift, with the State Police," the man said, speaking urgently now. But his eyes betrayed sorrow. "Do you have a teenaged son?"

Callie's body went completely slack in Mike's arms. He held her tightly as she brought both hands to her eyes, covering her face. Mike's heart was pumping hard and his skin felt numb.

"We do. Is he in some kind of trouble?"

He could have left the house and done something stupid. Like walked over to the neighbors. Maybe they'd freaked and called the police. They didn't know anything yet. Didn't know anything.

Didn't know. Didn't know didn't know didn't—

"He is . . . there is no easy way to say this. He is deceased."

Callie began to writhe in Mike's grip, and then she broke free, her elbow coming back and catching him in the solar plexus, knocking the wind from his lungs.

She shoved the detective aside as he sought to grab her. She twisted the doorknob, yanked it back and pushed her way through in one unstoppable motion. She had jumped off the porch and into the frigid night before either Mike or the detective could even straighten themselves out.

As Mike caught a glimpse of her, hair flying in the darkness as the storm door began to close, his only thought was, *She's not wearing any shoes.*

* * *

She ran through the darkness toward the red lights. They stuttered and flashed in the night. They made no sense, those lights. They shouldn't be there.

Yet they had always been there. Deep within her she knew. The lights had always been there, and this had already happened. Already happened in another life, and would go on happening, all through eternity.

She sprinted down the edge of the driveway, oblivious of her feet clad only in socks, in the snow, unaware of it coming down, melting on her face and sticking in her hair. The scene ahead seemed to get no nearer, like a mirage in a dream.

Her mind was empty as she ran. She was aware only of her breathing, the pumping of her arms and legs.

Where was she going?

She had forgotten, momentarily, why she was even here, running. And then she saw his face, with the mop of hair in his eyes, and the half smile on his lips.

Someone was trying to stop her. A big man in a uniform had his arms stretched out. His mouth was moving but she heard no sound. She surged past him. She felt his fingers brush her arm as he lunged for her. Then more men surrounded her. She ran until everything in her body sang in chorus, her blood, her nerves, the ringing of the night, all blended into one magnificent blast of sound, and her son was in the middle of it, light brighter than a thousand suns surrounding him, and he turned and looked at her.

Then it was gone.

She saw that they were gathered round something in the road.

Her gaze fell on the object of their attention. She saw his face, and she saw his arm, his hand, which seemed to be reaching out. They were clearing the snow off him. There was a woman crouched there, who now stood up.

Hands gripped Callie's arms. She pulled at them and howled. Yet no sound escaped her.

The woman was coming towards her. She was waving her arms and her lips were moving. Callie felt the grip on her release. She moved away as the woman kept coming.

Her eyes were kind but her face was set and determined. Callie ignored her and walked on. Then the woman suddenly had her in a monstrous hug.

The next thing Callie knew, she was on the ground. She was only a few yards away from him. The woman was talking about a crime scene, that Callie must help her son by giving them space to work, that she had to be still now, be still.

Callie was looking at him.

None of it made any sense. Not the shouts nor the lights, nor this woman lying on top of her. This was a dream, wasn't it? She was still home in Florida; she would soon wake up and go to his room, and he would smile up at her from his desk, the secret smile that only the two of them shared, because they had been through everything together; they had survived his biological father, they had survived the painful divorce, they had survived being on their own together before Mike. It had always been just the two of them, the last two people in the world.

They would survive this.

They would survive.

CHAPTER EIGHT

Mike was getting angry. He felt it rising, breaking in waves in his brain.

The detective was holding his hands out in a calming gesture.

"She'll be okay. You need to stay here with your other children. Please. Let me ask you a few questions. We think what may have happened to your son — we think possible assailants left the scene only a half hour ago, and we're trying to track them."

"What?"

There were words coming out of the cop's mouth that Mike didn't understand. Where was Braxton? Why had Callie run off? Had the cop said something? Had the cop said something fucking stupid about Braxton? Did he say he was out there? Out in the road? What was he doing in the road?

"Anything you tell me right now could expedite their capture. Sir? Do you understand me? We can get whoever did this, but time is critical. Did your son have any enemies? Anyone who might want to hurt him?"

"What? No." Mike kept looking out the front window. All he could see were those harsh lights in the trees. He was dimly aware of Reno crying in the other room. He needed to go to her. Just a second, though. Just a second. Hold on.

"You just moved here. He started a new school, right? Any problems with other kids? Arguments? Bullying?"

"No. Kids at school? No, no problems." Mike's lips felt waxy, numb. He couldn't see Callie. He wanted to go out on to the porch. This man must get out of his way.

Shhh, said a voice in his head. *Calm down, baby.*

Callie, where did you go?

"Ok. What about other people? Who did he hang out with?"

"Hang out? No one." Mike strained to see further. He pressed his forehead to the window. It was cold, so cold. He shut his eyes for a moment. "Did he get hit by a car?"

"We don't know yet. But it doesn't appear that way."

"Then why . . ." Mike struggled to find the words. He licked his lips. His tongue was chalky. "Why are you asking me all these questions?"

"The person who found your son out there said that moments after he arrived, there was a—"

The walkie-talkie on the detective's belt burst with static. Then, "Detective Swift, Trooper Bronze."

He pulled the device out, in front of his mouth and pressed a button. "This is Swift. Go ahead, Bronze."

"Swift, Troopers Day and Wyckoff got a . . . we've got a dark green Hyundai at Exit 30. New York plates. Three people. One Robert Darring from New York, one Hide-oh . . . I can't pronounce it. Hide-oh Miko? Asian kid; Philadelphia. The third has no I.D. He says he's fifteen. The other two are older. Over."

"They say they were at the scene?"

Static, then the trooper broke over again. "Affirmative. Say they are friends with the decedent."

Swift pressed the button, scowling. "Say what they were doing up here at three in the morning?"

"Coming to visit. Saw the kid in the road, the old guy next to him, thought he'd done something bad, and turned and hightailed it."

Swift made a dismissive sound, blowing air out of his lips. "Hmm," he grunted without pressing the transmit button. Then he pressed again, and said, "Have Day and Wyckoff bring them in. I'll contact the prosecutor. Keep old Lenny Duso handy."

"Copy that."

Mike withdrew from the window and watched Swift as he placed the walkie-talkie back on his belt. Swift fixed him with a level gaze.

"Okay, Mr. . . ."

"Simpkins." His voice sounded far away. Reno was still crying. He needed to go to her now. He felt as though some explosive charge had just detonated, silently, as if underwater, bursting apart his family and flinging them all into different shoals.

"Mr. Simpkins? New York State gives us seventy-two hours to bring formal charges against the arrestees. I'm going to be honest — there's not a lot of physical evidence out there. The wind and snow have destroyed a lot. But these kids — you just heard — might know something. And if so, they could lawyer-up real quick; obtain a writ of habeas corpus and, if there's no charge, a judge will let them go."

Mike tried to absorb the words. Why was the cop saying all this? He moved towards his daughters in the other room.

The detective nodded. "You stay with them. I'll be back. We're going to need to find out how your son knew these three, if he did. So you be thinking about that. Think about anyone who may have wanted to do him harm. Don't worry about your wife — we'll take care of her. We'll bring her back so you can all be together . . . Mr. Simpkins. I'm very sorry."

"Thank you." His words seemed to come from someone else.

He turned into the hallway in time to see Hannah emerge from the bedroom, sleep in her eyes, her mouth turned down into a sad frown, Reno beside her, tears streaming down her face.

His heart broke.

CHAPTER NINE

Swift stepped off the porch and into the snowy night. The wind blew and bit into him, chapping his face and hands. He pulled his parka tighter around him and looked up the road.

The scene was still lit up, all those lights turning the snow pink, the trees a darker purple. He walked briskly down the driveway of the Getty place — now the Simpkins place. He'd had to deliver such news to many people during his years as a homicide detective, but this one was bad. The look on that woman's face. And the father — though for some reason Swift didn't place him as the biological father. It was just a guess; something in the man's body language, something in the way he spoke. Like he was overcompensating a little, the way stepparents maybe sometimes did. Biological parents, they got the child's love unconditionally. *Steps* had to work a little bit harder, had to earn that love. It wasn't fair, and for a job as thankless as parenting usually was, it probably made it all the tougher.

Swift himself had been raised by a stepfather. A brutal son of a gun, who had been a cop, too — for twenty-two years. He wasn't one of the nice cops, but one who took his badge and gun as a license to do whatever he wanted. To come and go and do as he pleased.

Swift didn't place Mike Simpkins as that sort of man, that sort of father. He sensed that Simpkins was a pretty healthy guy, mentally and all the rest, who genuinely loved the kid. But, you never knew. There was that itch in the back of Swift's brain that said Simpkins might be someone to look at. It could have just been that he wasn't the bio-parent, but it could have been something else, too, something that planted this little germ in Swift's mind. Such as the flare of anger he saw rise up in the man's eyes. Or maybe the way he had looked, just for a moment, when Swift asked if he knew of anyone who might hurt the kid.

Or maybe Swift was overreaching. This case was already tough, and he had a feeling it was only going to get tougher — for everyone. The irony was, he'd been courted by the Attorney General's office for the past two months; they were grooming him for a job much cushier than the life of a senior investigator with the State Police. He could've already said yes. He needn't be here, dealing with this, at all. He could be in Albany right now, he and his dog Kady in a nice little house on a nice little suburban street, dealing with white collar problems. But he'd said he had to think about it. Now he wondered what the hell he'd been waiting for. Dead body in the snow, in the middle of the road in the witching hours of the night — and a kid, no less. New family just relocated to town, and look what happens. And he was in the middle of it. When this thing was over, he was going to call Paul Greenberg at the Attorney General's office and say, "Yes, sir, thank you sir, be down as soon as I can shine and pack my shoes."

Huddled into himself in the cold, Swift turned towards the scene of the crime, a couple hundred yards away, the wind now cutting from the side, kicking up curls of snow, destroying more and more possible evidence, let alone a crime scene reconstruction.

The troopers were bringing the three from the Hyundai to the substation outside of New Brighton. The arrest had occurred no more than ten minutes ago, and they were half an hour away. Swift had twenty minutes before they would arrive at the station. It would be a good idea to get to them right away, certainly before any one of them acquired counsel. They'd be waiting for their out-of-town lawyers to get to the office, or, if they wanted public defense, a PD wouldn't be available until at least later that morning. They would be his for a few precious hours.

First he needed to check in with Brittney Silas, and see how she was coming along with the crime scene. And he needed to talk to the mother, if she'd calmed down. He hadn't even gotten her name.

As he approached, he watched as one of his troopers turned around a vehicle that was trying to drive west on Route 9N. He could see the driver ogling him through the bare window of the snow-encrusted vehicle as it passed.

CHAPTER TEN

Mike stood looking at the open laptop on Braxton's desk. He held both girls in his arms. Hannah weighed next to nothing, but Reno was heavier and pulled on his shoulder as he kept her against him.

As he looked at the computer screen, his mind was blank. He seemed to be having trouble putting even the most rudimentary thoughts together. A moment later, the screen went black, and the cartoon criminal disappeared. When the screen shut down, something in Mike's mind switched on.

"Daddy? Where's Mommy?" Reno snuffled against his neck. He could feel her tears soaking the collar of his t-shirt.

"A-mommah?" Hannah said on the other side of him.

"She's outside."

That screen timer is set to sixty minutes, Mike thought. He remembered having a conversation with Braxton about it not long ago. Braxton had been given a personal laptop on his thirteenth birthday. He'd had access to one before, an old one of Callie's, with limits to internet access that both Mike and Callie enforced. Prior to his thirteenth birthday, he had campaigned hard for an iPad Air or a Kindle Fire. He was an avid reader. He had canvassed Mike and Callie endlessly in his brooding, mumbling fashion. But they had decided on a laptop because it seemed the most useful for school. His homework assignments frequently required him to go online, and the laptop seemed like the wisest choice. And this time, it was agreed that there would be no parental control over online use. Instead, Mike and Callie monitored the number of hours Braxton spent each day. Two hours out of every twenty-four, for the purposes of entertainment. It seemed reasonable; two hours was either enough for one movie a day, or, should he choose otherwise, two hours of social networking or gaming — usually that game called *The Don*. No more than that.

In the beginning, they had been vigilant about checking how long Braxton spent online each day. But — life happened. They grew lax. Callie rationalized that it was no big deal, they could still count the days. Of course, though, they started to lose track. Without a system for who checked and when, and in the midst of dinners and work, and Mike putting his business back together, and the girls and all of their needs, monitoring web-time got lost in the family shuffle. It had been about a month since Mike could remember last looking at the stats — and Mike knew this because that was the day Braxton had shown Callie how to set a computer to sleep mode, and he'd demonstrated by showing her on his own computer. Seeing them together had reminded Mike to check how much time the kid was spending online.

Braxton was a tech whiz, like most kids these days. The scariest thing about the digital generation was how much natural aptitude the youth seemed to have. It was hard to mount a real argument against technology when it came to kids so readily. Hannah, at two, could already navigate around iPads and smartphones. She knew where the apps were on Mommy's phone and would scroll to them, double-tap to open them, and then play Counting-Sheep or Animal Farm Jigsaw or Cake Factory. Couldn't speak yet, not in full sentences anyway, but could operate wireless media devices with aplomb.

Braxton was doing things that were already beyond Mike's capabilities. He could see that the time restriction, loose as it was, was preventing Braxton from doing much more online. If given free reign, the kid could probably live online eighteen hours a day. Mike didn't doubt that Braxton would be able to write code for Flash websites if he wanted to, or even begin to design his own video game.

With one arm cupping each of the girls against his body, Mike leaned over, stretched a finger to the keyboard and tapped the space bar. The laptop woke up. The face of the mobster reappeared. It grinned at him and arched an eyebrow.

One hour. If Brax's computer sat dormant for more than an hour, it would go dark. An hour after that, and the CPU would go into hibernation.

One hour. So Braxton was at his computer one hour ago from now, playing this game.

The clock on the lower right side of the screen read that it was 3:48 a.m. At about 2:48, his son was probably sitting right here.

Mike leaned over again, feeling his daughters turning to lead in his arms. Hannah was sucking her thumb, her head on his shoulder. Reno was still burying her face in his neck. When she spoke, he could feel her lips move against his skin. She'd just asked where her mother was. Now she asked a more difficult question.

"Where's Braxton?"

"Braxton is outside, too, with Mommy."

His own words sent a spike through his heart, and Mike felt his lower lip tremble. His eyes stung for a moment with tears. But he couldn't lose it. Not now.

"Come on. Who wants something to eat? You girls want some breakfast?"

The notion of putting them back to sleep had crossed his mind, but Mike didn't think it very plausible. Hannah might go back to sleep for fifteen minutes or so, but Reno was much too upset at this point. He needed to ply them with food, fill their bellies and plop them in front of a TV show or something. There would be men, anyway, he realized, coming through the house in their boots with their pens clicking, their heads swiveling, asking questions, jotting things down. Men like the one who'd just been at the door, men like scavengers picking through remains.

The media, too, ogling and watching, and asking their questions.

He needed to feed the girls and get them situated so that he could get back to Braxton's computer for a moment, just to check a couple of things. Those men who would come and rake their way through the house would take away the laptop. Mike had to get something off of there first. Something better not seen by anyone.

"Here we go," he said to the girls, bouncing them a bit as he carried them down the hallway. "Here we go," he said in a sing-song voice.

CHAPTER ELEVEN

Someone wrapped a blanket around her, but she wasn't feeling cold.

They put him in a black bag. Then they were putting him in the back of a van. Someone told her it was the mortuary service. She would go with them.

They told her no, you need to go home, get warm. We'll need you to come down and formally identify the body in just a couple of hours.

She said if you touch me again, I'll rip your throat out. She got in.

They let her stay with him.

She looked at the man who had come to the door — *Death*, she thought of him as. He reminded her of something buried deep in her memory, something she had studied in school; *The Pardoner's Tale* by Geoffrey Chaucer. It was the plague; death was in town.

To Callie, this man in his black slacks and parka, his thinning hair blowing in the wind, was death. That look of detachment on his face as he watched her. They closed the doors of the van and his face shrank in the small rear windows.

And then she was alone with her son. She knelt down beside him as the vehicle drove through the night, and she put her head on his chest and held him through the body bag. She felt his arm and his hand and over it she placed her own.

Callie felt such a wave of sorrow and grief that she was unable to breathe. She gasped for air, her heart a drum beating in her chest. Her vision started to black out, and she felt hands on her. She fought and came to herself, pushing the groping hands away. She took deep, ragged breaths and regained control. They said he hadn't been shot or stabbed, that he didn't appear to have any broken bones. They were going to have to do some tests to determine the cause of death.

This made her throat and heart constrict again. She felt the blackness encroaching; she warded it off, she pushed it back — she threw her head back and expelled a long breath that felt like a geyser.

That great rush of air seemed to exorcise some demon, and everything became quiet. The van neared the mortuary and Callie was at peace. She kept her hand on the bag, even as they unloaded him and brought him inside. She never left him.

* * *

Swift watched the woman go. It was highly inappropriate and broke all procedure to let a victim's relative ride along to the lab. But there were trained professionals with her who knew how to handle such grief. Swift himself, despite all his years on the job, felt he did not.

Trooper Bronze opened the door to the police cruiser and looked out at Swift. Bronze would drive him to the substation, a few miles away. Another trooper would bring his own car along later.

He slid into the warm vehicle and felt his phone buzzing in his pocket. Expecting a call, either from the captain or the lieutenant, he pulled it out. It was another email message.

He grunted and asked Bronze, "You know how to deactivate email alerts on these damn things?"

"Sure. I'll fix it for you when we get there."

Swift sighed and gave the screen a series of touches with his fingertips, figuring out how to open the email. It wasn't that hard, actually.

"What a night," he said. He could still feel the adrenaline racing.

"You got that right."

There were two new messages, both from the same address. He thought he vaguely recognized the email address as having something to do with his bank.

The first one was about suspicious activity detected on his account.

He frowned and shook his head. Just what he needed at the start of a new case. He opened the next email.

This second one told him to take defensive action, with instructions on how to prevent future incursions.

"For God's sake," he muttered. Bronze glanced at him as he pulled away from the crime scene, engine roaring, lightbar flashing, tires kicking out fans of snow.

PART TWO

THE SUSPECTS

CHAPTER TWELVE

The State Police substation just outside New Brighton was a squat, one-story building with a few small offices and a single interrogation room. The main space featured basic equipment, including a copy machine, a paper shredder, an emergency medical cabinet, and a breathalyzer with its attending *Datamaster*. There was a kitchenette in the corner with a sink, refrigerator, and coffee maker. The interrogation room was a simple ten-by-twelve box, the walls institutional green, with a pane of one-way glass into a neighboring room the size of a walk-in closet that smelled of mice. There was no closed-circuit television; to watch a suspect sweat it out in the box, you sweat it out in the cramped space next door.

State Police Captain Tuggey was waiting as Swift came in. He watched wordlessly as Swift shrugged off his jacket and hung it up. He motioned the detective to sit down opposite him.

The bitter aroma of coffee percolating on the kitchenette counter filled the air. It looked to Swift as though Tuggey had dressed hastily. There was some black soot on his fingers, his white shirt was smudged with what looked like creosote and Swift could scent wood smoke.

Tuggey had a large ranch-style home ten miles away. Probably his wife had asked him to stoke the stove before he left. Life had to go on, even when you were a cop's wife.

"Mayor called half an hour ago," Tuggey said.

"Oh yeah?"

"Yeah. Lieutenant is en route. Know what the mayor said?"

"Tell me."

"'How long you gonna keep this road blocked off?' That's what he says."

Swift blinked. He remembered his conversation with Silas.

Tuggey puffed his chest out. "'As long as it takes,' is what I told him. But you got out pretty fast." The captain looked his hands, turning them over, examining the backs and fronts and in between the fingers.

"Cap'n Tug, Silas wanted to take her time, as she should, but we soon saw that the body was going to be our best evidence . . . and the three kids picked up in the car back on the interstate . . . Besides finding a piece of cardboard and some deer shit, there was nothing else at the scene."

"Fuck," Tug said softly. Profanity was unusual for the captain and he seemed to think that swearing in a low voice somehow reduced the level of venal sin. Swift watched Tuggey search the objects on his desk, as if the answer lay in the jar of miscellaneous pens or scribbles on the pad of paper.

"So, what's the play?"

"For now? I want to see what I get from our three teenagers. Or, is it two and a twenty-something. Troopers tossed the car on site — just a quick search incident to arrest. The two younger kids had phones on them, so we checked their latest messages, and we're pulling the laptop from the victim's room."

Tuggey nodded slowly, and resumed, "Mayor said his own phone was ringing off the hook. Says to me, 'I've got six inches of accumulated snow on that stretch of road the highway department can't get to. I've got people trying to get to work along the back way, one car in a ditch right now.'"

No doubt Mayor Engle had awakened as Tuggey had, alerted by the all-points bulletin. Deputy Cohen, first on the scene, had made a general announcement from the site that went out to all law enforcement bodies, including his own Sheriff.

Which made Swift ask, "Why isn't Sheriff Dunleavy running this?"

Tuggey all but rolled his eyes. "Oh, no doubt Engle had been hoping this case would have stayed within the Sheriff's Department so he could have polished his image. Amazing. Even someone dead in the middle of the cold road ain't enough to push politics aside.

"But, Dunleavy made the right choice, Swift. That's why you got the call. The Sheriff's Department doesn't have the manpower or experience for this. Dunleavy's good at what he does: the jail is a tight ship, the Deputies serve the community and the mental health offices, but he would be in over his head on this so he T.O.T.-ed it to us."

"He's worried about over-running his budget," Swift observed.

"Hey, you don't want to catch cases? Then you should have taken that Attorney General's job."

"I didn't mean that, Tug."

"Dunleavy can't stretch a dollar, so what? What's important is that we had a body in the road, a crime scene in the middle of a snow storm, and potential witnesses or suspects fleeing the scene. It's more than Dunleavy was prepared to handle. He made the right decision. What I'm just telling you, is that the Mayor was wadded up over it.

Says to me, 'When can we get this road cleared? We got people have to get to work.'"

"Should have asked him to make that statement publicly."

Tuggey threw his head back and laughed, dispelling the slight tension in the air.

"Exactly right. I should have." Tuggey grew serious again. "What I did say was: We don't rush a crime scene. We process it. We work up to the body." He looked shrewdly at Swift, his sooty fingers forgotten. "You sure you and Silas got everything? Last thing I need, Swift, is people saying we rushed it. The mayor wouldn't take any heat from that — he'd deny it. But did he or anyone from his office contact you, put pressure on you?"

"No, sir. We're getting the road open sooner than later because that weather isn't giving us anything. What we got is how that boy died and, right now, anything those three kids know about it. And I think we're in agreement that CLS headquarters in Albany is too far away and too long to wait for an autopsy, so I made the call and went with Doctor Poehler in Plattsburgh. Had the on-call mortuary service pick up the body and take it up." Swift felt a chill as he recalled the mother's face through the van's small windows. It haunted him. Why did a mortuary service van have windows anyway? "We can use the Albany FIC if and when we need the DNA databank. I'm on a first-name basis with two analysts there. Whatever we need will come quick. Okay?"

Tuggey pointed a finger in the air. "Okay, but listen. I'm going to keep the Sheriff's Department plugged in on this all the same. Alan Cohen is a good man and Dunleavy tells me he'd like him to get a little more experience. And they were first on scene. Least we can do is show him some respect for not going all cowboy on us."

"Long as he knows this isn't a ham and egg routine."

Tuggey narrowed his eyes. "He knows. Everybody knows."

"Okay."

Tuggey sighed and shifted his posture; the chair protested beneath his weight. "So, you said you wanted to see these characters one at a time. Two of them are juveniles, as you know. So for them we've got the video as well as the audio recorder in the room. I didn't know who you wanted first, so I gave you the Asian kid."

CHAPTER THIRTEEN

Tuggey swung open the door into the interrogation room. A frail-looking kid with stringy black hair, olive skin, and almond-shaped eyes turned his head to look back at them. He seemed terrified. He was maybe sixteen, and wore a track suit, black, with red-piping. Swift could smell the fear, like sweat and battery acid combined.

"Thank you," said Swift.

Tuggey promptly closed the door. Swift turned and looked at the kid, who lowered his head. Swift walked around the table where the video camera was mounted on a tripod. He looked it over for a moment before finding the record button. He fumbled with the DAT recorder for a second before turning it on. Finally he took a chair across from the kid. Once he was seated, he pulled out a notepad and pen from his inner pocket. He set these on the table and folded his hands in front of him.

"Hi," he said. "I'm Detective John Swift."

The kid looked up. His eyes were dark, but his face was open. He was obviously petrified. This thing could be over before Swift knew it. Things were looking up.

"Have you been given your Miranda Warning?"

"Yes," answered the kid, his voice so light and quiet it was almost inaudible.

"You understand you have a right to counsel. Would you like to contact an attorney at this time?"

"No."

Probably didn't want his parents to find out what was going on, Swift thought. He couldn't know that the troopers had already called them when he was brought in. His driver's license had been run, and the parents' number came up right away. If anyone was going to call a lawyer, it would be them. But the interview was on tape. Who knew what could happen down the line? All you needed was a sharp defense attorney claiming his client asked for a lawyer and didn't get one, and you could have an entire confession thrown out of court.

"Can you state your name and age, please?"

"Your name sounds fake."

Swift blinked and put on a smile. "My name? No, it's real."

"Sounds like a character."

"Oh I'm a character. Just ask my ex-wife. You want to know what? I'm actually John Swift the Third. And, get this, you want to know something even worse?"

Swift waited until the kid said, "What?"

"My middle name is Leslie. John Leslie Swift the third."

The kid was silent.

"But there's a good reason. My great grandfather was named Leslie. Back then, you could name your son Leslie and no one thought two ways about it. And he was a good man too. Know who he was?"

"No."

"Yeah, silly question. I'll tell you, real quick, just so you know how crazy this gets. He was one of the very first State Police Detectives; joined way back in 1925. Just seven years after the State Police were first founded. So. There's this guy named Sam Howell was murdered down in Westchester County. He was foreman of a construction company. But there was no local police department to investigate, so the state legislature put together the troopers. Just like here, in New Brighton, there's no local department. There's a Sheriff's Department, and sometimes they handle stuff like this, if they have detectives. But this one doesn't. That's why I'm here."

Swift sat back and fixed the kid with a level gaze.

"What's *your* name?"

"Hideo Miko." He pronounced it *Hid-aye-oh Mee-koh.*

"That's different, too."

"It's Japanese."

Swift gave him another smile. "Is it Hideo Miko the third?"

"No. My father named me after a Japanese baseball player. Hideo Nomo."

"Oh. Very cool. Your father a big baseball fan?"

"He's crazy over it."

"You get along with your father?"

The chitchat seemed to make the kid more comfortable; some of the fear he'd been exuding had abated. "Not really. Why?"

Swift shrugged. "Just asking. My old man and I didn't see eye to eye on anything. I'm talking about my stepfather. Practically everyone in my family is in law enforcement, though. That's how it usually works. My father was killed in the line of duty. He was a state police detective, too. My stepfather, though, he was a highway patrolman."

Hideo looked away and studied the wall for a moment. Maybe he sensed what was coming next.

"Point is, I guess it's in the blood and in the backstory. Know what I mean? So I'm going to ask you a few questions, and I really hope you can be honest with me. Alright? I just need to know a few things, and then I can get you out of here and back home."

The kid averted his eyes.

"What were you doing up here tonight? You and your family, you don't live up here. Do you?"

"No."

"So what were you doing up here?"

"Visiting a friend."

"And that friend was Braxton Simpkins?"

"Yes."

"Could you look at me, son? Would you mind?" Maybe it was rude in Japanese culture to look authority figures in the eye, but Swift needed to see what was going on there.

Hideo slowly brought his gaze back. The fear carved through his features. It made a knot of his mouth, as though he was afraid to blurt something out, or start crying.

"Thank you. Why were you visiting him in the middle of the night?"

Hideo shrugged his shoulders.

"Are you afraid to tell me something?"

No response, and then Swift saw tears filling his eyes. Hideo looked away again, up towards the corner of the room. He nodded twice, which caused the tears to spill over his eyelids and track down his face.

"Okay. So where do you live? Philadelphia?"

He nodded again.

"Do your friends, the two other guys in the car with you, do they live in Philadelphia, too?"

Now the kid shook his head, no.

"Where are they from?"

"New York City. And Short Hills, I think."

"Short Hills? Where's that?"

"Jersey."

"Okay. So we got three of you from three different states. How do you all know each other?"

"Online."

"And is that how you know Braxton Simpkins? From online?"

Hideo nodded. His whole mouth now was working, his mouth pursed, the lips crinkled, and his features contorted as he tried to staunch the flow of tears.

"What sorts of things online? Like Facebook? Social Media? That sort of thing?"

He shook his head again.

"Then what? Something else?"

The kid was very still. He stared at the desk.

When he finally spoke again, his voice trembled. "I don't want to say anymore. I'm sorry."

"Hey, no. Hey. It's okay. You're doing great."

"I guess . . . I guess I should call a lawyer after all."

His voice cracked on the word lawyer and he lowered his face into his hands. A few seconds passed, and then Swift thought he heard the kid say something. He leaned forward and listened to the muffled words.

I'm sorry, the kid was saying into his arms through the wet snuffle of his tears. *I'm sorry.*

One down, thought Swift.

* * *

Swift took a quick break and called Trooper Bronze, who'd gone back out to 9N to keep an eye on things.

Swift could hear the wind rattling around in the background as Bronze answered.

"You're still holding the scene?"

"Yes, sir, Swifty."

"Okay. I'd like you to call some relief. Leave the scene and head back over to the family."

"Sir?"

"Keep an eye on them, get the stepfather and his girls anything they need. I'll be there as soon as I can — these kids are opening up like flowers. I'm going to get a confession out of one of them."

"Excellent."

"But we still need to keep an eye on the stepfather. And while you're doing that, helping him out, we're going to get everything from the decedent's bedroom. Our CSI, Silas, is going to get the laptop — we need to make sure of that. These kids know each other from the internet. Emails, social networks, and whatever else they do."

"Copy that, sir."

"Thank you, Trooper."

"You got it."

Swift hung up and walked back to the interrogation room, which was now occupied by the driver of the Hyundai. This kid was twenty-three. His name was Robert Darring. He looked up at Swift. The look gave Swift a slight chill. He'd seen a face or two like that in his day. This kid was going to be a pisser, not like the Asian kid, but a tough nut.

Then I'll have to crack him.

CHAPTER FOURTEEN

Mike's hands moved over the keys of Braxton's laptop. The girls were sitting in the other room, eating snacks and watching cartoons on the TV.

He opened a new tab in the internet browser and went to Yahoo mail. His gaze swept the screen, registering what was there.

"Shit," he muttered.

Braxton had not kept his email account open with the password stored in memory. Mike clicked on "Sign in" and then sat back for a second, trying to think what Braxton's password could be.

Are you serious? You're looking to hack into your son's email right now in the middle of everything that's going on? Are you crazy?

Still, he had to try. They were going to go through this laptop, of that Mike had no doubt. A laptop was a modern person's journal, photo album, record of business transactions — a whole psychological profile, a veritable window on their soul. Braxton had been lying out there in the middle of the road covered in the snow. Some unknown kids had fled the scene. The cops would pounce on this laptop and Braxton's Kindle, too — anything that connected him to the outside world.

Mike tried something he thought might work. A couple of years ago Braxton had played *Minecraft* obsessively on the Kindle. There was a spooky character in *Minecraft* that just showed up at random, stealing your possessions and destroying whatever you had built. This character looked just like you, but had white, glowing eyes, an expressionless face. It was called "Herobrine."

Mike typed in the name and hit Enter. Red text appeared on the screen indicating that the password was incorrect. He tried another one, a character with long spindly legs and arms taken from a terrifying internet meme about a tall man who took children into the woods. "Slenderman." But this didn't work either.

Okay, made sense. It was a long shot anyway — Braxton had stopped being into *Minecraft* a while ago. What was he into now? He'd been given the laptop when he turned thirteen, four months before. So something that was important to him since his birthday.

Mike looked around the room. His gaze fell on the bookshelves, the top of the dresser, the closet. Any moment Hannah would start balking at something, or finish her snack and want more, or the episode of *Curious George* would end. He stood up so fast the swivel chair spun around. He hunted through Braxton's things. He looked at the two posters on the wall — both of them from *The Hobbit.* He knew Braxton identified with the Hobbits to some extent. Unlike himself, Braxton was small. He tried to remember the names of the characters.

He returned to the desk and tried some different possibilities. Every one of them came up incorrect. He could feel the panic starting to creep up his neck, his heart beating faster. He needed to go be with his daughters. Hell, he needed to go collect his wife. Callie was beside herself, out of her mind with shock and grief. He thought about Callie. She was strong, but her strength had a darker side — she was passionate, a gifted teacher because of her energetic style and her unconventional approach to learning — but this was the mother of all tragedies, the worst thing that could happen to a person, to lose their child, to outlive the love of their lives. He felt despicable and guilty over what he was trying to do.

What else? What else did Braxton like? What was special to him? What was secret?

He loved to skateboard and had gotten around Florida on those four little wheels for years. Mike had noticed that the skateboard had been left at home more frequently in the months before their departure.

Desperate, Mike tried a few brand names. Volcom, and Burton — though he thought Burton only made snowboards. He tried RUCA and Billabong. The red text kept flashing. Then the website prompted him to continue by entering a string of odd letters and numbers. It was attempting to protect itself from hackers.

Frustrated, sweating now despite the cool temperature of the room, Mike bent closer to the screen and squinted at the code, pecking it in with his index finger. Then he was again at the log-in field the idiot cursor blinking at him, teasing him to enter the correct phrase.

Or numbers, he thought. Or a combination of text and numbers. He could be here all day.

But he didn't think Braxton would've used numbers. It was just a hunch, but he felt like his son was more inclined to use a word with special meaning to him. The kid was into reading and writing, not math. What else was he into?

Braxton was fiercely dedicated to environmentalism and had some wild ideas about a whole new type of economy, what he called, on the few occasions they discussed it, a resource-based economy. This concern for the environment and the economy, coupled with his lack of debating skills, had caused some trouble between them on more than one occasion.

Mike felt a sudden light illuminate the back of his mind. An innovator Braxton had once expressed his admiration for. He had been watching some documentary about a man named Jacque Fresco who had created *The Venus Project*, an elaborate design for a utopian world, one that, to some people, would seem like pure communist fantasy, but that placed resources at the center of the world economy instead of the commodification and competition of capitalism.

Mike typed J-a-c-q-u-e- and F-r-e-s-c-o and then both together.

No dice.

He tried V-e-n-u-s-p-r-o-j-e-c-t

He hit Enter. Foiled.

He sat back for a second and rubbed his face. He leaned forward again and stared. He tapped the delete button until the word "project" was erased and then he stopped. He was grasping at straws here. There was just as much of chance that Braxton would be coy and have a password like "Password." Anyone who wanted to get anywhere they weren't supposed to go on the web didn't bother trying to crack existing passwords.

Mike was preparing to try a whole new angle when he hit Enter on "Venus," just for the hell of it and, a second later, Braxton's email account opened up in front of him.

Mike's eyes widened and his scalp tingled. He was in. He started flipping through the emails. He kept his eyes on the dates to the right of the email chain.

"Dad?"

It was Reno calling from the other room.

"I'll be there in a minute. Just put on another episode, okay honey?"

"Dad?"

"I said I'll be right there."

He heard a thumping.

"Dad there's someone at the door."

He froze. He had yet to locate the email. He peered at the screen and scrolled further down. There were not many messages. Mostly there were repeats from something called "Kapow." He quickly flicked the cursor over to the trash folder and opened it. He scrolled toward the bottom, and heard the knocking again at the front door.

Jesus, he needed to get out there. He strained his eyes, rolling up and down, scanning the screen. Nothing. Braxton had already deleted the email Mike was hunting for. It was long gone.

He pulled his face away from the screen and quickly closed down the browser window, collapsing both of the open tabs.

He got up out of the chair and turned to see that the screen was now illumined, whereas it had been dark in sleep-mode. The original browser window was now closed. He'd tampered with evidence, for God's sake.

He left the room, his pulse rate uncomfortably high. No one would notice anything, he reasoned. To check his son's laptop was a natural reaction that anyone could understand.

He entered the living room, turned and saw two shapes behind the window of the front door. They were here.

CHAPTER FIFTEEN

Swift pressed 'record' on the video camera, though he wasn't obliged to do so in this case. Robert Darring was an adult and it was only minors who had to be videotaped during interrogation. For adults the audio record was sufficient. But since it was already there, having the video on certainly couldn't hurt. Swift didn't have the benefit of a partner, not yet. He'd spoken with Kim Yom, who would be arriving shortly from BCI headquarters in Albany to head up computer forensics, but he didn't want to waste any time. His name suited him — as people all too often said. Justice should be timely. The kids were here now, and before the lawyers got to them, he wanted to hear their stories. He couldn't force them to say anything they didn't wish to, and he wouldn't. He would do it by the book. They had a right to counsel, but they could talk too. Maybe they even wanted to. The truth set people free.

Of course, it could also send them to jail

Robert Darring looked at him across the table. Now that he was in closer proximity, Darring didn't look his age. From afar, at a glance, yeah, he'd looked twenty three. He wore a hooded sweatshirt and sweatpants, the kind of outfit worn by college kids; only the sweatshirt displayed no collegiate logo. It read, simply, "OBEY." Swift had seen the word before, something to do with street art. It was usually accompanied by a creepy face, a rendering of the late Andre the Giant.

There were some faint lines around the boy's mouth and eyes, and pouches beneath eyes that were dark, so brown they were almost black. He wore his sable-colored hair close-cropped. He looked Italian or Hispanic, or a mixture of both, though his surname suggested Irish or Gaelic descent. Perhaps he was mixed-race with a white father.

"Could you please state your full name and age?"

"Robert Matthew Darring, aged twenty-three."

"And where are you from?"

"Originally or now, sir?"

"How about both."

"Originally from Queens, New York. Currently from Queens, New York."

Kid was trying to be smart. But Darring's face was blank. He looked like someone standing in line in a cafeteria or at a post office. The initial hard-ass impression was easing slightly. Or, he was playing it cool.

"And why were you on Route 9N tonight around 3 a.m.?"

Darring opened his mouth and proceeded to relate exactly the same story as Hideo Miko. They had come to visit Braxton. They saw a man standing over a body in the middle of the road and they freaked and turned around and got the hell out of there.

"Okay," Swift said, folding his arms. "Here's my problem with that story. One, it's the middle of the night — or very, very early morning. Two, you were *beyond* Braxton Simpkins' house. If you were coming from I-87 and turned off at exit 30, you would have been coming from the east. The crime scene is further *west* along the road."

Darring nodded soberly. "I understand, sir. It was the middle of the night for a couple of reasons. One thing, none of us have ever come up here before. We got a little lost. And I screwed up — I had the directions in my phone, but then I forgot my phone at home. So we had Sasha's phone and used GPS. I guess you could check all that, or whatever. But then as we got about to — oh, I don't know, I think exit 24 or so, not far north of Albany? The snow really started coming, and that slowed us way down. And that's why we went right by his house, too. This area is really small, like, really off the map."

"Oh don't I know it," smiled Swift. The kid was talking a nice little streak. Seemed happy to volunteer details about what and where.

"The GPS went wonky," Darring went on. "It couldn't tell us which house was his. Technology, right? I don't know, maybe we had the address not exactly right. He'd only just moved, so . . . but then we saw the guy in the road and it really scared us. If you say we were beyond Braxton's house at that point, I guess we were. But we had no idea."

"His parents were going to let you come visit in the middle of the night? Even if the snow hadn't slowed you down, or you hadn't gotten off track, you still would have arrived very late at night."

Darring lowered his head. "No, sir. His parents didn't know. It was stupid. The whole thing was . . . I don't know . . . We just thought it would be cool to take a road trip."

Swift took a breath and leaned back slightly. After a moment he said, "You know, when I asked Hideo Miko these questions, he had different things to say."

Darring looked up. For just a second Swift thought he saw something almost feral in the young man's eyes, something menacing. "He did? I don't know what. I mean, he was asleep for most of the drive. What we saw in the road really scared him. He's . . . he's different, sir. He has some problems, you know? I think he may have wet his pants, but don't tell him I told you that."

"Your secret is safe. But that's not what I mean. Hideo was afraid to tell me at first, but then he opened up. And his story does not match yours. So, let's cut through the guff and just talk straight. Alright? Here's what I've got." He leaned forward and counted off on his fingers: "I've got you at the scene of the crime. It's the middle of the night. I've got a witness see you speed away."

"Right. Which goes with what I'm telling you, sir."

"Uh-huh. Well, we have this kid's body on a slab right now, and within moments, we're going to have cause of death. And it's all going to add up to what you and your friends were really doing there tonight. It's just a matter of time."

Swift leaned back. For a moment he fixed the kid with a look that was fatherly, compassionate.

Then he leaned forward.

"Look Mr. Darring. I just need something to take to the DA. This is going to be an open and shut case. I don't even need anything from you; I've already got it. If we take this case to the DA right now, you're going to do time. Not easy time like your two minor friends, and not cozy county jail either. Prison time, Mr. Darring. I'm here to give you an opportunity to explain what happened. That's all. There's always two sides to a story, and if the DA hears your side, you'll get credit for it, and it can really help you out. You're going to need friends, okay?"

Darring's face remained inscrutable. He seemed neither alarmed nor angered by any of this. Instead, he too leaned forward.

"Sir. If this was really such an air-tight case? You wouldn't need to interrogate me. You would just go ahead and take it to the District Attorney for potential charges." Darring's dark eyes were lit with red pinpoints reflecting the record light on the video camera. His voice was even and light. "After I give you my 'explanation,' and it corroborates whatever evidence the state *does* possess? Then you go about trying to prove that I, the defendant, grossly understated my actual involvement."

Darring sat upright, his expression still blank.

Dammit, thought Swift. Okay, so the kid was too clever for the usual routine. That was fine; Swift had other cards to play.

As if on cue, his cell phone buzzed in his pocket. Swift pulled it out and looked at the incoming number. What perfect timing.

"It's my forensic pathologist." He stood up and walked briskly to the door, glancing back at Darring. "Let's see what she has to say."

He left the room.

CHAPTER SIXTEEN

Doctor Janine Poehler watched the woman in the adjoining room with a heavy heart. It was just before eight o'clock in the morning, and Janine's understanding was that the woman had been woken up in the middle of the night to be informed of the death of her son. She couldn't imagine a moment more tragic than this, a more horrific way to deliver such terrible news. Some part of the woman's mind must believe she was still dreaming, and soon she would awaken and the nightmare would be over.

The woman's name was Callie Simpkins. She was being comforted by two state troopers, one male and one female. The female trooper looked up and her gaze met Janine's through the glass that separated them, an unanswerable question blazing in her eyes.

The body lay behind Janine on the table, covered in an evidence sheet.

No way was Janine going to perform the autopsy with the mother watching. Simpkins was beyond grief; she was hysterical. Yet she refused to leave, and the troopers were pulling their hair out trying to figure out what to do with her. What the woman needed was a crisis worker, a mental health therapist from the county, who was supposedly on the way. Janine wanted to know who the hell had made the call to let the woman ride in the van in the first place. Simpkins had just spent forty minutes driving from New Brighton to Plattsburgh with her dead child in a body bag. She was out of her mind. Her eyes were locked on the body in the next room. Her mouth was open in a yawing, soundless scream, giving her face an eerie, misshapen look.

Janine turned her back on the viewing room. It was supposed to be there so that medical students and law enforcement officers could observe the autopsies. Janine did work with the college, but she also had her own practice in anatomic, clinical, and forensic pathology. Most of the referrals she got came from law enforcement, and sometimes medical students and criminal justice students were permitted to observe, depending on the circumstances. In fact, the local state university had just recently dispatched several students to witness a perinatal autopsy, during which two of them abruptly left. Imagine a bereaved mother witnessing her own flesh and blood child undergoing a postmortem examination. Even seeing the external examination would be devastating. She needed the troopers to get that woman out of the room.

The lead investigating officer was John Swift, a man she had known for many years, ever since she had been a medical student. She'd gotten his number from the female trooper and was now ringing him, keeping her back to the woman. God help him if he was the one who'd let the woman ride here with her dead child.

Janine put the phone to her ear.

After a couple of rings, he picked up. "Swift."

"Detective Swift. This is Doctor Poehler."

She heard some noise at his end, as if his phone were being jostled. "Yes, Doctor Poehler. How are you?"

"I'm in a bit of a situation."

"Yeah, this is one for the books alright."

She glanced at the body on the table. "That it is. Very, very unfortunate." Then with emphasis, "Made more unfortunate by the presence of the victim's mother."

Swift hesitated. "I appreciate you responding so quickly, Doctor."

"I'm an early riser," Janine said, letting it pass for the moment. "Autopsies are best performed within twenty-four hours of death. Organs deteriorate, embalming interferes with blood cultures and toxicology. But, Detective, I've never had to perform an autopsy with the family looking over my shoulder."

He was silent for a moment. She heard a door open and close at his end. Then he spoke, his voice low. "I know. This thing went off like a daisy-cutter. I made the call and let her go; she was so volatile . . . I'm sorry. I'll have my troopers get her out of there right away."

"Anything I'm looking for?"

"What's your initial perception?"

"I only glanced. Nothing obvious. No bruises, no blood. Normally developed white male measuring sixty-two inches and weighing a hundred and eighteen pounds and appearing generally consistent with the stated age of thirteen. Lividity is fixed in the distal portions of the limbs. There is one small scrape on the right cheekbone."

"Suggesting he fell to the ground?"

"Something like that, yes."

"Let me ask you — could this be some sort of illness? Something undiagnosed?"

"Of course that is possible. I have no idea at this time." She paused. "You know how this goes, Detective, I need time to . . ."

"I know. I just . . . I've got a suspect in the box right now. I really like him for this, but the crime scene was a wash and all else is pending."

Janine understood. Swift wanted something right now that he could turn around on whoever he had sweating in a small room beneath the lights. But she didn't have that for him. She didn't have medical history, nothing. "Best I can tell you that's pertinent right now, Swift, is that the kid is deceased. And my hunch — and I hate hunches — is that it's not from natural causes."

"Okay. Thank you, Doctor. I'll have the troopers escort the mother out of there."

"That would be very helpful. I'll call you as soon as I finish the external examination."

"Perfect. Thanks again."

"You're welcome."

Janine hung up. She turned around and looked into the observation room.

The mother was standing right at the window, her hands up on the glass. The troopers were behind her, attempting to gently but forcibly pull her away. The woman's mouth was moving. It looked as though she was saying something over and over again. Janine could just hear her voice, muffled, through the glass.

Please, she seemed to be saying. *Please.*

A moment later the male trooper took his phone from his belt and put it to his ear. Likely he was going to try for Mental Health to please come and medicate this woman. Janine had half a mind to do it herself, at least it would ease the poor woman's suffering. Or she could call the hospital and get her taken in to emergency care. Her anger had diffused somehow during her brief discussion with Swift. She found herself wondering if, before she was even aware of it, he had charmed her out of her righteous indignation.

CHAPTER SEVENTEEN

Swift had just put his phone back in his pocket and turned to re-enter the interrogation room when Trooper Bronze came walking briskly down the corridor, white snow still melting on his shoulders. Close at his heels followed Assistant District Attorney Sean Mathis.

"Detective Swift!" called Bronze.

Swift raised his eyebrows.

Mathis pushed in front of Bronze, slightly out of breath. "Sasha Bellstein. Your third from the car. He called a lawyer in New Jersey; he's advised the kid not to talk to you. Told him to sit tight, doesn't need to talk to anyone, 'they're not going to charge,' he says, 'and they'll have to let you go.'"

Swift held out his hand. "You're the new ADA. I'm John Swift."

"Yes, I know." They shook. Mathis was unsmiling and looked tired despite his crisp suit.

"We talk?"

"I'm in the middle of an interrogation, Mr. Mathis, and—"

"Really need to talk urgently," Mathis said. Swift saw a speck of sleep still left in the corner of the man's eye, and could smell the cologne rising from him in a fog.

"Of course," Swift agreed.

Swift looked at the trooper, who understood that the two men needed another room where they could have a private conversation. He glanced at the door to the interrogation room, and then back at Swift.

Swift winked. "He can sweat a bit longer. Good for him. Builds character."

Bronze smiled.

* * *

Swift and Mathis could watch Robert Darring through the one-way glass in the adjoining room. Mathis sat on the edge of the table, his hands folded in his lap. Mathis was young, still in his twenties, which, as far as Swift was concerned, was diapers. Mathis looked unhappy, like most young ADAs. They spent their time either preening for the cameras or reading the riot act in small, claustrophobic rooms like this one. Mathis didn't disappoint.

"The hell is going on?"

Swift blinked. "Come again?"

Mathis jerked his thumb at the next room, where Darring sat looking down at the table in front of him. The kid seemed almost meditative, Swift thought, not sweaty at all. Eerily inactive. Normally you had a suspect in a box like that, even if they were innocent, they became nervous and began fidgeting. Everyone had some dirt on them, everyone had lied about something. Whether it was taxes or unpaid parking tickets or the porn collection tucked away in the basement, everyone carried some measure of guilt. Being in an interrogation room with police breathing down your neck was like being in a sauna, it leached the poison out of you. Didn't matter if whatever you felt guilty about related to the investigation or not. Or, you had your zealots, your self-righteous types who talked about their rights being violated, and police harassment. Young men who drove drunk, let's say, got arrested, refused to be handcuffed, got pepper-sprayed, then turned around and started alleging use of "excessive force." Darring acted like none of these. He didn't seem nervous, nor was he claiming police abuse. In fact he did nothing at all. As if he were on pause. Barely there.

"You got this kid in there," Mathis growled, "you got a dead body, three suspects, two of them juveniles, in custody with, from what I hear, paper-thin stories — were you going to call me at some point? Gonna charge them with a crime, maybe?"

"We pulled these three in for questioning on probable cause for a felony, a good faith belief that they're involved, or, at the least, they know something about it. I didn't want to waste anyone's time reviewing the case until we had charges that would stick."

"Are you . . .?" Mathis gave Swift an incredulous look, as though he had just landed from another planet. "Are you presenting me the steps in a criminal case as if I'm your nephew at some family reunion, bouncing on your knee?"

Swift pointed at the one-way glass. "I had one of these kids in tears less than an hour ago, saying he was sorry, and the other one was just about to get the news from my pathologist that the victim's death was unnatural."

Mathis' expression suggested Swift was the dimmest bulb in the light factory. "I'll never understand cops. You want a suspect to talk, you charge them with a crime. Scare them, get them talking, put some muscle behind it. You make charges and then amend as you go. Let the law work for you."

"You charge them right off, they clam up, get lawyers, and you get nothing out of the interrogation. Right now, that's all we're subsisting on. What that kid in there has to say, and what the dead kid on the table has to say."

"Anyone thinking hit and run? Pathology look that way?"

"No. And to come from three different states, drive for hours through the middle of the night, to hit this teenaged kid with their car?"

Now Mathis dropped the look of long-suffering incredulity. His forehead creased. "They came from three different states?"

"Yes, Mathis. They car-pooled up here. And they first *arrived* and *then* drove away from the scene while the witness, Duso, was there."

Mathis closed his eyes for a second and massaged the bridge of his nose. "So it was Duso who gave the witness statement? Jesus. Okay. So, far as we know they arrived at the scene after the fact."

"Wait, what do you know about Duso?" Swift felt the hair on the back of his neck stiffen.

"Nothing. Relax. I know you and his son, Frank, have had a past beef, that's all."

Swift let it go for now. "Well, anyway, that's what we got from the witness. They arrived, they turned around, they drove away. Hence the probable cause, hence the questioning, but that's it for now."

"What about tire tracks? We've got the vehicle in impound?"

"It's dumped almost a foot of snow out there overnight. No tracks. We can impound the car if I make the call that there is evidence which couldn't be readily removed at the scene."

"You're doing it again."

"What?"

"The nephew bouncing on the knee."

"Jesus . . ." Swift waved a hand in the air. He wanted to get back into the box. Why was the frigging ADA hounding him now?

"Who's the CSI? Silas?"

"Correct."

"What do her logs show so far?"

"I left her at the scene. She found some snow. And some more snow."

"That's it?"

"That's it."

"And on the body? In his pockets? Anything?"

"He's dressed in pajamas. Nothing in his pockets."

Mathis turned and looked into the interrogation room again. Darring hadn't moved. "God." Then he looked back at Swift. "What else? What about the kid's home? Parents? Anything unusual?"

"We're going to go through the kid's things. His laptop." Swift nodded toward Darring. "So far two of them admit to knowing the decedent online only. They'd never met in person. This was their first rendezvous."

"Huh. Who do we have for that?"

"We have Kim Yom from the Cyber-crimes Division. She's got a bit of a journey to make, but she'll get here in a few hours. Meantime, Silas will pick through the kid's room when she's done with the core scene; she'll retrieve the laptop, hand it off to Yom. We'll keep good track of the chain of evidence."

Mathis looked down between his shoes and blew out a breath. Someone wasn't much of a morning person, Swift thought. The young new ADA was likely used to late nights in the city watching his money slide across the counter and come back as exorbitantly priced drinks. The only bar around here was *The Knotty Pine*. Probably not in Mathis' style. He seemed to be simmering down now, having come in on the boil.

"You know we'll have to kick these kids loose if we can't come up with something. You've got to formally charge suspects eventually, detective."

"Now you're bouncing me on *your* knee."

Mathis frowned. "Funny. And yanking the body out of there so quick? You think that was the right call?"

"You can't have it both ways, Mathis. You can't ride me for not calling you sooner so you can slap on charges and at the same time ride me for moving the crime scene along too fast. Plus, without a confession, these guys are going to ask for a grand jury, and you know it."

"You better hope not."

Swift turned on a smile. In his younger days he would have fed those diapers he was wearing right back in the young ADA's face. But his lack of control had gotten him into more trouble than it was worth.

Besides, Darring could wait a little longer. Swift decided he'd make a quick detour to Plattsburgh. Check on the mother. See what Janine Poehler had to say about the body.

CHAPTER EIGHTEEN

Janine spoke into her recorder.

"Name: Simpkins, Braxton Thomas. Date of birth: October 22, 2001. Date of death: February 17, 2015. Age: Thirteen. Body Identified by Callandra Mary Simpkins, mother. Medical Examiner's case 2014-227. Case number 003428-23E-2015. Investigative Agency: Bureau of Crime Investigation, New York State Police."

She circled around the table and continued to record her observations. "The autopsy is begun at 6:14 a.m. on February 17, 2015. The body is presented under a white evidence sheet. The hands have been bagged. The decedent was wearing black pajama pants and a long-sleeved t-shirt with detailed art work on the front. Socks and sneakers on the feet. No jewelry. Upon removal of the clothing, an odor of urine was detected. Areas of the body were swabbed and submitted for detection of uric acid, as were the pajama pants and t-shirt. Following removal of the shirt, various scars were observed along the left forearm that suggest possible cutting and at least one mark from ligature, as if the victim's left wrist had been bound at some point. A second ligature mark, which will be known throughout this report as Ligature B, was observed on the decedent's neck. The mark is dark red and encircles the neck, crossing the anterior midline of the neck just below the laryngeal prominence."

She stopped recording for a moment and took another long look at the young body. Virtually hairless. Thin, pale. A typical teenage boy. The marks on the forearm that indicated cutting were not surprising — in her twenty-five year career as both a pediatric and adult forensic pathologist, she had seen more young people who cut than she could count. It was a sad, disturbing trend.

The anomaly lay in the ligature around the one wrist. There was no matching mark on the left arm, which was pristine. Who tied up only one arm?

The mark around the neck was a different story. Upon first glance it looked like it could be caused by attempted suicide. But a closer inspection suggested otherwise. Janine began to envision an odd and rather gruesome scenario wherein the teenager had tied his wrist to his neck, and perhaps applied force to tauten the ligature and maybe to cinch the windpipe, shutting off the blood and oxygen to the brain. It could even have been a perverse kind of "high," or a new type of sadomasochism she hadn't yet encountered.

She clicked the record button, her gaze resting on the mark around the neck.

"The width of the mark varies between 0.7 and 1cm and is horizontal in orientation. The skin of the anterior neck above and below the ligature mark shows petechial hemorrhaging. Ligature B is potentially consistent with the apparatus that caused Ligature A. The absence of abrasions associated with Ligature B, along with the variations in the width of the ligature mark, are consistent with a soft ligature, such as a length of fabric, rather than a belt or a rope." She clicked off, thought, then resumed recording. "Or a soft belt. No trace evidence was recovered from Ligature B that might assist in identification of the ligature used."

She paused again. For a moment, she felt light-headed. She needed to take one of her pills — the early call from the State Police had disrupted her morning routine.

That job as Commissioner of Health looked better all the time. An office, not a lab. A desk, not an operating table. She'd heard through the grapevine that John Swift was also considering a slight career change, and that the Attorney General's office had made him an offer to investigate for them directly. Corporate and political malfeasance was a tropical paradise compared to the lab and the streets and the ripped-apart families. When this was over, she would offer to buy Swift a cup of coffee and the two of them would convince one another to make the transition without further ado. Just two aging divorcees, urging one another a little farther along the path. He was a handsome man, too, in a Clint Eastwood kind of way, so a coffee could have other perks.

Then she looked up from the body and into the observation room, and there was the senior investigator, raising his hand in a wave.

* * *

"You scared the hell out of me."

Swift smiled. "What've we got?"

She went through the external examination with him as they stood next to the body, giving him an overview rather briefer than her more detailed notes. "I'll have the whole Summary Report to you by midday," she said, searching his face. "But something tells me you don't want to wait."

"You mean other than the fact that I just showed up and scared the hell out of you?"

"Meaning I can see it in your eyes."

"Yeah. We're struggling with a spoiled crime scene and hysterical parents and an antsy-pants new ADA looking to prove himself to the District Attorney. I understand you offered the mother a mild sedative?"

"We did. Unusual, but I had to do something. She seems to be coming around. Where's the father?"

Swift pulled in a slow breath. "There are two little girls . . ."

"Oh God," Janine said, dropping her gaze and looking away.

"Yeah. And they're with him."

"Poor things."

"Yeah. So I'm going to go ahead and speak with the mother and father separately; try to get them together later in the day."

Her eyes opened wider as she looked at him again. "Don't overwhelm them, John. They've been through just about the worst thing that can happen to a person."

"I know. And I believe there are three kids sitting in Essex County right now who are responsible, or at least know who or what is to blame. But I need something to link them to it. Sounds like what you've got so far is taking me in the other direction — ligature marks, self-inflicted wounds."

"I haven't done an internal. You want me to do it?"

He scowled. He wanted her to do one. And she knew she was compelled to. But to cut open that kid . . . Her job had never before affected her like this. All through her career, friends and family had wondered, how do you do it? How can you cut open a dead human being and poke around inside them? She'd never been bothered by the biology of humans or animals. In high school she'd dissected insects and amphibians with total aplomb and made the transition to grad school cadavers without batting an eye. It was just how she was. She was easily able to compartmentalize. But it had become harder and harder over the past few days, or weeks. She was really feeling it today.

"I'll get started on the internal," she said.

Swift stood still, his eyes fixed on her.

She squinted at him. "You're not telling me to hurry are you? You're not telling me to rush the internal examination of a human being in a homicide case, are you, Detective Swift?"

He pursed his lips, suppressing a smile, and exhaled through his nose. "Of course not."

"Back later," he called on his way out of the door.

She watched him exit the room and took some small comfort from the fact that his job was, in many ways, as tough as hers. She had to internally examine the boy who lay on the table; Swift now had to go talk to the mother.

CHAPTER NINETEEN

"He was very gifted."

"How do you mean?"

Callie Simpkins had composed herself somewhat. She must have gone into the bathroom and splashed some water on her face, tying her long, sun-streaked hair back into a ribbon. She and Swift were sitting in a small café down the street from the morgue. The place was quiet, the only sounds coming from the cook in the kitchen, banging around with steel pots. The air smelled of fresh coffee and old bacon grease.

"I mean, gifted." Her eyes were red from crying, the surrounding skin shrink-wrapped. But her look was focused, despite the sedative she'd been given. "And like most gifted people, that came at a certain cost."

"Special schools, that sort of thing?"

She was shaking her head emphatically. "No. No special schools." She took a deep breath and her gaze wandered, leafing through the scrapbook in her mind. "We had him tested once. We didn't know what to do — he was very quiet and withdrawn a lot of the time. And he fell along the autism spectrum. Not quite autistic, however they test for that. But they said he had Asperger's syndrome. And if he was diagnosed, we could get insurance to cover his therapies and any meds, and I was like, 'What?' You know?" She looked at Swift now. "Like, 'What?' I don't want my kid on pills, going to see shrinks all the time. I didn't think it would be good for him. Plus, I think as a society we over-medicalize. First they wanted to tell us he had ADHD. Then I read that, you know, they take these kids who are younger — I started him in kindergarten early — and they're maybe a little less emotionally mature and they say, 'the kid has a disorder.' Today's world, you walk just a little out of the marching line, you know, because maybe your left foot turns a fraction of a centimeter, you've got 'Left Foot Turn-out Disorder,' or something. You know what I mean?"

Swift nodded. He kept his opinions to himself. They didn't matter here. But she was genuinely funny, and he cracked a smile at her comments. He liked her immediately. He could see that, through all the grief she was battling, Callie was a survivor, a firebrand. Probably had a tattoo hidden away somewhere. Maybe two.

"I wanted to nurture *who he was*, does that make any sense? Not try to change him . . ."

But then, inevitably perhaps, Callie Simpkins lost herself to sorrow again, and Swift's smile faded as he watched her face crumble, and her eyes fill, then overflow with tears. She averted her gaze and took a breath, her lip trembling. She took her hand and rubbed at her eyes, smearing away the moisture, and pressed her fingers to her lips, as if to stop them from quivering. Swift seized the moment, and redirected the conversation.

"Mrs. Simpkins. What do you think Braxton was doing tonight? Why do you think this happened?"

She gave him a hard look. "Do I think this happened because of Braxton's limitations?"

"No, no. That's not what I mean at all. I mean, what was he doing? Did he wake up because something disturbed him? Or was he already awake?"

She lost some her defensiveness.

"Oh, he was probably up. He wakes up in the night. Almost every night. Never bothers anyone. Just sits there in his bedroom. Lately, he'll play his game."

"His game?"

"Yeah, some game on his laptop. It was on when I came into his room tonight. Is it still 'tonight,' or is it 'last night' now?"

Swift was jotting down some notes. "I think we can say 'last night.' Do you know what the game was called?"

"Uhm, I don't know. I can't think of the name. Mike would know. Brax played all sorts of games. He loves them. I know you're supposed to . . . what's the word . . . to moderate what your kids do with games and computers and phones, and we do all of that. Reno, that's our six-year-old, she already wants a phone. You know? She says it's not fair that the three of us have cell phones and she doesn't."

The tears spilled now, and she took a hasty swipe at her cheekbones.

"Braxton had a cell phone?"

"Well, sort of. We call it the 'house phone' and he only has it if he's going to be out somewhere. Lately he's been taking it more often because we've moved and are getting into a new routine and there's been a lot to do. But Braxton and his games." She shook her head, in a mixture of pride and disbelief. "He's always been something. Can solve any game in, like, minutes flat." She snapped her fingers. "He would play the games on my phone when he was younger. You know, the apps. And he would just chew through them in minutes." She snapped her fingers a second time. "Amazing." Then she grew troubled again.

"So that's what you mean when you say he was gifted? I mean, one of the ways he showed it."

"Sure. Yes. Definitely. He had that sort of mind. Problem-solving. Way ahead of other kids his age. But that's not . . . that's not everything."

"What else?"

"He was . . ." She fought hard against another tide of emotion. "You know . . . he'd get upset."

"How so?"

She shrugged, but Swift knew she was certain of what she was talking about. "He'd get very down on himself if he lost at something. Not because he was competitive with others so much, but he was competitive with himself. Does that make sense?"

"Absolutely."

She searched Swift's face with that penetrating look she had. "But don't think for a minute I mean he was violent. Brax was incredibly kind. Ethical. He was protective of others, never wanted to hurt anyone."

Callie bent forward and buried her face in her hands. She sobbed silently, her shoulders rising and falling.

Swift was tempted to reach out and comfort her, but it was best he didn't. "Mrs. Simpkins, we can do this later, when your husband gets here."

Her head came up and she sniffed back mucous and wiped away tears from her face again. "No," she said. "What, am I going to sit around here and lose my mind? No, let's figure this out."

Swift nodded. He admired her attitude. She brought to mind a younger Janine Poehler. She was a bit like Brittney Silas, too. That reminded him; he needed to check in with Silas as soon as possible. Between preliminary autopsy results and the statements of his mother, self-harm — in this case fatal — was beginning to sound more plausible.

Swift took a sip of his coffee and set the cup back down.

"Everything okay at bed time last night? Anything out of the ordinary?"

"Well, everything's sort of out of the ordinary. We just moved two months ago."

"That's stressful."

She gave him a look that seemed to detect criticism. "Sure. But we've done alright."

"I'm sure you have. How's he adjusted to the new school?"

"He's done fine."

"And he was in which grade?"

"He's in seventh." She paused for a moment. Swift wondered if she was aware how she switched back and forth between the past and present tense. That was usually the way of things soon after losing someone. Likely she was not cognizant of it. "I said that we started him early, but after all the other stuff, we had him repeat a grade. Second grade. We thought that would take the edge off, and it did. It helped."

"When you say, 'we,' you're referring to you and the educators, or your husband, Michael? Any others involved?"

"I mean Michael . . . But sure, there were other people too . . ." There was a hint of a question in her voice.

"I know that Braxton is not Michael's biological son. What sort of role does his biological father play?"

Her look instantly hardened. "None. Mike and I have been together for eight years. When we met, Braxton was five. I had been raising him alone for three years. Mike adopted him, that's why his last name is the same. His biological father has no involvement."

"His name?"

"His name is Worthless Deadbeat Dad."

"Any aliases to that?"

Her eyes narrowed, but her mouth twitched in a smile. "Tori McAfferty."

"And where does he live?"

"I don't know. He never paid child support; I never wanted to see him or think of him again."

Swift made a couple more notes. When he looked up, Callie was staring at his notepad. "I know what you're thinking."

He set his pen beside the notepad and looked at her.

"You're thinking that Braxton is a troubled kid. Parents divorced, raised by a stepfather, recently moved far away from home, started a new school, and has a different mind than most people. You're thinking he did something to himself."

"I just need to get as much information as possible. In no way am I jumping to any conclusion."

"He wouldn't do that."

"I believe you." Of course he did; a mother never thought her child would do such a thing. There was no mechanism that could support the idea. Swift took a moment to deliberate if now was the right time to tell Callie about the three kids who were picked up. If anything, he was wondering if Braxton was *pushed* into doing something to himself. Peer pressure. It happened more and more these days, especially with the internet and on social media. "Have you spoken with your husband since you left the house?"

She looked remorseful. "No. I left my phone at home. I haven't called. I need to."

"I think that's a good idea. But, before you do; your husband was standing beside me when I got word that the troopers picked up a car which had left the scene just after the witness arrived."

Her eyes lit up. "And . . .?"

"And I've questioned two of the three young men who were in the car."

"Are they suspects?"

"I think what we would say at this point is that they are persons of interest. They have not yet been formally charged as suspects."

She was sitting upright now, her back rigid, her eyes wide. "Who are they?"

So much for the sedative they gave her, he thought again. He flipped back a couple of pages in his notepad. "Are any of these names familiar to you? Robert Darring, Hideo Miko, Sasha Bellstein?"

"No. No, I don't think so. Who are they?"

He took a breath and shrugged. "We don't know, exactly. They say they were friends with your son. That they knew him from online. You say he played some games. So, maybe from one of these games. They're young. Two teenagers, and one older, in his twenties."

"What the hell did they say they were doing up here?"

She was getting agitated. Swift saw that same 'mother bear' who had run shoeless out of the house. He'd made the call to tell her about the three kids — he was seeking a way to tie them more definitively to Braxton, but it was at the cost of her trust in him. He could tell she would become adamant that the kids were prosecuted. He understood that. But it just wasn't so simple, and the ponderous machinery of the justice system was always hard for the bereaved to accept. They wanted fast action and instant results. Who could blame them? He merely tried to serve that up as best he could.

"They said they were visiting. That it was a planned occasion. They alleged that your son was involved in this plan, and expecting them. Did he give you any indication? Did he act strangely at all last night? Maybe he . . ."

"What? Acted like he was going to run away with them? No way. Braxton wasn't running away anywhere. Who are these kids? Have you contacted their parents?"

"Yes. The Assistant District Attorney spoke with the parents of two of them."

"The Assistant attorney? Why not the District Attorney?"

"Cobleskill? She might get involved down the line, might not. It all depends on the case. Anyway, none of the parents were aware their children had gone anywhere. None of them knew your son."

She seemed to be waiting for more, but there was nothing else, not yet. Swift knew in his bones that the three young men who'd come up to pay a visit were not telling him everything. The Asian-American kid had even shut down on him, acting afraid to talk. He doubted that Braxton Simpkins had invited them, or wanted them to come. It was instinct, but instinct backed up by some persuasive facts.

For one, Braxton had been in his pajamas. He didn't have a bag with him, packed and ready to go. He'd gone out into the dark and cold with nothing.

When she spoke again, breaking into his thoughts, Callie's words were soft, contemplative, and yet ruthlessly precise. "Three kids — or, a man and two kids — drive up to our town in the middle of the night and are seen leaving the scene where my son lies all alone in the middle of the road. Dead. My son is dead."

She regarded him levelly across the table. All the emotion had drained from her face. Swift had seen this before, usually in men, but sometimes in the women too. She was now a heat-seeking missile. She would want justice for her son. And she would stop at nothing.

Swift closed his notepad and stuck it in his inner breast pocket. He clicked off his pen and slid that in beside it. He began to feel the first smoky curls of fatigue creeping around the edges of his thoughts, his vision.

"You need to get some rest," Swift said, as much to himself as to Callie. "I'm going to have a trooper drive you back to your home."

"No. I'm not leaving him."

He leaned across the table, and this time he did touch her hands. They felt cold and dry. "Mrs. Simpkins, there is nothing you can do for your son here. The best thing you can do for him is to go and be with your daughters, your husband."

"Did you take his laptop?"

"We're taking a few things from his room. It's going to be tough, but we're going to need to search through any of his email accounts, Facebook, Twitter. I'm sorry that . . ."

"Good."

She surprised him by getting up from the table abruptly and looking around the empty cafeteria. "Take whatever you need and charge those three. I'll leave. I'm going to go say goodbye first."

"Mrs. Simpkins." *Oh no.* "You can't."

"I *can't*?"

"There will be the right time and place for formal goodbyes . . ."

"Thank you, detective, but please get out of my way."

Fine. Here it comes. He blocked her path. "Mrs. Simpkins, Your son is about to undergo an internal autopsy."

Her gaze speared him. "What?"

"We need to know how he died."

But it was too late. She pushed past him and charged out of the café, through the front door, a little bell chiming.

"Shit," Swift muttered, and started after her, pressing buttons on his phone to dial emergency services.

CHAPTER TWENTY

Swift drove back south to New Brighton. It was slow going. For a while it had looked like the storm was ending. The precipitation had tapered off to a few twirling flakes, but now it was back with full force, thicker than before. The day was grey, the trees streaks of brown, and the mountains silent behind the gauzy curtain of falling snow.

Callie Simpkins had the body of a star athlete in comparison to his. He'd been unable to reach her before she'd made her way back inside. She'd rushed ahead to the autopsy room. Mercifully, the curtains had been drawn in the observing area, and the door to the lab locked. While she banged on the glass and yanked at the door knob, Swift had finally caught up with her.

She'd fought him off like a wild creature, beating her fists against his chest and arms — he could still feel the impact of her blows. At last she had crumbled, leaning into him, all the sadness and pain released from her in a torrent of inarticulate cries that had finally dissolved into tears. Her body went slack, all the muscles turned to rubber, and he'd held her until emergency services arrived.

They took her to CVPH, where she was now under much heavier sedation. He hoped she would be able to get some rest. There was no doubt she was strong, and during their talk in the café she had shown that her mind was sharp, her instincts on point. He couldn't blame her for the emotion that overcame her. He could only imagine, after all she had been through with her child, now having to face this.

For a long time to come the waves would batter her, like a boat in a storm, offering only the shortest reprieves when her mind temporarily occupied itself with mundane things, basic, survival things like going to the bathroom, maybe eventually eating. But after each brief moment of forgetting, it would return. Even, in times to come, when she thought she'd reached the shore, she would be in danger of crashing on the rocks.

Swift drew a deep breath, hearing a rattle in his chest. He let the air out in a long, slow exhalation. He drove the car south, the wipers on high to sluice away the thick, wet snow.

* * *

"She's at the hospital," Swift told Mike Simpkins. "You're going to want to go be with her. You and the girls. My troopers will take you there."

"No," Mike said. "We'll go ourselves."

"Then they'll escort you. I won't take no for an answer. The roads are really bad out there."

Mike was doing the dishes. He had tucked the girls away in the master bedroom where they were watching a movie on his laptop. He said he felt guilty about all the TV they were watching, but he didn't know what else to do with them. He told Swift he thought with any luck they might go back to sleep.

"And how about you?" asked Swift. Mike had offered him a seat on a stool next to the woodblock island in the kitchen. "How are you holding up?"

"I've never been so awake, yet so tired at the same time," Mike said, turning from the sink with a couple of plates which he dropped into the nearby dishwasher.

Swift nodded. He watched Mike go through the routine for another moment. He knew some people coped with loss by keeping their hands busy. Mike seemed that sort.

"You know it can only help me the more we talk about Braxton," Swift said. "But this is a hard time; you need to be with your family."

Mike paused for a moment and looked across the woodblock at Swift. His eyes were puffy. "I will," he said. "I've called one of Callie's co-workers at the school. Another teacher. We had dinner a few weeks ago. She's going to come and watch the girls, and I'll go up to the hospital."

"I think that's wise."

"So we can talk while she makes her way here. Maybe fifteen, twenty minutes?"

"That's great. I appreciate that."

Mike nodded. He looked distracted. It seemed to Swift that there was something else that burdened him. The troopers had already cleared out the things from Braxton's room, under the guidance of Brittney Silas. There was no one else in the house at that moment, so Swift wondered what was occupying Mike's thoughts.

"Something I asked you before," Swift said. "Just . . . it's important. Did you think any more about anyone who might want to harm Braxton?"

"Yes," Mike said suddenly. He looked up rapidly, directly at Swift. "His father."

Swift felt something cold flicker through his veins. "You mean his biological father?"

"That's right. Tori McAfferty."

"And why do you think that?"

Now Mike glanced away. He took a step back from the dishwasher and leaned against the counter beside the sink.

His gaze drifted beyond Swift, through the windows and into the woods outside.

Mike suddenly looked less certain, as if he was going to backtrack from his statement.

"Everything is important right now, Mike. Every single thing. What makes you say you think his biological father would want to hurt him?"

Mike's chin fell. He reached up and ran a hand through his stringy, black hair. He took a deep breath and exhaled. In the other room, Swift could hear the voices of cartoon characters and calliope music as the girls watched their movie.

"He tried to get in touch with Braxton about a month ago. He lives up here."

Swift flipped through his notes, but more for effect than anything. He remembered what Callie said without needing to read it. "Your wife says she doesn't know where Mr. McAfferty lives. You do?"

Mike kept his face down, looking at the floor. His head bobbed. "He found out that Braxton was moving north. I don't know how. I asked Braxton if he'd been in touch with Tori before, but Braxton said he hadn't. But, you know, these days, Facebook, and all that. All you have to do is look. Callie's not a big Facebook person, and neither am I. But we both have accounts. And I have a Google Plus, you know, and who knows all the accounts Braxton might have, or what he says on them."

"We'll know soon enough how Mr. McAfferty found out. But, how do *you* know?"

Mike raised his head slowly. "We have this policy about how much time Braxton spends on the computer? On all the devices. You know, we read how harmful it can be for kids. Makes them sedentary, they can get addicted to it, the neuropathology of their developing brains, stuff like that. Especially Brax. I don't know if Callie told you, but he has Asperger's."

"She talked about it. That you avoided diagnosis, and sort of treated it yourselves and tried to blunt the edges where you could."

Mike's eyes were hard for a moment. "Well, you could say that. Did she tell you that, with no diagnosis, there is no insurance?"

"She mentioned it."

"Right, so, everything we've had to pay for, and I mean, Brax would only eat real particular foods for like five years, and Callie had him on all this holistic stuff, and vitamins — she had him do acupuncture, we've had speech therapy, we've had play therapy — I've paid for all of that. I mean, we've paid for it. Not cheap."

"I understand."

Mike hesitated. "So . . . we instituted this system where we would check how much time he spent on his laptop — which he just got for his 13th birthday. Two hours a day. Three on weekends. Some people might think that's too much. Some people think it's overbearing. It's hard to get the balance, you know?"

Swift was listening, making the occasional note. He was also forming a picture in his mind of the way Mike and Callie Simpkins operated together in their marriage. Mike seemed like the worrier. A man with something to prove perhaps. This was just a gut observation, and Swift knew he was no psychiatrist. Speaking of which — and he made a note — each of the parents would probably benefit from seeing one, Callie especially. Callie was all guts and emotion and rubato. Mike seemed more intellectual, compromised by a guilt complex, along with some resentment about what his family were costing, which he seemed to feel, at least to some degree, was excessive.

"I understand," Swift said again. "So you were checking up on the time Braxton spent on the computer and you . . .?"

"I'm not proud of it, you know? We had guests over for dinner. You know, the woman I've got coming to watch the girls. And all during dinner that night, Brax was a bit sulky, and then he made some crass remark. I confronted him about this after the guests left. He got pretty upset, and made a comment about going to go live with his biological father. Then we got into it, and I questioned him, and found out that they'd been corresponding. After that I did a little searching and found out that the guy's got an HVAC business not far from here. But this guy, man. You know?" Mike shook his head and stared off now into times past. "The things he did to Callie; what he put her through, and what he put that baby through at such a tender age. Man . . ."

"He was violent?"

Something fierce came across in Mike's gaze. "Oh yeah. That fucker was violent alright."

Mike ducked his head and glanced across the room in the direction of the rubbery cartoon voices. He made a face as though his hand had been caught in the cookie jar. Swift saw it was due to his use of forceful language. Then the anger returned. "Yeah, he was abusive."

"A drinker? That type?"

"Yeah, but more so other things. A huge temper. Violent. Mental problems. Drugs."

"Like what?"

"Oh . . . Callie told me so many things when we first got together. It took a long time for her to recover. I had to be patient. You know, she was pretty sure he was bipolar. OCD, all of that. Had to have everything just so. When the baby came, he couldn't deal with it. Too messy, too disorganized. Callie is . . . I like to call her Madam Chaos. Somehow she keeps it all together. One of those people who has a method to their madness, you know? Tori, though, he medicated himself. Speed, that sort of thing. To the hyperactive sort, speed actually mellows them out." Mike looked away, and Swift could tell he was longing for his wife.

"I've heard that." He made a note then looked up. "Sounds like Callie and him were mismatched."

"You ain't kidding."

"So . . ."

Mike got back on track. "So, I was checking on Braxton's computer one night; the time-check thing. He was in the other room, or something. And he'd left his email open. I just . . . I looked. I saw a thread of emails between the two of them. Tori talking about all these things, how he wanted Braxton to come stay with him, how his mother hadn't told the truth about him, all that sort of stuff. Calling her a liar, basically, and me an imposter. It really got under my skin. So I wrote back. Stupid. I know it wasn't right. But I wrote back, I identified myself, saying that this was wrong, to be getting into the kid's head like this. I don't know. I don't know what I said. And him, I mean, he was online right then and there because I sent the email and was looking through other stuff and an email came right back. And there was that same old temper, threatening me. So. I threatened right back."

Swift was very still. "What did you say?"

"I said I'd hurt him."

Swift waited.

"I said I'd kill him."

There it is.

Mike suddenly grew animated, defensive. "I know it was too much. I was so shocked by it, and hurt, and . . ."

Swift was nodding. "I understand. Well, we'll have a record of all of this, we can piece it together when we go through Braxton's laptop. We . . ."

But Mike was shaking his head. "It's deleted."

"What? As of when? How do you know?"

"I checked this morning. Before your guys came in."

"Why?"

"Why? Because I said I would kill the guy. I thought about him, when, you know, when you first came to the door about Braxton being out there. I panicked, and I'm sorry."

"Did Braxton see the email you had sent? Did Tori continue to correspond?"

Mike grew quiet. He wouldn't meet Swift's gaze. "No. What I said was, the whole thing I said was, if he continued to correspond, or tell Braxton I intervened, I would call the police, I would do everything in my power to wreck him, his business, everything, anything. That if he wrote back again, I would kill him."

"So he never wrote back."

"No. I checked."

"When you got on the computer this morning. After we notified you about Braxton's death."

"Yes."

Swift calculated all of this. "And you think maybe Braxton was affected. Did his mood change after that?"

Mike's chin started to tremble and he hung his head again. He nodded. "He'd been keeping it from his mother, but I could see it. I know it affected him. Made him depressed." Mike's hands flew up and covered his face. "Oh Jesus. Oh Jesus . . ."

At that moment, Swift's phone buzzed in his pocket. It hadn't seemed to stop for the past four hours. Mostly he'd been ignoring it. But he decided to take this one. He couldn't bear watching Mike Simpkins fall apart.

* * *

Swift stepped out of the room, leaving Mike sagging against the kitchen counter. He answered the call.

"We're about to open this road back up to the public." It was Brittney Silas.

Swift walked to the front window of the Simpkins place and looked west up the road. He couldn't see the core scene from here, and the lights were subdued in the grey daylight. Soon the troopers would be pulling out, and the massive plows would come through, scraping the roads down to salty rubble.

It was one of the fastest tear-downs of a crime scene he'd ever heard of. Normally you took your time with a scene. It was all you had. Silas was telling him the road was open because she was nervous. But they'd already gone over this. She wanted his approval, he decided, since he'd been calling the shots.

"It's okay," he said. "I think we got everything we're going to get from there. How you doing?"

"Doing okay," she said. It sounded like she was in her car, heat blasting away. "Little frozen."

"Yeah."

The silence lasted just long enough to be awkward. "You did a good job."

"Did I?"

"Yes. Let's just say I consider you more than a mere supplemental party."

"Shut up," she said, and he thought he could hear her grinning.

"You're more than just an evidence tech."

"Ha ha," she said. "No one has used the term 'evidence tech' since back in your day. Fifty years ago or whenever."

"Touché."

She laughed, but it wasn't a full laugh, it had no real joy in it. He couldn't blame her. Still, Swift could never resist the opportunity to get someone going, crack a smile, something. His ex-wife said it was because he couldn't handle unhappiness. "Well I picked the right career, then," he would tell her. But with Alicia, nothing. Couldn't get a half-smile out of her. It had been impossible to make her laugh. Maybe, he wondered, the new guy could do it. Maybe he was making her laugh right now while Swift was stuck working out of his tiny State Police substation in an office barely bigger than a walk-in closet. He could be in that box with some killer for seventeen hours, looking for somatic indicators, trying to draw a confession out, make a friend, always pitching and selling. When you were an investigator you had to be a salesman. You had to sell someone what they didn't want — ever — their own stinking, filthy truth.

Swift was making himself depressed.

"How *you* doing?" Brittney asked, perhaps sensing it.

He looked out the window, into the faint light of the day, watching the snow blow down at an angle, and the wind whip it up off the eaves of the house, spiraling it, spreading it like a crop dusting.

"I'm okay."

"Don't believe you."

"You shouldn't. You're right. Look, you did fine. You processed your scene, you didn't touch the body — we bagged it, and we've got the bag for trace analysis. There was nothing else anyone could have done at that scene."

She was quiet, considering. "Thanks, John."

"Sure."

"We'll catch up at the station? Or, what do you want?"

"I want you to stay with your evidence, keep me comfortable that we've got case continuity with all this moving around and shucking and jiving. And ask Cohen if he'll meet me at the diner in town in one hour."

"Altos?"

"That's the place. Oh, one last thing. When you talk to Cohen, give him a little assignment from me. Can you?"

"He'll like that. Sure."

"Have him just do a search on the name Robert Matthew Darring. He can cross it with Queens, and also just do a general search."

"Got it."

She fell silent again, and this time it felt heavy, like she was waiting for something else from Swift. He'd been prepared for that.

"Not asking you because I have other plans in mind for you."

"Oh yeah?"

"Dinner."
He thought she might just be smiling again.

CHAPTER TWENTY-ONE

Mike stood in the kitchen, staring off into space. The water was running behind him. He'd never felt anything like this before in his life. He had no idea how to handle it. The detective was talking to him again. Asking him something. Looking at him. He needed to get to his wife. Callie was in the hospital and he was standing here doing the dishes, answering this man's questions.

"What does your wife teach?"

"She, ah . . . she teaches art."

"Art?"

"Yeah. Studio Art. The kind where models come in and pose."

"She's a painter?"

"Painter, sketcher, illustrator, tattoo designer; she's done it all."

"That sounds great."

The detective, Swift, put on another one of his smiles that made Mike feel as if his blood were seeping into places it shouldn't. What did they call that when the heart stopped pumping and the blood drained down? It wasn't rigor mortis . . . livor mortis, that was it. Mike wondered if Braxton had livor mortis. What was happening to Braxton right now? Was he being cut open? Swift had mentioned the autopsy. But Mike hadn't heard anything much after the detective told him Callie was in the hospital. That she'd basically become unmanageable.

"Hey, Mike?"

"Huh?" Mike looked up at Swift. The detective was looking behind him. It took a second to register before he turned round and saw the faucet running. He hit the lever with the heel of his hand.

Where the hell was Callie's co-worker, Sarah? She'd sure picked the wrong day to take her time getting to where she needed to be. Of course, it was brutal outside, with the wind picking up into gales, dumping the snow all over the place, creating cowls and ridges like sand dunes. Mike checked the clock on the stove. Had it only been ten minutes since he looked at it last? Time was all over the place. One moment he lost whole chunks of it, and then it slowed to an agonizing crawl.

Braxton, somewhere in a room where they were digging into him and separating him with stainless steel tools that glinted beneath the fluorescent lights.

The kid had been standing there in the kitchen. Right where the detective was now. Last night. Eating his final snack before bed. He'd had a few handfuls of *Combos* and some milk. He only drank milk at Mike's insistence. All he really liked was grape juice, the kid. It used to aggravate Mike. They'd gotten in little heated battles over it. Mike had raised his voice about it once. It all seemed so stupid and petty now. Mike felt waves of guilt churning up, choking him.

He leaned into the sink and an explosive, unexpected regurgitation of his previous night's dinner splattered into the steel basin.

His body was shaking as he reached up and turned the tap on. He was beginning to lose his grip.

"Mike. Maybe you should be looked at, too. Let me take you, when your friend gets here to watch the girls."

Mike leaned down and put his mouth to the water frothing from the tap. As he let it pour over his lips and tongue he was reminded of the week-long crusade Braxton had undertaken not long ago, to conserve water. He'd seen a documentary or read an article online, and suddenly he'd been afraid that they were all going to run out of water — not today, but when the girls had grown up and were about to start families of their own.

"We waste water like it's nothing," he'd said, his eyes animated beneath the mop of highlighted hair. The only time Braxton ever really came out of his shell was when he was on some crusade. "People think the Third World is the only place to have water shortages, but we have it right here in the United States. Lake Mead is running out. Vegas is going to pipeline all the way up into northern Nevada and steal the water from there. Then *that's* gonna run out, too."

Over the years, Mike and Callie had held several private discussions about Braxton's bouts of anxiety over environmental and economic issues. They admired the kid for his knowledge, but worried that his concern, sometimes amounting to panic, was not healthy. He was easily agitated, and he blew the issues out of proportion, obsessing over it for days, sometimes weeks, like the water issue. Or he would champion something like The Venus Project for hours on end. Callie's biggest fear was that this behavior showed traces of his biological father's symptoms. The mood swings and the obsessive-compulsiveness. Braxton didn't have the signature peculiarities that were supposed to accompany OCD, like turning a light switch on and off, having shoes that didn't touch together in the closet, but he worried about things that were not yet happening, he perseverated endlessly over some eventuality that might just come to pass, and Callie described his father that way, too.

The detective was still behind him, standing just next to the woodblock, no doubt looking at him with that frown of empathy and concern that was making Mike sick. He was getting annoyed with the detective now. Standing there, asking questions about Callie, about Mike, about who they were; assessing what kind of parents they were.

He spun around, half-aware of the water running from the corners of his mouth.

"Why don't you stop, huh? Give us a little space. I already told you what I think. I think you need to look at the kid's biological father. Alright?"

The detective was nodding, still with that *I understand* expression on his face that Mike hated, wanted to smash, wanted to run away and hide from. He wanted to get away from this entire day, this whole nightmare. He wanted to wake up and have his wife next to him and the kids — all three— snoozing contentedly, soft sounds of sleep drifting through the air, as the house, satisfied with their warmth and presence, creaked and sighed around them.

Without another word, the detective named Swift suddenly walked out of the kitchen. Mike heard him leave by the front door.

Mike felt his heart turn cold, and his hands form into fists. He found himself thinking back to earlier times, back to the days when he'd been young and free in the city and pain like this couldn't touch him. Running around with guys like Denny Ford, guys like Bull Camoine, owning the night, taking what they wanted.

Back then, there had been nothing to lose.

CHAPTER TWENTY-TWO

"Can you tell me where this email came from?" Swift asked.

It had been two hours since he had left the Simpkins place, and it was now going on ten in the morning. The clock was ticking on the three young men from the Hyundai. They were being kept on ice in the back rooms of the sub-station, given meals, kept sequestered from one another, but time was running out. Like Mathis had said, they needed to be formally charged, booked, and dropped at the county jail to await arraignment. Janine Poehler was still performing the internal autopsy on the body, Brittney Silas had dusted for latent prints and turned over the laptop to the police officer now sitting in front of Swift. Kim Yom.

Yom was with computer forensics, a cyber-crime specialist. She was Filipino, with a Korean surname. Or, was it the other way around? Swift couldn't remember. She'd made the drive up from Albany through the severe weather in record time. Added to which, she'd attended the latest National Cybercrime Training Partnership a year before, so she was alright in his book.

"Here's what I've done," Kim said. She had two laptops in front of her. She referred to the one on her left. "After I fished this email out of the trash, I began at the bottom and worked my way up in the headers. First we've got original arrival time, a couple of months ago, you can see that here. Content type is plain text. But then already, in this next line, we have a problem. Most everyday emails are MIME. That means Multipurpose Internet Mail Extensions. That's a formatting protocol to encode any attachments and alternative representations in a single email. But this email is more dynamic than that. Okay, we can see here the 'To' field, it's to you, and the 'From' field, it's from this address. There is no X-sender, or X-originator or X-originating IP. Ah, but in the Received; here is where we would find the gold."

"Please tell me about the gold. Before my head explodes."

"The series of 'Received' headers are the trail we follow. This trail tells us where the message was sent from, and along what path or series of servers it traveled across the internet. And this is why we started at the bottom, as each mail server adds a received header to the top. So, you see all these? On and on and on?"

Swift bent forward and squinted at what to him looked like hieroglyphics. "Uh-huh?"

"That tells me that this email was bounced all over the world. There is no discernible return path. It's completely covered up. This email came through the deep web."

Swift looked blankly at the screen. *The deep web.* He'd heard the term, but couldn't remember where. Part of him felt foolish for asking, but he asked anyway. "The deep web?"

Kim pushed back from the desk and turned in her chair to better face him. "In a nutshell, everything you and I see and do on the web is just superficial. What the everyday user accesses — Amazon, email, even porn — that's just surface material. Like, cutaneous. The deep web, also called the dark web, is ninety-percent of the internet. Subcutaneous. Beyond that, really; the guts. It's where you'll find the black markets for prostitution, gambling, murder for hire; all that good stuff. It's where hackers go to rob bitcoin and Target and create massive viruses. Or, I'll give you another analogy. Think of it like the water beneath the ground. You're standing on dry land, but there's an enormous aquifer beneath your feet."

Swift considered this. It described how he felt to a tee.

"Great," he said laconically. "So the email is useless to us."

"I'm sorry detective. It could take months to track down the source."

"Well . . ." He looked at her and his eyes conveyed *If months is what it takes . . .*

She looked back at him like he was crazy. It was a look he'd become familiar with over the years. He smiled. "Okay, let me ask you this: this is pretty big league stuff, right? Hacker stuff. You think some guy who might have an anger management problem, maybe a drug problem, a deadbeat, is going to know how to do all this stuff? Hide his . . . whatever you said?"

"I really can't make that assessment, Detective."

He looked at her, hoping for more, but she was a stone. "Okay," he said. "Then please tell me more about the victim's activities on his computer."

Kim seemed happy to change track. She turned to face the second laptop, her own.

"Okay. Here I've cloned the hard drive to my computer and gone through the registry. I've been able to recover almost every deleted file from when the computer was first purchased and activated, which was only three months ago. Pretty normal stuff."

"Like what? What normal stuff?"

"Like there are a handful of school assignments. Just Word Docs. One Power Point presentation for an oral report, and one spreadsheet for a math class. Other than that, there's nothing. But the internet cache is loaded. It looks like he spent most of his time online. I'd say ninety percent of the time the victim was actively using the web."

"Doing what, mostly?"

Kim Yom's slim, delicate fingers fluttered over the keyboard for a moment and Swift watched as the internet browser opened and brought them to a website. The front page of the site depicted a bloody, Mafioso scene, a man in a classic mobster hat and trench coat, holding a tommy gun, stood over a fallen body.

"What's this?"

"This is *The Don*. Very popular game."

"What's it about?"

"Oh, building and managing a criminal empire, killing off your competition, that sort of thing."

Swift grunted. He leaned in and squinted at the image. "Can we play it?"

"We need to create a username and password."

"Yeah, but, doesn't he have one? Stored in memory? Just click that button there, 'play.'"

Kim glanced back over her shoulder at Swift. "Passwords are stored in log-in cookies. I'd need to use his computer." She was asking permission.

"Don't sweat it. Let's just take a peek."

Kim once again turned to the laptop on her left. With latex gloves on her hands, she brought up the same web page and clicked the start button. They waited a few seconds while the game loaded, a blood-red progress bar inching across the lower portion of the screen. Once it had fully loaded, they were looking at a rendering of a New York City neighborhood. The volume was faint, but Swift could hear the sound of traffic, cars honking, even birds in the trees.

Trooper Bronze and Trooper Day were in the office, both of them opting to pull double-shifts in order to stay with the case. They drifted over towards the machine to have a look.

"I'm familiar with this game," said Kim. "You don't need to download anything; it's all on the company's servers. Which means that whatever actions the victim took on here, we'll have no record of them from his laptop."

"Can we search for the names of the three suspects in the box?"

Kim shook her head. "Each user comes up with a code name for themselves. See?" She pointed a pink-nailed finger at the screen. Swift saw the name "Fresco."

"That was his nickname," Kim said. "We're in his game."

"What's that?" Opposite the name and other stats was a smaller window.

"That's chat."

"Chat?" Swift knew what online chat was, he just hadn't realized that it had integrated with computer games. He supposed it made sense. "So, he's playing with other people from around the world, and he's able to chat with any of them?"

"If they're online, yeah. More than chat, they can interface with each other wearing headsets, talk to each other. There's also this inner game email here, too." She made a few quick movements on the mouse pad and a new window within a window opened, showing a chain of emails.

"Let's look for emails with other players."

"No problem." Kim selected one of the four tabs on top of the email window; Reports, Messages, Tributes, All. She clicked on Messages, and a list of names appeared. Swift read a few of them. Mickey 2 Nines. Lefty Guns. Dixie Normous. They ranged from tough, mafia-sounding names to the silly, lewd, and sometimes completely obscure. One name was all alphanumeric symbols. The other was a nonsense syllable half a dozen characters long — HYLPMR.

"Can we print all of these out?"

"Absolutely."

Swift leaned back from the laptop, stretching, feeling the knots that had settled in his upper back throughout the morning. Driving, hunching over tables, standing around in the cold, it all took its toll, and he wasn't getting any younger. The two troopers stepped back and gave him space, as he rolled his neck and his shoulders for a moment. He brought his attention back to Kim and the laptop.

"Okay," he said. "So, what else can we do? How can we find who he was talking to? I need to place those kids in this game and find something they said to him."

But she was shaking her head. "That's not possible. Unless he took a screen shot of something, but I've found absolutely none. It's possible he uses his phone for this game, too, so I'll have to go through that next. Otherwise, we'd have to get a federal warrant, fly to San Francisco and lift the data from their thousands of servers."

Swift sucked his teeth for a moment. Then he dropped his palm onto the desk next to Kim and looked into the computer screen at the tiny objects moving around behind the open email window. The miniature buildings in the neighborhood, the tinny, faraway sounds of the streets, as if he was looking through a portal to some other world. Which of course, he was.

He turned to look at Kim. "You think he would've given out his physical address?"

"It's possible. A player can be friends with another player one minute, have an alliance with them, and then be enemies the next. In the game, and in their own minds, their reality. These games are becoming more real to kids than their everyday life. On the other hand, kids are always told not to give out information over the web. And, in my experience, they're pretty smart about it. It's possible he offered his information, but I think, if anyone found out where he lived, they did it another way."

"How? Why? What makes you say that?"

"Because this computer has been hacked. The basic operating system firewall, a network filter, was breached two days ago."

Kim turned her face from the screen and her dark brown eyes looked up at Swift.

He gazed back, unflinching. "This laptop was hacked?"

She nodded.

He instantly thought of Mike Simpkins. "By someone who came into his room and . . ."

Now she shook her head, "No. By someone remote. Through the internet connection. The Simpkins have broadband and a decent router. There's plenty of signal pumping through their home."

"How, though? I mean, I don't know the first thing. They just zero in on an email address and then, what? They connect to the computer and take it over?"

"Yes and no. That's what an IT person might do if you call them up and give them your passcodes because you're having a problem and you let them control your computer remotely. This is different. They came at this computer from a different route. From the deep web."

That phrase again. "Jesus," Swift muttered.

Kim looked at him straight-faced. "Personally, I think Jesus would be impressed. I consider Him a libertarian."

CHAPTER TWENTY-THREE

"So let's recap," Swift said to Deputy Alan Cohen over scrambled eggs, bacon, and toast at the local diner in New Brighton. Time was absolutely critical, but so was food, and so was delegation. They were later than the usual breakfast crowd, but the two cops still drew stares from the other patrons. The crime had come too early to make the news, but there were other ways of getting information, especially in a small town. Swift smiled at a few faces, aware of their curiosity. Then he dismissed them from his mind.

Swift was glad Cohen was able to join him. Cohen was enthusiastic, and Swift needed a sounding board right about now. The only negative rumor on Cohen was that he had terrible flatulence, and no one liked riding in a deputy cruiser with him. He would try to hide it, they would say, which was worse. A straight-up ripper would at least let you know what was coming, instead of the virulent sneak attacks that led to rolled-down windows and caused Cohen to whistle a tune like he didn't know who'd dealt what.

"We've got a family who moves up here from Florida two months ago, in the middle of the school semester," said Swift. "The wife is able to take a job mid-year as an art teacher at the college in Plattsburgh. They've got three kids, two in school, one just a baby. The husband is out of work, trying to start up a business here, or get freelance work as a camera-type guy. Photography or something. The teenager is in some ways atypical, possibly an undiagnosed Asperger's case. In other ways, seems pretty normal. He plays a game regularly, called *The Don*, with other players all over the world.

"This morning, at just before three a.m., he leaves his house in the middle of a snowstorm. We don't know why. Both father and mother say laptop was open and switched on when they checked the room for him, and that game was on the screen. Brittney Silas secured and documented the room and seized the laptop, and we've been going through it.

"He goes outside in his pajamas. So, either he rushed out, or he's got some kind of mental state he's in that doesn't remind him to put on warmer clothes, or he's under duress of some kind. Because the car that shows up while Lenny Duso is standing there in the road — we don't know that it just arrived in town. Those three could have been here earlier. Maybe they were returning to the scene of a crime."

Cohen was nodding, his gray-blue eyes shining as he absorbed what Swift was recounting.

"You arrive first on the scene in response to Duso's emergency call," Swift said to Cohen. "You arrive approximately five minutes after the call. You assess the scene and put out the APB for further assistance. Then you call your Sheriff, Dunleavy. Dunleavy calls my captain, Tuggey, who rouses me out of sleep — I'm on call. Tells me to check it out, looks like a homicide, Sheriff's Department is willing to T.O.T. I call my evidence tech, Brittney Silas, at the okay from Tuggey to get whoever I need, and he's making calls, too. I arrive approximately twenty-five minutes after the emergency call, Woodruff about thirty minutes, Silas, about thirty-five, forty minutes. Sound right to you so far?"

Cohen nodded. "Sounds right." He forked some hash browns into his mouth.

"Okay. I do the initial walk-through with Silas when she arrives. We're now forty-five minutes or so from the emergency call. With me? And we spend ten, maybe fifteen minutes before I leave her to process the scene up to the body. There's not much — everything is covered in snow — and we've got a description of the runaway car from Duso; working the scene for tire impressions wouldn't be worth it anyway — it's a main artery, there are tons of tracks, and there's the goddamn snow. So, we're pretty quick on the process. It's more the body we want to get into as evidence; we have that taken by the on-call service. Meantime, now, I've gone over to the Hamiltons, spoken to the neighbors there, and then on down to the Simpkins once we've got a solid idea that it's their kid. Troopers were ready to go door-to-door anyway, but it worked out that way. Point being, I'm at the Simpkins house at *least* an hour and twenty minutes after the call. Still with me?"

Cohen nodded again. "Still with you."

"So, let me ask you: how long does it take to drive from that spot on 9N to exit 30 on I-87 where my troopers picked up the three kids?"

Cohen narrowed his eyes and chewed his food, swallowed, and said, "I see where you're going. 'Bout twenty minutes, thirty in the snow, forty if you're barely crawling."

"Exactly. So, what were those kids doing for a whole extra hour?"

"Could've stopped at the gas station. Gotten something to eat. Messed around."

"But they fled the scene. They wanted to get away."

"Maybe they thought they did. Maybe they're just kids and it was out of sight, out of mind for them. Time for a soda."

"But the gas station is closed between 11 p.m. and 5 a.m." said Swift. He hadn't been eating while he talked, and his food was getting cold. He picked up a strip of bacon and chewed on it, took a sip of his black coffee. The food was greasy, the coffee strong, and he savored both tastes. He'd skipped breakfast and now his stomach growled in anticipation. He tucked into the meal and started after the eggs, watching as Cohen nodded.

"That's definitely interesting," said Cohen. "Who else do they know in the area? This 'we came up for a surprise visit' is obvious claptrap. But, maybe they *did* know somebody, and they laid low there for an hour."

"Totally possible."

Cohen looked around, seeming to gain mental momentum. "Something else I was thinking; maybe it's nothing."

Swift pulverized more bacon with his teeth, his gaze inviting Cohen to continue.

"Well, I was thinking about the family's situation."

"Yeah? Me too."

"They sound like they're on the ropes financially."

"Uh-huh. The dad started talking about lack of medical coverage. The kid had some special needs."

"There you go. And that's on top of a basic struggle, I mean — three kids, one salary? Okay, maybe they have some savings. Maybe they're secretly loaded. That Getty place they bought is okay; decent little plot of land, nice views of the mountains, but it's no castle. They picked that up relatively cheap — it had been sitting on the market for three years. So, if they have money, their home doesn't show it."

"Or their vehicles," Swift added, picturing the rusted Ford pick-up in the driveway and the small, ten-year-old Honda. "Not even an SUV to tote the kids around in."

"Exactly."

Swift put his silverware down for a moment, his appetite momentarily sated, his attention on Cohen. "Where are we going with this?"

Cohen shrugged. "Just that money is so often a factor. In just about everything."

"In just about everything," Swift agreed.

* * *

The bell chimed as a trio of patrons walked into the diner, gaped at the two cops for a moment, then made their way to an open table.

"Now let's talk suspects and possible motives," Swift said, picking his teeth with a nail. Their plates were cleared away and Swift had requested the check. He fixed Cohen with a studied glare.

"We've got the three in the box now. We can't hold onto them for much longer unless we charge them."

"Fleeing the scene of an accident?"

"Could be. If we can show the car has damage, and that the victim suffered from an impact. But as things are now, that doesn't look too likely. Appearances are that the vehicle and body never made contact. Brittney Silas will let us know."

"The online game . . ."

"Right. If Kim Yom can find something on the victim's laptop. She indicated that it could take a long time — longer than we have to keep them on suspicion. But I'm thinking about motive. Possible it was bullying, and it went too far. Happens all the time. We need a clear indication of that, though, and I'm either going to get it from the kids in the box or Yom will get it off the computer. Now, did you do a search on Robert Matthew Darring?"

"I did," said Cohen eagerly. "No record, which you already knew. I did a standard search after that. White pages address in Queens. Okay. I did combinations, too. There was a hit for 'Matthew Darring' on a website called 'zKillboard.' Some crazy shit over my head. I made notes.

But I saw one thing under this guy's profile that said 'I whip my slaves back and forth.' Other than that, Matthew just gets you to the Bible. Robert Darring, just the physical address. The name Darring alone, clothing manufacturer. Specializes in camouflage."

"Great," said Swift. "I'll take a look at the notes. In the meantime, though, we've got something else. Another person of interest is the victim's biological father."

Cohen's eyes widened as he listened to Swift relay the conversation about Tori McAfferty. "So we've got this unbidden return of the biological father, and a threat issued by Mike Simpkins, the stepfather. This is something I really want to look at right away. McAfferty is in the county, in South Plattsburgh." Cohen was leaning forward, those grey-blue eyes stormy. He was waiting, Swift could tell he was longing for some action.

"If you want another assignment, I'd like you to pay him a visit, just get an idea." Swift said.

"Absolutely." He was nodding vigorously. "Absolutely."

"Bring someone with you. Who's on shift this evening?"

"Deputy Trainer."

"I'm sure the Sheriff will dispatch him to you. Your department has been very cooperative. Is this something you could do?"

"Yes," he said. "Absolutely," he repeated.

"Okay. And I'll make the inquiries about the financial situation. I'll use a soft touch."

Cohen smiled, revealing a block of unstained white teeth. Guy didn't drink or smoke or anything. "You? A soft touch?"

"Got to. I've already spoken with Mike Simpkins twice. He's going to form a love-hate relationship with me, if he hasn't already made up his mind one way or the other."

Cohen nodded, took out his wallet and started pulling out bills to pay the tab.

Swift held up a hand. "It's on me. Take a look at McAfferty for me. Just a little one; don't get him worried."

"I'll use the soft touch, too," Cohen said.

Swift grunted. "We'll be just like mothers with newborn babies."

Deputy Cohen laughed.

Swift went to the register to pay the bill. He stood at the counter, leaning against it, feeling sluggish but a bit better after eating and talking things through with Cohen. He really liked the deputy. He'd only seen him in passing over the years, but Alan Cohen seemed like a good man, with much more going for him than the rumor mill had to offer. Swift hadn't been a hundred percent sure Cohen was the man to check out McAfferty; the cursory web search on Darring's name was partly a test. Now he felt better. Cohen would handle it.

"I'm sorry John," said the woman at the register. She was the owner of Altos, a woman in her sixties, with a beehive hairdo circa 1958. Swift was a regular. He frowned at her as she held up his card. "This got declined," she said. The other patrons were by now positively falling out of their seats to hear and see what was going on.

Swift took the card and looked at it. It was a debit card from his personal checking account. The last he'd checked, there was a little over twenty-five hundred dollars in there. He remembered the email he'd gotten that morning about fraud detection. He'd forgotten about that.

"Sorry," he said, and stuck the card back in his wallet.

The woman waved her hand in the air. "Come take care of it another time."

"Yeah, okay. Thanks."

He turned and saw Cohen watching. "Everything alright?"

"Sure," said Swift. They left the diner together.

CHAPTER TWENTY-FOUR

Mike's hand shook as he held the phone and listened to the ringing at the other end. Callie's friend Sarah was with the girls, Callie herself was sedated and sleeping at CVPH, so Mike stepped outside the hospital to have a cigarette and call his father. The sun was barely visible, smothered behind thick grey clouds. He hadn't had a cigarette in years. Callie didn't even know he used to smoke. No one did.

Jack Simpkins answered.

"Dad," said Mike, his voice cracking. "Braxton is dead."

"What?"

"He went outside in the middle of the night. They found him in the road."

Jack Simpkins was silent.

"Callie is in the hospital. I'm with her. She's a total wreck — they had to sedate her. The girls are okay; they're with a friend. The State Police are investigating."

After a long moment, Jack finally spoke.

"Where were you?"

"Where was I? I was in bed. With Callie. We were sleeping."

Mike felt his heart start to pound in his chest. Had his father just accused him of something? That Mike should have been there for Braxton, or something like that?

"It was just a normal night," Mike went on, hearing his voice sounding as if it was coming from someone else. "The girls went to bed, Braxton stayed up for a while, reading. Callie and I sometimes go to sleep before he does." A spasm clutched at Mike's chest as he felt the emotion well up in him. "He's gone, Pop. Braxton is just gone. There last night, gone this morning. I . . ."

Mike couldn't finish. He didn't know why he had called his father. Jack Simpkins had never been reassuring. When Mike had been facing the loss of his job, Jack had been unsympathetic. "Make yourself indispensable," he had said. "Make your case to the new firm, cut your rate, do what you have to do."

Jack had worked for New York Transit all those years and had never joined a union. He stood by the adage that hard work and sacrifice were the only things that paid off. Yet two years ago he had started dumping thousands of dollars into a 529 college fund for Braxton. It was as if he was incapable of showing sympathy for Mike, his own son, but someone an extra generation apart — and a grandchild not of his own line — was somehow deserving of a helping hand.

Mike wept silently, not wanting his father to hear. He could hear Jack breathing at the other end of the line. At last he pulled himself together and took a deep drag from the cigarette. "So, I just wanted to let you know. I'll keep you posted on the funeral arrangements, if you want to come. I'm going to have to see someone tomorrow about that."

"Do you have a person there?"

"No, Dad, I don't have an established relationship with a funeral home. It didn't cross my mind, what with looking for work, moving into a new house, taking care of the kids while Callie gets up to speed at the college."

Mike heard the ice in his voice, chill as the cold air outside the hospital. He dropped the cigarette to the ground and mashed it out with his boot. He found himself thinking about the old days again, smoking cigarettes with Bull Camoine on the Staten Island Ferry. Telling Bull things he didn't tell anyone else.

"Let me know," said Jack quietly. "I'll be there. Braxton was a good boy."

"Yeah," said Mike. "He was." *Not like me*, he thought, and then felt ashamed of being selfish and childish and jealous of his father's affection for his step grandson at a time like this. Still, it sat there, a bilious pit in the center of Mike's chest.

"Alright, Dad. Take care."

Mike ended the call without waiting for a response — or lack of. He turned and walked back into the hospital feeling worse than when he'd come out. As the doors slid open, he wondered why he'd even bothered to call. What had he expected? Some warmth and compassion at long last? A break in the freeze-out that had lasted for twenty-five years or more? Mike could smell the fug of his own cigarette on him as he walked into the hospital lobby, and it made him feel dirty. This whole thing made him feel dirty.

A moment after he stepped through the door, his phone rang. He glanced at the screen and saw a vaguely familiar number on the display.

"Hello?"

"Mike, it's Sarah."

His throat constricted. "Is everything alright? Are the girls okay?"

"The girls are fine. There's just — there are people outside. Reporters, a van parked at the foot of the driveway."

"Has anyone come up to the door?"

There was a pause, and then Sarah said, "On their way right now."

Mike realized that in the midst of all his shock and emotion, he'd forgotten about the press. And, given that Braxton's death had occurred in the wee hours of the morning, it had taken time to catch on. Probably someone on their way to work a few hours later had gotten rerouted, and they mentioned it to a friend, and it went on from there. The thought of reporters encamped in his front yard with his girls inside — girls who didn't even yet know what had happened to their brother — it was very troubling.

"Are there police there, too?"

"Yes there's been the same state trooper down at the end of the driveway since this morning. I don't see him, though, just the car. Mike, I'd like maybe to take the girls to my place. It's up Wolf Mountain and there's a gate at the bottom. I'm just worried these people will surround us as soon as I step outside with the girls. What should I do?"

"I'm going to call the detective in charge of the investigation. Hang tight."

"Okay."

"Call you right back."

Mike hung up. His whole body pulsed with anger.

CHAPTER TWENTY-FIVE

The Assistant District Attorney surprised Swift as he approached his car outside the diner. Mathis was crossing the street, his black coat collar turned up, his movie-star hair blowing about in the wind. Mathis had come up from New York, and no one bothered to hide the fact they thought he was a hotshot. He was young, yet a reputation for efficient, precise convictions had preceded him.

Swift had been avoiding his calls all morning since their run-in at the substation.

"John, hold up," Mathis said, picking up his pace to a trot. Swift's hand had rested on the car door, and now he withdrew it and tucked it into his pocket.

"How's it going?" Mathis said as he approached.

"Good," said Swift. He nodded towards the diner. "Great hash browns."

Mathis' look darted in the direction of the diner, but only for a second. His eyes were crisp and bright blue and fixed Swift with a glare.

"I've been trying to reach you."

"I know."

Mathis searched Swift's face for signs of guile or disrespect. Swift felt the breakfast settling into his stomach, and realized he was soon going to have to pee out all that coffee.

"Some place we can talk?"

Swift nodded at the car. "Step into my office. It's going to be a bit chilly though."

Swift opened the driver's door and slipped in. He started up the vehicle and turned on the heaters to full blast as Mathis got in the passenger side, an unconcealed look of disgust on his face.

"My dog, Kady, she sheds," Swift said.

Mathis looked like he was trying to sit with no single part of his body actually touching anything. Swift thought about offering him a napkin to put under his delicate butt, and had to force himself not to smile. He watched as Mathis did his best to get comfortable among the dog hairs. It wasn't quite working out for him.

"Look," he said, seeming to stare at every single hair with venom, "I know I came on a little bit strong this morning, and I'm sorry. I didn't mean to get off on the wrong foot with you. I respect you, and I think you've handled things the right way so far."

Swift wondered where this was going.

"So," Mathis said, "we're meeting with the press in a half an hour."

Ah that was it. "Speaking of the press, I just got a call from Mike Simpkins. Very distraught. They're sprawled out all over his front yard. News channels from Plattsburgh, Burlington, papers from Placid, Saranac, Westport, all of it. I told him we would get them off his back."

"How?"

Drive them all to a burnt down warehouse; tell them it's Disney World, thought Swift. "Hopefully our statement will slake their thirst. What are we going to say?"

"What do we know since three hours ago?"

"Mathis, you've got to let me work this case. We're focused on the body, the three kids, processing the car, and on the laptop. If we can find any of the victim's latent prints in the car, if we can find evidence of any correspondence that resembles a threat from one or all of our three boys in the box, then we can tie it all together."

Mathis was blank-faced. "The car, any damage, the prints, I get. That's our hope. But I've prosecuted cyber-crimes before. Searching for evidence by back-tracking is going to take too long. They'll be back at home way before we uncover anything."

"So, okay, we'll pick them up and charge them then." This was the last thing Swift wanted to do, deal with a sprawling, protracted investigation.

"Pick them up?" Mathis counted off on his fingers. "Pennsylvania, New Jersey, New York. Then we're talking about the FBI."

Swift shrugged. "Maybe we should make some calls."

Mathis seemed to be boiling beneath the surface. So much for making amends. Swift watched the young ADA's face darken. He knew Mathis wanted this case, had convinced the DA he could handle it soup to nuts. And New Brighton was a one-horse town; something like this came along once in a very long time. It was the ADA's chance to make a name. The last thing Mathis would want would be to relinquish it to federal authorities because it went over state lines.

"There's got to be something else," Mathis said.

"With the online thing?"

"Yes, with the online thing."

Swift swiped a hand across his chin. He felt the stubble there. "We'll work as fast as we can, that's all I can do."

Mathis' eyebrows went up. "Was the victim gay?"

Swift shot Mathis a look. "What?"

"Was . . . he . . . gay. Homosexual."

Swift scowled. "He wasn't anything. He was barely thirteen."

"Oh, come on, you know what I mean. But thirteen, you knew whether you liked boys or girls, didn't you?"

Swift thought back. Sure, he could remember middle school, a girlfriend here, a girlfriend there . . . But he hadn't lost his virginity until college. Partly due to his parents' religious strictures, partly because he was awkward and shy.

"I guess," he said. "But, no, I don't know."

"The parents didn't say anything?"

"About his sexuality? No, it didn't come up."

"What did you talk to them about? What have you asked them?"

Swift considered the mother's description of her son's unique personality, the autism spectrum, but he said nothing. It wasn't material yet. It would only cause Mathis to start hunting for ways to fly the Hate Crime banner. Maybe, Swift considered, something like that was involved. From the outset he'd suspected the gang of three to be complicit in some way, whether they'd harassed the poor kid to the point of breaking him, or whether they'd outright murdered him. In some way they had contributed. But there were no facts until the forensics on the car came back, until Kim Yom could find something substantial in her backtracking of internet correspondence, and until Janine Poehler finished her autopsy report and submitted it. He had no cause of death, no murder weapon, and no solid link to any suspects. Except, maybe, the biological father.

But then there was the money, too. The family seemed to be either in financial straits or fiscally backed in a way that they kept quiet about.

"John? I get the feeling there's something . . ."

"What's the situation with counsel?"

Mathis blinked, but answered quickly. "Two of them have lawyers now. Lawyers hired by their parents."

"But Darring isn't one of them."

"How did you know?"

"A guess."

"There was no family to contact. He's a foster kid."

Swift raised his eyebrows.

"And he's waived his right to an attorney," Mathis went on.

The two men looked at each other as the vents blasted warming air around them.

"Something's up with that guy," Swift said about Darring.

Mathis nodded. "About that we see eye to eye. And that's why you need to get back in there; you need to press him. He knows something, John, and you've got to get it out of him."

They fell into a brief silence, considering. Swift pulled a stick of gum from the console and unwrapped it. Another round with Darring? He supposed he'd been interrupted before, and never quite got back to it. Plus, Mathis clearly wasn't going to let it go. He wanted a confession.

"Call me Swift," the detective said. "Only my mother calls me John."

Mathis frowned. "Your mother still alive?"

Swift popped the piece of gum into his mouth. "No."

CHAPTER TWENTY-SIX

Swift was back in the small room looking at Robert Darring across the table.

"How come you waived your attorney privilege? And why do your friends think they need one?"

"I can't answer that. You've kept us separate. But my guess would be their parents hired them. They're probably just worried."

"Why do you think they're worried?"

"Miko and Sasha, they're rich kids. Their parents live in nice little suburban neighborhoods. They think places like this are the Wild West. Something out of *Deliverance*. Ever see that movie?"

"But not you. You don't worry about that, that we're going to keep you here unjustly, take you out behind the shed, drag you through the manure."

"No. I don't."

"And you don't have family to worry, either."

"I don't, correct."

"No one? You're not married, no wedding ring. Girlfriend?"

"No."

"What do you do for work, Robert?"

Darring shrugged. "Whatever."

"Odd jobs, you mean?"

"Sure."

"How do you support yourself?"

"I gamble."

"You gamble? Doing what?"

"Online poker, a little bit."

"How's that work?" Swift was pretty sure online poker was outlawed.

Darring's dark, muddy eyes darted at Swift. "It's legal in Nevada, Delaware, and New Jersey."

He left it at that. Swift wondered if the poker-playing had something to do with what they called proxy servers. He was learning from Kim Yom about that — you could trick your IP address to make it look like you were somewhere else. Like a state where online poker was legal. Or, maybe you hopped on the George Washington Bridge and played from a friend's house across the river.

He let it go for now. "And you also play this game, *The Don.*"

"I play a lot of games."

"And that's how you know the victim."

"Didn't we already go over this?"

"We did." *But there's a bigger audience now*, thought Swift. Captain Tuggey had been joined by the substation Lieutenant and the ADA, who were all observing through the other side of the two-way mirror. "I'm just being thorough. So, you were a foster child?"

"I was."

"Never adopted?"

"No."

"What happened to your real parents?"

Now Swift saw the homely, pock-marked face seem to fold in on itself. Darring's eyes seemed to glaze over. "They weren't suited for parenthood."

"What happened?"

"I was taken by Child Protective Services when I was two years old."

Swift made a note of this. He was sure that Mathis was also there in the observation room next door. They'd pulled a file for Robert Darring, but it was completely clean. No convictions, no priors as an adult. Not even a parking ticket. He lived in Williamsburg, Queens, NY. He had a valid driver's license. They were looking into employment records, too, but Mathis would have to tap the Department of Labor for that, which took time.

There was, however, a sealed juvenile record. Mathis was trying like hell, he'd told Swift, to crack that open. He needed a judge to grant permission, and he was working hard to get it.

"Really? Two years old. So you have no memory of them."

Darring was still staring off into some memorial distance. "I do remember my crib. I remember that I could push against it, you know, shove it from the inside, and it would move across the floor."

"So, you entered into the State's protective custody; how long until you were in a foster home?"

"Couple weeks, I guess." Darring wandered slowly back from his past. It was remarkable — like watching someone emerge from a trance. Swift made a mental note that the young man could be unstable. He was, at the very least, eccentric.

"How is this going to help you find out what happened to Braxton?"

"Ever heard the name 'Fresco?'"

Darring was silent for a moment. Swift watched him closely, wondering if he'd hit on something.

"Sure," Darring said casually. "Jacque Fresco. Real out-of-the-box thinker. One of my heroes, really. And Braxton's, too. Probably why he chose it for his player name."

"In *The Don?*"

"Yeah, right."

Swift could almost feel the Captain and the ADA buzzing behind him in the little observation room. The kid was freely admitting that he knew the identity Braxton had used in the game. It wasn't proof of guilt, but Swift felt it was a step in the right direction. The other kid who'd been interrogated so far — Hideo Miko — hadn't wanted to admit this. Now all they needed was a threat or indication of violence among the messages in the game or, hell, from the server in San Francisco if they had to go Federal.

"Every little thing might help us find out what happened to Braxton. Your cooperation is the best thing for us, to help us figure out what occurred."

Now that shrewd look returned. "I thought you knew what happened, you were ready for a conviction, but wanted to give me a chance to explain and show my side of things."

Swift smiled. "Okay . . ." He held up his hands for a moment, palms out. "I guess you caught me acting as-if. It's hard-wired into me, you know?"

"Hard-wired?" Darring suddenly seemed to grow interested.

"Yeah, you know. It's an expression. Hard-wired. Something you've been programmed to do. Or programmed yourself to do." Swift tilted his head to the side. "You're familiar with that expression, right?"

"Of course. It just struck me."

"Why?"

Darring let out a loud sigh, an exhalation that seemed to deflate his whole body, and he leaned back deeper into the chair he was sitting in. He turned his head to the side and stared at the wall. For a moment Swift thought he had just shut down on him. That the conversation was over, and the kid was clamming up.

Then Darring spoke again. "We're going to all live completely online someday," he said.

"Oh yeah?"

"Yeah. Like, right now, we have our phones and laptops and tablets. More and more we're online, we're checking our phones, sitting down at the desk. On email, social networking, conducting business. But soon, and I'm talking just a couple of years, we're going to be online all the time. Google Glass, Oculus Rift; just the beginning. And it's an awkward beginning. It's clunky. The future will look nothing like these."

"What will the future look like?"

Darring's dark eyes contained something that seemed to live behind them, shifting as he spoke, a shadow behind a curtain.

"I lied. Well, I didn't tell the whole truth."

Swift felt a tiny thrill. "About?"

"I'm a day trader, too. I take my poker earnings and I invest them. Biggest thing right now? Biotech stock. The things these companies are doing are amazing. Alzheimer's research. Oh man. They're able to outfit a chip, right here," and Darring put a finger to his temple, "that uploads your thoughts. And that's just the tip of the iceberg."

Now he turned his body to face Swift directly.

"Ever heard of Kurzweil? Another out-of-the-box thinker like Fresco. Kurzweil plans to live forever, and he's going to, too. Like that movie with Johnny Depp. We're living more and more digitally. Even now, if you die, you have an afterlife online, on all of your social media sites. Everything you ever did is still on the web. But that? Just the Stone Age. We'll look back on that like we look back now on living to age thirty and painting on cave walls."

"It's really something," Swift said, feeling a bit lost. He was aware that technology was growing exponentially, but remained skeptical when he heard claims like this about people living forever in a digital capacity. Or even in a physical sense — there were only so many pills and organ replacements. Nature designed creatures to rise and then expire. There was no cheating it.

Darring went on, as if reading Swift's thoughts. "Everyday people, they may know a little, and they may doubt it, or maybe they think it's quaint, but what I'm talking about is a complete evolutionary leap." He became reflective again, looking inward once more. Swift's ears pricked up; Darring's tone was confessional.

"I've been obsessed for a while with liminal trance states. The relationship between narrative and immersion. There's a great book by Janet Murray. What is it? 'Hamlet and the Holodeck.' Great stuff."

"What's immersion, Robert?"

"Hmm? Immersion is a phenomenon. It's where you enter a kind of hypnotic, trance-like state and lose all sense of body awareness."

Darring appeared to have floated in and out of the present moment several times already during the interview. Normally when you had someone in the box, even for suspicion, even if they hadn't done anything, they were on vigilant alert. They were completely present. If they weren't, they were either a career criminal who had become desensitized to the process, or in an altered state, or mentally deficient. Swift hadn't considered another possibility, that someone, like Darring, could have been institutionalized in a different way. By the internet.

"I like to read," offered Swift. It seemed to make a connection because Darring's face lit up — as much as the nondescript face of a twenty-three year-old poker-player could be said to light up.

"Exactly. That's one of the times when it happens. Or, when you're in a movie theater watching a film, and you just completely lose all of your body awareness, and the body, the mind really, enters a landscape of imagination, of archetype and myth. Know what that is?"

"No."

"It's a dream landscape. It's not bound by the normal Euclidean meat-puppet limitations. It's not bound by the rules you and I live with every day, the rules you try to enforce every day. Let's call it 'the enchanted space.' So, for me, you know, I'm extremely interested in the techniques and rhetorical technologies we use to hack subjectivity."

"'Hack' subjectivity?"

"Perception and awareness, man. Moment to moment; that's how Erik Davis defines subjectivity."

The kid was throwing out one name after another. Swift had scribbled the names *Fresco, Kurzweil, Janet Murray*, and now he wrote *Erik Davis*. While he wrote he said, "I'm trying to follow along here. Some of this stuff is over my head, you know?"

Then he looked up and flashed another smile. "Okay. Most of it."

Darring was patient. "Look, when you watch a movie, you're basically inhabiting a dream space for a couple of hours. Cinema is the spectral machinery of the mind."

"And that's how it is online, too? In a game like *The Don*?"

Darring shook his head. "That's different. That's interactive. That's a whole other thing."

Swift sighed and looked at his notes, all the names, and felt like scratching them out. Where was this taking him? The kid was enamored of technology, that was one thing, but how did it open up his connection to the victim?

"You said Google Glass . . . Oculus Rift; I haven't heard of that. Can you tell me what that is?"

Darring raised a hand and circled it around his head. "You know. Virtual gaming headset. But cooler."

Swift felt something in his chest, as if a knife had slipped under his skin and the cool blade pressed against his heart. Darring was gesticulating. He took his left hand and circled it around his right, saying, "You can wear the glove, too, but I think that's primitive. All you need is the wristlet, and you can use both of your hands. It just attaches here," and he clamped his hand around his wrist.

Swift suddenly felt the need to unbutton the cuffs of his dress shirt and roll up his sleeves. Braxton's body showed ligature marks around his neck and wrist. Could be from a helmet. Could be from a glove.

Darring's own hands returned to his lap underneath the table. He looked vaguely like a kid who'd been disapproved of, though Swift had said nothing, done nothing but adjust his shirt sleeves.

"I'm interested in engineering neural nirvana with chemical technology," Darring said quietly, now almost apologetic. "Electronic technology, rhetorical technology, whatever it might be. I want to make subjective experience a work of art. That's my newest obsession."

Swift felt the hairs standing up on the back of his neck. "And Braxton Simpkins, did he factor into this?"

Darring was silent for a moment, and then said, "Yes."

Swift could practically feel the ADA jumping up and down in the next room.

Swift leaned into the table, settling himself. He was going to miss dinner with Brittney Silas. But he could be in court by the morning.

CHAPTER TWENTY-SEVEN

Deputy Cohen listened as the GPS instructed him towards Tori McAfferty's home.

"Turn left on Military Turnpike," the emotionless voice commanded. After a few minutes, "Turn right onto Salmon River Way."

Along Salmon River Way, the homes of South Plattsburgh were modest, some well-kept, others in junky disrepair. Cohen had come from a neighborhood like this, but north of Plattsburgh, in Chazy. The median household income ranged somewhere in between twenty-five and sixty thousand dollars. ATVS and Snowmobiles decorated many yards. The houses were small, many of them single-wides, with double-wides and a few modest stick homes. One in five had an above-ground pool.

Tori McAfferty's house was brick red, a studs-and-drywall home built sometime in the past thirty years. There was a small garage off to one side, too small to fit a car in. More of a shed. Large elms and maples demarcated the back yard and surrounded the house in a semi-circle. There was a white van parked in front of the shed with a decal embossed on the side.

MCAFFERTY PLUMBING AND HVAC SOLUTIONS

Cohen turned the police car into the dirt driveway to the house and shut off the engine. He reported his position to dispatch. He ran the plates of the van on his Mobile Data Terminal and found the vehicle registered to McAfferty. Discreetly, keeping one eye on the house in front of him, he checked his service weapon. He pulled out the magazine and examined it and then slid it back into the grip. Cohen then opened the door, retrieved his nightstick from the passenger seat and slid it into the loop in his belt.

Deputy Trainer was en route, but had gotten held up at the jail dealing with an unruly inmate who'd been in county for a couple of weeks after a second drunk driving charge. It was the same kid who'd tried to turn his first arrest, the previous summer, into a case of excessive force against the troopers. Trainer was coming, he'd promised, and Cohen knew he should probably wait, but he couldn't help himself. He liked the Sheriff's Department, but working a homicide investigation was undeniably more engaging. Years pulling duty at the jail, or doing pick-ups for mental health, had left him bored and maybe even a little depressed. His wife could see it — she said he carried it on him. His kids, two of them, one in elementary and one middle-schooler, didn't look at him the same way they did when they were younger. Back then the uniform had impressed them, the gun on his hip, the insignia on his sleeves, the star-shaped badge on his chest. Now he no longer seemed to exist.

Cohen stood looking around. There was less snow here, just a windblown dusting. The area was lower in elevation than New Brighton and the air was a bit warmer, maybe by five degrees. There was even a hint of spring in the air, a humidity.

He started walking up to the house when he saw a shape darken the doorway at the entrance. A moment later, the door swung inward.

A woman with her dirty blonde hair pinned up on top of her head stood grasping the knob. She was pretty in a haughty sort of way, with cheekbones as sharp as scythes, and some acne blurred over with foundation make-up. She wore sweat pants, a sweatshirt, and a skeptical expression. Cohen guessed she was in her late twenties.

"Can I help you?"

"Good afternoon, ma'am. Tori McAfferty live here?"

Cohen stood at the bottom of a block of concrete stairs. She looked down on him, scowling. "This is my house."

"Okay. You're the owner?"

"I am. What do you want?" She was looking around, up and down the street, maybe to see if there was anyone else with him.

"Is Mr. McAfferty in? I'd like to speak with him."

"What about?"

No one had yet told Tori McAfferty about Braxton Simpkins' death, and the name wouldn't be released by the media since the victim was a juvenile. His last name was different, too, and no information had been given about the boy's biological father until Mike Simpkins had told Swift late that morning. Typically the Sheriff's Department assisted the County Coroner with death notifications, particularly when they were some way outside of New Brighton, where the coroner happened to live. Deputies were frequently dispatched to deliver the bad news. A year before, Sheriff Dunleavy had squeezed a few drops from the budget to send Cohen and two other deputies to a training session. Cohen was racking his brain as he stood in front of McAfferty's house for what, if anything, he'd really retained from that training.

"Are you his wife, ma'am?"

"I am."

"I'm afraid I have some sad news. I'd like to be able to deliver it to both of you, if possible. Is he in?"

The woman continued to glare down at him, and now she seemed to calculate something. "What's the news?"

"Like I said, ma'am, it concerns both of you and I'd like to be able to come in and speak with the two of you together if he's in."

"Well, he's not in at the moment, so I guess you're going to have to tell me."

"I would really prefer to speak to you together. Any idea when he'll be back?"

She turned away from him, and glanced at the van in the driveway. To Cohen's surprise, she started clucking her tongue. Like she was taking her time to think about something, deciding what her next step was.

Cohen felt a distant tingling sensation in his fingertips. *She's stalling me*, he thought. But at first he couldn't understand why.

The woman's head swiveled back around and she looked down at Cohen again. "He's, well, you know how men are," she said, suddenly playful, almost flirtatious.

She's taken a different tack. Now she's going to try to charm me while she continues to stall.

"I'm not sure I understand, ma'am."

"You send them to the grocery store and they're completely clueless." And she smiled, revealing a glimpse of her teeth.

Cohen's tingling fingers touched the holster strap at his side. His thumb and forefinger pinched the strap and unsnapped it. Fear and excitement rode in waves through his muscles and nerves. You had teeth like that when you smoked crystal meth, Cohen knew. He'd seen enough addicts come through the jail, more of them all the time as the drug snaked its way into the North Country. This was a pretty girl, could have been an actress or a model. But he realized her hair was pinned up because it was dirty, and her teeth were stained and rotting because she was a user.

"Ma'am," said Cohen, edging forward a little, "on second thought, maybe I will come in and just talk to you alone. How would that be?"

His heart was beating hard against his ribcage. So hard it made it difficult to hear his own voice. *Go back to the car,* said an inner advisor. *Go back and wait for Trainer.*

Another voice countermanded. *She's stalling because he's back there in the house, McAfferty, right now, cleaning up signs of smoking or cooking the shit, that's what she's doing. You wait for back up or go in later and it's all going to be long gone.*

Her expression changed as her smile faded and she seemed to fill the doorway with her body, blocking his path. "I'm sorry; I lied," she said.

Cohen's fingertips trembled against the cold grip of the gun on his hip. He raised his eyebrows and waited.

"He's not out. He's sick. He's in the house but he's real sick. We both are. The flu, you know? Both of us puking our guts out. It's disgusting, and I wouldn't want to get you sick. So let me just go get him, okay? If he can walk, I mean."

"I'll take my chances," said Cohen, acting fast against her attempts to dissuade him. "I've had my flu shot."

The woman openly grimaced. No poker-player here, Cohen thought; her face was a jangle of nerves, twitching as she ran the gamut of fear, contempt, and hatred.

Cohen started up the steps, his hand resting on the butt of his sidearm. In the back of his mind, jurisprudence stood watch. He was already preparing a justification, a probable cause for his actions. The woman was clearly lying, the van in the driveway was registered to McAfferty, had his business information on it, the woman said he was out at the grocery store then changed her story again. And she looked like an addict. It would have to be enough.

As he climbed towards her, he asked her to push back inside. Up close, he could smell perspiration and unwashed clothes. And the house behind her emanated further smells of unhygienic things, stale cigarette smoke, moldering food. But cutting through all these in sharp contrast was the smell of recently-smoked methamphetamine, a distinctly chemical, cleansing smell, like cleaning products or sanitary napkins.

Now he had every ounce of probable cause he required.

"Step aside, please, ma'am."

The woman suddenly lashed out with her hands and raked her fingernails down his arm. It was such a surprising, yet ineffectual gesture that it took him a few seconds to react. By that time, the woman had already darted deeper into the house. Cohen pulled his gun out.

* * *

There was a small untidy porch, the width of the small house but only a few feet deep, and then a doorway. There was no door, but Cohen saw hinges mounted to the casing. *Someone probably kicked it down.* McAfferty's license had run clean, aside from a few speeding tickets and a DWI from seven years previous.

"Sheriff's Department," Cohen called out. "Tori McAfferty, please come out with your hands where I can see them."

The smell was even stronger here, the air stale and full of old cooking smells, food smells, and unwashed body smells. The windows likely hadn't been opened in a long time. Directly ahead of Cohen was the living room. A flat screen TV sat in the corner to his right, its dark surface streaked with greasy fingerprints. There was a couch that had seen better days cocked at an angle to face it. The carpet was stained in various places. There was junk everywhere — magazines, food boxes, articles of clothing. A few framed pictures adorned the walls, one of them had fallen at some point and was leaning against the baseboard with a chunk of the glass missing. It was a shot of Jimi Hendrix on stage.

Go back outside now, the advisor in Cohen's mind said. *Go and wait for Trainer. Don't proceed any further.*

"McAfferty," he barked. "Come out here where I can see you, hands out in front of you."

The living room, which spanned from one side of the house to the other, fed into three doorways at the back. The one on the far left had light coming through, and Cohen could make out part of a sink. That was the kitchen. Two dark doorways sat closer together in the middle. Maybe one a bedroom, one a bathroom. The house had looked small from the outside, but it could have gone back a ways deeper than he'd first noticed — there might have been more rooms beyond those adjoining the living room.

He aimed his weapon at those dark doors in front of him.

He started walking deeper into the living room. He bet the place had a basement, too. He could be standing over a cooking operation, which would be a huge bust. It wasn't easy to tear down a cooking operation, they were complex and full of different burners and containers and precursor chemicals. Still, enough of it could be disposed of in a short period of time, enough to weaken the strength of the prosecution.

Cohen felt the nerves at the base of his spine jangle when his foot kicked something on the ground. He glanced down and saw a video game controller. He took a moment to consciously slow his breathing and heart rate. If he could just get McAfferty to show himself. For God's sake, he just needed to talk to the guy, be the one to deliver some pretty horrible news, and now look how things had suddenly turned. You never knew what you were walking into. You just never knew.

Something caught his attention and he swiveled around, face to face with a window. Through it he could see the top of the van, and beyond it, the street. He'd seen a car approach in his peripheral vision — another Sheriff's

Department vehicle. The car parked and Deputy Trainer stepped out.

Cohen felt the release of the tension in his chest. His back-up was here and everything was going to be alright. They were going to pull this tick out of the dark and he was going to turn out to be the one who'd murdered that poor kid in New Brighton. Cohen was sure of it.

He watched until Deputy Trainer passed out of sight. He would walk up the path and be at the door in just a few seconds. For now, Cohen stayed where he was, keeping his gun aimed at the back rooms, and the darkness there. It was only the second time in his career that he'd had to pull his service weapon and —

The ground heaved beneath Deputy Alan Cohen's feet. He felt a tremendous heat rising, and for a split second pictured in his mind's eye some enormous, fetid bubble swelling up from beneath him, inside it a raging and roiling furnace of blue fire. Then it released in a tremendous crescendo, and Cohen and the room and everything in it vanished in a deafening explosion.

PART THREE

THE GAME

CHAPTER TWENTY-EIGHT

Callie opened her eyes.

There was a blackness, thick as tar, closing off the passageways of her mind. She didn't know where she was. She didn't know what time it was, the day, the week, the month.

There was only one place in all the darkness that showed any light, only one clear feeling; a tear in the black. It took her a moment to understand what it was, and then she remembered.

Braxton was gone.

Once this fact had fully formed, a cascade of others poured through that slice in the darkness. She didn't know where her girls were either. Fear and anger flooded her, and she tried to get up.

It was as if she'd been filled with lead. Her limbs were thick and heavy, nearly unresponsive. Her mouth was dry, her tongue felt as though it was thick with liquor. The inky darkness lingered all around her, along the edges of her vision, obscuring her thoughts, trying to draw her back into its viscous fold. She tried harder, and the muscles in her stomach burned and ached as she sat up.

At first she could barely make sense of the room. Everything was sterile and white; an alien place, as though she'd been abducted and taken to some other world without color, without emotion, feeling.

She realized she was in a hospital. Then Mike appeared in the doorway, and came rushing to her side. He threw his arms around her.

She tried to push past him for a moment, her useless arms flailing about as he enveloped her body and squeezed. She clenched her buttocks and dug her heels into the bed and tried to slip past him, to leave this place immediately and return to her son, and to her girls.

You could always go back. A soft voice.

I could?

Just go back. Back to sleep. Back into that darkness. There is no pain there, no memory. Just fall back into it.

She considered this for a moment. "Mike," she said, through waxen lips, her cottony mouth.

He held her even tighter, and she struggled against him. She saw her son again as he sat in the car beside her on the morning ride to school. She saw him hunched over his desk as he pecked at the keyboard of his laptop, and standing on Flagler Beach, now a pre-teen with the wind blowing his hair across his face, and as a toddler, getting his leg over the red tricycle for the first time. And then he was a baby, he was in her arms, and she knew that life was going to be hard for him, because he was going to be different, he was going to get his heart broken, he was going to believe the world was kind and just and fair. The world that was going to subdue him, to press him into rank and file, to corrupt him with its culture industry, its competitive wiles, its insatiable appetite.

Her baby, soft in her arms, looking up at her.

Callie could feel the pulse in Mike's neck against her cheek as he held her, the warmth of his blood, the strength of his arms. And she gave into it.

But there were no tears this time.

Callie watched over Mike's shoulder as the last of the day's light drained from the single window. She could hear the sounds of nurses talking and the distant beeping of monitors outside, down the hallway. Dimly, she thought she smelled cigarette smoke.

Mike pulled back from her at last and his eyes were red, his face a mask of suffering. But his lips curled into a smile.

"How are you feeling?" He raised his eyebrows.

"Heavy."

He nodded, and glanced away, out the window to where the dusk settled.

She licked her lips. She needed water.

"Where are the girls?"

He looked at her again, and she saw he sought her approval. "I called Sarah."

"Oh. Good. They're okay?"

"They're okay."

She glanced down for a moment. The patient ID fastened to her wrist.

"What did you tell them?"

"I said that you got sick. You went outside into the cold and got sick."

She nodded. Callie knew she could be tough to deal with. She'd been edgy all through the past Christmas, for one thing. Lying about Santa Claus was something she found pointless, and she had been annoyed with Mike for perpetuating some stupid myth.

Such concerns seemed trivial but also profound to her now. "I did get sick," she said quietly.

"Do you remember what happened?"

She could tell he was treading lightly. Perhaps he'd been advised to do so, in case it set her off again. The thought made her feel lonely.

She often felt alone. Even after eight years married to Mike. Even with three children. Her own family was large but not close, her friends far flung. Mike once told her that she distanced herself. He said she needed to do so in order to create, and that he understood. At that moment she knew she would be with him for the rest of her life.

Besides, there was nobody else. Not her father and his new family in California, and all of their blond Jesuit prep-school kids, not her mother, mistress of the desert in New Mexico with her dopey, common law husband with his long hair and Miller Lite paunch. They seemed farther from her now than they ever had.

"I remember . . ." she began, and didn't finish. She remembered, alright. She remembered knowing that, as she sat here, her son was being cut open, his organs removed and weighed; his body systematically taken apart like a car in a garage.

She looked at her husband coolly. The sadness was settling within her, surf calm at sunset. Who knew what would happen later, what the tide would bring? Braxton walked along the water's edge, always away from her.

"What's happening with funeral arrangements?"

Mike swallowed. "Nothing, until after the autopsy. I mean, I've spoken with the funeral home in New Brighton. They've given me their available times but I can't really select one until the detective speaks to the pathologist and they decide what's next."

"Can you get me some water?"

"Sure." He looked around, walked into the small bathroom, and she heard him filling a cup. He came back and handed it to her. It was cold and good, and she drank it down.

"Good?"

"More, please."

He refilled the cup and she drank half this time, and then set it down beside her. As he moved about she caught another whiff of cigarettes. "Thank you."

She noticed him staring at the cup after she'd placed it on the bedside table. Something seemed wrong. She reached over and took his hand.

"What?" she asked.

"You won't believe it."

"What do you mean? Mike, what? You're scaring me a little."

He was shaking his head. "Something else I have to tell you. Something just . . . man."

"What *is it*? Spit it out."

"Okay. It's pretty major. They told me that I needed to be careful what I said to you."

Callie glanced at the door. Mike had left it open. She wondered if he'd been asked to do so, in case anything happened, and he needed help with her. She felt a pinch of embarrassment at the idea, and some resentment. It was time to focus. Her girls would need her. Mike would need her too — he had a way of dealing with things that was . . . different.

She kept her voice level. "Mike. I'm fine. I went a little bit . . ."

"Honey, no one is asking you to apologize. There's no . . . we have no idea how to do this. You can't prepare for this. Everything you do, everything we do, is exactly as it should be. Okay?"

She nodded. He was being a champ, and she loved him for it. There was always more to Mike than met the eye, and that was part of why she'd fallen in love with him. She might have wondered why a man already in his thirties had never married, never settled down — sometimes that was a red flag. But then she learned where he'd come from, and what he'd learned growing up. It hadn't been pretty. He understood the wreck of her family; she understood the absence of his.

He was watching her, appraising. Then he came out with it.

"Tori has been living in South Plattsburgh."

She swallowed. Her throat was dry again. "What?"

He looked down.

"Mike? What are you talking about?"

"He contacted Braxton. Started sending him emails. Trying to convince Brax to come live with him."

"I don't understand. I don't . . . he's living up here? I thought he left here a long time ago."

Mike looked at her. "I told the cops about the emails. I thought maybe it could have something to do with what happened."

She felt sick. Like she might throw up. The whole thing made her head spin. How could Mike have kept this from her? All the conversations they'd had over the years about open communication, and especially about the kids. How it never helped to keep something from the other parent, even if you were trying to spare them. It always backfired.

Mike looked away. He appeared hurt, and she squeezed his arm, perhaps harder than she should have. "Mike?"

"I threatened him. Callie, I threatened Tori's life."

She swallowed and found she had no saliva. Anger, fear, a sense of betrayal. But at the same time she realized now was not the time to chastise Mike — for his lack of trust in her — it would only make things worse. She eased her grip on his arm, and took a deep breath. She spoke softly.

"You did what you felt you had to do."

He looked at her again, unmistakable relief in his eyes. But then they darkened in self-recrimination. "What I had to do? I don't know. It was bad, Cal. It was a bad example for Braxton, for one, and it was stupid. It could have . . ."

Suddenly she shushed him and raised her hand to his mouth. "No. Mike, you were trying to do the right thing. What exactly did you say to him?"

"I said I would kill him."

She drew another trembling breath, and forced herself to stay calm. Then she nodded.

"It's okay."

"Is it? Honey, what if . . ."

"Stop it," she said. *How could he? And now to sit here and be so deflated about it, so mournful and pathetic?* "You were the best example for Braxton you could be. Even when you grew protective and angry, as you did. It may have been rash, but you showed him your love. You showed him your strength."

"I don't . . ."

"Mike, Brax and I talked about you, many times, and what a great dad you've been."

Mike's eyes filled with tears, and his lips pressed together as he tried to keep from crying.

She went on. "And I know how much it has always hurt you, Braxton's longing for his biological father and . . ."

He bent forward and hid his face in his hands. She placed a hand on his back and looked away. Why was he telling her now? It had come up with the cops, no doubt. Callie had been checked-out, sedated, and Mike had been left handling the inquisition. The subject of Tori had come up and Mike told them about the emails and his threat. That meant the investigation was going to include Tori.

"Have they spoken with him? Mike? What did he say to the cops?"

"He didn't say anything." Mike lifted his head, sniffed and wiped hastily at his face. "Not exactly."

"What does that mean?"

"A deputy was dispatched by the investigators to go and ask him a few basic questions. While the deputy was there, the place . . . oh man, the house . . . exploded."

"It *what*?"

"They're saying that Tori had a meth laboratory in his basement. Not the biggest operation, but enough that he figured the cops had come to arrest him and he self-destructed the place. The deputy is in critical condition. He's here, in this hospital."

Her hand covered her open mouth. Along the corridor she thought she heard not just nurses talking and monitors beeping, but static bursts and voices coming through on walkie-talkies.

"He's alive?"

"He's barely alive."

"And Tori?"

"They're looking for him. I've actually heard the word 'manhunt.'" Apologetically, he added, "There's cops outside the room who want to ask you questions. About Tori. He's a major suspect now. If you're up to it. I'll stay here with you the whole time."

I told you; you should have returned to me, the voice said from the blackness. *You should return to me permanently, because this is never going to get better, this is never going to go away.*

I can give you peace.

Callie swung her legs out of the bed at last. She slipped an arm around Mike's neck as she stood herself up.

"Babe, what are you doing?"

"I have to go to the bathroom," she said, keeping an eye on the door into the hallway. "I have to pee before we go any further with this thing, okay?"

"Okay," he said.

CHAPTER TWENTY-NINE

Swift sat at his desk in the substation, rubbing his hands together. He felt cold, even though the substation was toasty with all the heaters running. He looked away from the computer monitor for a moment and stared off into space. He was the only cop in the station except for Trooper Coates, who was in the next room, keeping the home fires burning. Everyone else was out on the manhunt for Tori McAfferty. It was going on seven in the evening, and, on top of it all, he'd missed his dinner with Brittney Silas.

The three boys from the Hyundai remained on ice, two sitting with Trooper Coates, instructed by their lawyers not to say a word to anyone, and twenty-three-year-old Darring, still with no counsel, alone in the interview room. They'd had the kids in custody for nearly fifteen hours. It was permissible, but it was dangerously close to giving defense lawyers ammo like "coerced confession." If this thing ever went to trial.

You had to be careful. Perpetrators and suspects in custody turned into claimants against the state faster than you could say "instant action" these days. Swift knew the routine all too well. His own troopers had been mired in allegations for weeks now over a drunk driver who'd been belligerent and uncooperative and gotten pepper-sprayed as a result. Frank Duso. Lenny's Duso's son. Frank was now alleging permanent damage to his eyes along with a slew of other things. Captain Tuggey had, in recent weeks, backed up his troopers in a statement in which he'd simply described the first five degrees of the use of force in ascending order as: (1) presence of uniform; (2) verbal command; (3) placing hands on arrestee; (4) use of pepper spray; and (5) physical force and defensive tactics.

There was, of course, a sixth, deadly physical force, which could be resorted to only when the conditions prescribed by Penal Law § 35.30 were present. Tuggey had maintained that his troopers had done everything they could to keep the use of force at a minimum, but that the claimant had driven it up the ladder of degrees. Swift had been involved because he'd been at the substation when the troopers brought the claimant in for the breathalyzer. He'd seen the whole thing, and been asked to give testimony at the upcoming trial.

You had to be careful. You never knew who you were dealing with, or what their angle was. Mostly, you expected lies.

For a few precious moments there it had seemed like Darring was veering towards a confession. He'd continued to wax philosophical about things like "liminal trance states," of which Swift himself had little grasp, teetering on divulging something about Braxton Simpkins, and how he fitted into all of this techno-philosophy. But the more the interview had gone on, the more it seemed like the kid was talking gibberish, nothing like a confession. It was beginning to look like the kids were just being kids after all, stealing away to visit some other kid they gamed with on the internet. If they had lawyers and parents with hefty bankrolls behind them, the aftermath could get ugly. Uglier than it already was.

The call about Deputy Cohen had come in during Swift's interview with Darring. The Captain and Lieutenant had rushed off, and Mathis had vanished too, indicating he'd be back. Everyone had deserted the place, but Swift couldn't rush out, much as he wanted to be part of the hunt for McAfferty, he had other things which couldn't wait. He needed more ammunition for his ongoing interrogation of Darring, but it was hard to focus.

Swift looked at the computer screen and felt the pressure mounting. He sat trying to think through what he'd been uncovering, while at the same time going over and over his last conversation with Alan Cohen. He'd told Cohen to take another deputy with him, and Cohen said he'd buddy-up with Trainer. Trainer had been at the scene that afternoon when the explosion happened, and he was currently being treated for minor cuts, abrasions, and third degree burns. Word had already come down that Cohen had entered McAfferty's house alone. Why? Why hadn't he waited? If he'd waited for Trainer, he might not be in critical condition right now.

Of course, it could have gone the other way, too, and Trainer could be right there beside him in Intensive Care, also about to undergo surgery that would remove embedded pieces of wood, plastic, and glass.

Dear Jesus.

Swift needed to see Cohen, needed to talk to him, but he wouldn't be able to, not for a while. He needed to see Cohen's family. He was going to have to take responsibility for sending Cohen up there to Tori McAfferty's place. Better that they hear it from Swift himself than second-hand. Another wonderful task to look forward to.

As he stewed over this, the door to the substation burst open, making Swift jump.

Mathis came walking in, a swirl of snow in his wake. Swift quickly closed down the windows on the computer screen.

The prosecutor sat down across from Swift. Mathis, for a change, didn't look his usual cocky self. His face was drawn, his eyes underscored with purple rings of fatigue. He looked wary. Maybe even out of his depth.

"How you doing?" Swift asked.

"I'm fine. You?"

Swift just stared across the table at Mathis until Mathis looked away. Swift wasn't trying to intimidate the guy, he just didn't have the words. Finally, he said: "I was the one who sent him up there."

The ADA shook his head. "We were following a lead, Swift. A good lead. And now this guy, McAfferty, with these messages to Braxton Simpkins, this operation he's got going on in Plattsburgh — it looks good for us. It's better than this *vel non* bullshit we've been scraping by with."

Swift shrugged. "Yeah." If he recalled, "vel non" was a legal term, Latin, meaning "or not," used when something was presented in a case because there was no other alternative. Even if it lacked any supporting evidence.

Mathis showed some of his familiar smugness for a moment. "It's not perfect, Swift, but it's an awfully big indicator that this guy is a wild son of a bitch."

Swift blew out a long breath. "I know."

Mathis squinted. "You're a skeptic. Hey, you're supposed to be. You don't exactly like McAfferty for this — much as you like those kids. I get that. But think of this. Maybe McAfferty didn't come down here and put hands on anyone. But maybe he called the kids up. Talked some real terrible shit to them. Threatened them. Have we got the phone records yet?"

"Still working on it."

Mathis drummed the desk with his fingers. He seemed to be growing more himself again, becoming antsy.

"Well, I see Braxton Simpkins with a target on his back, any which way you slice it. Biological father, estranged, shut out by the mother and step-father; they move back here after years and years, he gets in contact with the son, who knows what sort of poison he fills the kid's head with, who knows how he messes with him. I mean, you said the stepfather wrote to him? Threatened to kill him? I mean, come on. So, that right there, that sets McAfferty off, and he goes into some psycho mode, and he continues to contact the kid. Or maybe, maybe he's not spewing poison, but he's sweet-talking the kid, turning him against his parents. He convinces him that he needs to leave them. Maybe he tells him that they'll meet. But something happens, and the kid has some sort of attack out there in the snow. Still waiting on the internal?"

Swift nodded. He'd tried Janine Poehler twice already that evening on her phone and left messages. Now he cocked an eyebrow at the ADA. "That's a lot of maybes."

Mathis obviously felt the barb. "I can make it stick. The emails, the step-father's testimony, the meth-dealing; we catch this son of a bitch and we offer him a reduced sentence for the meth lab, we hatch a deal with the defense — he gets life reduced to thirty-years-plus-parole with a full confession for the murder of Braxton Simpkins."

Swift spoke low, his voice growling. "For Christ's sake, Sean, he nearly killed a cop."

"Nearly," Mathis said, his expression inscrutable.

"What if Cohen doesn't make it? How are you going to negotiate with that? No judge in the world, no jury, if it comes to that, is ever going to sleep at night knowing they traded one life for another. Especially a cop's life; you know how this goes. There's no room to proffer here. Besides, it's barking up the wrong tree; McAfferty *is* guilty, guilty of being a drug dealer and a piece of shit and someone who put a police officer in a life threatening situation and didn't hesitate to light the fuse. But I don't see him for this."

Mathis leaned back. Swift expected him to revert to his high-and-mighty pose, but Mathis stayed affable. He ran a hand through his spiky, purposely unkempt hair. "You got something else?"

When Swift just gave him a look, Mathis leaned forward. Then he sat bolt upright. "You got something *else*. Swift? What the hell have you got?"

CHAPTER THIRTY

It was after nine p.m. when Mike pulled the pick-up into the driveway. Callie had grown listless beside him in the cab of the truck. When they had first left the hospital, the two of them had been animated, upbeat, almost giddy. It had been a struggle to get Callie discharged, to convince the staff crisis worker she was not a danger to herself or others, and they felt a bit like kids escaping out from under their parents' house rules. Mike and Callie held hands, and cried together, and even laughed. The girls were safe, there were no meals to prepare or dishes to do or laundry to fold — for a couple of fleeting hours, it was almost a vacation. They had talked as they left the hospital and drove to the interstate to head the thirty miles south to New Brighton, but as their exit approached, the talk thinned out, and Callie seemed to shrink and harden in her seat, like something petrifying. As they turned onto route 9N, the truck filled with a heavy silence. The wind swept across the road, turning the fine-grained snow into waves. Their driveway was drifted with the powder, and the house looked small and windswept against the backdrop of the dark mountains.

A lone state trooper was parked at the mouth of the driveway. As Mike neared, he rolled down his window and the night chill immediately poured into the car, striking Callie's exposed flesh. She drew her coat around her as Mike leaned into the door and spoke to the trooper. The trooper was young, Mike saw, barely in his twenties, blond and pale but with hard, serious eyes.

"Thanks for being here," Mike said. "I appreciate it."

"Yeah we were able to convince the press to back off." The trooper glanced off into the dark night. "I'm surprised they didn't follow you from the hospital." His eyes came back to Mike and then looked past Mike at Callie who seemed to harden further under his gaze. "Press can be somewhat reasonable — just girls in there, I told them, and they didn't even know . . ." He trailed off. "Didn't know the whole story yet," he finished, and now he was looking around, anywhere but at Callie. "Anyway it was enough your friend was able to stay here with the two girls. I think the press rattled her, though. And I don't know how long they will stay away. So sorry for you folks, but this is a pretty major story for the area."

"Thank you," Mike said again, not knowing what else there was to say. The trooper looked impatient to be elsewhere; Mike could bet where. On the manhunt for Tori McAfferty. Where he wished he was himself.

"Okay," said the trooper. He dropped his shifter into Drive. "Someone will be by in the morning." And then he pulled away.

Mike sat for a moment, truck engine running, and then rolled up the window. Both he and Callie returned their attention to the house and he rolled slowly forward.

The girls were inside with Sarah, but that was all. The respite Mike and Callie had experienced at the hospital, the momentary lapse of reason and surreal giddiness only gave the reality more weight. Braxton was not inside the house. Braxton would never be inside the house again.

Mike parked the truck, and glanced at Callie. Her face was dimly lit by the console of the cab's interior, casting her features in amber. She looked back at him and they exchanged a wordless communication. They had spent their time together, and now it was time to be strong for their daughters. The next few days would be nothing but ugly business, and they had to show their daughters love and security.

Mike turned the key and the truck rumbled and then stilled. The silence was massive.

"What do we tell them?"

Despite all the talking, this was the one question they had both avoided asking.

Callie was quiet for a moment, unmoving, surrounded by the night.

"Tomorrow," she said.

* * *

The girls had both been asleep throughout the afternoon and were up now, active and bright, and Reno was asking questions about her brother, and about the reporters who'd been on the front lawn, the policeman she'd seen sitting there all day. She was six, sharp; there were plenty of clues, and she continued to suspect something despite Mike and Callie's evasive answers. They did their utmost not to lie. Callie said, "Something happened to Braxton, but we'll talk about it in the morning."

"What happened to him?"

"Let's say goodnight to Sarah and thank her for playing with you girls today."

As they said their goodbyes Callie couldn't look Sarah in the eye for too long, couldn't withstand the sorrow and pity she saw. She was resolved now to stay strong, to move forward, but she knew she had to avoid certain triggers. She would handle one thing at a time, put one foot in front of the other. Sarah had done their dishes and picked up after the girls, and her contribution was so generous that Callie didn't know how to acknowledge it. Sarah seemed to understand, leaving quietly, smiling at the girls. It was clear she was relieved to be gone.

CHAPTER THIRTY ONE

"I'm sorry," Callie said to Mike once they were in bed.

Mike rolled over on to his side and looked at his wife. In their many years together, he could count on his fingers the number of times she had apologized. Callie wasn't the apologetic sort. This didn't mean she was cold or crass — far from it. They made her feel vulnerable, and so she kept herself somewhat insulated.

"Don't be sorry," he said.

"I just . . . I lost it. I don't even remember . . . I barely remember anything. It was like I was . . . I don't know. I was someone else."

"No, you were you, and you were fine. No one faults you for anything. Especially me."

The girls were asleep in their room. Callie had asked Mike if they should all sleep together, but in the end both agreed that it would be best to keep things as normal as possible.

There was no manual for this, Mike thought. No road map to navigate something as huge as this. Sure, there were funeral services, and eventually there might be support groups (though Callie would balk at these), or websites. And of course, there was always the church, but neither Mike nor Callie had attended a church service in years.

Mike's mother had been a devout Catholic, his father agnostic. Callie's mother was a mixed bag of New Age philosophies, her father more faithful to football than anything else. Mike and Callie had been married by a Justice of the Peace, and had kept the ceremony small.

"When are you going to tell your parents?" Mike asked.

"I don't know. When we . . . when we know more. I just . . . I can't. Not right now. My mom would only . . . oh God, it would be a mess. And my dad would be on me every second, trying to call the shots."

Her tone was final. But they were going to need help, Mike thought. They had few friends here, if any. Really just co-workers of Callie's. There was Frannie, who'd brokered the house, but she was a whirling dervish. Mike's only real friends were back in the city. He hadn't kept in touch with anyone he'd worked with upstate. Moving south all those years ago had been a clean break. He'd never intended coming back.

"They're going to come at me," Mike said in the stillness of the bedroom.

Callie sat up a little. "What? What're you talking about?"

"The 529 for Braxton. Jack put almost a hundred thousand dollars in that account."

"So?"

"So, we're broke. I've been using a credit card to pay for things."

"What? I thought you said . . ."

"I know what I said. I'm sorry. I didn't want you to worry."

He could feel her hackles rising. Emotions would run high now, and he had to watch his step, for both of their sakes. He knew how she felt about keeping things from one another, and this had to be said.

"How much?"

"How much on the card?"

"Yes, how much on the card."

"A little under four thousand. Not too much. The plane tickets, some of the shipping, and setting up the utilities when we got here. His last session with Dr. Driscoll."

He looked at her carefully, prepared for her to react to this. Much as Callie lamented her mother's outlandish ways, she was a closet New Ager herself. Callie had never wanted Braxton to be treated traditionally. Driscoll was an acupuncturist. It was a way for her to deal with Braxton's condition without having to name it.

"Everything else I had went into the closing costs on the house."

Callie rolled onto her back and stared up at the ceiling. "Mike . . ."

"I know. I'm sorry. I thought we'd be okay. I've been putting together my bids, and there were a couple of jobs materializing, plus more coming down the pipeline. I figured I would make the payments, and with your income, we'd be okay. And we *would* have."

"And you think they're going to . . . to what? Think you had something to do with Braxton's death in order to collect on the frigging 529? Jesus, Mike. That's like—"

"The detective, Swift, he gives me these looks . . ."

"He's a cop. He's suspicious of everyone. That's his job." She propped herself up again on her side and he could see her eyes shining in the gloom. "And so what if he does think something? There's nothing for him to find out."

It wasn't actually a question, but her ensuing silence was meant to pull more out of him.

"No, there's nothing for them to find. But they're just going to look at me. I would if I were them. Like you said, they're cops."

"You would if you were them?"

"Well, I'm the stepfather and—"

"Oh Mike. Don't start. Please. Are you kidding me? Mike, his biological father just blew up a meth lab in his house, nearly killing a police officer. You think they're worried about you?"

They could hear Hannah suddenly start to wail in the next room. She often woke up in the night, but usually later, in the early hours of the morning.

"Shit," Callie said. She spilled out of the bed and padded quickly out of their bedroom.

The bit of poison from their last conversation hung in the air round Mike like putrid smoke. He didn't want to argue with Callie. Now, especially, they needed to stay solid and together. But it felt like something was trying to pull them apart.

The cops would look at him, of that he was certain. And they would surely look at Tori McAfferty for Braxton's death, if they caught him. And when they did, he would lie, or he would say whatever they wanted him to say in order to get his sentence reduced.

Mike couldn't stand the idea of Tori McAfferty in the hands of a wheeling, dealing justice system.

He couldn't stand the gnawing guilt. He was guilty of intervening between Braxton and his biological father, and threatening him. What if he had caused Braxton's death? It was the ugliest, most terrible, heavy thought he'd ever had, and it squatted there like a demon.

There was another scenario — what if they did look at Mike, and concluded that he stood to benefit financially from Braxton's death? The account was in Mike's name — Jack had never wanted to deal with the paperwork. What if they thought he'd done something to Tori — pushed the buttons of a mentally unstable, estranged father — something that had set him off with the idea that an outcome such as Braxton's death was not only possible, but positive?

There was a manhunt for Tori McAfferty. Cohen's critical injuries, the meth lab explosion, and the hunt for

Tori McAfferty would be making waves all over the media. The trooper said he'd convinced the press to leave, that they'd shown some compassion, and Mike figured this was possibly true, but more likely they'd been drawn to the incident in South Plattsburgh. They'd be distracted by the meth lab explosion for a while, but then they would be back.

Mike got out of bed and retrieved his laptop. He brought it back into the bed. In the other room, Hannah had quieted. Callie was with her girls, and Mike thought it was for the best.

He opened the computer and waited a few minutes for it to rouse itself out of hibernation. Then he opened the browser and did a search for the latest breaking news about the hunt for McAfferty. After a few minutes, and once he was sure Callie and the girls were sound asleep, he put on his shoes.

CHAPTER THIRTY-TWO

Swift and Mathis talked into the night.

"Mike Simpkins is the owner of a 529 account. Know what that is?"

"It's a tax deferred account for higher education."

"Know how much is in it?"

"I'm dying to."

"A little under a hundred K." Swift looked over the top of his laptop at Mathis. "Jack Simpkins, that's the grandfather, lives in Florida, near Jacksonville. Funny. Jack in Jacksonville. Anyway, he was an MTA worker. Not big money, but he worked his way up and was one of the highest paid in New York City by the end of his career. And he was a miser. Stuck everything away for his retirement, played the stock market and made investments. I put in a call to him and he was willing to talk to me."

"Even though it could implicate his son?"

"Even though." Swift looked away for a moment, recalling the tone of Jack Simpkins' voice when they had spoken an hour ago. "Seems like he doesn't hold his son in the highest regard. His 'life choices,' he said, something to that effect. Marrying some neo-hippie artist chick who had a kid and a deadbeat ex. Always struggling with work. Those were his words."

"Nice. Supportive."

Swift went on. "Mike was getting laid off from a company where he'd worked for a few years, and was trying to get back into freelancing, start his own business, something along those lines. They moved up here not just because of the wife's job op, but because Mike was no longer bringing home any bread. The father said he'd tried to get Mike into the business, as a tradesman for the MTA, good honest work, but Mike left home at seventeen, narrowly avoiding some trouble which would've sunk him."

Mathis raised his eyebrows. "Such as?"

Swift raised his hand and moved it from side to side. "This is where the father was vague. But, Mike got in with some guys, you know how it is, kids of other MTA workers, teenagers, kind of like our boys here." Swift jerked his head, indicating Darring and the others. "The father just said they got up to no good. He mentioned one name, a guy named Bull Camoine. Old childhood friend of Mike Simpkins'. I pulled the sheet on both Mike and his buddy. Mikes's pretty clean; Camoine's is a mile long."

"Interesting," said Mathis.

Swift got back on track. "Anyway, Mike left home, wanted to get into TV and movies and all that. Wanted to be a filmmaker, ended up being a cameraman for Golf and NASCAR, nothing solid until he got in with a mid-sized company that traveled him around as a fiber tech manager. Basically a guy who runs all the cables. For a few years they did alright, but Mike didn't save anything. So when he got laid off, all he had was the house, worth more in Pompano than a comparable home up here. So, they traded down, essentially. Anyway, Jack Simpkins tells me this stuff and tells me that his way of contributing was to open up this 529 for the grandson, Braxton."

Mathis absorbed the rest of the backstory with a look of growing excitement. "This is something."

"It is. So you can see why, even given Cohen, and McAfferty, and the whole thing, I'm not just leaping off in another direction. I've got a murder to solve."

"And Mike Simpkins can cash out the 529 account now?"

"He can. He's the owner — Jack put everything in Mike's name. I mean, theoretically, he could have accessed it at any time. It's not like it's locked until the kid goes to school. But with the kid dead . . . you know, the money's not going to just sit there."

Mathis was staring off into space. "Penance," he said.

"How's that?" Swift regarded him closely for a moment. He could have sworn he glimpsed something human in the young, hotshot ADA's face. As if Mathis wrestled with his own daddy issues. It reminded Swift of something he'd read not long ago, online somewhere — *Everyone you meet is fighting a battle you know nothing about.*

"Guilt about how he treated his son Mike. Guilt about not supporting him through his life, or something. Something he did, maybe. Some part of Jack Simpkins felt guilty, and the education fund was his way of making atonement." Then the moment was gone. Mathis was a hungry prosecutor again, scenting a kill. "How much again?"

"After the hit it's going to take with the taxes — you only get the full amount if it's used for education — it's probably going to be about sixty, sixty-five thousand. Which is still no chump change."

Mathis was clearly chewing this over in his mind. "Enough to solve Mike's financial troubles, maybe. Enough to start a small business, get himself going. But, shit, if that's not a stretch — when it comes to killing your kid that's a meager payday. A year's middle class salary. Lot of risk for a relatively small reward."

"Unless there's emotional motive, too," Swift said.

"Get back at the father for the sins of his past, resentment towards the favoritism shown to the grandson."

The two men fell silent. It was a long shot, but honestly, Swift thought, it happened every day. People killed each other for far less. And it was different when it wasn't your own flesh and blood, wasn't it? Sure some, maybe most step-parents loved their kids as much or more than the bio parents, but there were a few bad apples out there weren't there? Men such as his own Highway Patrolman stepfather, who liked to teach a lesson with his fists. In situations like that, a relatively modest payday was perhaps plausible. Plus, once you started to follow the dollar, the angels of empathy and compassion often disappeared from the scene. Cohen himself had been sniffing around that very idea — it was what had given shape to Swift's own suspicions. He credited Cohen with the insight. People did the most heinous things for money. There was jealousy, anger, sometimes pure psychopathy, but crime related to money reigned supreme.

Mathis spoke in a low voice. The two of them were practically whispering at this point. "So . . . let me throw this and see if it sticks — Mike Simpkins hires these three we got cooling their heels?"

Swift had already considered it. "Maybe, but how does he find them? How does he know them? They've already all admitted they knew the victim through the online game. There doesn't seem to be a connection."

"Unless that's their story. That's what they were coached by Mike Simpkins to say. That they knew the kid from playing some innocent game online and became friends. That was to be their story in the event they got caught."

"In the event? They had an hour to get away, and yet we still picked them up at exit 30, before they even got on the Northway. The troopers were sitting there for ten minutes, and the kids drove right up."

"Because they're paid to be the fall guys?"

Swift shrugged. "Doubtful. Now we're talking even less money for Simpkins if he gives them just a small fee."

Mathis drummed his fingers softly on the desk. Swift could see the prosecutor's mind working. They had all of these pieces, the drug-dealing emotionally disturbed biological father, the sizeable savings account which could now become cash in the step-father's pocket, and three kids from three different states who all said they knew the victim from an online game — and at least one of the three seemed out-there enough to Swift to actually be a plausible killer. It was how these components went together, if they did at all, which was eluding Swift and the prosecutor. It felt like some game of its own, something played out with real people instead of characters on a screen.

"We need that autopsy," Mathis said, thinking aloud.

"We'll get it."

Mathis glanced up at Swift, and his eyes shone with worry. "We need it an hour ago, Swift."

Swift sensed there was one more skeleton in their midst. "What is it?"

"The two in there, the younger ones, both their lawyers have filed a writ of habeas corpus. Their parents are enraged that we're detaining them and haven't booked them yet. One set of parents is actually on their way north as we speak."

"Oh Jesus." Swift pushed back from the desk and ran a hand across his jaw, grazing the stubble there.

"I've got to charge them and put them in county or kick them loose. And I've got to do it now."

Mathis continued to stare at Swift, and the detective got the sense that his assistant district attorney was actually looking to him for advice. Swift took a deep breath, and sat up straight.

"Kick the minors loose. We keep Darring, and we book him tonight with suspicion of murder."

Mathis was nodding. When he spoke, it was to himself. "I'm not bound by the initial charges. Can change them once more evidence is obtained . . ."

"We'll be able to drive it home with the autopsy, or we'll do whatever else we have to do. We'll go full forensics on the vehicle, too, when we charge Darring. He's got no counsel, and so far his interviews suggest there's more than a simple friendship going on. At least something rotten in the state of Denmark. You can show a judge the interview tapes if need be."

Mathis was nodding emphatically, sitting up straighter too. Then his gaze connected with Swift, and to the detective's surprise, the prosecutor stuck out his hand.

Swift shook it.

CHAPTER THIRTY-THREE

Swift stroked Kady's fur and stared into the fire burning in his woodstove. It was almost one o'clock in the morning. He'd been up for nearly twenty-four hours. It was time to get some rest, otherwise things would start to go to shit, become messier than they already were. The young bucks out there would find McAfferty. The old geezers needed to rest their eyes and their addled brains. No matter what was going on — aliens landing or complete economic collapse, a serial killer tearing through town or a mass murderer at large — people still needed to eat, pee, sleep. Soldiers passed out on watch. Prison guards caught secret naps in the broom closet. Even the President of the United States occasionally rested his bones on one of the Oval Office couches.

Only human. Only flesh and blood.

Still, he had one more call to make.

Sheriff Dunleavy sounded older on the phone, more tired than Swift had ever known him.

"I appreciate it, John," Dunleavy said after listening to Swift's few well-chosen words. "But it was my call. I was the one who asked for you to keep Cohen around. We're both big boys, we can handle it. The only person who is at fault here is the son of a bitch who did this."

Swift felt a pain in his heart, but also the release of his culpability for Cohen's death. He hated that he felt this relief, yet there was no denying it was there. Why else had he called the Sheriff this late?

"And we're going to catch him," said Dunleavy, with a little enthusiasm coming back into his voice — as if prompted by vengeance. "Your whole State Police force and my Department are all out looking for him right now. We'll catch him."

"That's right," said Swift. There didn't seem to be much more to say. They had already gone over all of the details and each had exhausted their stores of useful information. There was certainly a connection between the Braxton Simpkins murder and the man, Tori McAfferty, who had struck a match to his meth operation — biology for one — but the anything else was an outside guess. And both Dunleavy and Swift were too long in the tooth to waste much time on wild guesses.

"If this cold and snow keep going on like this, I'm going to break into the sacramental wine," Swift said.

Dunleavy laughed, but it was thin. They lapsed into silence again.

"Alright," said Swift.

"Alright," Dunleavy echoed.

Swift hung up his phone and dropped it on the couch beside him. Kady's ears perked up, she looked at the phone, licked her chops, and then set her head down on his knee. Swift stroked her behind the ears. His eyelids were growing heavy, but his mind still buzzed. It was tough to shut it all out. Hard to put the images away in a box somewhere, but he'd gotten better at it over the years. The religious said you gave it over to God; you lay your burdens at His feet. Swift didn't know about God, not in a world like this, not in a place where teenage boys dropped dead in the middle of the night and their bodies turned to lumps in the snow. And as he drifted off to sleep, he couldn't help but think about the victim's family, and what a thing it was to have children, something he'd never had. That boy had wandered off into the night, the dark trees surrounding him, the snowflakes melting on his warm body, and he had drifted into the road, somehow, yet there had been no footsteps, and he felt sure that when they tossed it they'd find no evidence that the boy had ever been inside that car with the three others.

It was like he just manifested there, in the road. Swift could still see him, a shape in the falling snow.

Swift began to descend into sleep, and as he did, he saw the boy turn, and Swift found himself right there, out in the road, just a dozen yards away from the teenaged Braxton Simpkins.

And the boy looked at him through the white flakes, and raised his arms out to either side, and there was a sound in Swift's ears, something like a chiming, a ringing in the background, a kind of radiation, and the taste of metal on his tongue, not unpleasant, but somehow clean, like blood.

They stood like that in the snow, and then the boy's mouth opened, and he spoke to Swift as he dreamed, and showed him things.

He showed him everything.

CHAPTER THIRTY-FOUR

Kady was a mild-mannered dog; she seldom barked. Swift sat up and rubbed at his face and blinked and looked to where Kady usually lay sleeping on the floor beside his bed, but she wasn't there. He groaned and got up, swinging his legs out and groping the floor with his feet for his slippers, not finding them, not bothering to look further. He stood, the bed springs squeaking, relieved of his weight.

"Kady!" he snapped, more irritably than he wanted to. Then, in a more friendly tone, "Kady? Huh, girl?"

He grabbed the long black Maglite from his bedside table along with his sidearm, still in the holster. With these items in hand he walked out of the bedroom and into the kitchen.

Kady continued to bark. She was standing by the back door, her nose raised towards the knob, her tail down between her hind legs, her golden hair iridescent in the gloom.

"Kade. Kady-girl."

She briefly jerked her neck around to look at him and her tongue came out for a moment, pant-pant. She turned her head back to the door and started yapping again.

"Okay, okay," Swift said. He approached her, bent low, his hand out, and as he reached her, smoothed his hand alongside of her and patted her soft stomach. She reacted with a jump, gave him a quick kiss with her moist tongue, and licked her chops. "Shh, shh," he told her. "Still." Now that he was beside her, her tail started to wag, whacking against the back of his legs. He was wearing pajama pants, no shirt. The woodstove in the living room was still cranking and the house was warm. The digital clock above the stove read that it was just after four a.m. He'd been asleep for barely three hours. He stood at the back door and unfurled to his full height, feeling the joints of his spine clicking in protest, and leaned toward the window to look out.

The rear door of the kitchen looked onto the back of the property. There was one lamp post about ten yards from the house that stayed on all night, glowing a Halloween orange. The night was still, showing no snow, only the crystal glints of the powder that had fallen that day, unbroken in drifts and ridges.

Kady barked again. "Shh. Shh. What?" He saw nothing but the snow and the sky, a smudge of jagged treeline in the distance, the humps of the foaling shed, the dilapidated barn, and beyond these, the edge of the outbuilding.

He set the flashlight down on the shelf next to the kitchen door and used both hands to remove his pistol from his holster. He set the holster on the shelf and took the flashlight. He clicked it on, shone the beam towards the glass, which only succeeded in reflecting a bright supernova of light back at him. He set the gun on the shelf, unlatched the door, took the gun and put his hands together; one holding the light, the other aiming the gun where the light shone.

The door swung inward with a gust of wind and banged against the radiator behind it. Kady barked again and took several steps backward. Swift stepped through the kitchen door.

The kitchen was up a few rickety steps from the ground; in the spring the concrete blocks beneath the subfloor were visible until the perennials his grandmother had planted years before bloomed into life. The steps were now covered in snow. Swift was in his bare feet, the bitter cold knifing into him, clamping around his legs and ankles and arms. He did a sweep from right to left, the light beam playing over the buildings, the old post-rail fence greyed by the sun and listing with age. Behind him, Kady was silent. Right to left he swept, then back the other way.

"Kady," he said softly. "What is it?"

When he turned to look back at his dog, she wasn't there. Instead, she was a few feet away on the other side of the kitchen floor, drinking from her water bowl.

Swift lowered the flashlight and the gun and stepped back inside. He set the light and the weapon down on the shelf and closed the door. A few moments outside and the cold had gone right through him. He looked across the parquet floor at his golden retriever. "Hello? You with us, there, watchdog?"

Kady's head came up, water dripping from her black gums, and then she ducked back to the bowl and resumed lapping up the water for another few seconds before trotting into the living room where she lay down in front of the woodstove.

Swift watched her affectionately, and then, taking his cue from the pooch, went to warm himself by the woodstove beside her.

CHAPTER THIRTY-FIVE

"He was dragged."

"He was dragged?"

Swift sat across from Janine Poehler. He had invited Brittney Silas to join them, and she had her evidence folder with her and a laptop. They were meeting at Poehler's office. It was going on noon, approximately thirty-three hours since the estimated time of Braxton Simpkins's death.

Janine Poehler nodded and took a sip of her black coffee. There were croissants and bagels on the table, but no one was eating. This could have been partly due to the photographs Poehler was displaying on her desktop computer.

She pressed play on her digital voice recorder.

". . . Following removal of the shirt, various scars were observed along the left forearm that suggest potential cutting and at least one mark from ligature. It's as if the victim's wrists were bound together at one point. A second ligature mark, which will be known throughout this report as Ligature B, was observed on the decedent's neck. The mark is a dark red ligature and encircles the neck, crossing the anterior midline of the neck just below the laryngeal prominence."

She clicked it off. Brittney Silas was looking through her own photographic log of the crime scene, clicking through a slide show of photos and squinting at the screen. Now she looked up at Poehler.

Swift was looking over Brittney's shoulder at pictures of route 9N. "You think he was tied up and dragged? By the car?"

"My report shows that the victim died from ligature strangulation. That is an asphyxia caused by closure of the blood vessels — hence the petechial spotting — and closing of the air passages by external pressure on the neck. My conclusion is dragging. The mark is sloping, indicating that the ligature was pulled upward from behind, and the position is high up at the level of the hyoid bone. I see evidence of violent compression and constriction of the neck. This was obtained from the presence of bruising and ecchymosis about the marks on the neck, hemorrhages in the strap muscles, under the skin, in the sides of the tissues around the trachea and larynx, in the larynx and in the laryngeal structures themselves. The ligature mark alone is not diagnostic, it's more indistinct, suggesting a soft material used."

Brittney spoke up. "Like what?"

"I don't know. Something tensile enough to create the compression without snapping."

"A garrote," Swift said.

Poehler raised her eyebrows, perhaps appraisingly. "Precisely."

Brittney frowned. "What's a garrote?"

"It was first used in Spain," Swift said. "It's where convicts were tied to a wooden stake and a rope was looped around the neck. A wooden stick was slipped down the back of the neck between the cord and the skin and twisted."

"Jesus," said Brittney. She grimaced. Janine Poehler sipped her coffee and watched Swift, who went on.

"So then other countries got into it. Garrotes have been used as a stealthy way to eliminate sentries and enemy personnel. They also teach it to special forces now, how to improvise garrotes and make special ones suited to particular tasks." Swift finished speaking and rubbed his jaw absently, looking off.

"But not a rope," Janine said. "There were no fibers of any kind and the ligature marks for both A and B are more consistent with a softer material."

"Well, we're not looking for a woman's silk scarf," Brittney countered.

"I would say no, not exactly. I think you're looking for a cord. Something higher end, not any cheap extension cord, which could leave traces of rubber embedded in the skin. Something strong, but elastic."

Swift continued to rub and itch his jawline.

Poehler looked at him. "Growing a beard?"

Swift's eyes seem to find focus again and he looked at her. "Too lazy to shave."

Brittney looked back and forth between the two of them. Swift knew she was tough and as a CSI had seen her share of horrors no doubt, but death by strangulation was hard to take. And they now had to reconcile the possibility that the body had been dragged, with a crime scene which had been scraped over by a highway department plow just ten minutes before Braxton's time of death, according to the timeline, and then covered in snow which had accumulated that night at a variable rate of around four inches per hour. There had been no evidence to show a body had been dragged behind a car. No way to obtain casts of tire tracks either. But, Swift remembered, and it concurred with Brittney's observation that night — she had found no footprints left by the victim.

"This kind of thing — the garrote — has even made its way into the mainstream by way of movies," Swift said. "Ever see James Bond in *The World Is Not Enough*?"

Ever since meeting with Darring he'd found himself referencing movies.

Poehler shook her head, and then fixed Swift with her green eyes.

"It's in *The Godfather*, too," she said.

"That's right. That's exactly right." He drifted away again after that, putting something together in his mind.

Brittney interjected. "So what are we talking about here? In layman's terms."

Poehler nodded and pushed back the swivel chair, rotating to face the two of them more directly. She demonstrated with gestures as she spoke.

"The victim was tied at the left wrist and around the neck by a sash cord of some kind that left no fibers behind. This cord was then likely attached to the back of something powerful, probably a car. And he was dragged. There are minor abrasions consistent with a dragging. At first I thought they were cutting marks. Which is, sad to say, because I've seen a lot of that in my pediatric work. It was a gut reaction. Now I see those marks as drag marks. So, I think he was towed like this, dragged like this behind the car. The hemorrhaging isn't severe. There was very little putrefaction — I was able to see that, aside from the petechial markings, the bursting of the capillaries in the eyes was moderate. It's possible to conclude that, yes, asphyxia, or even hypoxia, is the official cause of death, but there is also the massive dose of cortisol, adrenaline . . ."

"Fear," said Swift.

"Yes. Fear, the cold, the exposure. All of these things contributed."

No one spoke for a few moments. Then Brittney finally broke the silence.

"There was no cord found in the car, or at the scene. What do we do, Swift, do we go back and sweep the woods again?"

"Absolutely. I take full responsibility for pulling us out of there."

"What about the car?"

"Now that we've got it, officially, we can take a close look at the rear bumper. There's no hitch — it's a Hyundai, for chrissakes — so there's got to be somewhere they tied that cord on. We need that cord."

Poehler asked, "Where are they now?"

"Two are gone. Let go this morning. One is processed and sitting in county jail. It's his vehicle, so it stays with us. Mathis laid charges on thick, but they won't stick without the cord, or some weapon."

"He didn't lawyer up?"

Swift pursed his lips and shook his head. "No. He didn't. He's going with a public defender."

"Huh," Poehler said.

"Yeah."

Now they needed to go and find something which their first search had shown just didn't exist. The crime scene had been as bare as an empty cave.

Swift considered one other place he ought to look.

CHAPTER THIRTY-SIX

"Mike," said the voice on the other end of the phone. "Been a long time, man."

"I know, man. Totally."

Mike could hear the sounds of city traffic in the background on Bull Camoine's end of the conversation. Mike experienced a wave of nostalgia for the city, and his misspent youth.

Bull was born Paul Anthony Camoine to a middle class Italian family on Staten Island. He'd had his name legally changed to "Bull" two days after his eighteenth birthday. There was, as one might predict, a tattoo of a huge, snorting *Bos taurus* covering the left side of his back, most of it over the shoulder blade, the tattoo a process of needle and patience that Bull had once called "the sweetest pain you'll ever feel." He was an ardent libertarian, and a conspiracy nut. He championed an orthodox capitalism, which was pitted against a bloated government that spied, pried, and taxed the holy shit out of every last citizen. They would do this, he believed, until the citizenry had nothing left, in order to render them powerless against a military takeover that the liberals were instituting in order to completely socialize the country, so that no one had to work, no one had to go to church, or stay married, no one had to do anything but hang onto the teats of government while the super-rich got even super-richer.

He was a lot of fun at parties.

Bull never used a cellular phone, only a pager. He switched the number every six months. His parents' home number, however, was still the same. Bull's mother, who shared her son's concerns about over-governing and the secular agenda, guarded it like a sentry. In order to earn her trust, Mike had to remind her of the times when, both eleven years old, he and Bull had eaten brownies in her kitchen after a Cobras football game. When that wasn't enough, he'd reminded her about her own father, who had played for the Stapletons in 1932 under Coach Hanson. And that her father had arrived from Italy, playing professional football only three months after landing at Ellis Island. All because of a bet he'd made with his brother, who'd remained in the home country.

She'd given out the pager number after that.

"What's been going on?" Bull asked. There was the characteristic wariness in his voice, but Mike felt it had softened since they last spoke. Bull had gone to work for the MTA, and had actually worked for three years under Mike's father, who took credit for taking Bull under his wing after Bull's father had died in a tunnel accident. The boys had originally met at Bull's father's funeral, and Bull had been at Mike's mother's funeral, many years later, which was the last time the two of them had seen each other. Thus, the two funerals bookended their brief but potent friendship.

"I moved," Mike said.

"Yeah, I heard."

"You heard?"

"Linda keeps a Facebook account. No matter how much I tell her it's just free information for the NSA and the CIA, she keeps it. Thinks I don't know. But then she comes up with things, like, 'Oh, Callie and Mike bought a house in upstate,' and when I ask her how she knows she has to come up with something. It's a sickness."

Mike didn't know whether Bull was referring to his wife's lying, Facebook, or social media in general. It didn't matter. Mike wasn't calling Paul Anthony "Bull" Camoine because of his theories on privacy invasion.

Aside from his doomsday philosophies, Bull was also the person who had physically assaulted more people than anyone Mike knew of, except maybe professional boxers. He'd been in jail at least a dozen times in his thirty-nine years, not to mention all the times he could have got sent up, but the person he'd assaulted was so petrified of retribution they didn't press charges. Bull's stay behind bars usually never lasted more than a couple of days; he would be arraigned, his mother would post bail and he would have to pay a fine. None of this seemed to faze him, however. Since the government lacked any legitimacy, he couldn't see why he should pay his debts. His longest stretch had been a year, and he'd spent it in Sing Sing, a State Correctional Institution. There his doomsday philosophy had really coalesced. Capital, Bull professed, was not paper currency. There was certainly money circulating in prison, but currency was not about dollars. It was about connections. It was strength by ownership. The more guys you owned, the more powerful you were. Bull was a powerful ally to have, and the worst enemy. Plus, he had a lot of guns.

"Yeah, we moved," said Mike. "And we've had some . . ."

"You've had some trouble?"

Mike knew Callie hadn't posted anything public yet about what had happened to their son. He was sure she hadn't sounded off on any social networks, mostly because she wasn't ready to break the news to her parents. Bull was just picking up on the tenor of Mike's voice, and making a guess backed by his usual skepticism.

"Yeah. We've had some trouble."

"Tell me."

Mike took a breath. He told Bull about losing his job, about his financial straits, about the move towards Callie's career. He spoke little of Braxton until he mentioned the emails from Tori McAfferty. He told Bull he'd threatened McAfferty.

"Fucking A," said Bull. "Put that son of a bitch in his place. Up and leaving Callie and his baby like that. That's not a man."

This made Mike feel a little better. Just a little. He continued recounting the events, bracing himself for the part where he described Braxton's death. Surprisingly, he got through the telling without getting choked up, and Bull was silent, listening, some daytime soap on his mother's TV warbling in the background. By the time Mike was finished, his hands were shaking. But not with sadness; they shook with anger.

"Sweet Holy Mary," Bull said at last.

"Yeah."

"So this guy, this piece of shit, he's up there and he's got a meth lab in his basement. Probably wants to get the kid working for him, the sick son of a bitch."

"I don't know. Yeah."

"Whatever. He's not thinking right. He's fucked up, Mike. You know that. You did the right thing telling him to piss off. Don't think for a second you didn't."

"Oh I think about it every second, Bull. I think if I hadn't done that, Braxton would still be alive."

"No. This psycho would have wound his way around Braxton's life some way or another."

"Then if I hadn't lost my job. If I'd had savings. We wouldn't have had to move."

"Bullshit. Life happens. Callie got a job offer, you said. You looked for the signs, you saw them, you acted."

"I don't know."

"Sure you do. Look, Mikey? You call me up for a confessional? You call me up to talk about how bad you feel, how you feel responsible, and you want to cry on my shoulder? That why you called me?"

"No."

"They haven't caught this guy yet. I don't watch the TV news — it's all owned by real estate corporations and banks — but I can bet, I can just bet, they haven't gotten him yet. Bunch of backwoods cops up there running around, banging into each other, couldn't find their asses with two hands and a flashlight. So, you're maybe a little worried? You're right to be."

"They have to get him. Eventually they'll get him. In the meantime, they're looking at me."

"At you? The fuck you talking about?"

Mike then explained to Bull about his father setting up the 529 account for Braxton. About how, now that Braxton was dead and the account was in Mike's name, he stood to collect. How the cops were using this as a reason to sniff around, how the detective, Swift, had asked him if he wouldn't mind coming down to the station for a bit that very evening.

"Cocksuckers," Bull said, typically profane. "This is just what I'm talking about."

Mike could feel heat creeping up the base of his neck. He may have felt better getting some friendly, manly mojo from Bull, some reassurance that Mike wasn't to blame for this horrible tragedy, but now a new form of guilt was rising up. What exactly was he doing, winding Bull up like this? What purpose did it serve?

"You need help," Bull said. It was a statement, matter of fact.

"No. I mean, yes, but this has been helpful. Just talking."

Bull made a dismissive sound. "Nah, Mikey. Come on. I know you. I've known you since you was a kid in that cold apartment downtown. I remember seeing the look in your eye then, and I bet you got that same look now. That take-no-shit look after your father . . . you know. Mikey, you didn't take it from your old man, you sure as shit ain't gonna take it from your son's old man."

The comment about Mike's old man was like a cold sock to the jaw. He hadn't expected that, for some reason — and he had let Bull lead him right into it. Into a dead end where bad things happened, and the walls were on three sides, until something came up behind you, trapping you in.

"Same thing," Bull went on. "Sorry to say — and hey, it sounds like your old man is trying to make amends with this deferred tax account, okay, I'll give him that, even if it wouldn't-a bought half a semester by the time that kid was going to school — but your old man made his grown up choices. So did Braxton's. You want to play a man's game, you pay man prices."

"My dad had an affair," Mike said, feeling the ice of it in his gut. "It's different."

"No. Not different. Same shit. You got outta there, is what happened. Maybe — hey, for all you know, maybe this was Braxton's way of getting outta there, too. I hate to say it; I know it's tough. But listen, you did what you could do for him, Mikey. You did alright by that kid."

"Thanks."

"While he was *above* ground, Mike. You did what you could do while he was *above* ground. You see what I'm saying? Now you gotta do what's right for the kid's soul, Mike."

Bull was an impassioned orator when he got going. Punctuating everything, cursing, using Mike's name, again and again. Mike knew Bull. He'd heard all the speeches over the years.

"Alright," Mike heard himself say. "Thanks, Bull. I'll keep you posted."

He could almost hear Bull Camoine grin down the phone connection. "Whatever you say Mikey. Just know; I know what you and your mom went through. Yeah your pop helped me out, but I never forgot, you know. I never forgot the things he did to you and your ma. I got your back. You pull the Bull trigger when you're ready, Mike."

CHAPTER THIRTY-SEVEN

The house on Salmon Run in South Plattsburgh looked like a meteor had struck. Half of the roof was gone. The walls were eviscerated. The yard was a charred, black ring.

The police and fire department were everywhere. Crime scene tape flapped and twisted in the breeze, cordoning off the home and the street both ways. All vehicle traffic had been rerouted and the street was filled with gawkers surging against the police tape and traffic cones.

The McAfferty scene was a jurisdictional nightmare. State Police, Clinton County Sheriff's, Essex County Sheriff's, and DEC still hadn't sorted out the chain of evidence. Evidence techs wore head-to-toe Hazmat suits. News vans — Plattsburgh, Burlington, Albany, even Montreal — were parked beyond the police barricades; photographers vied for the best shot of the smoldering wreckage. A reporter was mouthing into camera as Swift walked past, and her eyes broke away from the lens for a moment to follow him before he ducked beneath the yellow tape. He'd parked well out of range along the shoulder of the road and had moved quietly through the packs of onlookers, making his way inconspicuously towards the scene.

He was so low-profile that one of his troopers tried to prevent him from going inside the crime tape until Swift looked up and locked eyes with the young man.

Just yards from the house, which still gave off heat and a stench like singed brake pads, Detective Remy LaCroix stood looking out over the crowd huddled in the street. There was a steely drizzle coming down, pattering Swift's overcoat. Rain so cold it was almost snow. The crowd didn't even seem to notice it.

"Reminds me of something," said Remy, as Swift walked up the slight rise towards the detective standing in the burnt grass. "There are three types of people in every civilization: The killers, the victims, and the bystanders." Remy nodded over Swift's shoulder at the gathered crowd.

"Somebody's got to watch," Swift said. "Otherwise, it might not be real."

Remy paused and looked Swift up and down. "You feeling okay, Swifty?"

"Yup."

The two men were standing shoulder to shoulder, facing in opposite directions. While Remy surveyed the crowd with disdain, Swift looked at the cinders and ash which were all that remained of the house.

"Whose place is it?" It had occurred to Swift that Tori McAfferty was a man with a pretty flimsy business in HVAC contracting. No employees, not even a yellow pages ad. Remy LaCroix was part of a task force seeking to nip the burgeoning North Country meth industry in the bud. But McAfferty was barely on their radar. So he was either independently wealthy, or he was living off someone else.

"Funny you should ask," said Remy, still looking through the gauzy rain at the gaping collection of neighbors. "Place is Tricia Eggleston's. McAfferty's girlfriend."

"Eggleston? Oh boy," Swift said.

Remy scowled and smiled at the same time. "Yeah."

Swift shook his head, and briefly glanced up at the dark, wet sky. The Egglestons were a family of regional prominence. They were everywhere around Lake Champlain from Plattsburgh down to Schroon Lake. Thomas Eggleston had a car dealership. Anita Eggleston was a teacher at New Brighton. There was also a criminal defense lawyer, and a notable realtor.

"Then she's probably Tom's daughter." Swift said to himself. Thomas Eggleston, or Big Tom. He had a few car commercials that played in several counties. Unlike McAfferty, Big Tom did very well on paper.

No doubt every one of the Egglestons, in-laws included, were cringing in the shade right now, embarrassed, ashamed, or outraged — or all three — by their relative who had shacked up with a cooker and a dealer and was peddling tooth-rot to the community. Thing was, meth addicts weren't hard to notice. They were all stringy, evasive, and unhygienic. It was likely the family had known of, or at least suspected Tricia's involvement with meth.

Big Tom would either make a big fuss, or keep a low profile and hope to stay out of the media. It was tough to know how he would play it.

"You think her uncle will represent her?" Swift asked. Tricia's uncle, Warren Eggleston, was the lawyer.

"He already is."

"No qualms about representing family? No conflict of interest?"

"Nope."

"And she was picked up for questioning early this morning?"

"Yeah, at a girlfriend's. Says she ran out when the cop came in. No idea about where McAfferty went, or the explosion, nothing. Warren is guarding her like a pit bull."

Swift nodded. Warren had the reputation of being a tenacious lawyer. It was he who'd represented Frank Duso for his drunk driving charges, and, rumor had it, was the one who put an idea in Duso's head about how he maybe couldn't see so well after being pepper-sprayed.

"So why you up here, Swifty?" Remy turned his head and looked at Swift with a half-smile.

"I love the smell of burning meth labs," Swift said.

"Yeah, me too." Remy turned to face Swift. The wind picked up and pierced both of them with shards of icy rain. "Took half the night to knock that fire down. Twenty-odd hours later, and this place is still chaos. For a while everyone kept back — sometimes you get a couple of canisters of something exploding after the fact. I don't know — I'm no expert. I started with pharmacy rip-offs of pseudoephedrine, stuff like that. But this place, you know, there's been some activity we've seen here." He looked at Swift. "You want me to keep you in the loop, yeah? Your thing going on down there with the kid in the road?"

"Simpkins, yeah. I would appreciate it."

"Well shit, Swift. You could've just called. You didn't have to drive all the way up here. I know I'm a pleasure to be around, of course."

Swift smiled. Remy was French-Canadian, about half a foot shorter than Swift, round in the middle, with a small dark goatee and a fedora. He was the only cop Swift knew who actually wore one. It made him look like some PI from a pulp novel out of the 50s. Swift liked him. He reached into his overcoat pocket and pulled out a small pair of needle-nosed pliers. Swift held them in the air and opened and snapped them shut once.

"You are a pleasure," Swift said. "But it's more than sharing information. This guy is a possible suspect for murder one; my case. So, I've got to go have a look around for myself."

Remy stepped back and smiled broadly. "Be my guest," he said. He swept an arm towards the ruined home. "There's everybody in there but K-9. And I guess they're on their way; it was just cleared for the dogs. Here, take this."

Remy handed Swift a small white mask to put over his mouth and nose.

"You may have to wait in line before you walk through. I'm working on the concession stand. Give me a minute and I'll have popcorn."

"Could probably cook it off the floor in there," said Swift through the mask. "If there's any floor left."

Remy burst out laughing, and then put a hand to his mouth, possibly so the crowd wouldn't see. "Or hot dogs," he said in a lower voice. As Swift began to walk away Remy said, "That's all I want. Nice little hot dog stand. One of those push-carts. That's how I'm going to retire. Make a killing with those things. I could set it up for the bystanders at a scene just like this. Hey — how's your thing coming with the Attorney General's office?"

Swift tossed Remy a look back over his shoulder as he approached the house. "I've been playing hard to get," he said.

Remy's voice floated back, serious now. "Not after this you won't be."

"No," Swift said, as a trooper in a rain jacket pointed him into the devastated house. "Probably I won't."

* * *

Inside, he was once again overcome with culpability. He pictured Cohen walking into the place the previous evening. How long had Cohen been standing in the house before it had blown up?

Swift shrugged this off. He needed to concentrate. The scene before him was absolute mayhem. Remy LaCroix was right; there were people everywhere. Evidence techs were still scraping residue from every conceivable surface. A trio of firemen were in the back, under the supervision of another State Detective — Swift recognized him as a man named Ashburn — and they were erecting some temporary support beam to prevent the roof over the kitchen from collapsing. The ceiling — what was left of it, mere ragged tatters, was dripping. Everything was sodden. The carpet squished under his feet around the mouth of a gaping hole that had eaten up eighty percent of the living room floor and part of the rooms at the back.

All over the walls were dark stains. Swift thought he saw the outline of a body. As if the flash of the explosion had somehow imprinted a silhouette of Alan Cohen against the wall.

Goddamnit. Stop it.

He needed to get through this muck. He needed to take someone out to dinner. Forget Silas, she still had most of her career in front of her. Poehler was more his speed. He would slip his hand down to the small of her back, circle it around the rise of her hips, pull her to him. Crude, he knew, to think such thoughts. But he had to think about something. Anything to get his mind off Cohen.

He had to get to the room which the investigation had deemed McAfferty's bedroom, and that was straight ahead. Anything back in that bedroom which might relate to Braxton Simpkins, Swift needed it. Of course, Tori himself would be the best evidence, along with what he might have to say about his biological son, but there was no telling how long it would take to find him. It could be in the next few hours, if he was stupid, and hiding close by. Or even stupider, and tried to cut across the border into Canada, or take the ferry across Lake Champlain and into Vermont. But he could have been smart, too. He could have gone downstate, where the population grew denser every mile closer to New York City. Yeah, if he was smart, he would have hopped on the Amtrak the first chance he got after striking that match, and would have already arrived in Penn Station to be lost in the crowd.

Swift didn't know what kind of a man he was. Callie Simpkins seemed pretty bright. She was emotional, for sure, but her son had just been found in the damned snow. She was an artist, and she was easy on the eyes. We all make mistakes, thought Swift, sometimes we try on the wrong clothes, but there had to be something redeeming about Tori McAfferty if this intelligent, reasonably sane woman had spent time with him, and even had a kid with him. But with every hour Tori McAfferty wasn't in custody, the less likely it was they would ever find out.

Until he made a mistake.

Most criminals on the run screwed up eventually, and that was how they got nailed. They needed resources — food, shelter, money — and they were apt to go about it in an aggressive, or illegal way. It was all many of them knew. Others, it was impulse. It was entrenched in them, the need for violence. And often part of them wanted to get caught, knew they needed to be taken down.

He reached the back bedroom after hugging the wall to circumnavigate the crater. The room was dark, the floor spongy under Swift's feet as he snapped on his flashlight and swung it around.

The place was a wreck. The bed was a twisted mass of box springs poking out of wadded blankets. The dressers had mostly burned and were soaked and blackened. There were a few crispy photographs on one, however, and Swift approached and picked one up with his pliers.

He lifted it off the top of the dresser and squinted at it. It was hard to make out, but it looked like a man and a woman standing together. The woman was probably naked.

He moved on to the next picture, which was curled up into a tube. He unrolled it, but it was useless. The image was burned away.

Swift put the photo back. His nose was starting to itch inside the mask and he could smell the coffee on his breath. He looked around the room again. The walls were streaked from the ceiling down to the floor with tar — probably from the melting shingles on the roof. There was a strip of what might have been a poster still tacked to the wall. A mangled guitar sat wet and glistening beneath the poster. Swift crossed the room towards a door at the back of the bedroom, mindful of his footing; he didn't want to go crashing through the floor. The entire building was a deathtrap. He felt bad for the investigating team, moving gingerly about in their white space suits, looking like astronauts in some alien atmosphere. Swift knew that the prize was out there in the afternoon storm, on the run.

The door from the bedroom led to a small room, even darker, but in better structural shape. Off to his left, Swift could see the firemen and troopers in the kitchen. Standing right in front of him was an evidence tech, a CSI in a Hazmat suit, who was going through the dryer.

It was a pantry and laundry room, Swift figured, looking around. There were a few canned goods left on the shelf, and signs that some of them had exploded in the heat. Spilled boxes of dry goods, a couple of tools, and a mop and a broom had managed to stay propped upright in the corner. He smiled at the CSI.

"Howdy."

"Howdy," the tech echoed back in a muffled voice. He sounded like Rick Moranis in that movie, the spoofy one — *Spaceballs* — that was it. Swift was about to excuse himself and leave by the back door when he saw something hanging from the hooks next to the top-load washing machine.

You've got to be kidding me.

There were belts hanging next to the washer. One of them, with a huge buckle, looked like it belonged in a Texas rodeo. A couple of others, while wet and blackened in places, were clearly a woman's, and there was also an orange extension cord, plus another cord, pure black, coiled up next to it.

Swift took the cord coil in his hand. He reached over with his pliers and lifted the cord up off the hook.

It was slender, strong, about a half-inch gauge. A good, tensile cord, stronger than a typical electrical cord. Judging from the coil, it was about twenty, twenty-five feet long.

Swift looked at the ends. He grabbed one end with the pliers, as if taking a snake just behind its jaw, and lifted it up to eye level to get a better look. It was a guitar cord. The end was called a quarter inch end, or a tip-ring-sleeve. Probably was used with the mangled instrument he'd seen in the bedroom.

The CSI was watching him.

"I'm going to take this," he said.

The tech responded with that same muffled voice. "You're going to need to sign for it."

"Whose clipboard?"

The tech looked around. In the other room, there was a loud crack, a splintering that could only mean a floor giving way, and Swift heard men's voices cry out. The firemen and cops in the kitchen had just fallen through.

"Shit," said the tech, and turned and leapt toward the kitchen. He gripped the doorway and leaned in. "Everyone okay?"

An embarrassed-sounding voice floated back. "Yeah . . ."

Swift slipped out the back door.

CHAPTER THIRTY-EIGHT

"If he left the house," said six-year-old Reno Simpkins, "it was because he was trying to protect us."

Mike and Callie sat together on the couch while Reno stood in the middle of the living room floor. Hannah was nearby, absorbed in playing with her toy doctor kit. The sun was going down outside — daylight saving was getting nearer, but for now darkness fell at 6 pm. Callie realized that neither she nor Mike had even thought about putting together a dinner.

"I bet you're right, honey," said Mike. Callie glanced at her husband sitting beside her. Each of them held a cup of coffee in their hands. So far, broaching the terrible subject to their daughters had gone much better than they had feared. Of course, who knew what a lasting impact this would have on Reno. She seemed to be taking it in her stride. She was a smart girl, and her parents already knew her to be capable of managing her emotions to some degree.

Callie leaned forward a little, sitting cross-legged with her coffee resting near her abdomen. "Why do you think that, honey? Why would Brax be trying to protect you?"

Reno stuck out her lower lip and lifted and dropped her shoulders in an exaggerated shrug. "Because he always protected us. That time when Hannah was at the top of the stairs and he caught her before she fell? And he came into my room sometimes."

"He came into your room?" Mike now leaned in a bit, too.

"He plays on his 'puter sometimes and I see the light when I wake up and one time I came into his room and then he walked me back into bed and I had a bad dream."

"You had a bad dream that woke you up?"

"Yeah and Braxton was on his 'puter and he came into my room and he told me that bad dreams were just atoms and couldn't hurt me."

"Atoms?" asked Callie.

"Yeah, atoms, and he told me that he could protect me from the atoms by a magic trick."

"Maybe you mean 'Phantoms,'" said Mike.

"Yeah, bantams."

Callie frowned. Mike could see she was attempting to hold back her tears. "What did he do, honey?" she asked. "How did he protect you from the phantoms?"

Reno held her hands out in front of her and then clasped them together and drew the coupled fists towards her heart. "He took them and he put them in his chest, like this."

Mike fully expected Callie to break down at this, and could feel his own tears rising against the backs of his eyes, threatening to spill over. But Callie slowly sat back and then took a sip of her coffee with both of her hands and then smiled at her daughter. "That was very nice of him."

"Yeah, very nice of him so I think that when he left the house it was maybe to release the bantams outside. So that they wouldn't stay here in the house with us but be outside and then they could fly away. He was probably doing that and then he got hit by the car."

Mike felt the stone in his chest that had settled there the moment they'd told Reno the white lie — that Braxton had died because he'd been outside in the dark and a car hadn't seen him. And as if his daughter was able to read his thoughts, she now crumpled up her face as she asked a question. "I don't understand how he would get hit by a car."

"Why not?"

"Because he had his headlight," she said, pointing to the middle of her forehead.

The police hadn't said anything to them about a headlamp being found. *What headlamp?* Mike wondered for a moment. Then he remembered his father gifting one to Braxton as they'd traveled north two months ago. "How do you know he had his headlamp, honey?"

"Because when he went outside he had it on."

"You saw Braxton go outside the other night?"

"Mmhmm, I was awake."

Mike's body had grown rigid. He spoke deliberately, with clear enunciation. "Reno, did you see what happened to Braxton? Did you watch him outside and see?"

She shook her head, her feathery hair flopping. "No, I just watched the light go away."

"You watched the light go away? You mean it just went out?"

"It went into the snow. It just got darker and darker and then gone."

It sounded like she was describing him head up the road, but Mike still had to press. "But you didn't see anyone out there with him? Maybe a man, like me?"

No, she shook her head again.

Callie broke in. "Honey, did Braxton say anything to you before he went outside?"

This time, Reno nodded her head.

Mike felt his pulse start to race. He could feel Callie beside him, feel the heat emanating from her body.

"What did he say?"

"He told me goodbye."

"He said goodbye? What, exactly, honey, if you can remember — what exactly were his words?"

She shrugged. For a moment she seemed much older. "Just goodbye. He said, 'Goodbye, Reeny.'"

Mike and Callie exchanged a look. She was holding on now, but it couldn't last. Her flesh-and-blood son had been taking on the nighttime dreams of their eldest daughter. Unknown to Mike and Callie, he'd been getting her back to sleep. And he had put on his headlamp and said goodbye to her the night of his death, walking off into the snow, his light, literally, fading.

He'd known what was going to happen. Yet he had still left in his pajamas. It meant he wasn't going to run away. It meant that he had planned to walk outside into the snow and cold to meet his death.

Mike got off the couch and went to call Detective Swift.

CHAPTER THIRTY-NINE

Swift called Brittney Silas on the way back to New Brighton. The Simpkins daughter had reported that the victim had left the house with a headlamp on. Swift advised Silas to redouble the search of the woods along 9N. It would be like looking for a needle in a haystack, and a lot of manpower had been drawn off by the manhunt for McAfferty, but it was paramount. Silas was on it.

He also informed her that he'd found something which matched Janine Poehler's description of the ligature used to strangle the victim. He realized that guitar cables, extension cords, and all the rest could be found everywhere. Probably one in four households had a resident musician, someone with an electric guitar. And Swift was no audio technician — for all he knew the cable could be used to hook up stereo speakers, too. Which put it at just about every household. But it was something.

"I need you to cover my ass here, Brit," he said to her.

"What? What did you do now, Swift?"

"The McAfferty house was a mess. They were up to their eyes in it."

He heard Brittney sigh. "You just took it?"

"I didn't want to wait until hell froze over to pull it from their chain. Listen, all you have to do is call Remy LaCroix. We've got interlinking investigations. He'll sign off on it. He's a good guy."

"Did you pack it up already?"

"I did. Sent it to the lab." The quarter-inch cable would be tested for DNA in Albany. It took time to be couriered there and run through the examination. Swift wanted to keep things moving.

"Alright," Silas said, sounding resigned.

"Hey," Swift was nearing the substation. The setting sun was blinking through the hardwood trees beyond the shoulder. Silas would be out there all night looking for a headlamp, in the cold, under the glaring area lights. "Thanks, Brit."

She paused for a moment. "I'm beginning to think you're a smooth talker," she said.

"No. Too many eyes spoil the pie, is all."

"That's another one of your lines?"

He smiled. "Thanks, Brit."

* * *

Time to shift attention to Kim Yom, the computer forensic specialist. Kim had overnighted at a local fleabag motel, but looked as prim and fresh as if she'd spent the previous evening at the Waldorf. She was immaculately dressed in a linen pantsuit and smelled faintly of perfume and shampoo. They sat side by side at Swift's desk.

"Tell me more about the deep web," Swift asked.

"I'll tell you what I can. What do you want to know?"

"How does it work?"

Kim sat back in her chair and gathered her thoughts. She was an articulate woman, and chose her words carefully. "Like I said before, ninety-nine percent of the internet is deep web territory. And by that I mean, the accepted definition is sites that aren't indexed by standard search engines. We're talking about dynamically generated sites, very hard to reach unless you know exactly what you're looking for — and how to find it. We used to work with Turbo10, which was a sort of deep-mining type of search engine. But that's defunct. If you think of the deep web as a pie chart, the largest slice is databases. NASA, the Securities and Exchange Commission, others. Then there's fee-charging sites like LexisNexis and Westlaw which host government documents. About twelve percent is Intranet stuff for companies and universities. Then you get to the darkest wedge of the pie. That's Tor. Here's where you can buy LSD, AK-47s, human body parts, you name it."

"How do you access that?"

"Well, you don't. It's not like that. Tor browsing is what keeps a user's internet activity hidden, bouncing them all around the world."

"How?"

"It's communication relays."

"It's all automatic?"

"No. Well, yes and no. But the relay network is run by volunteers."

"Volunteers?"

She nodded. "People who believe in anonymity, and stand against Big Data. See, we're really in Federal territory here. Personally, I work a lot with the FBI and the National Center for Missing and Exploited Children. Child pornography is a federal offense. Eighty-five percent of the perps are doing it both locally and on the internet. Agents pretend to be kids and get into chats, careful not to solicit a rendezvous, but to lead a perp into it, and then they nab him. But the deep web is tricky — you've got to catch criminals in the act, because these websites are shifting constantly. And because a lot of times, you have more than one person acting in collusion. Acting as one entity, bouncing things around, making their moves to hack or whatever they're doing."

Swift pinched the bridge of his nose for a moment and shut his eyes. He hated the sense that he was completely out of his depth. Jumping off the horse to chase the fugitive down on foot? He was the guy. Pursuing a criminal through a labyrinth of shifting websites designed to keep all footprints concealed? It was worse than a foot of snow on the crime scene.

He opened his eyes again, and saw Kim watching him carefully. "Alright," he said. "So we know — or, we're fairly certain — that someone out there used these . . . methods to learn Braxton Simpkins' location?"

"No."

Swift was stumped. "No?"

"Okay," she said, and turned to her own laptop, a shiny new Mac, slim as a magazine. Her fingernails clicked against the keys. Swift watched the screen, his head starting to pound. When they'd been together the previous afternoon, Kim had claimed that the victim's computer had been hacked — he was sure of it. He thought she'd said that the hacker had accessed it through the deep web, a term Swift knew he'd heard before; now he remembered how. Kim had mentioned NASA. Swift recalled that, before rising to more global fame, Julian Assange had been a hacker who'd broken into NASA over a decade ago.

Then it made sense. You hacked in to a deep web site, not necessarily a laptop's hard drive itself. Did that mean Braxton Simpkins had a website? Swift was still confused, and hoped Kim would clear it up.

"I've cloned the victim's hard drive like I showed you yesterday," Kim said, "and I have a Tor browser bundle on my computer."

"So you can hack NASA?"

Kim remained unsmiling. "There have been major hacks into other companies besides NASA over the years. Google, AOL, Verisign, Heartland Payments, Monster, Fidelity Nation, Stuxnet; they've all been hacked. So has, I believe, Kapow."

Swift perked up. Now they were on some familiar territory. He remembered the name Kapow.

"That's the company that administers the game, *The Don.*"

"Correct. All of the user data — the player data — is stored in the Kapow servers in San Francisco, maybe other places, too. They have a lot of users. Over six million. What I'm doing with my own Tor is searching the deep web hacker sites — there's a few — where hackers might brag about their victories, or swap information, in some cases."

"Excellent," said Swift. He thought he was beginning to get some of the bigger picture. At least, he could grasp that Kim Yom was actively searching for the hacker who had gotten a hold of Braxton Simpkins information. There was still one piece left missing.

"But what about the firewall breach? Is that part of the same thing?"

"Once the hacker had the data from the Kapow theft, they targeted the victim's laptop directly."

"Why? They already had all of his info, right?"

Kim lifted her shoulders awkwardly and let them drop. It was almost as if this self-possessed woman didn't take naturally to a shrug. "They were looking for something else."

"What?"

"I don't know."

Swift blinked at the screen. Pages were opening and closing rapidly. Nothing looked like anything he'd seen before; the usual website was a blitz of advertising and buzzwords and branding. These sites were stripped bare, filled with cryptic information. In some cases, as Kim's fingers flew, the pages onscreen didn't even appear to be in English, but code. Swift thought it was called *html.*

"Pinpointing just where the hack came from is basically trying to find a needle in a haystack. The digital tracks have been very well covered. The best I've been able to determine so far is that it originated in the U.S."

This jolted Swift out of his brief hypnosis. "That's great." He nodded at the hieroglyphics in front of him. "You're able to prove that the victim's computer was hacked, and from the U.S."

"Yes. And I have a date, too, in the registry."

A couple of flicks of her fingers and a window popped up, with more icons and graphics. Something Swift could finally recognize. She opened a folder and started to scroll through about a zillion file addresses. Then she stopped. "So, we've got this Kapow data theft happening December 28. The firewall was breached a day later."

Swift reached into his inner pocket, pulled out his small notebook. He licked his thumb and flipped back a few pages. "That was the day the Simpkins were moving. They weren't even here yet. Two months before the crime."

"Looks that way, detective."

Swift sat back in the swivel chair beside Kim, thinking. Then he leaned forward again and put on a winning smile. "Any chance we can narrow the trace? Three hundred million people in the United States."

Again, Kim was stone-faced. "That's a real long shot. Next to impossible."

He sat back. Stumped again.

"What about the messages? The email messages from within the game."

Kim turned and pulled a stack of paper from a very chic valise at her feet. She flopped the papers on the desk beside the computer. "I read them all."

"And?"

"You've got your basic stuff. Definitely a lot of rivalry going on. These gamers are vicious. Lots of wummers."

"Wummers?"

"Wum. W-U-M. Means 'Wind-up Merchants.' Internet slang for someone who intends to cause as much disruption as possible by goading others online."

"Like a troll." Swift had heard the term somewhere.

"Sort of. Trolls tend to be characterized by spewing negativity everywhere. Wummers are really looking to stir things up, to get a reaction."

"And you've found 'wumming' going on in there?" Swift glanced at the stack of papers.

"I certainly did." Kim began to leaf through the printouts. "There are messages between players, and there are also battle reports. From what I could gather — and this is going back about three months, before the messages were last cleaned out of the inbox — a player named Billy Sweet Tea had attacked Fresco — that's the victim — and wiped out a good portion of his defenses, and stolen vast resources. So, Fresco then goes what they call in gaming circles, 'berserk.'"

"How so?"

"He retaliated by hitting Billy Sweet Tea every single day for the next three months."

"Wow. Berserk."

"What I found in other messages though was that Billy Sweet Tea had been terrorizing other gamers, too. Sweet Tea is a big player. Though it's free to play, you can spend real money in the game for 'bullion,' and use that as currency to buy troops and speed up building and training processes. Sweet Tea was a giant compared to other players."

"But he didn't appreciate it when Fresco started hitting him day after day," Swift said, trying to follow along.

"No. He most certainly did not."

"Are there direct threats?"

"There's one."

She handed Swift a sheet she had already pulled out and set aside. Swift snatched it and read it eagerly.

> fresco i see you got your try-hard pants on today, good 4 you. now listen here you stupid fvck, u keep this shit up go right

> ahead private tryhard, i'mma find u, not in the game, i know all your hideouts in here dumbshit but I'm gonna find you in real life and I'm going to kill you. you and everyone in your fucked family. you failed to even help your little butt-buddy too. You probably fail a lot in life don't u? you hear me u stupid little fck? U must be a little kid LMAO. But you're playing a big boy game now little kid. I'll be seeing you. keep yer light on for me. – billy

"Jesus," Swift said, leaning back, holding the sheet up in front of his eyes with one hand, pawing at his jaw with the other. "This is it, right here. Sweet Tea says he's going to kill Fresco. Find him and kill him and kill his whole family."

Kim Yom looked at Swift, expressionless. She was capable of divorcing herself from any emotion during a case, which was partly why she was so efficient, Swift knew. But he couldn't help get excited himself.

"This could be the threat that gives us intent."

"Or it could be two kids talking tough. You build that into your prosecution — worse, hinge it on that — and the defense shoots it right down, saying that the language only refers to in-game strategy. Rile your opponent. Get them to make a mistake."

"Yeah but this is the kind of stuff that causes kids to jump off bridges." He thought of Mathis, who'd been looking to carve out a possible case of cyber-bullying, maybe a hate crime.

She blinked at him. He knew just by looking in her eyes and hearing the words come out of his mouth that what they had was still circumstantial, no matter how scathing and brutal it read.

"How do we connect Sweet Tea to Robert Darring? I mean come on. We've got the kid admitting he played the game. Got him at the scene of the crime, with a real, real shaky story about why he's there. What if we got his personal computer?"

"That might help."

She sounded doubtful. Or just unenthused, and it was starting to irk Swift just a little bit. They *had* this kid, dammit. He was five miles away, sitting in county lock-up, cooling his heels. They had him, and here was his online alter-ego, issuing threats. There was motive now — revenge for Braxton Simpkins' aggressive retaliation in a war game.

"We get a warrant, we search his place, we get his computer, we find, just like with the victim, he plays this game online and there's his username and there's his password and boom, we got him." Swift slapped the printout against the palm of his hand.

"It's possible," said Kim.

He searched her face. *Dammit, Kim.* "Or what? We get the data from the servers in San Francisco. You said we could do that, right? With Federal intervention?"

"We could do that, too. That could take much longer, but have far more evidentiary value."

"Why?" Swift's angst was coming through in his voice. "Why would getting this guy's computer and showing that it's him, he's this Sweet Tea player . . . why wouldn't that hold up? Why are you skeptical?"

"It's not my place to say."

"What? What are you talking about, Kim? Of course it's your place."

"You're lead investigator, John. I'm your cyber-crime specialist."

"Well, this is a goddamn cyber-crime." He glared at her, and then took a breath. "Please excuse my French."

"Oh I speak French. It's not a problem."

She fell silent. She was letting him work it out.

"You think he's smart," said Swift.

"It takes a certain intellect to navigate the deep web effectively."

"You think there's no way his computer is sitting on his desk in an apartment in Queens with an incriminating username and password waiting to be discovered."

"It crossed my mind."

"And you don't think he's entirely alone in his . . . activities."

"Probably not."

Swift felt himself deflate, and he sat back. He tossed the paper onto the desk in front of them. After a moment he said, "Well, we're going to try anyway."

"I would expect no less."

He glanced at her. "And you're going to see about getting the data straight from the gaming servers."

"Say the word."

"I'm saying the word. Let's put the spark to a bigger barrel. Go federal. Put me in touch with whoever. I'm assuming there's an investigation into the Kapow hack?"

Kim nodded.

"We've got to tie this kid to these messages, to this game."

"I understand."

He sniffed, and scratched at his jaw some more, looking around the room, his gaze at last falling on the computer screen. "Why's he just sitting there?"

"Darring?"

"Just sitting in lock-up. Like this is all in a day's work for him. Like he's not afraid."

"Because of one other thing I have yet to tell you."

Swift's eyes opened wide.

"Probably because the Billy Sweet Tea player is still active. He was online just this morning."

CHAPTER FORTY

Mike found Callie standing in the kitchen, staring into space. He came up behind her and put his hands on her shoulders.

"What's next? You talked to the detective earlier?"

"I did. He said he was working on something, closing in on the bad guys, and blah blah blah."

"Did he tell you what the autopsy report was?"

"He said he wanted to meet with us first thing in the morning."

"First thing in the morning?" She buried her face in her hands in front of him. "I don't know if I can take this anymore." She pulled her hands away. "Mike? What are we going to do with him?"

He didn't have to ask her what she meant. He'd put in a call to the funeral home and made some preparations, but, ultimately, he hadn't known what to tell them. Their son was, at the moment, evidence in a homicide case. They didn't know how long it was going to take, and they didn't know what they were going to do once they got Braxton back.

"Mike, we have to decide."

"I know."

They both heard the vehicle turn into the driveway. Mike and Callie moved side by side to the front door and peered out together at the news van pulling up. As the doors of the van opened, Callie was already putting on her shoes.

"Honey," Mike said.

She grabbed a coat off the rack by the door.

"Babe," Mike said. "Let me."

But she threw open the door and stepped out without responding to him. At first he was tempted to follow and scanned the floor for his own shoes, but then thought of the girls. Hannah, having a much-needed nap late in the day, was not clinging to her mother at the moment because she was sleeping. Reno was lying on her stomach on the living room floor with a book. Mike looked at her, and she back at him, her head in her little hands.

"S'okay, honey," he said. He turned and looked back outside as Callie reached the van. Already she was gesticulating, and Mike could see her lips moving, her eyes wide. The reporter and the cameraman looked like they'd experienced this sort of thing before, but the cameraman started to get back in the truck while the reporter shouted across the hood at him. Then Callie turned to the reporter and stood toe-to-toe with her — and her hands were really flying.

"Go easy, go easy," Mike whispered against the windowpane.

The reporter stumbled back as Callie got in her face, inches away from the woman's beak of a nose. It took the reporter a moment to steady her footing, and then she shouted back at Callie with righteous indignation.

"Ah shit," Mike said.

But, it worked. The reporter got back in the van, too, pointing and shouting holy hell at Callie, no doubt arguing that Callie's situation was tragic, yes, but it was no excuse for this kind of assault, that she was just a woman with a job to do.

Yeah, Mike thought. *You got a job to do. Spread more misery.* Did the world need to learn about yet another tragedy? What good did it do anybody? They might lament a tragedy with their social networking friends, maybe donate their ten dollars via text. Then they'd forget about it all twenty-four hours later.

Callie strode back to the house as the van made a hasty exit down the driveway. The reporter cut the wheel so hard to turn around that the van slid in the snow. For a horrible moment Mike thought it would plow right into the snowbank and then they'd have two highly agitated news people stuck in their front yard. But the tires grabbed some traction and the van stopped, turned, and shot back out and onto 9N.

* * *

Callie came in the front door, a blast of cold air on her heels. "Bitch," she said under her breath.

"Honey, listen . . ."

She snapped a hard look at him. "What? We're in it now, Mike. Know what she said? She saw the detective from our case. Yeah, up in South Plattsburgh. She knew, Mike. She was saying things about . . ."

"Mom?"

Callie looked down at Reno. "It's okay honey." She took Mike by the elbow and led him to the kitchen. Mike could smell the crisp winter air on her skin. "Be right back, baby," she said to Reno over her shoulder.

In the kitchen, her voice was breathy and frantic. "You hear what I'm saying? What happens when the rest of the press knows who his biological father was? What happens when they all make that connection? There'll be more like her. I won't be able to back them off with a few idle threats."

"Well I'm pissed at the troopers. That one cop said there would be someone posted here." Mike put his hands on his hips and looked out the front window. He debated telling her that he had called Bull. That maybe there was a way to get some outside help. That they didn't really have any friends here. Sarah was one thing, but hers wasn't the type of help Mike was thinking of.

"I'm upset, Mike."

"I know that."

He stepped closer to her and put his hands on her shoulders. Her arms were trembling at her sides. "We'll have Brax . . ." she said. "We'll have him cr . . . He can be crem . . ."

She was trying to say *cremated.* She'd jumped back to the conversation they'd been having before the reporters arrived. Her face contorted as she struggled not to lose her emotional footing.

And then her shaking subsided. The transformation was something to behold; an expression came over Callie's face like he hadn't seen since the early days, when she was coming to grips with the wreck of her first relationship, the abuse she'd endured, the child she'd had in the middle of it all.

"We need protection," Mike said.

"Protection?" She pointed out of the room, indicating the reporters who had sped off into the snow. "From them?"

"From them, from anyone. From Tori."

She glared at him for a minute. Then she turned and walked off. Mike glanced into the living room. Reno's head had ducked back into her book. She'd been watching, listening. How much more of this could his daughters take? He followed his wife.

* * *

She was in Braxton's room, compulsively folding clothes that sat in a laundry basket. Mike dimly realized that neither of them had gone into Braxton's room since the night before his death. There was dirty laundry in there. An unmade bed. Investigators' footprints. They had tramped through, looking over all of his stuff, taking his computer and his phone and his school and personal notebooks. He had wondered if she would ever be able to go in there. She was trying to be strong, but this was a living nightmare.

She slowly turned and looked at him, and he moved close to her.

"Brax was trying to protect us, to protect the girls."

"She didn't know what she meant. She's just a girl."

"Come on, Cal," he said, reaching for her, taking her arm. "You know better than that."

She pulled away. "Don't tell me what I know." But her words had lost their vehemence. Being in Braxton's room calmed her somehow. It was like she was recharging in here, centering.

Mike spoke in a whisper, leaning close. "He's out there. Tori is out there. He had contact with Braxton and wanted to take him, I don't know — maybe kill us all. Braxton went out as a peace offering and . . ."

"I can't believe you kept that from me."

". . . And he was trying to keep us safe. Now that's my job. I'm going to protect us, but not like Braxton."

He looked around his son's room. The bed in the corner with the plaid sheets still a mess. The poster of *The Hobbit* on the wall. The old video game console piled in the corner, forgotten. His sneakers, unlaced, tongues out, on the floor. For God's sake the kid hadn't even been wearing his shoes when he left.

"You kept that from me and you didn't tell me about the money problems either, Mike." Her voice was low, too. Calm. She was folding a shirt of Braxton's — a *Hurley* shirt, with a bright yellow X-shape on the front, and keeping her head down. "What else don't I know about my husband?"

He felt taken aback. "What?"

She looked up. "You want to tell me when you started smoking?" Her eyes were cool and distant.

She must've smelled it on him.

"That what you were doing last night when I woke up and you were gone?"

He didn't have anything to say.

"Or at the hospital?" She dropped a folded pair of jeans and crossed her arms. It was like being in her son's room had not only centered her, but emboldened her. Not that Callie needed much to embolden her; Mike just hadn't been expecting this.

"Honey . . ."

"All these years you never smoked. I'm not that stupid. And I don't care if you do smoke. It's just, you know, something a husband tells a wife. 'You know, I used to smoke.' Right? Simple. Not telling me that. That's fucking weird, Mike. Makes me wonder. Makes me wonder about other things. About you in New York, and your friends. You never say much about that. I know you and your dad had it out somehow, but I let that go. I figured it was normal father son stuff. But Jesus, Mike, you never told me you smoked. You've picked it up *again*, you're going off in the night. We have money problems, you don't tell me. Braxton's fucking biological father starts emailing him, you email back and threaten the guy's life, you don't tell me. Who are you, Mike? You want to tell me that?"

"Callie, I'm not him. I'm not Tori. Don't treat me like this." Mike could feel the hurt and anger begin to rise.

"You're a man," Callie said. He'd never heard her speak like that before. Totally detached. Unemotional. As if medicated. So much for being centered. "You're all like that. Your idea of protection just gets people hurt. Just like Braxton got hurt. You tried to protect him by threatening Tori, and look what h—"

Mike slammed his fist down on the dresser. Braxton's things — his wallet and chain, a necklace, a belt, trading cards, a cup still half-filled with grape juice — all shook. The belt slipped off the top, the cup spilled and grape juice ran down the side of the dresser and pattered onto the carpet.

Callie looked at him silently. Her expression was flat and mournful and righteous at the same time. It said everything. He had just proved her point.

She pushed past him and walked out of the room.

CHAPTER FORTY-ONE

A day passed. McAfferty was still at large. The search grid covered half the state of New York, into Vermont, and border patrol was on high-alert all along the edge of Canada. Video surveillance was scrutinized, passport checks were vigorous, tourists were pulled over and searched. Kim Yom continued to surf the web using Tor. She'd retreated to her motel. She said it was quieter there, and Swift knew the substation was cramped. He spent three hours during the afternoon ignoring the phones and business of the station, tucked over the keyboard of his own desktop PC, trying something he never had before.

Since his last meeting with Kim Yom, he hadn't been able to get the child pornography racket off his mind. It wasn't really something you wanted invading your thoughts, but Kim's mention of the FBI stings had given him an idea. Once online, he surfed to the Kapow website and selected the game *The Don.* To join was fairly simple — you needed a legitimate email account and had to create a user name and password. He worried about the integrity of Kapow, about giving out his personal information. So he created a new email account for himself, replete with a fake name and birthdate (he made himself twenty-five years old), and used this for the game. As he went through these simple steps he realized that, even without Tor, there were simple tricks for hiding your identity online. He was sure his true identity was still discoverable to anyone with the know-how to access it. He wondered about the strange emails he'd continued to receive over the past couple of days, and how his debit card had failed to function, despite having sufficient funds in the account. He thought he would mention this to Kim at their next meeting and see what she thought. She was like an IT therapist. He grinned to himself.

And then grew serious as he wondered if it was somehow connected — the hold on the debit card and the hack of Kapow, the incursion into the victim's laptop.

Setting himself up with the fake email and user account had taken him nearly an hour. He felt like an old dog, willing to learn but slow to grasp new tricks. Then the next obstacle. He needed to introduce himself to other players in the chat window. He watched the stream of chatter for a while, and noticed that you could click on each player name, which brought you to a profile. Each had varying levels of Power, Respect, and Experience. Here he was, what the gaming crowd called a "noob," without any experience points to his name — Kady. If he started asking questions, or looked for another player, he might arouse suspicion. So he spent the second hour teaching himself how to play. It was slow going. Each upgrade to a resource building in the game took time. The more advanced the level of building, the longer the time it took. The same went for building the troops, his army, to attack others. Within an hour he'd exhausted his resources and had built little.

It would have to do. He began to insinuate himself into the conversation, deciding to take a passive approach. As other players chatted, he occasionally dropped in a "LOL" if something was funny. He had a second page open on the browser for internet slang. If something was unbelievable, or incredible, he'd type in a commiserative "SMH," which meant, "shaking my head." After about twenty minutes of this, a player started talking to him directly. The name was Jubilax. Swift sensed that it was a female player, but of course he couldn't know for sure.

Jubilax: Hey Kady. U r new? Or an alt?

Kady: Hi Jubilax. Yeah I'm new. Whats an alt?

Jubilax: alt is a player who has more than one acct. kinda cheating, if u ask me

Kady: Oh I see. Ty

A minute passed and there was no more from Jubilax. Other players were having conversations simultaneously, and these interpolated through the chat stream. Swift's fingers hovered over the keyboard. Then he typed again.

Kady: actually have a friend I'm lookin for

He waited. Nothing from Jubilax. A full two minutes passed. He thought she must have left the game. Then:

Jubilax: oh yeah? who that be?

Swift felt a little ripple of excitement.

Kady: name is Billy Sweet Tea. U know him?

He waited. His fingers left the keyboard and drummed the desk as he stared at the screen. Half a minute went by. He guessed that players didn't focus exclusively on chat, but played the game and glanced down occasionally. It was not a priority. Finally she came back on.

Jubilax: Nope. Sorry. U sure hes on this server?

Hmm. Swift scratched his chin.

Kady: This server?

Jubilax: lol. U are new

Swift leaned back. He wondered if this was what Kim Yom had meant when she said that there were multiple servers. Swift figured it made sense that all of this information couldn't be stored on one server, not with tens of thousands of gamers. He hadn't considered that, while the data might be divvied up, the players themselves played on each different server. He hunched forward and pecked at the keys some more in his one-fingered style.

Kady: lol yeah. guess I knew that. Hey how many servers do you think there are?

He waited another agonizing two minutes for her response. In the meantime, he watched the chat flow among the other players. Some seemed good-natured enough, but he caught racial remarks, concealed profanity (the game didn't allow straight swearing, but you could add a period or a dash to a curse word), and the occasional insult. He thought for a moment. This chat window represented people from all over the world, thrown together, communicating with one another from a presumably safe distance, free to say whatever they wanted. Some players rose to the challenge and played with respect, others used the opportunity to spew poison.

The game was a microcosm of the world, Swift thought. Building troops and resources took time, but you could spend money on "bullion" and speed those times up artificially. As he glanced at the profiles of chatting players, he noticed quite a spread in the levels of power and respect. Clearly, some players were moneyed. After forty minutes of watching the screen, it was obvious that there were game politics going on. Players from warring families would form alliances, particularly if it gave them a better shot at winning in tournaments, which were ongoing. So you had the "rich" players supporting one another in order to stay moneyed and in power. A system which theoretically started out with every player on equal ground, quickly skewed in favor of those more financially equipped.

Jubilax: Uhm, think maybe almost a hundred by now. Why?

Christ, thought Swift. Nearly a hundred servers. Here he'd thought his player would be automatically incorporated into the same server Fresco and Billy Sweet Tea had played on. He'd never thought to ask Kim Yom about that, and now he'd spent the better part of the afternoon chasing his tail. And what was more, the idea that Sweet Tea was even Robert Darring was now doubtful, because Darring was locked up while Sweet Tea was apparently still playing.

Swift — as Kady — thanked Jubilax for talking to him and prepared to sign off. He stopped short when he saw a flashing indicator in the lower right corner of the screen. There was an icon that looked like an envelope. He clicked on it and it took him to his player message inbox, feeling a momentary flare of excitement.

There were three messages. The first was a general welcome message from Kapow, telling him what fun was in store. The second was an advertisement to buy bullion and purchase various goods in the game store — already they were trying to sell stuff to him. He wondered how much money players spent. The third message said: Reminder: Scheduled Maintenance Downtime.

He opened this message and read that the game would be down — worldwide — for two hours the following day. From the tone of the message, this wasn't the first time. *The Don* was a "beta" game, meaning it was available while the creators continued to work on it and tweak it. What was far more interesting than the message, though, was the image which accompanied it.

Swift scrambled to do one of the few things he was proud to know how to do on a computer. He took a screen shot. After exiting out of the game at last, he opened the image, cropped it neatly, and printed it.

CHAPTER FORTY-TWO

Swift met with the Simpkins couple, later than planned, apologizing profusely for the delay. He then shared with them — sparing the graphic details — the results of their son's autopsy — and the possibility that Braxton had been strangled to death. It was no easier to deliver this information than it had been to report the child's death. The parents were a wreck. They said they'd been shooing the press off their steps all day. Swift thought they had been fighting — there was a freeze-out going on between them; they stood apart and barely looked at each other. The stepfather, Mike, seemed to have retreated somewhere inside himself, and Swift was worried about how the man looked. He didn't ask any questions about the 529 account. The Simpkins needed a chance to absorb the autopsy news. He assured them he would talk to the press again about respecting boundaries, and get his captain to assign a permanent detail to the house. They appeared to be even more devastated than when he had first come by. When the phone call came, he felt grateful for the interruption.

He stepped out onto the cold front porch. Swift didn't recognize the incoming number, though it was a local call.

"I have some information," said a voice.

"Who is this?" Swift thought he heard music in the background, people, perhaps the clinking of ice cubes. A bar.

"Can you meet me at the *Knotty*?"

The voice was vaguely familiar. "Is this Frank Duso?"

A pause. "Yeah. It's me. I've got something you might be interested in."

"What are you talking about? How did you get my number, Frank?"

"I called the station. Trooper Bronze gave it to me."

Swift winced. Bronze was one of the troopers involved in Duso's DWI arrest.

"So tell me," Swift said. "What have you got?"

"In person," Duso said, and hung up.

Swift took the phone away from his ear and looked at it for a moment, staring at the red Call Ended icon.

He put the phone away and looked through the window into the Simpkins' living room. The parents looked like zombies. The children were morose. He needed to let them be, come back later.

* * *

The Knotty Pine sat on the edge of town. It was a small, single-story building on a dirt parking lot, surrounded by evergreen trees. The sun had set, and only a dark blue glow remained on the westerly horizon. With the darkness came the cold. Swift went inside.

Frank Duso was belly-up to the bar. He was a young man who appeared older, afflicted by premature balding. He tried to hide this beneath a trucker cap. He turned to look as Swift approached, and took a drink from his pint glass.

There were a handful of other patrons in the place. They all seemed to be watching Swift as he crossed the gloomy space, walking over the gritty wood floor, boards creaking beneath his weight, music from the jukebox playing in the back corner, the air pungent with stale beer and body odor. Swift recognized most of the faces. New Brighton's population was small. A few of the people in the *Knotty* had been through county jail. Others he knew from around town. He smiled and dipped his head at a couple of them and then slid onto the bar stool next to Duso.

Duso looked straight ahead, at the rows of liquor behind the bar. "Buy you a beer?"

"What do you have for me, Frank?"

"Come on. Let me buy you one."

"Fine. I'll take a Labatt."

The bartender was an older woman named Rhoda. She'd been down at the other end of the bar pretending not to stare at Swift, turned towards the *Powerball* screen in the corner of the room — the only technology in an otherwise timeless place. She came over, wiping her hands with a towel, immediately Frank raised a finger.

"A bottle of Labatt for the detective," Frank said.

"Hi Swifty," said Rhoda.

"Hey Rhode."

Her eyes rested on him for a moment. She was a skinny woman, all gristle and wrinkles, her copper-colored hair pulled back in a loose pony tail that was fraying around the edges. She turned away and bent into the cooler to fish out the beer.

Frank was apparently not going to make a peep until Swift had a bottle of suds in front of him, so Swift waited. They watched Rhoda remove the bottle cap, slide a cocktail napkin over the wood and set the bottle on it.

"Thanks," Swift said. He reached out and wrapped a hand around the bottle. He looked at Rhoda who faded back to the other end of the bar and tried to look busy. Swift turned to Duso.

"Out with it."

"So, I just got out of County," said Frank.

"I'm aware."

Frank's voice was low. He played with some condensation on the bar, pushing the liquid around with the tip of his finger. "Interesting guy I met in there."

Swift leaned a little closer. "You talked to Darring?"

"Sure. We had lunch. Sat down next to each other. Seemed like the only other sane guy in there. Half the people you got in there, Swift, you know, those are mental people. They don't belong in jail. They got problems."

"Spare me the lecture," Swift said. "So what did you talk about?"

"You're looking at this guy for murder, huh? The kid? The young kid on the road? The one my dad found?"

Swift watched Duso, who kept his eyes forward, taking a long pull from his drink. He was really enjoying this, Swift thought. Having his moment.

"I can't discuss an ongoing investigation with you, Frank, who we're looking at or not. But if you think you've got something, if someone said something to you, I need to know."

Now Duso did look at Swift. He set his drink down slowly and then turned his head. He was a tall kid. At well over six feet, he should've been a hundred and ninety pounds of country-boy muscle, but he was gaunt. His eyes looked beyond Swift for a moment. "You know, you and your boys caused me a lot of trouble." He blinked a few times, as if to demonstrate the harmful effects of the pepper spray.

Swift took a deep breath and blew it out slowly. "Frank, you know I'm not going to discuss that with you either."

Swift glanced around, suddenly feeling as if he were in a fishbowl. He caught some looks as the bar patrons, sitting in the three dark booths against the back wall, standing near the jukebox, at the two high, round-top tables by the front door, bent over the pool table in the center of the room, quickly turned their eyes away.

"I'm not looking for *discussion*," Frank said. He closed his mouth after that, but the sentiment carried on in Swift's mind. *What I'm looking for is a big old fat apology. Maybe right here in front of all these people.*

"Okay," Swift said, playing dumb. He brought his gaze back to Frank. "What are you looking for, Frank? You called me here in the middle of the night to tell me you had something for me."

Frank's gaze had wandered past Swift again. Was he waiting for something?

"Spit it out," Swift said, making to leave. "Or I'm outta here."

Frank lowered his eyes and stuck his bottom lip out. He raised his shoulders. "I just, you know. I would've liked to hear you say, 'Yeah, Frankie, I'm sorry my boys went fucking apeshit on you like that.'" He looked up and dropped his shoulders. "But you're not going to. Are you?"

"Alright, Frank. Nice to see you." Swift got up to leave. His beer, untouched, sat on the bar.

"Darring said a lot of things," Frank blurted in a loud whisper. "He talked a lot. One of those types. Talked about shit . . . I don't know. He was going on about the internet. Stuff like that."

Swift stood still, listening.

"Seemed like the kind that needs attention or something. You know those types. Wanted someone to listen. So we were at lunch, and he's told me who he is, and why he's there, and how it doesn't matter. Because he knows how to manipulate people. Something to that effect."

Swift said nothing. He was looking at Duso, but his mind was elsewhere. His mind was on the two kids. Hideo Miko and Sasha Bellstein. The two kids they had let go. Then he focused on Frank again.

"That's it?"

Frank looked hurt. "That's it? I mean, sounds like he's working with other people, dunnit?"

Without thinking, Swift reached out and grabbed the beer and took a good, long, swig of it. He saw Frank watching him, smiling a little. He needed to call Mathis. He pulled the beer from his lips and swiped at his mouth with the back of his hand. "Thank you, Frank."

"Hey," Frank said. "Hey wait. Stick around for a bit. Bury the hatchet."

"Maybe another time."

Swift turned and headed out of the *Knotty*, feeling the eyes on him. He flung open the door and stepped into air, blasted by the cold. He was still holding the beer bottle.

* * *

He dialed the ADA's number with his free hand. Mathis picked it up before it had rung a second time. He sounded edgier than ever, probably squirming inside his skin.

"Yeah?"

"Lab tests came back an hour ago," Swift said into his phone.

"Thank God. Wait — Jesus, why are you just telling me now?"

"I had to see the Simpkins family. Then I got a call from someone."

"A call? Who?"

"In a minute. Test results are that the prints on the guitar cord are a match for Tori McAfferty . . ."

"Right . . . and . . ."

"Initial testing confirms Braxton Simpkins's DNA."

"Shit!" Mathis sounded like a gambler whose horse had just paid off. Then the ADA said, more quietly, "Holy shit."

"There are two tests that have to be done for it to be conclusive. This was a favor to me — friend I have there — but it still needs confirmation."

"I know that." Now Mathis sounded like Swift was the dark cloud coming to rain on his win. "It's McAfferty. What's the matter? You still don't like McAfferty?"

"I like him fine," Swift said, "but he's missing. And his girlfriend is a clamshell, protected by her uncle lawyer."

Mathis fell silent. Then he said, "Let me work on that."

Swift took a pull of the beer. He felt something in his bones, something he couldn't shake. Rather than things getting clearer, they were only becoming more opaque. It made him highly uncomfortable, all the more so because he couldn't put his finger on it. Swift had that feeling again, like things were happening that he wasn't privy to, like a puppet in a game. He thought of what Frank Duso had said just now, how Darring said he manipulated people. Swift felt trapped. He didn't like feeling unfree. His ex-wife knew that. His colleagues and captain knew that. He did what he wanted, when he wanted, and he stayed in control.

"Way I see it," Swift said into the phone, "we got one suspect, sitting there in County, charged, awaiting arraignment, and we've got nothing solid on him. But he's pulling strings somehow. He's . . . shit, Mathis. I think those two other kids were into more than we got out of them. And we let them go."

"Swift," Mathis said, sounding like he was trying to be patient. "We've got nothing but circumstance to link Darring to the murdered kid. You yourself helped convince me of that. Even the player in the game you thought was him doesn't look like it now."

"That's because . . ."

". . . And then we've got McAfferty, and we've got emails with his name on them, sweet-talking the kid, the threat issued by Mike Simpkins, and the drug dealing, the meth lab, Cohen . . ."

"Yeah, well, he's gone, Mathis. And I don't know that we're going to hear from him anytime soon."

"Come on. We'll get him. The whole state is looking for him. Like I said, I'll see if I can work the girlfriend. Cobleskill is working with the task force on the meth lab explosion."

That was good, Swift thought. If the DA was warming up for the meth lab prosecution, maybe Mathis could get somewhere with Tricia Eggleston after all. Maybe she would sing a little tune.

Swift heard a vehicle approaching. He turned and looked as a news van came down the road and began to brake as it neared the bar. It plowed into the snow covering the dirt lot and jerked to a halt next to *The Knotty Pine.*

"Ah God," Swift muttered.

"What?"

"Someone in the bar just made themselves happy by calling the press."

"You're at a *bar*?"

"Frank Duso. Fuck. That's what he was waiting for."

"Swift, you're at a . . . Duso? Lenny Duso's son?"

"Yeah. I gotta go."

Swift hung up and slipped his cellphone in his pocket. Then he dropped the beer bottle behind him in the snow. He started walking up towards the van as a reporter who couldn't have been two years out of college, trailed by a fumbling cameraman, scrambled to get their shit together. Swift thought he recognized her — had she been at the McAfferty scene the day before? She was cute, with a big nose that was somehow sensual.

He could jump in his car and probably be out of there by the time the news team got their thumbs out, but it would only stir up more controversy. So he smiled at them as he approached, and prepared a short, generic statement for them in his head.

As he passed by one of the windows in front of *Knotty*, he turned to look inside. Frank was there at the bar. He looked at Swift through the window, smiled, and raised his glass.

CHAPTER FORTY-THREE

Hey, Mike?

How many times had he heard that voice and been irritated, because it interrupted, was inconvenient, and he resented having to be patient with the boy? What would he give now to hear those words spoken again in Braxton's voice, that beckoning, that question?

Hey, Mike?

He could almost hear the words said out loud. And wasn't that what had stirred him from the brink of sleep?

Mike turned his head, reached over to the end table and fumbled to pick up his phone. He looked at the face. 2:33 a.m.

At first he thought he'd woken up because he'd imagined this voice, because his sleep was fitful, but when he looked at his phone he saw that he'd received a text message. He grabbed the phone and put it in front of his face. Callie was in the girls' room once again, so he had the bed to himself. His fingers poked at the screen and the message came up.

Check out the cop, it said, and a YouTube link followed.

The message was from a number Mike didn't have programmed into his phone, but he recognized the prefix

— 917. It was a New York City cell phone. Bull Camoine didn't have a cell phone, but he might have gotten one of the pre-paid versions.

Mike clicked on the link and watched with a growing sense of unease as the YouTube page opened. The video had already garnered over a few hundred hits. It had been posted only a couple of hours earlier, by *NewsNinja.* With some trepidation, Mike pressed the play button.

A bright young reporter, all of twenty-five, maybe, stood before the camera with a kind of wound-up energy. Mike recognized her right away as the woman who had been in his driveway the evening before. Behind her was a vaguely familiar building. "We're here at *The Knotty Pine*, where an anonymous tip-off informed us we could find the lead detective on the New Brighton case of a murdered thirteen-year-old boy."

Mike's stomach knotted at the mention of his son. Despite their efforts to stymie the press, the death had been reported dozens of times over the past couple of days, maybe more, on the evening and morning regional news, perhaps as far down as Albany, over in Burlington. A homicide in the boonies of rural, upstate New York was still a big deal. Of course the media was still talking about it, and surely by now the prosecutor's office — Mike thought the DA's name was Cobleskill, and the ADA, a young hotshot named Mathis — would have issued their statement, along with the Captain and Lieutenant of the State Police. Mike and Callie had tried to ignore it all, but it just kept coming.

As he watched the video he could see Detective John Swift walk over. The camera work was a little shaky, but Mike could see a smile spread across Swift's face.

Only the smile did not seem friendly, and the knot in Mike's stomach tightened.

"Detective Swift," said the reporter. Mike thought he heard a slight tremulousness in her voice. There she was, a little slip of a thing, fresh out of the local SUNY journalism program, dressed in a smart pantsuit and a jacket with a puffy, furry hood surrounding her coiffed coils of blonde hair, standing out in the middle of nowhere at dusk. Mike recognized the place now; it was the bar on the far edge of town. Rumor had it that the local cops spent as much time there dealing with domestic disturbances as they did doing pick-up orders for the local mental health clinic. It made sense. The bar was just a way to get a different type of medication. But what the hell was Swift doing there? Maybe he was off-shift. As far as Mike knew, there were no other detectives on the case. Swift had a support team — at least a handful of others doing administrative tasks for him, Mike guessed — but he was pretty sure that Swift carried the investigation.

"Detective," the blonde reporter said again. "What can you tell us about the status of the investigation into the recent murder in New Brighton and the possibility that it's related to the meth lab explosion in South Plattsburgh?"

Maybe there was a bit of glassiness to Swift's eyes. How many beers had the guy had?

Check out the cop, the text message had said.

Swift spoke. "You know I can't comment on that. We're doing everything we can to follow each and every lead, to exhaust all possibilities."

There was a moment of silence — hesitation, Mike guessed, on the part of the reporter, before she said, "With all due respect, Detective; at a bar?" The cameraman, as if on cue, swung the camera to the right to show the ramshackle establishment. There were several patrons looking out the window. One in particular, wearing a trucker cap over black hair, stood out. He seemed to be enjoying himself. Then the camera quickly swung back to face Swift.

"Yes," said Swift flatly, with that fake smile still on his lips. "I've stopped at a bar."

"Oh Jesus," Mike muttered. What the hell was this?

The reporter seemed to grow bolder, though Mike still heard the quiver in her voice. "Is this the first time you've stopped for a drink while on duty, during an active investigation?"

Swift scowled then. "It's *because* this is an active investigation that I can't comment. Thank you, now if you'll . . ."

"Detective, I smell alcohol on your breath."

Mike felt his muscles contract as Swift fixed her with a dark look. Even through the slightly pixelated video on his phone, Mike could see the menace in the aging detective's eyes.

Shit. Thought Mike. He didn't have any reason to worry for Swift or his career, but this was the investigator on his son's murder case. And Mike had thought Swift was on the ball. Seasoned and capable of getting the job done. Why was he letting some punk reporter get to him?

"Is drinking part of an active investigation for you, detective?"

Ooof. Mike reeled from that one. This was like watching some terrible prank unfold, one where the victim doesn't know they're being tricked. It was uncomfortable to witness.

"No, this is not a part," said Swift, simmering. "It's none of your business. Good night."

Swift started to turn.

"Do you have a drinking problem, detective Swift?"

He had almost gotten his back to the camera, and now he stopped cold. He slowly turned back around.

The reporter, incredibly, pressed further. "Is that why you were divorced several years ago?"

"What did you say?"

Mike cringed, yet, watching this, he was somehow galvanized, ready to get up, to get out there and solve this terrible mess on his own. Just like Bull Camoine suggested he do.

"And your case last year. There was some attention about the manner in which you handled your suspect? A man who pressed charges for police harassment and aggravated assault, which your department was able to sidestep. Is that accurate?"

Swift had completely turned now, and loomed in front of the camera. His expression had become a mask of contempt. "I'm not going to discuss that. You need to get back in your van now, miss, and take it back to campus. This is not reporting. This is sensationalizing. You should strive for better."

Swift turned around to walk away again.

"What do you think the parents feel about this? The lead detective investigating the murder of their only son is at a bar. A divorced bachelor with a history of violent behavior and questionable stability. How do you think they feel knowing that their son's justice is in your hands?"

Oh no, Mike thought. While he was pretty sure the young reporter with the blonde curls and hawkish nose didn't give a shit in the begonias about how "the parents" felt, after her display in his own driveway, the question was still an indictment. Mike glanced down at the timeline on the YouTube video and saw there were only seconds left. He sensed what was coming.

Swift took a few great strides towards the camera. The image jostled as he wrested the device from the cameraman's grip. And for just a couple of seconds, the video footage took to the sky. A shaking aerial shot showed, for an instant, the bar, the parking lot, the van, and two people standing and looking up while a third was walking away — Swift had taken the camera and chucked it into the air.

A moment later, the screen went black. End of video.

PART FOUR

IN THE POCKET

CHAPTER FORTY-FOUR

"This is insane," bellowed Captain Tuggey. "You want me to be that guy, Swifty? You want me to be the guy who's got to discipline you now? Suspend you? Fire you? Is that what you want?"

They were in the Captain's living room. It was after ten, but Tuggey was a night owl. His wife was asleep in the other room — or, more likely, pretending to be asleep and listening in. Their three children had all left the nest. Tuggey had a nice home he had built with his two sons a decade before, with cedar beams and a south-facing bank of solar windows. He wore white tube socks and a pair of grey sweatpants. His large, married belly was spanned with a polyester athletic shirt, unzipped down to the sternum.

"John, you've got an opportunity to get out of here, to go work for the Attorney General — you're letting your emotions get to you. You've been good, Swift, you've been real good, you've run a clean game for years since your last troubles with this kind of shit. Now this thing with the Duso kid is a mess. Was I wrong, Swift? Did you lose it with this kid? Okay, I don't want to know; he was never going to get far with that suit and he knew it, even if he's not the wooliest sheep on the hill. That was more Warren

Eggleston's play to get a little TV time like his big brother Tom. But now this . . . this thing with the reporter, John . . . talk to me . . ."

"She was coached," Swift said quietly.

"She was coached? By whom? Where did she come up with that information on you?"

Swift was standing inside the door, still in his boots. Tuggey had lit into him the moment he'd stepped into the house. The Captain made no move to offer him hospitality beyond the entryway.

"I could see it in her face," Swift said. "What she was saying was rehearsed. Somebody fed her personal information about me."

"That's usually how it works. Who? Duso?"

"Maybe."

"He's not bright enough for something like that."

Swift said nothing.

"But you think he was the one who tipped the reporter."

"Yeah."

Tuggey put his hands on his hips and sighed. He looked around the room, chasing the floor trim with his eyes, a builder's habit. He probably always saw something that needed improvement, was always judging his own work. The room smelled of the balsawood flooring they'd freshly installed in the dining area, and the pine-scented candles Tuggey's wife liked to burn. There was, however, a lingering fart smell underneath all of these olfactory notes, as if Swift's situation had upset Tuggey's stomach. Or, possibly, the dog's — Like Swift, the Tuggeys also had a pooch, theirs a shiny brown chocolate lab, the kind you saw in a calendar-with-a-dog-each-month, perfectly groomed, with teeth-cleaning biscuits and spotless feeding bowls.

"But maybe Robert Darring had something to do with it, too."

"Darring? What in the hell does this have to do with Darring?"

"Frank Duso called me down to the *Knotty*, Cap. Said he had something for me on the Simpkins case."

Tuggey was wide-eyed now, grandstanding forgotten. He looked oddly childlike, still poised for a sermon, but his eyes wide, his arms limp at his sides. "He what?"

"I'm not saying Darring knew Frank would be in lock up. I think Darring even screwed up a little, saying stuff to him about working with others. But they also talked about me. And Frank probably told Darring what he knew about me — whatever Warren Eggleston filled his head with when they were pursuing that claim of excessive force. Frank took the opportunity to call me up. And he also called up the reporters."

Captain Tuggey's arms lowered. "Shit," he said. "Shit."

"I know."

"Why'd you react like that, Swifty? Are you drunk? I can smell the liquor on you."

"Oh come on. Please. You can't smell anything, Captain. You've tipped three or four yourself. I had one. One beer, Cap. Frank bought it. I just . . . I wasn't thinking; I took it outside when I called Mathis."

Tuggey had his large mouth open like he was going to protest, but then he closed it.

"She was coached," Swift repeated. "Darring and Frank talked to each other, and Frank played the hand. Frank even called the reporter ahead of time. That's the part Darring probably helped him with. Planning. Getting the timing right. Because Plattsburgh's half an hour away."

Swift turned his head and looked away. Something shook loose in the back of his mind, as though a pile of thoughts had settled and then been disturbed. *A half an hour to Plattsburgh*, he thought. From *Knotty's*, yes. From the center of New Brighton, maybe forty minutes.

Swift glanced down at the ground for a moment and then back up at the Captain. "I'm sorry, Tug. I screwed up."

Tuggey's mouth turned down in a kind of aww-shucks frown. His bluster and anger had passed. "Well, we'll take care of it, Swifty." His voice suggested it was time to leave — that they would deal with this more fully in the morning. The wheels were set in motion now. There would be an internal investigation, probably a mandatory psych visit; the works.

"Alright," said Swift.

He turned and opened the door and walked back out into the night.

"Go home, get some sleep," Tuggey called from the doorway.

Swift raised a hand as he walked away.

CHAPTER FORTY-FIVE

"Mike, I checked your phone."

It was the middle of the night. Callie had been in the bed in Hannah's room and now she crept into the bedroom she shared with Mike. She was standing just inside the doorway. Mike had been lying awake. He sat up and struggled to see her in the dark.

"What?"

"You've called New York. And you've got text messages. 'Check out the cop.' What does that mean, Mike?"

"You've been checking my *phone*?"

"Who are you calling?"

Mike sat up further, feeling adrenaline spilling into his veins. "What do you mean you've been checking my phone? Callie, listen to me . . ." He swung his legs out of the bed and got up. He walked around the bed to the doorway and stopped in front of her. He could see her only a little bit better. Her eyes were shining in the gloom.

"You're talking to Bull? Is that who? What are you doing?"

"Honey, the cop, Swift, he . . ."

"I don't care about the cop." Although she was whispering, her words were still harsh. "I care about my girls. I care about my son, my sanity." She paused. It was so silent Mike thought he could hear their hearts beating. "I care about you," she said finally.

"And I care about you." He reached for her, touching her hand, but she withdrew.

"I want to take the girls and leave. Go back to Florida."

He was unable to speak for a moment. Florida? Was this a dream? She was waiting for his response. Finally he managed the words. "Callie, that makes no sense . . ."

"I can't take it. I can't take it anymore. The cops, the press, not knowing what's going on with you, what's going on with Brax . . . I can't take the looks from people. Like you said, we don't have anybody here . . ."

He wanted to tell Callie about the video the previous night, but seeing the lead investigator on their son's case acting like a loose cannon in some cop show would only add one more reason for her to go. He wanted to tell her that help was a phone call away, but she would never go for it. Not now. Not after he'd kept things from her. Especially his past.

"Callie. You've got to hear me out. When we met, you needed someone stable. I knew I could be that guy. I *was* that guy. I'm nothing like him, okay? Okay, Cal? Nothing. But I knew, I just knew, that if you knew about some of the things in my past, when I was just a kid — nothing more than a kid, Callie, but all the same — I knew I would lose you. Before I even had a chance." He looked at her in the dark, trying to read her face. From what he could make out, she wore her determined look. "Time went by," he said. "And some things just never made it into the conversation. They never needed to." He could feel his words failing to make their intended impact.

"We're going to go stay with your father for a little while," she said. "The condo never sold. It's still half-furnished. It's still ours." She was talking about their place in Stuart, in Turtle Bay.

"There are renters."

"Until the end of the month. Then we can move back in."

"Callie . . ." He stopped and rubbed his face with his hands. His wife had always been strong-willed. Defiant. But they used to talk, work things out. They had been a team. It felt like all that was fading.

"It's not open for discussion," she said, as if to highlight the point. Then she added, "You get our son when they're done with him and bring him home to me."

"You don't trust me," he said.

"Mike, don't . . ."

He could tell from her voice she was on the edge of tears, and he reached for her again. This time she allowed him to take her hand. They stood there like that in the doorway for a moment, and then she left.

CHAPTER FORTY-SIX

On the third morning after Braxton's death, a Tuesday, Mike booked flights for Callie and the girls. The plane would leave from Plattsburgh Airport the following afternoon. Mike helped her pack the girls' stuff. As he moved suitcases into the back of the truck, he realized his wife had a point; she wanted to put a distance between herself and the nightmare that had become their lives, the dark pageantry of hospitals, grim faces, and cops with no answers.

The cops had remained a disappointment. Detective Swift had come by the other night and, after sharing the gruesome news about Braxton's cause of death, indicated that they still had no number one suspect. Even Tori McAfferty was someone they would "question thoroughly once apprehended," but Swift seemed to Mike like he didn't have his shoulder into it.

He could tell, too, that the cop had been holding something back. Something he'd been reluctant to bring up, and Mike thought he knew what it was — Swift was biding his time before questioning Mike about the 529 account. Maybe it was best that she left. Let him deal with things on his own.

After packing, he slipped out in back of the house and called Swift directly from his phone. The day was crisp and bright and cold, and Mike's breath rose like smoke.

Swift didn't answer. Mike left a voice mail.

"Detective, it's Mike Simpkins. We're making some family decisions here; there are things changing on our end I need to speak to you about. Please give me a call back when you can. Thank you."

He hung up and went back inside. As he entered the house, he heard a sound that was unfamiliar at first, his heart began to race and he quickened his step, thinking that one of the girls were hurt, or something was wrong. As he turned into the hallway he saw first Hannah dash from one room to the next and then Reno after her, wielding a stuffed animal. He realized what it was. They were playing, and both girls were shrieking with laughter.

They ran into Braxton's room.

Mike's sudden smile faded, and he continued down the hallway to Braxton's room. He turned in, ready to corral the girls and get them out of there before Callie discovered them.

But Callie was already in the room. She was sitting in the middle of the carpet, Indian-style, like a teenager herself. It looked as though she'd been in the room for a little while. Things were put away, boxed up, posters taken down.

She looked up at him. Tears were running down her face, glistening in the lamplight. But she was smiling.

The sight of her, and of her tears, tore at Mike's chest. The girls, in the meantime, were running circles around their mother, until Hannah leapt up onto Braxton's freshly-made bed.

Mike dropped to his knees. He let himself fall forward onto the carpet. His entire body seemed to go limp, and he sagged there on all fours, letting his head fall down so that his chin touched his breastplate, and he felt the emotion mount in him as he crawled towards his wife.

When he reached her and looked up, she still had that expression on her face — a profound mixture of joy and sadness, and something that transcended both. She took him in her arms and he lay across her legs, and then the girls came piling on top of him. His face wet, he smiled, he ached, the four of them, now, all piled together.

* * *

Swift called back an hour later while Mike was shoveling a fresh dusting of snow. The precipitation wasn't much, but he needed the air, the movement, the rhythm of shoveling.

"Detective Swift, thanks for calling me back." It was an unfriendly greeting, purely formal.

Swift got right into it. If he was worried about Mike having seen the news video, he didn't show it. Or, he was compensating by barreling into the conversation.

"Mike. Good morning. I was planning to drop by in a bit so we could . . ."

"That won't be necessary," Mike interrupted, leaning on the shovel. He took a deep breath, inhaling through his nostrils. "From now on, after all she's been through, all *we've* been though, we need to give my wife and family some room."

"Mr. Simpkins, we've had some developments that I need to—"

"There have been developments here, too."

They were cutting each other off, stepping on one another's words, frustration in each of their voices. Mike grabbed the shovel like a staff with his free hand, and proceeded before the investigator could interrupt again.

"Callie is leaving. She's taking the girls and going back home."

This time, Swift was silent for a moment. "Home?"

"Back to Florida. We think it's the best for everyone. She can't imagine going on up here like this. Neither can I. The girls, in school . . . Callie, at her job. The press, hounding us. But that's just the short term. I understand that. This is a small town. An even smaller region. Something like this follows you around for years. For the rest of your life. And this investigation, this whole thing, especially the way it's been going . . . she just can't. She needs to have closure with her son. So if you're done with his body, you need to turn it over to us."

Mike dropped the shovel to the side and stripped his coat off, keeping the phone to his ear by switching hands.

"I understand," said Swift.

"Yeah," said Mike. *You understand*, he thought. *All the cops understand. The neighbors understand.* Everyone *understands.* People kept their distance, but they understood just fine. Mike couldn't blame them.

"So what do you want to tell me?"

He heard Swift take a breath. "I still would prefer to talk to you in person, Mr. Simpkins. I can tell you this, though; your son's body is free to go."

Mike felt something in him deflate. As if he'd been stoking the anger necessary to stay on top of the pain and anguish. Almost wanting Swift to say that Braxton's body was still evidence and critical to the investigation and they couldn't release it back to him at this time. It would give Mike further fuel for anger and frustration. He hadn't expected Swift to tell him he could have Braxton back. It was a mild shock.

"You can have the funeral service tend to the body," Swift said. "I can give them a call if you'd like. It's not a problem. They will take over and will be in touch to set up a time convenient for you to decide how you would like to proceed. I highly recommend Kristofferson's. They'll help you write the obituary, pick out the tombstone, the casket, the—"

"Yeah, okay," Mike said, deliberately cutting Swift off.

"I'd really like to speak with you this evening . . ."

"Is it critical?" Mike felt his hackles up again. "Is it going to make or break my son's case? Do I have vital information for you, detective? Or do you have my son's murderer in custody? If it's none of those things, then I need to spend the rest of the day with my family, who I'm not going to see for a little while."

Another silence from Swift. Then, "I understand."

That word again.

Mike closed his eyes for a moment, and rocked back on his heels, inhaling once again the bright scent of the late winter. Was it possible the trees would be budding soon, in just another month? They'd only been here for eight weeks, and hadn't even endured much of the winter, but it had still seemed to go on forever.

The winter that would never end. "I'll speak to you tomorrow," Swift said. "You call me after you see your family off, okay, Mike?"

It was the first time Swift had called him by his first name.

"I'll do what I can."

A pause. He could sense Swift going through his options. Was the old cop going to get heavy-handed now, or wither and shrink away?

Mike realized that he found the older man perplexing in a similar way to his father. Somehow always slightly obtuse, distant; men who prized their personal freedom and independence above all else. Hadn't Swift even said something that betrayed this just now? *Your son is free*, he had said. A telling choice of words.

Mike was surprised Swift was still on the case. Maybe there was a shortage of state police detectives, but he didn't think so. Possibly it would take a little time to transition someone else in, and bring them up to speed. Probably that was what Swift wanted to talk about anyway. To give Mike some bullshit about how the department thought it best that, for personal reasons, he turn the case over to another investigator who would do a stellar job and blah blah blah. Mike didn't want to hear it. Swift could save the speech. What Mike did want to hear, though, was something else.

"I know you want to talk to me in person. But just tell me who you think did it. Can you do that? Are you even going to be around tomorrow? I know what happened to you. I saw the video. So just tell me now before I have to look at some fresh-faced replacement of yours."

He hadn't expected any of that to come out. His words had tumbled from him in a rush. He almost cringed, waiting for Swift's response. Just like back home in his childhood. Until one day, Mike couldn't take it anymore.

"The report indicates that your son died from ligature strangulation."

"You told us."

"We believe we found the ligature. It was in Tori McAfferty's house, and it has your son's DNA on it."

Mike's throat constricted. He was dizzy, his balance off. *I knew it.*

Somewhere he thought he heard a bird singing under the bright sun. The warbling of the creature sounded sweet, but haunted, like a dirge.

Mike stood in the driveway, half the snow shoveled, the other half an inch of powder. The shovel lay at his feet. Holding the phone absently to his ear, he bent and picked up the shovel, as if he needed to grasp something solid, something tangible. He waited for the world and his thoughts to come back into some semblance of sensory order again. The birds singing in the distance, the wind low and stirring the light snow on the ground into delicate eddies, and Braxton, the image of Braxton being strangled to death. He wondered about the last thoughts that might have passed through his stepson's mind. The terrible sorrow at the thought that Braxton had been scared in his last moments of life, terrified, and alone.

"Mr. Simpkins? We're looking into several possibilities . . ." The detective's voice brought Mike back around again. Swift was hedging. Typical. What possibilities?

"Mike?"

"What?"

"Mike . . ." He heard the detective sigh. "I wanted to speak to you in person. But, okay. Mike, I also have to talk to you about the 529 account that was opened for Braxton, in your name."

"No," Mike said, feeling far away.

"Oh . . . Uhm, 'No'?"

"That's got nothing to do with anything."

"You understand I need to cover everything."

"And you understand that it's been four days since my son died and the biggest news is that you can't find the guy who did it — he's out there now, running around while you tip them back at a local bar!"

Mike ended the call. He put the phone away and gripped the shovel with both hands. He started back down the driveway, scraping and heaving, going faster this time, his breathing deep, his muscles flexing.

CHAPTER FORTY-SEVEN

Leaving Mike behind, leaving their new house, was not nearly as painful as Callie had feared. The house was nothing but boards and tar paper as far as she was concerned. They'd only been there a couple of months and she'd spent the bulk of that time tending to the kids and preparing her syllabi for the courses she was teaching up in Plattsburgh. And it had been the middle of winter when they'd arrived. She'd planned on spring cleaning, making the place cozier and more her own, even doing a little painting, but that time had never arrived, and so the house she left on 9N was just a building, nothing more.

Mike was a different story, but she still felt relief at their temporary separation. She loved him fiercely. All this would have been difficult for anyone to cope with. Beyond difficult. Downright Atlas-carrying-the-world difficult. For Mike's part, he was bearing a huge and weighty chunk of guilt. She knew he felt guilty over what he thought of as his complicity in his own stepson's death, and she felt terrible about this. But something more had changed in Mike. She supposed she had changed, too. But whereas she felt vulnerable, raw, exposed, Mike had become murky.

Getting in touch with someone from his hidden past. It scared her. It worried her that Mike was not just calling up any old friend, but an old part of himself. A violent part. She had vowed never to live with violence again after Tori. And so far with Mike, there had been none. But she could see the look in his eyes, the set of his jaw, the way his knuckles pressed white against his skin as he curled his hands into fists. He hadn't been up front with her about a number of things. Major things.

In truth, if she were to be honest with herself, she didn't know what to make of the thing with the money. When Mike first told her that his father was setting up an education fund for Braxton, she'd been thrilled. She'd gone to college, she believed in education; it was Braxton's future. His special character made it tough for him in some social situations. Grade school was tough. But, in college, he would flourish.

Mike had explained how it worked, to some extent, and she'd left it to him. He told her that Jack had entrusted him with ownership of the account; his father didn't want paperwork and phone calls bothering him. It all seemed normal enough.

Yet she knew that part of her reason for leaving was that she didn't want to be there when the cops came knocking again.

His guilt and anger were palpable; guilt about what? The email to Tori, lying to her, maybe even something to do with the money? She just didn't know. Whatever it was, he seemed to be always looking to her for some sort of expiation, some release from the prison he seemed to find himself in.

And wasn't she complicit, too, in a way? Had she not allowed Mike to take a background role in the family, afraid of what might become of them if he were allowed to express his true nature? All those times Mike had tried to discipline his stepson and she had come between them, unable to overcome her protective instincts, her self-reproach over what Braxton had gone through when she'd left Tori — had she not robbed Mike of some of his due authority as a father? Had she not done this selfishly, to make herself feel more comfortable? And had this precipitated Mike's lashing-out when he felt threatened by Braxton's biological father, after he came poking his deadbeat, drug-dealing nose back into the family?

She needed just to go away. It wasn't escape, it wasn't running away from her emotions — because there was nothing more hurtful that morning than the thought that she was leaving without her son.

There was a profound emptiness in that thought. It had the finality of a door slamming on a room to which she knew she could never return.

Whatever it was Mike needed to deal with, whatever he had to get through, he had to do it alone. She couldn't risk harm to her other children. Above all, this was why she was leaving. To protect her other babies.

They stood in the small airport terminal. Mike had insisted on coming with them through security and waiting until they boarded the plane.

They held one another, and she felt Reno's arms encircle her thighs as the six-year-old girl joined in the family hug. Next to them, Hannah watched and babbled and said "A-daddah," at her father.

And then they were waving, and she walked down the gangplank to the airplane that waited on the tarmac. Callie watched Mike recede from her as he stood there in the terminal in the jeans she'd bought him that past Christmas, his flannel shirt and the black coat with the fur around the hood, his dark, wavy hair, his eyes silver in the light shining through the giant windows of the terminal.

CHAPTER FORTY-EIGHT

Mike finished his call to the funeral home. Braxton's body would be incinerated that night.

He went to the refrigerator, pulled a bottle of chilled vodka from the freezer and poured himself a straight drink. It was only four o'clock in the afternoon, but he didn't care. He gulped it down and poured another. Then he went to the couch in the living room and sat down with his laptop. The place felt completely different now, alien; too quiet with the girls gone. He took another pull from the vodka and did a Google search on the computer, looking for Detective John Swift.

There were several stories in the local paper about Swift's involvement in a case where a young man, Frank Duso, had claimed police harassment.

Duso, Mike pondered. *Duso.* There had been a parade of people tramping through his life in the past seventy-two hours, but he seemed to remember that Duso was the name of the man who had found Braxton and placed the emergency call. Who was Frank? His brother? His son?

Troopers popped Frank Duso for driving under the influence. Not once, but twice. Some people just didn't learn. The first arrest had happened during the previous summer. In that initial incident, according to the state police, Frank had been unruly and uncooperative and his actions had warranted use of force. Pepper spray. His second offense had occurred several weeks ago. He was drunk again, speeding on the interstate between Plattsburgh and New Brighton. Speeding, inebriated, and under the influence of another substance: crystal meth. Frank Duso wasn't in possession of the drug, just had it in his system. So the mandatory minimum sentencing laws didn't apply. He was put in county jail for three weeks.

Mike leaned back into the couch, feeling his scalp tingling. South Plattsburgh was where Tori McAfferty lived. Where he, apparently, had a meth operation. Duso's second arrest report said he'd been driving back from there. Mike thought for a moment, then started a new search.

Was McAfferty already a known entity? What was going on behind the scenes? It seemed as though Swift and Duso had some kind of feud going on. Maybe it had to do with the pepper-spray incident, but maybe there was more. The prickling sensation intensified. Now Mike's fingers started to tingle as he typed.

The lead Investigator working Tori McAfferty's meth lab explosion was named Remy LaCroix. There was a picture of LaCroix in one of the articles — a funny-looking guy with a pot-belly wearing an old-fashioned fedora. LaCroix was part of a task force going after all the meth operations in the region. There was a related article in which the Plattsburgh Police Chief vowed that the city wouldn't allow this rot to infest his community like so many other places in the country. They were going to "stamp it out."

Mike cross-referenced LaCroix with the name Frank Duso. There was nothing. Even if there was something, realized Mike, it likely wouldn't be in the papers. But he had a hunch, a guess that Frank Duso was getting his meth from McAfferty. Or maybe even selling for him.

There was some connection between Swift, Duso, and McAfferty, though nothing certain apart from what Mike felt in his gut. That McAfferty had hurt Braxton. That McAfferty had killed him.

So when the email alert popped up a few minutes later, it felt like someone had reached down inside of him and squeezed.

* * *

The email was from Tori McAfferty.

Mike. You ought to check the balance of your 529 account. Then we should talk.

He brought up the page for the education fund, his nerves chattering. He plugged in his username and password. Then he held trembling fingers over the keys. The page to his account profile opened, and his eyes scanned down to the bottom where he read the balance.

The balance was zero.

He stared into an abyss; his brain could form no rational thoughts. *McAfferty. The whole thing. I knew it all along. I should have killed him when I first saw those emails.*

Memories of his childhood crept into his mind, long repressed, specters materializing from the shadows. Images of his father, hands black with the tar and soot of the tunnels, his face smeared with it, his white teeth flashing as he yelled at Mike's mother. Mike getting in between them. Turning on his father.

McAfferty. No different. Abusive psychopath. Everything starts and ends with him.

He got back on his email and sent a reply to McAfferty.

Tell me what you want.

He pressed Send. He got up from the couch and wandered aimlessly through the house, unable to focus. He was trying to locate something in his mind, but was unable to see clearly through the fog of swirling thoughts, each one more vicious than the last. He heard the chime that signified an incoming email, sat down and opened McAfferty's new message.

Tonight. 10 pm. You and I meet. Father to father.

You call the cops, and the whole thing is off.

Mike sent another message.

Why?

He waited another agonizing minute for the reply. It was an address, nothing more. Mike didn't recognize it, but found a piece of paper and a pencil in a kitchen drawer and scribbled it down.

He picked up his phone. He dialed the number from memory. He listened to the ring, and a woman answered. His own voice seemed to come from far away. She told him just a moment, and then another voice came over, and the sound of a man eating something like potato chips.

Bull Camoine said, "Hey, Mikey."

Mike let it all out in a rush, his whole body shuddering as he stood with the phone to his ear, looking out over the windswept front yard, the drifts of snow, the scabs of oak bark and branches darkening the white in places.

When he was done explaining — about McAfferty, the 529 account, the messages, everything — he added, "Callie and the girls left."

"Probably for the best," Bull said, as if this sort of thing happened all the time.

"You think?"

Bull was silent, seeming to calculate. "Not my place to say; I'm sorry. So aside from getting all this off your chest, to what do I owe the pleasure? Is it time?"

Mike was silent. He could feel his mouth working, but his lips had gone numb.

Bull let out a laugh. "Always did have a problem coming to the point, didn't you, Mikey? Come on. Nice to be catching up and everything, but Jesus, out with it."

Mike took a huge breath and exhaled slowly. "I was just thinking, you know? For protection."

"Absolutely, absolutely. We say no more, here, now, okay?" Bull would of course be worried about Big Brother listening in. And who knew — maybe Mike was worried too. Calling up an old friend to help you get yourself a gun was risky.

"Hey Mike?"

"Yeah."

"I've got my bags packed, Mike. I'll be there in a few hours. Sit tight."

Mike felt his lips quivering, and they parted. The objection rose in his throat, and then stayed there.

Let him come. Let him come and together you will shoot Tori McAfferty to death. Maybe first drag him behind the truck until he shits and pisses himself and then stop and let him think he is going to live and then do it again. Pull his arms from his body so he can't even wedge into the ligature like Braxton did. Pull him through the dark and snow until his head shears away from his body.

On the other end of the call Bull Camoine said, "I'm on my way to you, buddy."

CHAPTER FORTY-NINE

The phone sat on the desk between Swift and Captain Tuggey.

I spend half my goddamned life on the phone, Swift thought.

A voice came through the speaker. "Captain Tuggey, Senior Investigator Swift, Assistant District Attorney Sean Mathis. Hello."

"We're here," said Tuggey. "Hello Deputy Inspector Jonas. How's life in the big city?"

"Dandy. You trying to show us up out there in God's country? Quite a case."

"It is," said Tuggey. He glanced briefly across the desk at Swift before his gaze fell back to the phone. "We appreciate your help, Jonas."

"Well, I wish I had better news. As you know, warrant came through and we did a thorough toss of Darring's apartment in Queens. Seized a laptop, a smart TV, a gaming console, a few personal effects, that's about it. Guy lives like a monk. Place was spic and span."

Swift scribbled down a note in his pad, and Tuggey played with the Windsor knot in his tie. "Tell me."

"You know, like I say, not much to tell," Jonas went on. He had a thick New York accent. "Cyber-crimes spent the morning going through the computer." The word sounded like *computah*. "But there's nothing that has stood out. Normal usage, I guess. Amazon, Netflix, various news media, a little porn, two basic email accounts; one Yahoo, one Gmail."

Swift leaned forward. "Deputy Inspector, this is John Swift. Anything interesting in the emails?"

"We're still going through them. The Yahoo account has over a thousand. So far, looks like emails to some buddies. But no Branson Simpkins."

"Braxton," Swift corrected.

"Right."

"The other two? Hideo Miko, Sasha Bellstein?"

"Yeah, they're in there. Right up at the top. Just a couple. Uhm . . ." It sounded like Jonas was rustling paper. "This one here is a group email, arranging a time and place to meet. Time stamp is 4:22 p.m., Saturday. It says Darring is going to pick Miko up in New Jersey first, and then going to meet the other one outside of Philly at 7p.m. Something about when the Philly kid gets off work . . ."

"But no intent?" asked Swift. Tuggey gave him another glance, which Swift ignored.

"I know what you're looking for, Detective. No, there is nothing we have seen so far that indicates any intent to harm. Looks like they're just kids planning a visit to another kid."

"That kid is dead now," Swift said.

This time Tuggey didn't just glance, but gestured, drawing the ridge of his hand across his neck, indicating to Swift to *quit it*.

"I understand that, I understand," said Jonas. "You know what I'm sayin'? I wish I could tell you what you want to hear. But we just haven't found it."

"Thank you, Deputy Inspector," Tuggey said, before Swift could speak again. "We appreciate all you've done."

"My pleasure. You two take it easy up there, huh?"

"You bet."

Tuggey pressed a button on the phone to end the call. His eyes were fierce. “What the hell are you doing?”

“Trying to solve a murder.”

“You’ve already got two strikes against you, Swifty. Big ones. First, last summer’s fiasco with Frank Duso. Now this gaff where you’re caught boozing while on active duty — that’s punishable by termination alone — and you destroyed private property.”

Swift put on a humorless grin. “You loved that one. Admit it.”

“Now you want to badger the Deputy Inspector in New York City? You like this Darring kid so much for the Simpkins murder, you show motive, you give him a murder weapon, and you explain all this other shit with McAfferty.”

Tuggey pushed back from the desk and sighed. He played with his tie, smoothing it out.

“The arraignment is in two hours. Mathis is busy preparing. And you know what’s going to happen. Darring is going to see the judge, he’ll be advised of his charges, he’ll plead Not Guilty, Mathis will try to show he’s a flight risk, but Judge Stenopolis is a light touch with first-timers, and he’s got nothing but a sad, foster kid story in his background. No priors, no convictions. He hasn’t sought counsel, so he’s getting a PD. Bail will still be set high, but from what this kid has told us, he can afford it. And then, —vipp — he’s out. The burden of proof is all on Mathis, and he’s got none.”

“Which is why I’ve got to see Darring again.”

“No. For what?”

“I’ve got a theory.”

“You’ve got a theory. Jesus Christ, Swifty.” Tuggey was mad. “This is a small town, Swifty. You’ve probably noticed. Your recent actions make it look like we’re losing control, John. Like we’re frustrated, with nothing on the ball with this case.”

“Third time’s the charm, Tug.”

“Get out,” Tuggey yelled. “Get out!”

CHAPTER FIFTY

"Detective Swift. You look like you could use a cup of coffee."

The man standing in the receiving area at the Essex County Jail in Lewis offered Swift a wide smile. He was Brad Escher, county undersheriff. He stuck out his hand. Swift took it and gave it a brief pump. They stood looking at one another for a moment.

"I'm serious about that coffee. You want one?"

"I'd like to get right to the tough stuff." Swift looked over the undersheriff's shoulder and through the bullet-proofed glass into the jail.

"Absolutely," said Escher, his smile fading. "Right this way."

Escher led Swift through an entryway of piston doors and down a long corridor to an interrogation room. The room was much larger than the one at the substation. Here, Swift knew, the rest of the law enforcement team wasn't watching on the other side of a one-way mirror, but on monitors in another room a few doors down. Mathis and Tuggey were there, along with Sheriff Dunleavy.

Everything was being digitally recorded, and archived instantly to a hard drive. Swift found himself thinking that the reason why his own substation didn't have the budget to take on a homicide investigation like this one was because all the money went into the jail's technology. Even the chairs were cozier than the hard-backs in the substation.

Robert Darring was rotating back and forth in a swivel chair. Now booked into the jail, he wore the black and white striped jumpsuit over a grey hooded sweatshirt. He smiled politely as Swift entered the room and sat down across from him, setting out a file folder on the table between them. Darring's homely face and mud-colored eyes were open and guileless as his gaze dropped to the file.

"Frank Duso," Swift said.

Darring looked up from the file. "I'm sorry?"

Swift paused, letting the moment linger. He folded his hands together.

"Did I ever tell you about my father? No. I never told you. I told your pal, Hideo Miko, from Philadelphia. You know . . . Just before he broke down and cried."

"You can't take kids anywhere these days."

"My father was a state police detective, like me. So was my great grandfather. It skipped a generation, though; my grandfather was a farmer. But I bet you already knew that. That's just how smart you are. A foster kid, you've said. Spent a lot of time reading books, maybe, like what's-his-face in that movie. *Good Will Hunting*. What's that like, being a foster kid?"

"I don't have anything to compare it to. I wouldn't know."

Swift smiled. "Good point. Bet you felt alone at times though, yeah? Maybe . . . a little unwanted?"

Darring looked away, and Swift felt a momentary thrill that he might be getting under the kid's skin at last.

"You feel right at home here in this place. In an institution."

"Oh yeah, I love it," Darring said, flashing his teeth in an ironic smile.

"You feel comfortable. You open up to people. People like Frank Duso."

Darring's smile faded.

"You told him things. You talked to Frank. But, see, Frank's got a big mouth."

Darring glared, saying nothing.

"You didn't know that Frank and I had business, did you? See because he turned right around and got this big idea to call me up. Tell me he had something for me. In Frank's mind, he was setting a trap, trying to get back at me for some old business. So he called me up, invited me out for a drink, and told me all about you, about how you seemed like you needed someone to listen to your rap. How clever you are to work with others behind the scenes, throw off the cops, be in more than one place at a time."

"I'd like to see a lawyer please."

Swift hurried on. "Know what I think? You're Billy Sweet Tea."

Darring looked paler than usual. "Oh yeah?"

Swift pulled out his notebook and pen and set them on the table. He nodded. "You have other people, friends — I'm thinking Hideo Miko, Sasha Bellstein, maybe others — people in your little club, who play the same account, and that's your online persona in the game *The Don*."

"My persona?"

"Your character. What do they call it? An avatar? I played the game."

"You did? What did you think?" He was acting nonchalant again.

"Ah, you know, I'm an old guy. But I saw some interesting artwork. You know those pictures they show after you've waged war with somebody? A mean-looking thug walking away from a burning building? Or the one where there's a casket with flowers on it and mourners gathered around. Really great artwork. But this one's the best."

He leaned forward and slid a photograph from his file, the one he'd printed earlier. He spun it around so that Darring could look at it, while Swift watched his face.

"As you can see here, this is the image they use for their downtime, for maintenance. Or maybe fixing some security breach, who knows. But this one shows them digging a hole to dump a body in. The car lights shine so they can see to dig. And you can see the body there — see it? It's tied up behind the car, tied around the neck and the wrist. The way it's tied like that, it kind of cinches itself when someone pulls on it. A version of the garrote. Pretty gruesome stuff."

"Yeah, they really get into the brutality of it," Darring agreed.

"Did you get into the brutality of it?"

Darring looked up, his expression inscrutable. "It's just a game."

"You believe that the game continues on outside, in the real world, don't you? Or, at least, that what goes on in the real world is sort of inconsequential. Here's what you said the last time we met." Swift picked up his notebook and quoted. "'We're going to all live completely online someday.'"

"It's true."

"And this: 'I'm extremely interested in the techniques and technologies we use to essentially hack subjectivity.'" Swift looked up. "Do you consider yourself a hacker?"

"I asked for a lawyer."

"'The subjective experience,' you said. You know, you use a lot of big words. Like I said, you're a real smart guy. But I'm a little bit smart, too. Just a little. I think that what it means is, you mess with someone's perception of reality."

"You think so?"

Swift put the notebook down.

He leaned across the table and tapped a finger on the wood. “Remember couple days ago, when I admitted I was acting as-if? Well, now I’m not.”

CHAPTER FIFTY-ONE

Janine Poehler worked her way past security at the front of the county jail, and through the heavy doors. The guards smiled at her as she checked in, turning over her ID, her belongings and her jewelry. Unadorned, she continued to the room where four men sat watching Detective John Swift interviewing the suspect in the Braxton Simpkins case.

The men all turned and looked at her as she stepped into the room. She was wearing a crisp white shirt, the sleeves rolled up past the elbows, Sateen slim cargo pants and a pair of classic platform pumps on her feet. Four sets of eyes scanned her up and down, and then returned their attention to the monitor in front of Captain Tuggey. None of them asked why the forensic pathologist was here. They were too engrossed with the interview, for one. The whole town was waiting to know who killed the boy in the middle of the night, and she would be no different.

Janine made her way a little further into the room, stopping beside Undersheriff Escher, a lumberjack of a man who'd been in the armed forces before joining the Sheriff's.

She turned her attention to the screen.

* * *

"So tell me," Swift said to Darring, "how much manipulation are we talking about? Two kids, Miko and Bellstein, they're out there playing *The Don* on your behalf. You've hacked game servers, emails . . . bank accounts. What else?"

Swift's phone buzzed in his pocket. Brittney Silas. He couldn't take the call right now. He stared across the table at Darring, who looked smug.

"Let's try this. When I looked at the timeline, what always perplexed me was why you and your friends didn't hightail it out of there sooner. Why'd you wait around for nearly an hour and then come back? That left just enough time for you to do something. Like drive up to Tori McAfferty's house, plant evidence, and then head back south. And, theoretically, because you're not familiar with the layout up here, you backtracked instead of hopping on the interstate right from South Plattsburgh. You got picked up at the same exit you got off the highway on."

Darring scowled. "You're not giving me much credit."

"Then I thought, maybe you wanted to get caught. You drove right back through New Brighton and out the other end because you hoped you'd get picked up."

"Makes no sense to return to the scene of the crime."

"Sure it does," said Swift. "If you forgot something."

For just a moment, Swift thought he saw fear pass over Darring's features.

"In your story," Swift went on, "you never got out of the car. You never had contact with Braxton Simpkins. You were on your *way* to see him. Just arriving, just pulling in when you mistakenly drove past his house in the dark, you overshot, and then you saw this man in the road, plow-truck driver, standing over a dead body, and you turned, and you ran away, scared. But I think you were coming back."

There was an interruption, and Captain Tuggey's voice came over the intercom.

"Detective, we have to cease the interview. Darring's public defender is here."

Swift looked up towards the ceiling, then into the camera in the corner of the room, then down at Darring, whose look of resignation had lightened into a smug smile.

"Better stop," Darring said. "I think your job is already in danger, isn't it?"

Swift sighed and sat back. "Yeah."

"You've come along further than others might have."

"Oh yeah?" Swift raised an eyebrow. He wondered what the other cops thought of that one.

"Yeah." Darring maintained eye contact, gazing across the table at Swift. "I hope you realize something, Detective."

"What's that?"

"That you, and all the men and women, classics that you are — what a vintage, really. God bless you. Your fuck-ups weren't directly your fault. In the 70s and 80s you Baby Boomers had no idea what to do. And the Generation Xers, they just inherited a mess, which they've been whining about and trying in vain to fix. Neither of these two generations can be expected to know, to be able to do, what my generation can."

Swift leaned forward and put his hands, knuckled down into fists, on the table in front of him. "Is that what this whole thing is, Robert? You trying to prove something to the world about your generation? That the Millennials aren't really lazy, spoiled brats? Instead they're murderers?"

Darring almost flinched, and then smirked. "Oh that was tacky."

"So's your speech, Mussolini." Swift said.

Darring laughed out loud. "That's good. What I'm saying is that I'm a digital native, Detective. I may know more than most, but my whole generation is more fluent than yours'll ever be. So I'm just trying to concede that the playing field isn't really level, and I'm sorry for that. It seems capitalism once again favors those with early, unfair advantages."

"The playing field has never been level," Swift said. "That hasn't ever stopped me."

The intercom interrupted again. "Swift . . ."

Swift stood up, walked to the door and turned the lock. Interrogation rooms weren't supposed to have locks — but Sheriff Dunleavy had permitted it. Swift silently praised the man. He was too close now, goddammit. He had the kid right on the ropes.

"Swift!" Tuggey's voice roared over the speakers. There was a pounding on the other side of the door.

Swift was nonplussed. He and Darring stared at each other. "You created a whole web of lies to confuse and distract Braxton, and everyone else he knew. You created what you thought was a perfect screen for you to hide behind. Nothing in your little apartment in Queens, nothing on your so-called personal computer. Because you got those two other kids shilling for you."

Swift watched Darring closely. The young man's face had taken on that dreamy expression he'd gotten before. Like he was a radio signal fading out.

Suddenly, Swift flew across the room. In a few giant strides he was back at the table, and he slammed his hands down. He yelled in Darring's face. "What did you do to those kids to get them to do what you wanted? Why did you kill Braxton Simpkins?"

"Swift! Stop it, Swift!" Swift thought he heard the jangling of keys. Escher was opening up. The seconds were melting away.

Darring barely flinched at Swift's outburst. He looked up at the detective.

Swift gnashed his teeth. "Come clean, Robert! You know I'm going to find out anyway. You got people working for you; I got people working for me. Tell me! What are you doing?"

The door flew open.

CHAPTER FIFTY-TWO

"Let's go get this motherfucker," said Bull Camoine, setting down a black bag. He stood in Mike's living room, snow melting off his combat boots forming a puddle at his feet. Here in this place, Bull seemed larger than life. Living up to his name. He stood over six feet, and was at least two-hundred and twenty pounds of muscle and fat.

Mike, on the other hand, felt vaporously thin. A ghost. He couldn't recall the last time he'd eaten. Had they eaten breakfast this morning, he and the girls, before he took them to the airport? His head was swimming with the four vodkas he'd pounded, and a fifth glass was held in his hand. Nearby was a cup filled with spent cigarettes. He hadn't been drunk in months. Maybe a year. It was hitting him hard.

Bull clapped his hands and rubbed the palms together. "Tell me where he is."

"He's here in town," Mike said.

"He's *here*? What the hell are you talking about?" Bull's eyes were bulging with excitement.

"I got directions from him. He's right fucking here in town, man."

Mike felt dizzy and needed to sit down. He walked to the couch and dropped so fast it felt like the cushions jumped up and hit him in the ass. His drink sloshed in his grip.

"Whoa, whoa, hey Mikey," Bull said. He strode across the floor, his dripping boots tracking more slush and water. Mike stared at the melting trail on the floor. Bull grabbed the drink out of Mike's limp grip. "You've had *tee many martoonies* or what?" Then Bull lifted the glass to his mouth and drained it. He smacked his lips and said, "Ahh."

"I feel like shit."

"Fucking nuts. This guy is just something else." Bull strode away, presumably to get more drinks. Mike looked into the empty hand that had held his drink, still curled in a grip around a non-existent glass. When Bull came back a moment later with two fresh vodkas, he wore a thoughtful expression.

"So how did he get to your money?"

"I don't know. But, it's gone."

Bull slurped his drink and looked down with a quizzical expression. "Aren't you the only one who can make a withdrawal?"

"I'm the account owner, yeah. But the one putting the money in is my old man."

Bull shook his head, drank until the ice cubes bumped against his lips. "Uh-huh."

Mike felt like he was floating, attached to his body by a string.

"Your old man," Bull repeated.

"There's got to be something else going on."

"You call them?"

"Callie? No. I couldn't. I can't."

"You able to see who made the withdrawal?"

"I am."

"Your old man?"

"There was one more email," Mike said, starting to shake. It seemed to come from inside of him, his whole being rattling like an engine. The laptop was on the couch beside him. He tapped the mouse pad and the screen came to life. The last email was there. Bull, standing with his drink like a man at an art gallery opening, casually bent and squinted at the text. He read it out loud.

"Don't call the cops. Or the girls will get hurt."

Bull stood back up. He didn't look at Mike. He finished the vodka and stared off for a moment, thinking. Then he turned and walked across the room where he bent down to the black bag he'd placed near the front door. He reached in and pulled out a handgun. He came back towards Mike holding it out in his palm.

"This is a Glock 19, Mike."

He held it up. It was small, all black. Mike shifted the vodka between his hands, reached up and took the weapon by the grip.

"That's a Modular Back Strap design," Bull said. "Dual recoil spring assembly inside."

The grip was gritty in Mike's palm. He turned the gun back and forth in the air. He slipped his finger into the trigger. It had been years since he'd held a gun. The last time was when he was in his teens. He'd pointed it at his father.

"That texture you're feeling is called Gen4. And that's a reversible enlarged magazine catch. You can change that in seconds. I've got nine-by-nineteen safe action ammo for you. You'll have ten rounds in the magazine. But all you need to know, Mike, all you need to worry about, is that's your trigger, right there."

Mike imagined standing as he had stood decades ago. Holding a gun. Pointing it. Only this time, squeezing the trigger. Jack Simpkins' face became Tori McAfferty's. It all came crashing together — along with vodka on an empty stomach — and Mike got up and stumbled into the bathroom.

He dimly heard Bull calling after him, “Get it up, Mikey. Get it outta ya. We got business.” And then he heard the slap of a steel magazine as Bull loaded the gun.

CHAPTER FIFTY-THREE

"You're done, Swifty," said the Captain. "You're done."

Swift felt a hand clamp down on his arm and he shrugged it off. He strode out of the interrogation room and stalked down the hallway, putting the phone to his ear.

"Swift!" The Captain chased after him into the corridor. Swift looked around but didn't stop what he was doing, checking the message from Silas.

"You're done, I said, Swift." Tuggey was closing in on him. There was a dangerous edge to his voice. Swift knew he was one step away from being forced to resign. This was it. His new job might possibly be salvageable, if he stopped right now, if Tuggey could be convinced, after all this, to provide a glowing letter of recommendation to the Attorney General. But if Swift didn't press, didn't go for broke, the kid would walk. He knew it. If he gave in now, if he turned and bowed out gracefully, saving what little face he had left, then Robert Darring would get away.

He held a finger up to the Captain, who stood fuming. Swift listened to Brittney Silas' recorded voice.

"John, it's me. Listen, we found the headlamp. Two days out here in this shit, but we found it. Way down the road, like it was lost maybe while the victim was dragged behind the car. PETZL brand. I've checked it for latent prints. There's prints we cleared, which are Braxton's. And then there are a second set of prints, but they're nowhere in our database. Nothing. We've got clear-prints on the Simpkins family, and it's none of them, so . . . Anyway, we've got it logged into evidence. Call me."

He hung up.

* * *

Swift gathered all the cops into the room they had all been watching from earlier. He was surprised to see Janine Poehler there. He gave her a brief smile and touched her shoulder before turning to the others. Tuggey, Mathis, Escher, all there. Dunleavy was busy elsewhere; Lieutenant Timberlake was out commanding the manhunt for Tori McAfferty.

Swift told them all about the headlamp.

Mathis spoke up first. The ADA looked like he was choking on a piece of meat.

"It's too late, Swift. Darring's PD has the gag on him. We're not getting another word, you're not getting another second with him. This thing with the headlamp? My God. What a screw up. What an epic screw up. No way to enter that into the evidence file now. I'm sorry, man. I know you're a legend around here and I'm just the shitty new guy with the attitude, but you fucked up."

"Listen, Sean, I don't think so."

Mathis waved his hand in the air and turned away.

"The headlamp was dusted for latents," Swift said. "And nothing."

Mathis spun back around with raised eyebrows.

"Nothing? Well, what the fuck? We booked and printed him two days ago. He's in the system." Mathis pulled on his hair and paced. "Ah, shit."

Swift looked from Mathis to Tuggey, Escher and Janine Poehler, then glanced at the monitor. He watched Darring sitting there in the interrogation room along with his lawyer. He looked small from here, nothing like the big, unshakable personality of the past few days. From this distance he was just a kid, alone.

But, not entirely. He'd never been alone.

"He's not showing up for the prints because he's not who he says he is."

"What? Swift, you're losing it. You already lost it."

"I want to get the Feds on this," Swift said.

Mathis rolled his eyes. He plopped down into a swivel chair in front of the monitor and recording gear. He waved his hands. "Swift, we talked about this . . ."

Swift looked at him, cutting him off. "I know you want this one. But I'm sorry, Mathis." He looked around. "And the rest of you. I've got a feeling about something. I've had it for a little while."

Tuggey gaped. "For Christ's sake, John . . ."

Swift pointed at the screen, and they all turned to look at Darring's small, digital shape there in the center of it. "The prints don't match? That's because he's not who he says he is."

Mathis scowled. "What are you talking about?"

"Who the hell is he?" asked Tuggey.

"I'm going to find that out."

"We go to *court* in less than an hour," Mathis bellowed.

"I know," said Swift. He caught the scent of Janine Poehler beside him, her perfume, shampoo, aromatic traces of good coffee. He let his thoughts rest there for a moment. Escher was giving him a dirty look — he'd just had to unlock a room and haul Swift out. Tuggey had been riding him since the beginning. Mathis wanting to run the show. Swift was trying to keep it all in the pocket. It wasn't easy. Goddammit, it wasn't easy. A cushy job in Albany would be much better. Time with Kady. Time to think. To get out from under all of this.

"Tricia Eggleston," said Swift.

"Yeah? What about her?"

"You said you'd work on her."

Escher spoke up. "She got picked up in Plattsburgh, over the line, Clinton County. So she's up there."

Swift was looking sharply at Mathis, waiting.

Mathis raised his palms. "Swift, you think Remy LaCroix and DA Cobleskill haven't thrown everything at her? She's not talking. If she knows where McAfferty is, she's not going to say. Warren has got her locked up like Rapunzel. Anyway, we're talking about two different things here. I'm here because of the kid in that room, okay? Your case, the Braxton Simpkins case. We can't stick anything to this kid, headlamp or no. We cannot introduce anything else at this point. We're done. Over." He enunciated every word.

"Call her."

"Cobleskill?"

"We need to talk to Tricia right now."

"Swift," Tuggey said, "We're at the end of the line. Time's up."

Swift looked them all over. Mathis was rumpled with doubt and something like jealousy; he didn't want Federal involved, stealing his glory. Tuggey just looked bewildered, his mouth hanging open a little. Janine had a slight smile playing over her lips. Swift saw she had just a touch of lipstick on, or maybe lip balm, so that they shone. To hell with what they said about younger women. Janine Poehler was where it was at.

Swift pressed on. "We're going to need Kim Yom, too. Let's get her in here. We're going to meet tonight." Swift glanced at his watch. "Right now we need to have Tricia Eggleston tell us where McAfferty is."

Janine spoke for the first time. "What makes you think she's just going to open up?"

Swift looked at her and smiled. "I have that way," he said.

CHAPTER FIFTY-FOUR

Back out in the cold. The frigid wind edged into Mike's coat. Bull Camoine's Pathfinder sat in the middle of the driveway, the engine still running, the headlights turned off. Mike thought he saw someone sitting in the passenger seat.

"Who's that?"

"That's Linda."

Mike stopped walking, halfway to the car. Now that he'd thrown up he felt empty, as if someone had taken a steel wool brush and swiped it through his insides. His thoughts were still nebulous; things in his peripheral vision danced and darted. "Jesus, Bull. You brought Linda?"

Bull kept his voice low. His breath puffed out between his lips. "She's my wife, Mikey. We do everything together."

It had been years since Mike had seen Linda Epstein. He hadn't gone to Bull's wedding — no one had; the two of them had run off and married in Vegas, much to Bull's mother's endless chagrin. Linda had been a year behind Bull in school, and Mike remembered her coming to some of the old football games, a mousy girl with glasses who clutched her books against a flat chest.

The woman who greeted him as he piled into the back of the Pathfinder was very different. Now Linda Camoine, as she turned and smiled and held out her hand, Mike could see the tattoos that started from between her thumb and forefinger and wound around her wrist and disappeared beneath the sleeve of her black, body-hugging shirt. She'd either developed breasts, or bought some, and they bulged against a taut sweater. More tats rose from the collar, one tine of some probably tribal design snaked up and came to a point right between the back of her jaw and her neck. Her hair was no longer dull brown, but dirty-blonde, with a streak of purple or blue in it — he couldn't tell beneath the dome light.

"Hiya Mike," Linda said. "Been a long time."

Inside the Pathfinder the heat was blasting. And it smelled like lamb gyros and falafel sandwiches, odors which immediately called up in Mike a cascade of images and feelings; the hot rush of the subway tunnel, the streets around Washington Square Park, the warm linoleum of the third floor walk-up apartment kitchen where the afternoon sun hit it.

Bull got in and snugged himself behind the wheel. His weight rocked the vehicle on its axles. He turned and looked back, and a second later Mike thought that Bull Camoine must have supernatural powers, as he seemed to read his thoughts.

"The city misses you, Mikey. You woulda stayed? Oh man, we'd-ah had things wired."

Bull glanced at his wife. "I mean, me and Linda, we do alright. We do real good. We've got a couple of businesses, and we make a comfortable living."

"I thought you lived at home, Bull."

The husband and wife team exchanged another glance, and Linda seemed to shoot Bull a look of encouragement.

"After Bull's last incarceration," Linda said in a soft voice, "he was on parole when he got out. The parole officer was on him every second. We decided to base operations at his home for a while. We got him a job at the dry cleaners on Hylan Boulevard. We laid low for a year, didn't we, honey?"

"We did."

"And we just got used to running operations from there. Katrina liked having us. A mother likes her son around, you know? To help out. So we turned Bull's old bedroom into an office and we keep that, plus our space in the city."

Mike nodded "That's good, you guys."

Now Bull twisted around further to face Mike directly. "Listen, Mikey. This is about the life of your kid that was taken from you."

"I know."

"But, you know, if you don't want to do this, you say the word."

"He's in there. What about you? You sure?"

"Sure as the Pope wears a funny hat. Let's—"

Linda's hand darted out, quick as a snake bite, whacking Bull on the shoulder. "Hey. Ow."

"Watch the blasphemy."

"That ain't blasphemy."

"Of course it is. Making fun of the papal wardrobe is the same thing as taking the Lord's name in vain."

"No it ain't."

"Remember? Remember the smoke watch? Remember how long we waited? What did you pray for during that time, Bull?"

"Linda, come on . . ."

"What did you pray for?"

"I prayed to be more kind. Okay? You happy?"

Linda faced the back, looking at Mike with an apologetic smile. "We've been doing a lot of work on Bull's anger, his social interactions. It's the little things that matter most."

"Right," said Bull, clearly eager to dismiss the subject. "Now, Mikey, what do you say? This son of a bitch pops up out of nowhere soon as you try to start a new life, starts trying to coerce your son to leave you, leave the family — he's a home-wrecker. And when he can't have the kid, he . . . So you tell me, Mikey. We gonna do this?"

Mike sat in the middle of the backseat. The heat blasted in his face, and he liked it. He was so sick of the cold. He liked it hot. He ran hot. That was who he was.

"Yes," said Mike. "We're going to kill him."

"Booya!" said Bull, and spun back around, dropped the gear shift in reverse, and started backing out of the driveway and into the night.

CHAPTER FIFTY-FIVE

Swift made the drive to the Clinton County Sherriff's Department in forty minutes. But the weather was worsening, it was going to be hard driving as the night came on and the temperature dropped.

Tricia Eggleston was wearing the red and white fatigues worn by females at Clinton. Her face had a pinched, fuck-you quality that Swift could see even around the girth of Warren Eggleston. Eggleston, her uncle and lawyer, stood between Swift and the girl like he was her sovereign protector. Beside Swift stood the District Attorney, Elena Cobleskill. She was in her fifties, with short grey hair and a sharp navy blue pants suit. She dropped her briefcase on the table and invited Swift to sit down.

Warren, his eyes on Swift, walked around the table and sat on the other side next to his client. Swift turned to Cobleskill and Warren, and gave them his most pleasant smile.

"I'd like to sit with her alone, please."

Warren barked a laugh that wobbled his greasy double-chin. "I don't think so, John."

"I'll tell you what," Swift said, his smile gone. "I'll reverse my claim in the Frank Duso case. I'll go on record and say that I was a party to unwarranted use of force against Duso. You can appeal the court's decision to throw out your claim."

Eggleston's lips and cheeks sagged in disbelief. Beside him, Tricia wrinkled her nose in a scowl, her upper lip peeling back to reveal her stained and rotting teeth. She would have been pretty if it weren't for the ravages of the drug, Swift thought. "What is he talking about?" she said.

Swift watched Eggleston work it through. There was no way the man was going to be able to resist. He'd taken a pounding in court over the excessive force claim. It had sullied his reputation and humiliated him. The chance of vindication was too enticing to pass up. Swift could see his decision already forming. Then Eggleston turned and whispered into his niece's ear. Swift took the opportunity to look at Cobleskill. Her eyes widened and her thin lips curved into a grin.

"Alright," Eggleston said getting to his feet. It took some effort. "You have fifteen minutes. But I've advised my client not to say anything. So you're going to sit here and gaze lovingly at one another for the duration." His eyes darted towards Cobleskill, his expression urgent. "And you've got paperwork for me?"

Cobleskill opened her briefcase and pulled out a document. "I had to do it quickly," she said. "The detective didn't allow much time. But here is his sworn statement." She gave Swift a pen and he signed. Eggleston leaned in, his belly pressing into the table, and snatched up the paper. Swift watched his eyes work it over. Then he glanced across, a glimmer of triumph in his eyes, and left.

Cobleskill stood up.

"Good luck," she said, a hand on Swift's shoulder. The door closed behind her, and he and Tricia were alone.

"I'd offer you a smoke, but, you know how that goes," Swift said. She looked away from him. Her hands were on the table, fingers drumming. She kept tonguing her teeth. He wondered how bad her withdrawal symptoms were.

She seemed to be holding up well enough. When an inmate first came in, they wore solid colors until they had been medically evaluated. She was wearing the stripes, so she had already been seen by a doctor. Maybe she'd been given something.

He thought of Callie Simpkins, also sedated. It seemed so long ago, Swift thought, but it was just a few days. The wreckage caused by that one body in the snow. He looked at Tricia and waited until she met his gaze.

"You know where your boyfriend is," he said.

"Oh yeah?"

"And you're going to tell me."

"I am?"

"Not because Cobleskill out there and your Uncle will bid back and forth for how much less time you get in prison, because you probably don't care."

She didn't have anything to say to that. She looked down.

"But because," Swift continued, "I'm the one you're supposed to tell."

Her eyes came back up. Swift leaned back from the table. "Tell me about Robert Darring."

"Who?"

"Whoever called you. Set this whole thing up. Whoever told you the cops would be coming, and to ready explosives, be prepared to run, whoever gave Tori the address of a safe place to hide out."

She ran a tongue across her mottled front teeth again. Her eyes narrowed. "You're pretty cocky. But, you're a cop. Not surprising."

"You're supposed to tell me because your boyfriend is supposed to look guilty of murdering his biological son, Braxton Simpkins. The person who's doing this isn't looking out for his interests, or for yours. So whatever you were promised, it's a lie."

Her face changed dramatically. Her tongue fell away from her teeth, and she reached up and hugged her thin frame.

"Somebody called, yeah. Said our place was going to be raided. Task force; all that shit. State Police, DEA working together. Told us if we wanted out, we had to blow the place soon as the cops showed. There was a place for Tori. Me too, but I didn't want it."

"What place?"

"I got told an address."

"An address." Swift leaned forward again, slipping his notebook from his pocket and clicking a pen.

"Some old farm."

"Give it to me."

"I just wanted to cook, you know? I just wanted to fucking get small. I didn't love Tori no more. He's an asshole."

"Give me the address, Tricia."

"You gonna do this right? With the lawyers?"

He stared at her. "Now, or you get nothing."

She told him, and Swift started to write, and then his hand stopped, and he set the pen down, and he just looked at her again.

A moment later Swift got up and banged out of the room, leaving his pen and notebook behind.

CHAPTER FIFTY-SIX

Bull's Pathfinder sat parked at the mouth of a driveway that wound its way down to a dark house. A mailbox on a stake listed to one side with a frosting of snow. The driveway had been freshly plowed, scraped down to a glassy compaction of snow and ice, the banks piled high.

Mike looked out the windshield from the backseat. Something didn't feel right. And it wasn't the idea that he was here to kill Tori McAfferty; that felt fine. Any lingering doubts about that had passed through him and splattered onto the toilet bowl half an hour ago. This was something different. He was new to the area, didn't know one place from another, and there were many places like this, broken down farms amid rolling hills, with dilapidated barns and unused foaling sheds, but something here tolled familiar. He couldn't put his finger on exactly what.

Then he peered through the darkness at the mailbox beside the road. He suddenly got out of the back of the vehicle.

"Hey, Mike, what the fuck?"

He shut the door on Bull and stepped into the cold, feeling the wind and snow sting his face. He walked briskly to the mailbox and swished away the snow. He read the name.

SWIFT.

Bull came around the car all hunched up in the frigid temperature, scowling.

"What's going on?"

Mike felt hollow. Confused, betrayed, but mostly hollow. Like nothing mattered. Like nothing was sacred.

"This is the detective's place." He turned and looked through the night at the dark buildings strewn across the land.

"The detective? You mean the *statie*?"

"Yeah."

"Ho-lee-shit," Bull said. Mike wasn't sure whether Bull was going to want to back up and get the hell out of there, or if he was going to stay with it. It didn't matter. Bull had given him the support he'd needed, but now Mike was ready to go it alone if that was what had to happen. Nothing else mattered anymore. Nothing.

Bull looked off into the dark. He seemed to relax. "That's pretty fucking smart, man. Guy hides right there at the statie's house. Ballsy. Who's going to look for you there? Right?"

"I guess," said Mike. He turned to the vehicle. Time to get moving.

"*Or*," Bull said following, "the detective is in on it somehow. You say McAfferty had a meth lab, right?"

"Yeah."

"That's the way they operate," Bull said. The two men got back in the car and Bull continued talking. "That's the way it shakes out of the bag, Mikey, every time."

"What's going on?" asked Linda.

"That detective is probably on the take. For all you know, he's abetting McAfferty."

It rang true. Or, at least, possible. What else made sense?

"Whose place is this?" She was looking back and forth between the two of them.

"There's this guy," Mike said, "Frank Duso. I think Duso was buying from McAfferty, maybe selling a little for him. Duso was the one that called the press on the detective, Swift. The one you told me to have a look at. That video."

Bull had been nodding his head vigorously, but then stopped. "The one I who-and-what now?"

"You texted me," Mike said.

"I don't text nobody."

"He doesn't text," added Linda.

Mike looked at Bull, his thick neck and square jaw, limned yellow in the dashboard lights. "You didn't send me that text, the link to the video?"

"Nope."

Then who sent it? Mike sat back in the rear seat. He wondered if it could've been this Frank Duso kid. If he had called the press, which seemed likely, then he might've somehow gotten Mike's number in order to tip him to watch the video. Make Swift look like an unreliable investigator.

Wherever it came from, Mike had already begun questioning Swift's abilities. And his motives. And now this.

"There's a massive manhunt on for this guy . . ." Mike said quietly, as much to himself as to the others. "But Swift never said anything to me about McAfferty being into a meth operation. Not even when I mentioned the emails and practically handed the cops the son of a bitch on a sliver plate did they say, 'Yeah, we know this guy, we've been closing in on his operation for months.' Nothing. It was like they'd never heard of him. And now this guy's at the detective's *house*?"

"Yep," confirmed Bull. His eyes gleamed in the rear view mirror. "S'what I'm telling you, Mikey."

Mike looked down. His head was in a fog again. There were too many questions. But did they matter? He could sit here all night debating whether or not to call the cops and tell them about McAfferty's email, about the money taken out in Jack's name. But he'd been warned that the girls could get hurt. And Bull was already here. Things were beyond fucked up — too fucked up to trust the cops, who'd done nothing so far anyway.

And, if John Swift really was working secretly with McAfferty, or at least caught up in backdoor deal with Frank Duso, how would Mike know how deep the corruption spread? Who could be trusted?

Swift had seemed like an upright enough investigator. But then, he'd been busted while drinking on duty. He had a tarnished record. He lived alone, did what he wanted when he wanted, a kind of maverick cop with few people to answer to.

Plus, he knew about the 529 account. Swift and his team had been the ones to commandeer Braxton's laptop and lift all its information. It sounded too sinister to be true — cops complicit in the death of a minor so as to cash in — but Mike knew that worse things had happened. He and Bull were both raised in a pre-Giuliani New York, they were on the streets in the 1980s when police corruption was a plague and the criminals ran the show.

Still. This was a nice small town in the North Country. There were government buildings here — a mental health clinic, a hospital, a DMV. It just didn't seem like the type of place to harbor dirty cops, not the best place for criminals and corruption to get a real foothold. It was too policed.

Unless, of course, that was what made it work.

"Mikey, you alright back there?"

He still felt the effects of the vodka. His stomach had hardened, however, his nerves had steadied. Being with Bull, hearing the accent again, smelling the smells of the car, seeing Linda after all these years, it was doing something to him. It was making him feel stronger. More confident. More like his old self before fiber-teching and marriage and kids and domesticity. Like a man again.

"I'm good."

The car sat with the engine idling and the headlights turned off. If McAfferty was here, he would be hyper vigilant and on the lookout. Surely he would have seen them by now; Bull had just boldly pulled into the driveway, for God's sake. Now he was checking the firearm. Linda had one too — Bull had said it was a SIG, very compact, mean-looking. Mike felt the hard shape of his own handgun pressed against his abdomen where he'd tucked it into his pants.

"Then let's go," Linda said.

It was now or never.

The SUV rolled forward. The wind buffeted the vehicle, hitting against it from one side. Mike looked out over the large property at the shapes of other buildings, mere charcoal sketches in the dark. Tori McAfferty was hiding in one of those. The man who had killed Mike's son. Hanging out. Protected by a cop, maybe multiple cops. Somehow connected to Mike's own father. Threatening the lives of his wife and children, right now, right at this very moment.

His phone buzzed. Mike took it out and looked at the incoming number. "Speak of the Devil," he said. He rolled down the window and threw the phone into the freezing night.

You couldn't trust anyone. He looked at Bull and Linda, who were both turned around in their seats to face him. Not like you could trust old friends.

CHAPTER FIFTY-SEVEN

Swift had taken his emergency light and placed it on the dashboard where it flashed red. He careened along the highway, snow smacking against the windshield, the back of the car occasionally fishtailing in the greasy covering of snow over the road. Mike Simpkins wasn't answering his phone. Frustrated, Swift tossed his on onto the passenger seat.

It made sense now. It all made sense if you thought like Robert Darring. If you had a reason to want to make someone else's life a hell, to manipulate them, to choreograph a series of events that would have them right where you wanted them, thinking what you wanted them to think.

Robert Darring didn't just want to frame Tori McAfferty for the teenage boy's murder. Above all he wanted Mike Simpkins to think McAfferty was guilty. And then he wanted Simpkins to kill McAfferty, and so spend a life in prison. Darring had interfered with everything — he knew about the 529 account, somehow, knew the cops would look at Mike for that. He knew about the deadbeat bio dad McAfferty. That McAfferty was into cooking and distributing methamphetamines.

Why not just frame Simpkins in the first place? Why not just make it look like he did it for the money? The cops had already been looking that way, all they'd needed was a nudge. It happened all the time, all over the world, people killed for their life insurance policies, murderers out to get an early inheritance. So why not just make Mike Simpkins look guilty?

Because it wouldn't have stuck. He maybe had problems — who didn't — but Simpkins was basically a good guy, Swift thought. And Darring knew it. Maybe that was why he hated Simpkins. Maybe that was sufficient, but Swift didn't think so.

The wheel spun in his hand as the tires slid over a stretch of ice, grabbed a patch of blacktop, then hit more slush. The conditions were at their worst. The day had gotten warm enough to melt some snow and then the temperature had dropped, freezing chunks of slush into ice where the roads went high, but staying mushy through the valleys. He caught the wheel and straightened the car, pulling it out of a skid. His heart was pumping, but his foot stayed on the gas, pushing the car up to sixty through the dark, howling weather.

He passed a tractor-trailer with its hazards flashing. Someone up ahead hadn't got completely past the big truck and was travelling alongside it. Swift's light flashed; he slapped the horn and toed the brakes. "Come on!" He yelled. He swiped the air with his hand as if to push the vehicle aside. "Come on!" He was halfway there. Twenty minutes from his home. The place would be crawling with his troopers and the Sheriff's Department. He had to get there. In his mind's eye he saw Mike Simpkins going down. Torn to shreds by Swift's fellow cops.

CHAPTER FIFTY-EIGHT

A dog was barking in the main house. Mike stood in front of a smaller outbuilding, a ramshackle tenant house. A remnant from when the place was a working farm and the laborers lived on the property.

"McAfferty!" called Mike Simpkins.

The wind cut across the open land from the west. Mike felt it buffet against him, heard the sound of wind chimes banging together somewhere in the distance; the dog barking. He stood in a foot of snow. He felt numb.

"McAfferty!" he called again. "I'm coming in."

In his peripheral vision Mike could see Bull Camoine sliding up along one side of the small building, and Linda along the other, each of them with their firearms out and ready. They moved like predators in the night. He stepped towards the small, rambling front porch, its steps buried in a drift of snow. There were fresh foot prints leading up to the door.

He stopped, hesitating for one last moment, turning over the variables in his mind. Why was McAfferty here? What was Swift gaining by conspiring with a lowlife, meth-cooker like McAfferty? Was the meth industry really that powerful that someone like Swift could get taken in?

Of course, Mike rationalized, as the wind swirled around him, gusting up the snow, you never knew anything about people. It was naïve to think anyone was all good, or all bad. People were just animals, reacting, adapting, surviving.

Mike saw Braxton's face, the mop of hair in his eyes, as he sat playing with his sisters on the carpet of their home in Florida.

Braxton had been good. He'd been unspoiled by the world. Mike had ruined him, dragging him up here, back to the place he'd escaped from with his mother so many years before. Back into the belly of the beast. The beast on the other side of that door. Mike's hand gripped the gun tucked into his waistband and he pulled it out.

Then he launched himself up and took the door by the handle and yanked it open.

* * *

Tori McAfferty sat in a straight-backed chair, aiming a hunting rifle at Mike Simpkins.

The place was a single room, with a water closet at the back right. Opposite that there was a small kitchenette, and a back door. The floors were bare wood, with a single braided, oval-shaped rug that was probably once colorful but now worn to shades of brown. Beside McAfferty was a simple, Amish-style table. The place was cold, but smelled like propane — McAfferty had activated the small heater that stood in the unused fireplace. There were a few other odds and ends of furniture — an antique end table, a chest, and there were four dark windows.

Mike stopped just inside the room. The door slowly closed on his heels, then a gust of wind slammed it the rest of the way home. He held the gun out in front of him, pointing it at McAfferty, just as he'd pointed it at another man, all those years ago.

"I don't think we've ever met," Mike said, his heart pounding. "I'm Mike Simpkins. I'm Braxton's father." He kept a close eye on the rifle aimed back at him.

Tori McAfferty sniffed, like he had a bad cold. He looked terrible. There were large circles beneath his eyes, and his skin was blotched with acne. He was in his forties, Mike knew, but looked fifty, or older. Patches of grey were scattered through his messy shock of hair. Mike couldn't help seeing how Braxton had inherited that thickness, the wild cowlicks. McAfferty was dressed in a pair of Carhartt work pants and a Carhartt jacket, discolored all over by paint and stain and roofing tar, and wood glue and caulk.

"I read about what happened," McAfferty said from behind the rifle.

Mike blinked, kept the Glock level. "Oh, you read about it?"

"Saw it on the news, too."

The room smelled foul, closed up for too long. And now it also stank like McAfferty, of a man who hadn't washed in several days, a man on the run.

"So, I'm here. What's the deal, Tori?"

"The what?"

Mike narrowed his eyes. Bull and Linda were waiting on the other side of that back door. The plan was to let Mike talk to McAfferty first — he'd insisted, much to Bull's disapproval. Bull wanted to rush in and dispatch the guy straight away. Any delay only invited complications. Mike figured he was right, in principle, but he needed something from McAfferty first. He wasn't quite sure what he needed, only that he did. Maybe it was atonement.

"What did my father say to you? How long have the two of you been talking?"

McAfferty scowled. "How am I gonna talk to your father if I don't even know you?"

"You know me," Mike said. "I'm the guy who said I'd kill you if you ever did anything to hurt Braxton. And here I am."

McAfferty's scowl turned into a bitter smile. "Oh you're a tough guy. You and Callie probably fit just right together. How's she doing, that psycho bitch?"

"You've got one minute — one minute — to tell me what you want from me."

McAfferty's grin widened, and he threw his head back and laughed. The laughter was short, and turned into a coughing fit. He leaned forward again, doubling over, with a fist at his mouth, coughing and gagging. He dropped the rifle onto his lap, and spat out a gob onto the bare floorboards. His face was hectic, and red from the coughing, but his eyes still glinted with amusement. He spread his legs out wider, boots planted firmly on the floor, lifted the rifle and edged forward in the seat. Mike wondered for a moment where McAfferty's laptop was. Surely he had an internet phone. He saw neither. "Somebody's been fucking with you, huh?"

"Tell me, Tori."

McAfferty's expression changed. He looked both hurt and angry at the same time. His lips curled back in a sneer, revealing dark places where molars were missing. "You giving me orders now?" He renewed his grip on the rifle and aimed it straight at Mike's chest. Mike felt something flutter in his stomach; the muscles in his legs and arms emulsified. They were both just a squeeze away from putting a round into one another.

"Look," McAfferty said, "I don't know what you think you know. I blew my fucking house up."

"Why?"

"Why? Cops. So I took my shit and ran."

"Why the hell would you come here? This property belongs to a state police detective."

McAfferty looked around for a moment. "No wonder it's a dump." He pressed his face to the rifle again, glaring down the barrel at Mike.

"Somebody told you to come here. Who?"

"Who? My guy, that's who. He's supposed to be here, standing right where you are." McAfferty looked worried. "What the fuck is going on? I'm supposed to be on my way to the city tonight. And you're standing here."

Mike's arm was shaking, but he kept his aim tight. He asked through gritted teeth, "Why did you do it?" The nerves in his face were stretched tight. "Why did you kill Braxton?" Suddenly he exploded. "You worthless fuck!"

The back door crashed open. Bull charged in, followed by Linda. McAfferty tried to spin around, but it was too late — in a couple of giant strides, Bull had closed the gap between them and slammed McAfferty in the head with the butt of his gun. McAfferty sprawled forward and hit the ground, his rifle clattering across the floor, where he landed in a heap and was still.

Bull towered over him, chest heaving. He righted the handgun in his grip. Linda was pointing her own firearm down at McAfferty. Bull glanced at Mike, a worried expression on his face. "Cops, Mike. Fucking cops are on the way."

Mike stood there, confused and unable to move. He could hear it, in the distance, the sound of sirens. His gaze fell on McAfferty's gun, which had slid across the floor towards him.

"Pick it up, Mikey. Quick. Pick it up and let's finish this thing and get the fuck out of here. Might as well use the rifle. Keep the Glock clean."

Mike remained motionless for a moment, and then forced his body to respond. He slid the handgun into his pants. Then he bent forward and picked up the rifle.

CHAPTER FIFTY-NINE

Mike Simpkins wasn't going to take any more shit. He took a couple of steps over to Tori McAfferty and placed his boot on the man's shoulder and attempted to roll him over onto his back.

Tori groaned and his eyelids fluttered.

Mike had McAfferty's gun in his hand. He pointed it down at the man's head.

"Is my family in danger?"

McAfferty's eyes opened and rolled around, attempting to focus.

Mike kicked McAfferty in the arm. He brought the tip of the rifle within inches of McAfferty's forehead. "Tori. Is my family in danger? Did my father put you up to this?"

McAfferty moaned, still dazed from the pistol-whipping.

"Mikey," Bull Camoine said. "Let's be quick."

The sirens grew louder, closer.

Mike cut Bull a look. Bull had seen the look before, just once, long ago. "Get out, Bull. You and Linda. Get out."

"Mike, somethin' stinks here. Somethin's not right."

"And you feel like *now* is the time to say so?"

Bull frowned. "Yeah, Mike, I feel like now is the time."

McAfferty grimaced and touched the back of his head. "Ah, damnit," he said.

"Answer me, Tori. Did my father put you up to this?"

McAfferty looked up, pure malevolence in his eyes. "Fuck you."

Mike aimed the gun between those hate-filled eyes. "Did you kill Braxton?"

"Of course I didn't."

"Mike," Bull said, "he's going to say anything."

Mike yelled at him. "Get out, Bull! Now!" He looked down at the man crumpled at his feet. "Tori, why did you blow up your house?"

Some of the enmity drained away and for a moment, McAfferty looked pathetic. Mike felt a tiny stirring of sympathy for him. The drug had cooked him, his body, his brain, and everything else in his life. Probably he could have made much more from the business if he wasn't his own best customer.

"I told you," Tori said.

"When the cops were coming to call on you, you struck a match to the place."

"Yeah."

"Okay," Bull said. He took Linda by the arm and they slipped out the back door, looking back urgently over their shoulders. Mike didn't watch them go.

"That's lucky," Mike growled at Tori. "How come you're not bits and pieces all over your own yard? Huh? How did you get out of there in time?"

"Look," McAfferty said, flat on his back now, his hands up in front of him, warding off the gun, Mike, everything. "Okay? It takes about a minute for the charge to go off. I used a special incendiary device. I lost everything, man, My *Les Paul*, my Jimi picture, my good leather jacket . . ."

"That's tragic, Tori."

Tori licked his cracked lips. He looked up at Mike, standing over him. "Trish was the one who set this up, me coming here."

"Who?"

"My fucking girlfriend, man. Tricia Eggleston. Her brother is a lawyer."

Mike glanced away for a second and stared at the black windows. As the cops drew nearer Mike thought he could hear the roar of engines beneath the wail of the sirens. He thought he was close to putting it all together at last.

"Look," Tori continued. "Eggleston is a lawyer for Frank Duso. Duso is a guy who did a little dealing for me, and then he got popped for a deewee, and the cops Maced him or something, and he sued. Made the cops mad as hell. Made Eggleston mad too, 'cause he lost the case."

"So they had you hide here to what? Make the detective look guilty of something? That's pretty far to go for a pissed off lawyer and a young kid who wants payback against the cops. What does this have to do with my son, Braxton? Or your guy, the one you said was supposed to be here?"

Tori scowled up at Mike. "You think I know what this has to do with Braxton? I don't have a clue. My guy said he was your brother, so you're the one who should be telling me what the fuck is going on. You've got one fucked up family, man."

"He what?" asked Mike. Things were starting to get confused again. Faces flashed through his mind; his father's, Callie's, the girls, and Braxton's. What the hell was Tori saying?

There were noises outside. Doors opening and closing, the sound of boots on the ground, weapons loading. The dog was barking harder than ever. *His brother*? McAfferty must be crazy. His brain must be more mushed up than Mike first thought. He must be talking about his father. Mike didn't have a brother. His grip on the rifle slackened.

Tori sat up and looked around, listening to the commotion outside, a bewildered expression contorting his features. "I didn't kill the kid, okay? I didn't kill my own kid."

A voice boomed out of the night. "McAfferty. Simpkins. Come out with your hands up."

Mike took a breath and looked at Tori. "Did you email him? Braxton?"

"I don't even have an email account, man." McAfferty looked petrified.

"So you never corresponded with him. You never got an email from me, telling you to back off or else?"

"No, man." Tori was now looking at the blank windows, trying to see through, to get a look at the nightmare awaiting him. Red pulses of light silently flashed through the windows. Mike recalled that first night, the red in Braxton's room. He renewed his grip on the rifle. His finger moved at the trigger.

"No, I never got an email. Tricia, she uses the computer on her phone, or whatever. We don't even have a laptop in the house. I never sent any emails. The only way I knew Braxton moved back was when I saw it in the paper. Oh fuck man, oh shit . . ."

McAfferty looked utterly broken now, sitting there on the floor, legs sticking out in front of him, dirty clothes, mussed hair, rotting teeth. His eyes had grown droopy and glassy. "I loved that kid," he said.

"Tori McAfferty. Mike Simpkins," boomed the voice in the night. "You have thirty seconds to put down your weapons and come out or we're coming in."

Then Mike heard shouts, followed by gunfire. It didn't seem to be directed at the house. It was out there. Where Bull and Linda were. McAfferty stared up at him. "Please," he was saying. "Please, man."

All he had to do was squeeze just a little bit harder.

Braxton, dragged through the night to his death. Lying there alone, terrified, hurt, trying to protect his sisters. Trying to protect his family.

Mike looked down the barrel at Tori McAfferty, and for a moment, he closed his eyes.

He saw Braxton's face, saw him standing in the road, as if looking back at Mike, waiting for him to catch up. The boy held out his hand.

CHAPTER SIXTY

When Mike stepped out of the small cabin and down into the knee-deep snow, the whole world lit up. Headlights snapped on, bathing him in a harsh light. He heard shouts on the other side of the blinding glare. "Down! Get down on your knees!"

His heart in his throat, Mike could feel the ground vibrate as men pounded towards him. Their shapes loomed. He did as he was told.

"Put your hands on your head and drop all the way to the ground!"

The shapes became men — State Troopers — their weapons trained on him. Mike laced his fingers over his head, and lowered himself forward onto his belly in the snow.

Seconds later they were at him, guns inches from his face. One trooper grabbed him by the wrists and pulled his arms behind him, another slapped on the cuffs. They weren't gentle. Mike stared up into the white lights.

Amid the thundering of his heart and the pounding in his ears, the shouts of the men and the dazzling lights he found that his thoughts had gone to Callie and the girls. If anything had happened to them, if any harm had come to them, it would be over. It would all be over. There would be no point left to any of it.

The cops hooked their hands under his armpits and hoisted him to his feet.

As he was being hauled away, he saw a familiar face. Detective Swift fell in beside the troopers holding Mike. Swift's face was harried, he was out of breath, and he wore a look of sympathy. "It's going to be okay," the detective said, as Mike was shoved into the back of a trooper cruiser.

"My father," Mike said before the door closed. "This is all him."

Then he was driven away. Swift's face receded into the night. Mike stared out the windows as cop after cop, probably every last man in the county and then some — blurred past, watching him as he was taken away. Their faces looked blank and distant.

PART FIVE

TIES THAT BIND

CHAPTER SIXTY-ONE

"We were too late," Mathis said. His usually coiffed hair was matted, he looked disheveled, as if he hadn't slept at all in the past twelve hours since he'd been to court.

Swift sat across from him, at the same table where he'd confronted Robert Darring the previous day. After all that had happened, culminating in a spectacular end to the manhunt for Tori McAfferty, at his own property, Swift felt like he was carved from wood. Nothing could faze him. He watched Mathis strutting the same way Kady watched squirrels running about on a tree branch outside the window.

"Darring is off the hook," said Mathis. "Eggleston played the cord, the DNA, the McAfferty situation, everything. Judge threw the charges out. Says we can arrest him again on conspiracy or accessory, but the murder charge — dismissed. Darring spent the rest of the night in County and was processed out this morning."

He paused for a moment, and his eyes seemed to search those of Swift.

"Darring is free as a bird. Dunleavy said the kid was headed over to impound to fill out the paperwork and get his car back. I don't get it, man. I don't fucking get it."

"What's to get?" Swift asked. "We didn't have it," he said. "We didn't have anything in the car, anything at the scene until too late, and that's my fault. I'll take full responsibility for that. We didn't have anything in his computer or accounts, and no confession that could prove rational motive, let alone any homicide."

Mathis suddenly moved forward. He glared at Swift and jabbed his finger at him. "For Christ's sake, *you* had something. You had the fucking headlamp. I don't care if you take 'full responsibility.' Jesus, Swift. Come on. Too late for me to put in the discovery file, too late to introduce in court? And I ask for an adjournment, I get shut right down."

Swift shook his head. "Wouldn't have mattered."

"But that's not *your call*, detective! You're not the lawyer, not the judge, not the jury. You act like this is all some sort of game."

Swift looked at Mathis with a level gaze. "It is. It's his game. We've all been playing."

"No — *you're* playing. And you lost, okay? Darring is toddling off to impound as we speak to do the paperwork on the vehicle. An hour from now, tops, and he's out of here. We got the perpetrator, Swift. Last night before nine p.m. Pretty sure you were there. Tori McAfferty has been booked for first degree murder. We've got motive." Mathis counted off on his fingers. "He had no custody of his son, who was legally adopted by Simpkins, we've got the emails showing their heated exchanges. "And," he said, pausing for effect, "we've got the victim's DNA on the piece of cord used to strangle the boy, which *you* found, sitting in McAfferty's laundry room. Case closed, bye-bye McAfferty."

Mathis straightened his spine. He raised his hands to his neck to fix his tie, but he had taken it off earlier and it lay nearby on the floor.

"That's the game," Swift said.

Mathis gritted his teeth. "Fuck you, Swift."

At that moment, Captain Tuggey came into the room, with Sheriff Dunleavy close at his heels. After them, two people, a man and a woman, wearing snappy suits, whom Swift had seen once before. They were from Internal Affairs. They took up stances against the back wall, arms folded, watching like hawks.

Swift looked at the Captain.

"How you doin', Tug?"

"Better than you, Swifty."

Swift looked at the two IA investigators, who averted their eyes. Swift said, "We're going to do this now, Cap?"

"Swifty, I've given you the benefit of the doubt all the way here. I've given you time. You've been a good investigator, John. But lately I think you're having some trouble. That incident with the reporter, fair enough. But we just had the prime suspect in our murder case walk out of court. No bail, nothing. Stenopolis practically apologized to him." Tuggey held out a hand towards Mathis. "And the guy who blew up his lab and nearly killed a cop was picked up at your house. I think it's time you took a beat. You know? Step back and let us re-evaluate."

"We got Camoine and his wife shooting at cops on your property," Dunleavy interjected. "Couple of wild nutjobs. Who the hell are they; what were they doing there?"

Swift looked away. "They were muscle for Simpkins."

Mathis snarled. "And how would you know that?"

"Because no one is going to protect a scumbag like McAfferty," Swift said, jerking his head around to look at Mathis. "He had no friends. Simpkins does. Not a lot, but a couple. And he's the type to call on some muscle because he wouldn't have gone up to my place alone."

"What about this money?" Mathis demanded. "That's a hundred grand that was in the 529 account. Simpkins says it's no longer there; I think he could've withdrawn it, maybe used it to pay Camoine and his wife for something."

Captain Tuggey came closer. "Why, Swift? Why was McAfferty at your place?"

"He was told to be there," Swift said. "Tricia Eggleston said they had a contact, someone who set it up for them."

Mathis was relentless. "But Tricia *knew* it was your place. Why would she send her boyfriend off to hide out there? How did some guy she never met, whose name she didn't get, convince her of that? And why was your property chosen in the first place?"

"Because he *worked* her, that's how." Swift ran a hand through his thinning hair. "Darring did his research. Knew where my house was, knew that if he or his accomplices wrote fake emails to Simpkins, he'd lose all faith in the police. In me. So he'd keep quiet. Darring brought Tricia what she wanted — he cut her loose from McAfferty. Her uncle is going to put up a fight, but if Cobleskill gets her emails, they're going to find correspondence between her and Darring. I bet she was promised money, too. They both were."

Swift looked directly at Mathis. "But no one ever got any money, Sean. Which, by the way, wouldn't be the full hundred yards, remember? It would be taxed when it wasn't used for educational purposes. It would be more like sixty-five, seventy grand. But there are only two people who could extract that money — Mike Simpkins and Mike's father, Jack Simpkins, through a long, complicated paperwork process."

Now Swift moved his gaze from Mathis to Tuggey to Dunleavy. "This was all a game, like I said. Mike Simpkins would look at the missing money and, knowing he didn't take it himself, believe that there was only one other place that money could possibly be."

Swift leaned back and hung a boot from his knee. "But Darring never cared about any money. This is a revenge story, boys. For something that happened a long time ago."

CHAPTER SIXTY-TWO

"Dad? How's it going?"

Mike had been brought through the booking process by deputies who, when they looked at him at all, acted like they were viewing livestock. One was giving him the stink-eye now as he used the payphone in the men's pod. Even after lying awake on a narrow bed all night, he could still smell the vodka leaching out of his pores. What a mess he was. What a mess he'd always been. When his mugshot was taken he realized he probably looked like any other goon he'd seen on television, popped for meth, or child neglect, or any other scumbag thing — eyes bloodshot, hair sticking up, skin cheesy. What people never saw when they looked at those mugshots was the fact that all those guys had started out fairly decent; at least with some semblance of health and sanity, before they ended up shipwrecked on the craggy rocks of whatever tragedy their life contained — and everyone had at least one tragedy in their lives.

"Turn to the left," they'd said.

He'd turned, and the light had flashed, and they took another picture, and then they finger-printed him. He was stripped of his belongings and clothing and processed along with Bull and Linda, who had been arrested unharmed. Lucky for them that in all the dark and snow they'd never hit anything. Still, the two of them were facing stiff charges — fleeing arrest, firing on State Troopers — these things weren't small matters.

"Dad, you there?"

"I'm here, Mike."

"Let me talk to Callie and the girls."

Mike heard his father draw a deep breath and then sigh. "Where are you?"

For a moment, Mike considered lying. But his number would've come up blocked on his father's phone. And there was that distant beeping on the line as the jail recorded the call. Added to the fact that there had already been enough lying and half-truths lately to last a lifetime.

"I'm in jail, pop."

"Uh-huh," said his father. "A man can get into trouble when he's away from his wife and kids, can't he? It's like you're a different person. It's like you're your old self."

"I'm nothing like my old self. Can I talk to them, please?"

"You really think that's the best idea, Mike?"

"I need to know that they're okay."

"Why wouldn't they be okay?"

Mike felt himself sink. He was weak from dehydration along with the adrenaline still buzzing through him twelve hours on; he barely felt able to support his own weight, and he leaned against the pea-green wall. The hallway smelled like bad breath, old food, sweat, the end of dreams.

"Maybe you just need to cool out," Jack said.

"Put them on, pop. I don't care."

"No."

"No? Why did you take the money? I don't understand. To pay this guy? To pay McAfferty? I could've killed him, pop. I could've killed him . . ."

"Now you listen to me," Jack Simpkins growled. "You listen because this could be the last time we ever talk."

Mike felt a jolt. The old tapes started replaying in his mind — that father he'd left behind over two decades ago, sounding close enough to be standing right beside him.

"The girls are safe *now*. Safe from you, and your fuck ups, and your anger, and your violence. You know, Mike, you started out a good kid. So you got it in your head to be a filmmaker, cameraman, whatever you call it; you didn't want to follow in my footsteps and work for the MTA. Fine. But you didn't know, Mike, you didn't know what it would be like to raise a family, what it was like, day in and day out. Now you know, Mike. Now you know what it's like. It can drive you crazy."

Mike almost gave way to that old familiar rage. He contained it as best as he could, and kept his voice level, his internal gears grinding. "You don't know anything. You went to work, you came home, ate dinner Mom prepared, then went out to the bar . . ."

"You disrespectful—"

"Then you had your affair. And I found out. And mom never recovered."

"She never recovered because of *you*. She *knew*, goddammit, she *knew* about it and she let it be, Mike. It was you, you standing there pointing that goddamned gun at me that she never survived, Mike!"

The resurgence of those decades of repressed feelings was making Mike dizzy on his feet. He closed his eyes, leaned harder into the wall, and begged for God's mercy, something he wasn't sure he'd ever done in his life. After half a minute of silence, he wondered if Jack had ended the call. Mike spoke in a soft voice.

"Put them on the phone, please."

"No. You do your time, for whatever mess you caused yourself up there. You do your time and then you can have them back — if they'll take you. They'll be fine with me. We have everything we need."

Mike opened his eyes.

"What about my brother, pop? Huh? Do I have a brother?" Mike waited for an answer. Jack Simpkins said nothing.

"Was that what happened to you? What happened to us? To mom?"

Mike realized he was shaking all over, on the verge of tears. He listened, he waited, needing something desperately from his father. But after a few seconds Mike realized he no longer heard the beeping noise in the background. Jack Simpkins had hung up.

CHAPTER SIXTY-THREE

Swift had called a meeting with Tuggey, Mathis, and Kim Yom, who was back in Albany, and going to conference in. The two IA agents had invited themselves along, scrutinizing Swift's every move.

A few rings, and then a voice emanated from the phone. "Hello?"

"Kim, hi, it's John Swift.

"Hi John."

"You're on speaker. Captain Tuggey is here, Sheriff Dunleavy, ADA Sean Mathis, and two fine folks from Internal Affairs."

"Sounds like a party," Yom said in her usual deadpan voice. "What can I do for you, John?"

Swift glanced from the phone at the faces crowded around. Then his gaze dropped.

"You said you had some results for me. What we spoke about yesterday afternoon, before Darring went to court."

"Ah yes," said Yom. It sounded like she was clicking some keys on a computer. "I have those results right in front of me; thanks, in part, to our friends in New York and our friends at the Bureau."

"Kim, I would love it if you could share the information."

"Absolutely. So, Robert Darring was born in Manhattan as William Simpkins."

Swift glanced at Mathis, who seemed to have gone pale. Then he asked, "And how did you obtain this information?"

"As you had instructed, John, we did a Bureau search for new birth records coming online in the NYC metropolitan area for the past five years and found a hit for Robert J. Darring, dating two years ago. As you know, New York City police, under Deputy Inspector Jonas, did a search on Darring's apartment and seized his laptop, which yielded little. But in the apartment a few photos were found. Those pictures were scanned and sent to me. One photo clearly identifies Jack Simpkins, currently residing in St. Augustine, Florida."

Swift raised his head again for a moment. Everyone was rapt with attention.

Yom went on. "The woman, we didn't have a comparison for. So I used facial recognition software to cross-reference her image with any image of Darring's. None were found. I also cross-referenced the image with all of the players involved in the Simpkins' homicide case, including his grandfather, Jack Simpkins, the one in Florida, and there was a match. There were actually two matches. The woman is Pamela Falcone, and she's a Facebook user. She had a picture on her account of her and Jack Simpkins; our best guess the shot was taken twenty years ago. The other was on another social media site, not as popular anymore, called Myspace, and it showed Pamela Falcone again with Simpkins in a group photo. The Myspace page was for a bar in lower Manhattan."

Mathis could no longer restrain himself. "Fascinating," he said. "And what does it all mean? We're supposed to believe Robert Darring is Jack Simpkins' son? His bastard or something? There's no way the man would sign a paternity statement if he—"

"We found the paternity statement at St. Luke's Hospital," Yom interrupted, "and records for child support payments dating back to his birth, but ending when Darring — or, William Simpkins — turned eighteen. Juvenile records are confidential, and I've been working on trying to get them open, but from the outside alone it appears that Simpkins was in all sorts of trouble with the law in his youth, went into rehab at sixteen, saw counselors, the whole works."

"Thank you, Kim," said Swift.

"You're welcome, Detective. Good luck."

Tuggey leaned forward and pressed the button to end the call. Mathis' expression was still a picture of skepticism. "This is . . ."

"This gives us motive," Swift said. "Jack Simpkins signed the paternity statement not because he was coerced or blackmailed. He signed because he was going to leave his wife for Pamela Falcone. But then his wife got cancer. And his son, Mike, found out about the affair. As far as William Simpkins a-k-a Robert Darring was concerned, he lost a father, who had probably never spoken to him or acknowledged him beyond the paternity statement. Probably shut the mistress out, too. Sent the payments until William was eighteen. Then, nothing. So, William, with an obviously antisocial personality, oppositional-defiant, like Kim said — 'the works' — he harbors this hate, and it festers, and he grows into this astute hacker. And he plans his revenge."

"Jesus," said Mathis, all trace of skepticism vanished. "But what about this whole thing with the game — *The Don*? I don't know everything about these games but I believe it would be like trying to find a needle in a haystack, just jumping in and expecting to be able to find someone — for Darring to find Braxton Simpkins, who was using an alias, and on any number of servers."

Swift was ready. "Kapow was hacked into almost three months ago, just before Christmas. It wasn't as major as some of the other dark web hacks — didn't register on the top five lists, or anything — but it was enough for Darring to be able to find Braxton Simpkins, push him around a little, toy with him, threaten his family. We're still waiting for the full disclosure, but I'm sure when we see the rest of Kapow's data we're going to find that Braxton was threatened to the point where he believed he had to sacrifice himself, or else his family would be murdered. He had no way of knowing who the aggressor was, only that they had his identity, knew where he lived, and if he told anyone, went to the cops, anything at all, they would be killed. Plus, to his young mind, these types of things might not have seemed extraordinary. These games are violent, they encourage use of threats, as well as cheating and lying; the perfect place for someone like Robert Darring."

"And we just let him go," said Tuggey. "Christ, guys, how did this happen? Darring just walked away. I don't understand."

Mathis spoke up, and his tone had changed, becoming almost wistful. "Because we arrested and charged him as Robert Darring. A person with what we thought was a valid birth certificate and social security card. He did all of this as William Simpkins, who was kept entirely concealed from us."

Swift nodded. "We can't connect Robert Darring to this murder, show motive; we've already tried."

"But as William Simpkins," Mathis said, "We have a whole new case."

"We get him as William Simpkins, we show the paper-trail to his alias Darring, and once we have him for motive and opportunity, we get his real computer from him, and Yom takes it apart and shows every spurious email and account transaction, plus we get all the FBI data on the Kapow servers, the hack, the chat threats, all of it."

"What about the fingerprints on the headlamp?" asked Tuggey.

"That's even better," said Swift. "We can match those prints to William Simpkins, but he was a juvenile when he got into trouble. He became Darring when he was eighteen. So we need a judge in New York to unseal those records. Then we've got him a hundred percent."

The atmosphere in the room became suddenly electric. Everyone seemed to recall at the same time that their number one suspect — a different version, but in the same body — was still in town, getting his car out of impound, taking his sweet time.

Billy Sweet Tea, Swift thought. *William Simpkins.*

"Let's go," said Tuggey. He strode out of the room already with his phone at his ear to give his troopers the order to pick up Robert Darring — William Simpkins.

Mathis looked at Swift, chastened. "Better late than never?"

"This is a Federal case now. You're not going to get your big win."

Mathis grimaced. "Well aren't you something," he said. He lowered his head and looked up at Swift from beneath knitted eyebrows. Swift saw that Mathis was grinning. Just a little.

CHAPTER SIXTY-FOUR

"You're out, Simpkins."

The door slid open and Mike Simpkins was free to go. It had been both the longest and the shortest time he'd ever spent in jail, just over eighteen hours. His only time.

He collected his things in a daze. The past couple of hours he had thought of very little apart from his conversation with his father. A public defender named Ashcroft had come to see him through his release, and had unleashed a volley of information, which failed to penetrate his thoughts about his talk with Jack. Mike had been curious, without a doubt, as to why he'd been released, and the lawyer, who admitted to only having part of the story, had tried to explain. It was possible McAfferty had been set-up by someone, meant to take the fall. A good thing Mike hadn't pulled any triggers, the lawyer had said quietly and warily.

There was still the possession of an unregistered gun, they told him, and he had a court appearance for that coming up.

He left the jail after calling the single taxi service in the area to come and take him home. He supposed he could take responsibility for all of it, if he wanted to. For his mother, for Braxton, now for Callie and the girls, gone, apparently trapped by his maniac father back in Florida. As he drove through the evening with the sun setting on another day — five had now gone by since Braxton's death — he knew what he had to do. He knew that nothing else mattered, not his anger, nor his sense of guilt, nothing from his past, not even his father.

All that mattered was his wife and daughters. If his father did have something to do with all of this, with the money, with what happened to Braxton, then they could still be in danger right now. Court appearance be damned, he needed to get to them.

Maybe Jack Simpkins had been right about at least that much. Family was hard. Maybe now Mike was beginning to understand what his father meant.

* * *

At home, he sat in the living room and looked out at the snow-covered front yard, at how the ridges of snow cast small shadows beneath the light of a full moon, the drifts settled in serpentine patterns. He went and built a fire in the woodstove. It was ten minutes to seven p.m.

The seconds slowly dripped into minutes. He was tired, too tired to sleep. He hadn't slept at all last night. Driving to Florida was going to take everything he had. Along with every last cent. There was nothing left. Credit cards were maxed out. Checking account was empty. He had a little over three hundred in cash — just enough to buy gas for the twenty-four-hour drive. He'd packed the Honda with everything he needed. For a moment he considered cracking into the vodka again and drinking until he passed out. But that wouldn't do. He'd even thought of getting on the road right now, sucking down energy drinks until his skin cracked, but that wouldn't do either.

He couldn't leave without Braxton.

He sat, and tried to calm his mind, think rationally through the things he needed to do. He needed to pick his son up from the funeral home the next day. He needed to start getting his life in order again. Maybe he could even place a few calls and emails in the morning to his contacts in Florida and get some fiber-tech work down there again.

This got him laughing. He laughed until he cried, and then he just sat. The long hand of the clock in the living room dragged around to half past the hour, and his eyes started to grow heavy, and his head lolled on his shoulders. Then a car appeared on the road. It slowed and turned into Mike's driveway.

Mike stood up, fully alert again. He still had on his boots and jacket. He opened the front door and stepped outside.

He thought he recognized the vehicle.

Mike walked across and came up along the driver's side. The window came down. John Swift looked up at Mike and smiled.

"You look tired."

"I'm exhausted."

"Little time in the hooskow will do that to you." Swift turned his head and looked at the Honda parked in front of him. His headlights beamed into the back of the car where there was a puffy duffel bag standing on end.

"Going somewhere?"

"I can't. I've got charges to stand for."

Swift nodded, then he winked. "Can we talk before you go?"

Mike stood where he was for a moment, trying to read Swift's features. The detective looked back, eyes hooded, crinkled with crow's feet, his hair grey around the temples — to Mike he looked older than he had even just a few days before, but there was something spirited in his eyes.

Mike walked around the car and got in the passenger side.

It was warm, the heat pouring out of the vents. Swift twisted around to see behind him and started backing out of the driveway, on to route 9N.

At the road, he turned and drove up the half mile, passing the Hamiltons' on the right, and the open field. He slowed the car at the site of Braxton's death, his bumper slicing a groove into the snowbank on the shoulder.

Mike could feel the emotion rise as he looked out at the dark road. He imagined Braxton lying there as the snow fell down on him.

"You're probably pretty unhappy with your old man."

Mike cut a sideways glance at Swift. "He's got my wife and two girls. For all I know, he's the one who's responsible for this whole thing."

"Did you call the police in St. Augustine?"

Mike looked back out the window at the dark road. "No."

Swift took a breath and nodded. "Good. Don't think you need to."

Mike gave him another sharp look. His fatigue had completely vanished. He felt alert, pellucid, ready. More so than he had in days. "Oh no?"

"You don't think so either. You and your father may have problems, but you know he wouldn't hurt them." Swift turned to look at Mike directly. "We know who murdered Braxton."

"Yeah? You do? Let me tell you, detective, I wonder two things: I wonder if I care what you know anymore, that's one. And I wonder why I should believe you anyway. Why didn't you go after McAfferty right when I told you about the emails? You knew about him, didn't you?"

Swift was shaking his head. "No, we didn't. Despite what you might think. Different departments, different troops."

"Was Tricia Eggleston the one who told you where McAfferty was?"

"Yes. She proffered with the DA, who's going to put her through some rehab and a lighter sentence."

"You're keeping Bull and Linda locked up?"

"They're quite the characters. They've both got outstanding warrants in addition to the new charges. I know they're your friends, but they're probably going to be sent back down to New York to deal with some other business after they deal with shooting at cops on my property."

"They were just here to help me."

Swift raised his eyebrows. Mike could barely make out his face in the dashboard lights, just a bit of flesh tone, the shape of his head, the glittering points of light in his eyes. "I know."

"What else do you know?"

"Robert Darring is behind all of it. The fake emails from McAfferty, the manipulation of the funds in the 529 account; he baited McAfferty to set explosives and is responsible for Alan Cohen's severe injuries — and he tied up and dragged your son behind his car until he died, right there."

The two men stared out at the spot in the road in silence.

"That's a lot for one kid," Mike said after a while.

"He wasn't alone. He had the other two with him. And I believe there could be even more; compatriots from *The Don*. They have groups of players in a Crew. And I think they switched off and on and played one another's characters. So other kids played Darring's character in the game while he was in custody. Sent you emails, too. They even messed with my own personal life, managing to convince my bank to put a hold on my cards. All designed to distract, to throw me off. To throw us all off."

"It worked."

"I want to tell you who Robert Darring really is. But I think it's best you just hear it for yourself. You up for one last ride, Muchacho?"

Mike breathed deeply through his nostrils. "Alright."

Swift popped the car into Drive and they got moving.

"When did you know?" Mike asked. "About Darring?"

"I never knew. I went step by step. Made some mistakes."

"That's got to be tough on your career."

"That's the job. You never know anything. But I'm suspended, pending review. Which is a nice way for them to tell me I have to cool my heels while Internal Affairs mounts their case and has me totally canned. Which won't happen; I'll resign. It will all be cordial and quiet. I've cut a deal to revise my previous statements about the excessive force against Duso. He'll likely get a settlement now. It all means bye-bye Attorney General's office."

Mike wasn't sure he understood all that the detective was saying, but he offered, "I'm sorry."

Swift got the car up to speed. "I'm not too worried about it. I got a date with Janine Poehler out of the whole thing. Taking her to dinner as soon as I'm done tonight. Hang on," he said.

He surprised Mike by stamping on the accelerator and blowing the back end of the car around in a wide arc, tires spinning, snow and ice flying. He handled the wheel deftly, snapping the vehicle right back into the lane and rocketing back towards town.

CHAPTER SIXTY-FIVE

Robert Darring smiled at the federal agents as he walked into the room. He looked right at home, Swift thought. He wondered if Darring had been seeking attention all along. Although that might have been oversimplifying it somewhat. During all his years on the force, Swift had come across every kind of criminal. Many were driven by financial need. Others were compelled by unbridled passion. Emotion. Vengeance. Greed. And some, a few, left the investigators scratching their heads, long after the case was over.

Despite being picked up just moments before leaving town, Darring was his usual self, expressionless, smug. He sat at a long table surrounded by three Feds. Swift stood beside Mike, who had been permitted to stand in and watch the interview. Swift had had to move mountains in order to let that happen, but now here they were. It was something Mike needed, Swift had decided, before moving on with his life.

The federal agents had set up their cameras and brought their own recording devices. The place looked like a Best Buy showroom.

A federal agent leaned forward, speaking into a microphone resting on the big table. The Feds were extra starchy this morning, Swift observed, more machine than human. The agent proceeded to "let the record show" and bespoke the date, time, place, and purpose of the inquiry.

Unprompted, Darring suddenly began to deliver a speech. As he spoke his gaze seemed to track some interior place, as if seeing a world the rest of them could not. "A hundred years ago, Arthur Rimbaud said 'We are having visions of numbers.'" Then Darring looked into the cameras, at the agents, and through the one-way glass, as if he knew Swift and Mike were there. "'I am an oracle; everything I say is true.'"

He sat up straighter, projecting his voice. "It's just like the game. It *is* a game, and nothing more. We all have our little bundle of resources. We watch the numbers go up and down on a screen. Press a few buttons. But I can change those numbers. I change those numbers, and I can influence behavior. I can make people do what I want them to. Just like the people who play *The Don*, we're all just playing a larger version of that game every day. And it's getting easier and easier to control. All digital, all ones and zeros. What's easier than ones and zeros? A kindergartener can understand that."

The agents looked at one another grimly, and broke in with their questions. For over two hours, Swift and Mike observed. The Feds were meticulous, and the inquiry painstaking, even to Swift, who knew the virtue of being thorough, even if he did like to cut to the chase. He was happy to see it in their hands now. Happy, honestly, to be free again.

Finally, the line of inquiry turned to the question of Darring's real identity. The Feds had with them files thicker than the King James Bible, and they produced document after document, and at last Darring was forced to confess who he really was.

"William Simpkins." After nearly three hours of questioning, he was finally beginning to look beaten.

Swift watched Mike covertly during this revelation. He stared through the one-way glass, saying nothing. He uttered not one word throughout the whole procedure. When the federal agents took him aside after they were done with Darring, Swift wasn't privy to their exchange.

Swift left the county jail, walking out into the night, inhaling the crisp air, looking up as the stars snapped on one by one overhead. He needed to get home and feed his dog. He needed to get ready for his dinner with Janine. He needed to get moving with the rest of his life.

Maybe, he thought, walking to his car, feeling his coat flap around his legs, it was finally time to put some work into that sprawling property his grandfather had left to him so many years ago.

EPILOGUE

The wheels barked on the tarmac and the plane touched down in St. Augustine airport. Mike looked out the window. He knew he wouldn't be able to see them — they'd be on the other side of the security checkpoint, but still he looked, and pictured them there, Callie and the two girls, Reno now standing to her shoulder, Hannah at her waist. For a moment, he almost thought he actually saw them.

The wait was agonizing. The canned music in the plane. The ill-concealed tension of the passengers as they all did their best to maintain decorum. Stay calm. Wait your turn. Be polite to the people around you. And get off this goddamn plane as soon as humanly possible.

He'd spent the flight trying to put the past behind him, but he recalled one final visitation as he stood in the cramped quarters with the plastic-smiling passengers, waiting to disembark. Just seven hours ago, minutes before he headed out to the airport in the old Honda (where he'd left it, for all he cared, for anyone who might want it) a black sedan with a, tall, silver, wobbling antennae had pulled into his driveway. Two men in dark suits had bade him goodbye, with a look in their eyes that told him not to drop off the face of the Earth, they just might need to contact him again.

After interviewing Robert Darring they'd taken him into another room, sat him down, and flicked on a tape recorder. They'd taken that thick file out again, setting out the same photographs and documents they had displayed for Darring, like Blackjack dealers.

"William Simpkins," The first Fed said, tapping a birth certificate with his finger. There was a picture attached by a paper clip, as if Mike hadn't just seen the man in the flesh in the next room. "This is your half-brother?"

"I've never seen him before, never met him, had no knowledge of him until a few minutes ago."

The agents looked at each other. "You have any idea why he would want to murder your son?"

"Step-son," the second agent corrected.

". . . Your step-son?"

"I think it was to hurt me."

Those looks again. Then the agents pulled out pictures of two other kids unfamiliar to Mike. "These two were accomplices of Darring's . . . of Simpkins'."

"We're talking with them now," the second agent said in a manner suggestive of omnipresence. As if he was there with Mike, but simultaneously somewhere else entirely. "Darring blackmailed these two young men in ways similar to how he blackmailed Tricia Eggleston."

The first agent sat back and folded his hands across his stomach. "Darring contacted Eggleston over a week ago. He told her the cops were looking into her boyfriend, McAfferty. That there was a task force that included a detective Remy LaCroix, and that there were witnesses getting ready to testify before a grand jury. Former addicts, people in trouble."

"It was a bluff," said the second agent. "LaCroix and his task force were nowhere near McAfferty. Darring learned about the task force, though, in the papers. He knew McAfferty was Braxton's biological father through their online interactions; he gleaned this information over a couple of months playing *The Don* with your stepson. He sought out Eggleston, McAfferty's girlfriend. So she'd do her Lady Macbeth part."

"Naturally, McAfferty was skeptical. But, he was also paranoid. He bought an incendiary device."

Another document. "We have the records of his online order for several parts here. Built the device and had it at the ready."

"Just two days prior to the explosion, Darring contacted Tricia Eggleston. He never really corresponded with Tori directly, but through the girl. He convinced her that the cops were closing in. And then he gave her the location of a safe house for her and Tori to run to. She was supposed to join him, but she never did. Wanted out, I guess, no matter which way."

"So you've never heard of William Simpkins?"

"No."

More photos were pulled out. One showed Mike's father standing beside a dark woman with gypsy hair and eyes, in a group photo. It was hard to be sure because of the other people crowding the picture, but it looked like Mike's father had his hand around her waist. Mike stared at the woman, her eyes, the Mona Lisa smile on her face in the grainy photo. The first agent placed his finger on the face.

"This is Pamela Falcone. Know her?"

Mike swallowed. It took him a moment to find his voice — when he tried to talk all he produced at first was a scratchy grunt. "Yeah, I remember her," he said. Then he looked out through the windows and into the snow where the tree shadows morphed into memories rising up from his past. "I went down to the bar once where my father spent just about every night. I remember seeing her standing near him, the way she looked at him. I was only fifteen or sixteen. And that's when I understood. That's when I knew. But, then, my mom got sick." Mike looked down at the floor, at the pictures, at one showing Mike with his father and mother in Battery Park. He didn't even know where it came from — maybe a passerby had snapped it. Mike was Hannah's age, just a tot. He looked at his mother, her thin face, her small mouth, her large, baleful eyes. "I think I was even relieved she got sick," he said, his voice dangerously close to cracking. "Because then he stayed. He let the other woman go and he stayed with my mom. But I never forgave him for it."

Mike pulled in a deep breath and looked away from the photos, anywhere but at those faces. He put his head in his hands for a moment, ran shaking fingers through his hair, and finally looked up at the agents, both of whom watched him intently. The second one asked, "Maybe just like Robert Darring — William Simpkins — never forgave you for being the son your father raised? Watching you all of these years, resentment eating away at him, hatred? Forming his plan? How he could hurt you the most?"

Mike let out a breath. He hadn't even realized he'd been waiting to exhale. The two sets of eyes were watching him extremely closely. Now they blinked, all four of them, in eerie unison. Mike could smell Dial soap on the first agent.

"I raised a gun to my father when I was a kid. That's probably in your file, too. When I found out about his affair. So I don't know. I don't know if he stayed because she was sick, or because of what I did. I don't know if he just . . ."

They were looking at him with detachment.

"You realize this is a formality," the first agent said.

"We have to be thorough," said the second.

Mike nodded, swallowed, and said, "I understand."

He thought of Swift. *I understand.*

The two agents stood up, collected their files, and proceeded to the door.

Mike had remained seated, not sure his legs would support his weight if he should try to stand.

The first agent had opened the door and the second agent looked back over his shoulder. "Thank you for your cooperation, Mr. Simpkins. We'll be in touch. Good luck in Florida."

And they had left.

When his turn came he filed down the aisle with his single carry-on duffel. He had checked no baggage onto the airplane. He only had the duffel and a box, about the size of a bowling ball case, handsome bound-leather, black, with silver edges and rivets.

He nodded at the captain and stewardess, bid them farewell and stepped off the plane, leaving its chilly recycled air and into the balmy blast of a Florida spring. The humid air blanketed him with wet, fuzzy nostalgia; all the years that had passed down here in the sunshine state. And here he was again. For a moment, his stomach turned viscous as he remembered what he had lost, what his family had lost. But Braxton was home now.

As Mike had expected, they were waiting for him on the other side of security. Callie was wearing a pair of short-shorts that showed her long, smooth legs. Those legs had never quite lost their tan. Her bra strap was showing under a soft tank top, her dirty blonde hair piled up and pinned behind her head, her eyes wet, her mouth quivering with a smile. The girls were in their cutest outfits, Hannah in a little one-piece jumper thingy — Mike didn't know, didn't matter — Reno in jean shorts and a t-shirt that read *Aloha!*, a salutation from the wrong state that filled him with love and longing. And standing behind them, almost lost in the crush of passengers exiting and preparing to board, was Jack Simpkins.

As he walked towards them, Mike shot a glance at his father. Jack nodded back, and Mike felt something loosen in his chest. He dropped the duffel bag, almost running, like a guy in some frigging movie. He didn't care. There would be nothing hidden in his life ever again, no withholding. He grasped the box, saw Callie's eyes rest on it, saw her quivering lips part, as a heavy sigh escaped her, and she put the back of her hand to her mouth and looked at Mike.

He reached them, and set the box down. Braxton's ashes, there, in the middle of his family, Braxton who had bound them all together, who had been at the heart of these four people's lives, who now stood arm-in-arm, laughing and crying a little.

Mike pulled them all in tight. The crowd bustled around them; he caught one brief frown and one bright smile among the faces.

People were the same wherever you went.

THE END

TJB
Etown
February 12, 2014 — January 22, 2015

Acknowledgments

Writing this book was possible thanks to Keith Hall, his experience and knowledge of law enforcement. Accuracy of procedural detail is to Keith's credit, any errors are mine. Thanks also to Jennifer Bulkley, Oak Clement, and Stephen Buzzell for helping me to keep my head in a gunfight. Acclamation must go to my tireless publisher Jasper Joffe and everyone at Joffe Books, especially Anne Derges, for her surgical and companionable edits. And endless gratitude for my wife, Dava, for her work with real-world tragedies, her attentive support, and the mothering of my three children – those best stories of all.

Thank you for reading this book. If you enjoyed it please leave feedback on Amazon, and if there is anything we missed or you have a question about then please get in touch. The author and publishing team appreciate your feedback and time reading this book.

Our email is jasper@joffebooks.com

http://joffebooks.com

Also by T.J Brearton

HABIT

A young woman, Rebecca Heilshorn, lies stabbed to death in her bed in a remote farmhouse. Rookie detective Brendan Healy is called in to investigate. All hell breaks loose when her brother bursts onto the scene. Rebecca turns out to have many secrets and connections to a sordid network mixing power, wealth, and sex. Detective Brendan Healy, trying to put a tragic past behind him, pursues a dangerous investigation that will risk both his life and his sanity. Habit is a compelling thriller which will appeal to all fans of crime fiction. T.J. Brearton amps up the tension at every step, until the shocking and gripping conclusion.

ABOUT THE AUTHOR

T.J. Brearton is the Amazon best-selling author of 'Habit,' a crime thriller set in Upstate New York, and 'Survivors,' the second book in the Titan Trilogy.

He is the author of 'Highwater,' a supernatural crime thriller set in the Adirondacks.

Short fiction publications include The Rusty Nail Magazine, Orange Quarterly, Enhance Magazine, Third Rail, Atticus Review, and Nonsense Society.

He lives in the Adirondacks with his wife and three children and can be found at tjbrearton.com.